STONE

A Castle Sin Novel

Book One

A Dark BDSM Suspense Novel

By

Linzi Basset

Linzi Basset

STONE: CASTLE SIN

Copyright © 2019 Linzi Basset
Edited by: Kristen Breanne
Proofreaders: Marie Vayer, Melanie Marnell, Kemberlee
Snelling, Charlotte Strickland
Published & Cover Design by: Linzi Basset
ISBN: 9781688226982

Contents

Acknowledgements

I am amazed by the number of fans my first bestselling series; Club Alpha Cove, has. It truly is humbling to hear that many of them refer to it as their go to series and have read it over and over again.

To all of you, I wish to offer you my gratitude. I can't express in words what it means to me. Because of that ... the Castle Sin series is for those who kept asking for something in line of the CAC series. I truly hope you'll enjoy the Castle Sin Masters; Stone, Hawk, Kane, Ace, Parker, Shane and Zeke.

To my ARC team on Stone, you're an amazing group of readers and I'm blessed that you're always ready to start reading the moment the book lands in your kindles.

My super reliable proofreaders; ladies, you're a blessing. Marie Vayer, Melanie Marnell, Kemberlee Snelling and Charlotte Strickland, I salute you every month. Thank you for all your support. It's truly appreciated!

As always, my editor on Stone, Kristen Breanne, is a woman with patience untold. Thank you for never complaining when I'm late and for doing a superb job in all the books we work on together.

Finally, to a very special friend and one of the best bosses I'd ever had, Blaize Wulfsohn, whose real-life experience during the 2004 tsunami in Phuket, Thailand, was used in this book.

My constant mentor and soulmate; honeybuns, you keep me grounded and unbeknownst to you, you are the one who gives me inspiration.

Author's Note

Dear Reader,

Castle Sin is a dark BDSM suspense series

Castle Sin
Seven Masters
Seven Dungeons
Seven Times the Kink

STONE: MASTER EAGLE

"I should warn you, Master Eagle, I bite and have been known to scratch."

Peyton Jackson was a Pulitzer Prize winning investigative journalist, the best in her field, but in Castle Sin, she was known only as Sub PJ.

Peyton had stayed away from the ocean for a reason, yet there she was, on a remote island in Key West, surrounded by the sea, gazing at the majestic castle meant to become her home ... at least, that's what she made the seven Masters believe ... In reality, she was there for only one reason: to get her cousin off the island.

One unexpected perk ... or detriment ... was that it placed her directly in the sights of her biggest celeb crush. In contrast to finding herself wanting to please her Master at every turn, she also smelled a story, a scoop ... and she had every intention of taking advantage to find out exactly what went on inside the walls of Castle Sin.

Until she awoke the Beast inside the King of the Castle.

"And it's going to be such a pleasure to make you crawl and beg," he promised in a deep growl. "As meek as a little kitten."

He was known as Stone Rothman in Hollywood ... Stone Sinclair to his family ... and Master Eagle to everyone else in Castle Sin

A powerful Master, a compassionate man, and a hungry and demanding Beast created the enigma that was Stone Sinclair.

Trust and honesty were paramount in every aspect of his life and he expected the same from those surrounding him. As the king of his castle, it took a lot to crack his armor ... but this time *she* had peeved him off. *She* was one of the trainees who had applied to be a submissive at Castle Sin ... and *she* was a fake. A liar and an impostor. Two traits this powerful Master had no patience for.

The moment he laid eyes on the tall redhead, the Beast inside his soul began to stir. She was a deceiver, and he was going to enjoy transforming her into exactly what she'd applied for.

A submissive … his submissive.

Meanwhile, unbeknownst to both of them, a conspiracy threatened to yank their entire existence apart. It endangered not only their lives, but spelled disaster for the entire nation, and Peyton was forced into an impossible situation she had no way to get out of.

With lies and lust and fear at war inside her, helpless to fight the domination of the Master and his Beast, she attempted to find a solution … but no matter what she did, there was only one way it all would end.

With Stone Sinclair hating her.

Editor's Note:

Stone will make you want to go out and apply to all the local BDSM clubs in the hopes of finding your very own Master Eagle. Sexy as hell, sweet like candy, with just a vein of mystery and danger that we have come to expect, Stone is woven in such a way that will have your head in the clouds, your blood pounding in all the right places, and your heart cracking as you wonder what you would do if you were in her place...

I truly enjoyed writing the first book in this exciting new series. I hope you'll find the same enjoyment reading it.

Warm regards,
Linzi Basset

Linzi Basset

Chapter One

"Ugh! I hate all this water."

Peyton Jackson couldn't suppress a shudder of disgust as she stared over the wide expanse of the ocean surrounding her. For once it was all it was, there wasn't the usual terror associated with being on the water. The streaks of the sun danced over her face, turning the amethyst color of her eyes to a deep violet. Her only salvation was the sight of the green patch in the distance growing bigger as the speedboat carried them rapidly closer to their destination.

She hated everything associated with island life. To her, idyllic wasn't the description she'd use, rather hot, sticky and uncomfortable with sand …

lots and lots of sand surrounded by water. Too many dangerous gallons to mention.

"Five minutes, ladies."

Peyton glanced at the tall, muscled man at the helm of the boat. The way he handled her was poetry in motion, effortless, and skillful. Danton Hill was apparently the acclaimed Rothman cousins' Security Director.

Gmpf, imagine that, a Security Director! I suppose being celebrities they do need 24/7 protection. I wonder if he swaps their diapers for them too.

The strangled laugh that escaped her lips drew the big man's eyes her way. She quickly swallowed her mirth at the childish notion her wayward thoughts brought to mind, but a broad smile remained on her lips.

She looked at the other six passengers. All of them women, who stared with anticipation and excitement at the lush island that loomed ahead. Peyton had been surprised when she got on the boat to find them already waiting. Not because they were there but because they didn't fit the stereotypical woman she imagined would willingly submit to a life of servitude on a remote island ruled by seven men.

Masters, actually, she corrected herself. Powerful Dominants who knew how to make even the strongest woman bow to their command in willing submission.

Or so she'd heard.

Castle Sin, on the privately owned, The Sevens Keys Island, in Key West was a hush-hush establishment. Only approved celebrities, politicians, and executive businessmen were members of the exclusive BDSM club.

Four of the six women were older, at a guess in their early forties, and the other two, she surmised to be her age, mid-thirty, which left Peyton dumbfounded. It shot all the information she'd gathered over the years about the seven Rothman cousins to smithereens. She had expected to find a myriad of young females under the age of thirty on the island. A place that was inaccessible to the public, only paid members—which consisted of male Dominants—or as a submissive or slave employed by the reclusive owners.

Reclusive my ass!

The Rothman clan had risen to stardom fifteen years ago when all seven of them had been cast in a Marvel action movie that became a blockbuster on release day. Everyone thereafter had followed the same track. That first motion picture had set them up for life. The producers were clever enough to ride on the wave of success. They'd turned it into a series that released a new feature film every eighteen months. Of course, all seven men thrived on being in the spotlight. The regular articles in the tabloids about their sexual exploits and the strings of women that always hung on to them like leeches were proof of that.

The cousins hadn't stopped their lives the moment they made it big in film. Apparently, they all had various degrees but kept that part of their lives well hidden from the public eye. *Apparently*, being the key phrase. Peyton had been unable to find any concrete evidence of exactly what they did off the movie set.

No one knew where they disappeared to in between filming; Peyton had a theory that it was nothing but a smokescreen for the dubious shenanigans on the island.

"You haven't joined in the excited blabber since you got on board."

The deep voice of Danton yanked her from her musings. She did her best to glance at him in a subservient manner, an insecure flicker of eyelids as she peeked at him through her lashes.

"So, tell me, Peyton Jackson, why are you here?"

She was hard-pressed not to snort at his haughty demeanor as he looked at her from his towering height at the steering wheel.

Of course! He's probably also a Dom.

Like *that* mattered any to Peyton. She was beyond irritated. If not for her aunt begging her to talk sense into her impulsive cousin, Savannah, who had already been on The Sevens Keys for close to three months, she'd be happily chasing worthwhile and newsworthy stories—well as soon as she was back at work from the forced vacation she was on. As an investigative journalist for CNN and who made the front pages of all the major newspapers and magazines across the U.S., Peyton could afford to choose which stories she chased. Celebrities and movie stars didn't interest her unless they committed a noteworthy crime.

"I asked you a question, Miss Jackson."

The sharp intonation of her name seared through her. She cursed herself for not having the foresight to use an assumed name. If the Castle Sin Masters did a background check on her, it would put them on guard. It was the one thing she didn't want.

"I don't believe I need to tell you. There's only one reason all of us are here, isn't that right?" she hedged with a tight smile. She fluttered her eyes and looked down as Danton's gaze sharpened on her. It wouldn't do to harvest suspicion about her. She had to blend in and get her cousin off the island.

"Lies aren't tolerated at Castle Sin," he rasped, and a deep slash drew his eyebrows together as he studied her intently. Peyton did her best not to squirm under his piercing stare but failed when an evil smile twitched his lips. "Especially from you.

I have a feeling you're going to catch the Beast's eye."

"Th-the Beast?" Peyton cursed at how small her voice sounded. She couldn't help the rapid beating of her heart as he chuckled darkly.

"Yeah, the overseeing Master Dom." His eyes did another slow foray over her dark red hair blowing behind her in the wind. "I think this time, he's going to break his own rule."

"Ehm ... what rule?" she asked, unable to listen to her brain that kept telling her to shut the hell up.

You sound like a scared little girl, for god's sake!

Oh, shut up!

"Not to take a sub for himself." He nodded as his eyes roamed over her curvy body. "Yeah ... I think our Master is gonna take time to have a little fun for himself."

Peyton pressed her lips together, lest she say something that would give her away. She couldn't afford to be kicked off the island before she even made it through the castle doors.

She had avoided digging deeper into the lives of the seven Rothman cousins for six years, ever since rumors about their dubious sexual proclivities had been doused as the actions of a woman scorned. At first, she'd started investigating the claim by the woman, Leigh Simms, that she'd been held prisoner by the cousins—treated and abused like a slave. She'd publicly retracted her claim within days, and Peyton had lost interest, especially as there was nothing at the time, linking them to The Seven Keys Island. Still, her curiosity had been pricked and she'd done some research on and off when time permitted. She'd found nothing outside of what the public already knew about them, which didn't interest her as a reporter chasing dangerous criminals, syndicates, and corrupt politicians. Seven drop-dead gorgeous, self-made billionaire movie stars was nothing but sensationalism.

Until her aunt had shown her the secret file with information about Castle Sin on The Sevens Keys Island she'd found hidden in the room Savannah used when she stayed over during visits. Leigh Simms had also mentioned an island in her claim six years ago, but she hadn't given the name or the coordinates of where it was, except somewhere in Key West. It was the first time she'd come across information about the privately-owned club, Castle Sin. Peyton didn't live under a rock and knew exactly what happened at an exclusive BDSM club. She'd even joined as a member at such clubs since—purely for investigative purposes, of course, or so she tried to make herself believe. She grimaced at the memory of her first visit. She'd been daring that time and ended up with a crisscross butt that had her standing for a week before she could sit down again. To this day, she still didn't understand why she'd gone back a second, third—*hell*—a lot more times since.

Finding out that her younger cousin had signed an employment contract that included a tight non-disclosure agreement, to live on the island for a minimum period of one year after being trained as a submissive slave, had stumped her. It made her wonder if her attitude toward Savannah over the past five odd years had perhaps driven her to it. She'd shrugged it off. It was too farfetched. But the woman's claim from six years prior had come back to haunt her. She began digging deeper and elicited the help of her bestie and next-door neighbor, Taylor Banks. Taylor was a real estate attorney. She'd pulled a few strings to uncover the locked information of the corporation The Sevens Keys Island was registered to.

It listed seven names. The surname wasn't familiar but the names sure as hell were. They might be known to the world as the Rothman cousins but in real life, she now knew they were from oldest to youngest, none other than Shane, Kane, Stone, Hawk, Ace, Zeke and Parker Sinclair. Suddenly, she had an angle that sparked the interest of the bloodhound inside her for a story. One she had every intention of writing. Finding her cousin became secondary.

No matter that she was about to come face to face with the 'Beast' who would apparently claim her for himself or that *he* could be there … the one Rothman or rather, Sinclair cousin, who caused her ovaries to break out in a slow foxtrot until her loins throbbed with lust every time his face appeared on the big screen or television.

Cousin number three.

Stone Sinclair.

Chapter Two

"Taylor Banks? I've heard of her. She's a highly sought after real estate attorney, especially by big corporations and property developers. Why would she be interested in information about Seven Keys?" Hawk Sinclair rasped. He got up to fill his cup with coffee, dragging in a deep breath as the rich aroma filled his nostrils.

His dark eyes sought out his cousin, Stone, who stood in front of the large mullion bay windows of the boardroom at Castle Sin gazing out over the ocean surrounding them. His straight shoulders and aristocratic tilt of his rigid chin was a clear indication of his anger.

"Peyton Jackson." The name spat from Stone's lips. He didn't bother to hide the disgust he felt, nor the violence that swirled inside him. If there was one thing he abhorred it was dishonesty. He spun around and looked between the six men sitting at the large boardroom table. "Any of you heard the name before?"

"Fucking hell, the investigative journalist that never leaves a stone unturned once she smells a story?" Ace straightened in his chair as he gave Stone an inquiring look.

"The same, known in the industry as the bloodhound bitch." Stone sat down at the head of the table.

He was the CEO of Be Secure Enterprises. A company that no one in the acting industry knew about or was aware they owned. They had made sure the ownership papers were locked tight and not available for public scrutiny.

Acting was a career Stone and three of his cousins had never coveted but had been drawn into when the two oldest family members, Shane and Kane—who had been successful actors since their youth—had coerced them into a onetime only Marvel movie eighteen years ago. It had been more of an adventure than a challenge for the cousins to do something that big as a team. They'd enjoyed it and the experience had brought them closer as a family. Unfortunately for them, it hadn't ended there. The movie became an overnight blockbuster and they all shot to instant stardom. The producers immediately signed them up for an entire series of the action filled, Marvel themed films. Each of them was forever encased in action figures of the parts they played in the movies.

Mostly, it had been fun but for Stone, Parker, and Hawk; it had run its course. Stone was the first to indicate he wanted out, five years ago already. Of all of the cousins, he hated the limelight the most. He had always been a private person and the one who kept to himself outside of shooting movies and attending the bare minimum of social gatherings. Hawk and Ace, along with him and his younger brother, Parker, had concentrated over the years on quietly building an empire they could fall back on when the time was right. All seven cousins owned shares and had supported and been involved in Be Secure Enterprises to a certain extent over the years, knowing at some point, stepping away from acting was inevitable.

For Stone, who had just celebrated his forty-fourth birthday, the time had come. Be Secure Enterprises was already a well-known international company that developed and designed top level security systems. Software and hardware, as well as supplying a full system security portfolio to the corporate world, government, and legal institutions all over the globe to safeguard their data, buildings, and people. Acting had become a chore to him, and he hated the months it dragged him away from the company and being involved in the operations on a day to day basis.

Then there was Castle Sin. The kind of club that had been Stone's secret fantasy from a young age. It had come to fruition when he'd inherited billions when his grandfather passed away ten years ago. It had taken him two years to find the perfect island, another year to design and build the exclusive club to his specifications. It didn't take much to convince his cousins to buy into the idea. Although registration papers indicated Sinclair

Corporation, a secret addendum showed Stone as the sole owner of the island and the primary shareholder of the club with the rest of them owning a combined forty-five percent in shares. Over the past four years, Castle Sin had become home to them.

"Do you think one of the women we kicked out of the club is trying to exploit us again, like Leigh Simms a couple of years ago?" Shane, at fifty-one, was the oldest of the Sinclair clan, a couple of months older than Kane, who was also his best friend. He didn't suffer fools easily. As the resident psychologist of Castle Sin, he was also the best judge of character and spotted fake submissives the moment they set foot on the island.

"It's possible. If memory serves, she was the bloodhound on the story at the time until Leigh retracted her claim." Stone shrugged. "I suppose chasing a dead lead didn't interest her. She's more into hardcore investigative journalism, not sensationalism."

"Which poses the question, why would she be digging into the ownership of the island?" Zeke grumbled. His tall frame was relaxed as he slumped in the chair, chomping on a sandwich he'd just pinched from the plate in the center of the table.

"Parker, care to fill everyone in on what you found?" Stone's moss green eyes turned to his brother.

"Sure thing." Parker quickly linked his tablet to the large overhead screen against one wall. A picture of a petite blonde flashed on the screen.

Ace straightened and leaned forward. "That's Savannah Thorne, aka sub ST. She's currently in Hawk's dungeon, isn't she?"

Each woman who signed up for an employment contract or applied to the training program with Castle Sin as a slave or submissive, was called by their initials from the moment of their arrival. It was done to keep the lines clearly drawn between the seven Masters and their trainees. Each cousin was in charge of his own dungeon, where all the slaves or submissives received specific training. Only once they successfully passed their training in all the dungeons, were they christened with a club name and allowed to attend to the members in the club. Those who only attended the training program were offered the opportunity of employment first before they returned to the mainland.

"That's correct," Parker said. "And from all reports, she's doing very well and completely embracing the new life she signed up for as a Castle Sin slave."

"I forgot how innocently young she looked." Shane stared intently at the picture of the beautiful young woman on the screen. He recalled the assessment interview he had with her clearly.

"We were all surprised at how much older she is than she looks. She just celebrated her thirtieth birthday last week." Parker tapped on his tablet and Savannah's social security details appeared on the screen.

"So, what does she have to do with Peyton Jackson?" Shane tapped his fingers on the desk as he searched his memory banks for useful information on Savannah Thorne.

"That's what triggered our suspicion. There's some kind of connection between them. A couple of searches kept connecting their names but we have no idea what. Even on the dark web, any data seems to just disappear into pixels," Stone said. His expression turned thunderous as he paged through Peyton's application as a Castle Sin submissive.

"That does raise a red flag. Who has the ability to erase someone's life from the dark web *and* why would a Pulitzer Prize winning investigative journalist apply for a yearlong submissive employment position?" Kane looked at Stone. "And sub ST? If I recall, you and Shane had your reservations about her too."

"Care to fill me in?" Zeke said. He had been on a business trip to Australia and had decided to extend it a couple weeks longer for a well-deserved vacation. Therefore, he hadn't met Sub ST as he'd only returned a couple of days ago.

"According to our background checks, sub ST had been laid off as part of a merger and that led to her marriage falling apart and not too amicably either. Shane and I believe that sub ST's decision to apply as a live-in slave at Castle Sin was part of cleansing herself of past demons and regaining her confidence." Stone continued to page through Peyton's file.

"Which in itself isn't a problem, but she's completely new to the lifestyle and we weren't sure she understood what being a BDSM slave entailed," Shane said.

"And are you still of that opinion? The first month of her training was spent in your dungeon, wasn't it?" Ace sipped his coffee, watching Shane.

"Oh, she now understands what would be expected of her. Personally, I'm not entirely convinced she's slave material. She'll make a much better submissive but she's too feisty for a slave. I'm still scheduling regular talks with her. Deep down, she's a very troubled young woman. I got the feeling she came here not just to face her inner demons but to hide."

"The question is, from who," Stone muttered. "And with the possible link to sub ST, one thing is for certain. Peyton Jackson's interest in The Seven Keys Island isn't a coincidence or something to be taken lightly."

"Why do you say that?" Hawk narrowed his eyes. He was aware that Stone was angry. It was there in every taut line of his body.

"Because she's one of the new applicants I approved as a Castle Sin submissive." His head turned, his jaw rigid. He watched the speedboat slowing down as it approached the mooring bay at the marina of The Sevens Keys Island. The new trainees had arrived. "Miss Jackson scratches where she has no business. She's here for a story, mark my words."

"Relax, Stone. She might have details on the owners of the island but she also signed a tight NDA. If she blathers about Castle Sin and the training she willingly applied for, I'll make sure she's discredited and caught in litigation for years," said Hawk, the resident attorney.

"Peyton Jackson is a prize-winning journalist, Hawk. She's not stupid. I'm sure one way or the other, she's already got her escape route planned and found a way to write her story." Stone grimaced ruefully. "Blackmail comes to mind."

Ace frowned in thought. "Blackmail? Do you think she's already put two and two together about us as actors?"

"It wouldn't take a genius to figure that out, Ace. We might have changed our surnames as a protection mechanism when we joined Shane, Kane, and Zeke on that movie but our first names are the same. Trust me, the moment she noticed that, she made the connection." A volatile frown darkened Stone's face. "She's here for one reason only. To get the scoop of a lifetime."

"Which is why I drew up the NDA with the sub clause, Stone. To ensure our identities remain intact. Our asses are too well known out there not to take the precaution. So, unless Miss Jackson has written approval to publish or disclose any information about us, she's going to be locked in litigation for years and the station she works for will be sued for millions. No news station will touch her afterward, I'll make sure of that. Besides, not one of the other trainees, live-in subs or slaves will corroborate her story. You know everyone who comes here is one-hundred-percent loyal to us.

Leigh proved that—in the end at any rate. And I'll make sure to kill the story before she even puts anything to paper," Hawk said in a gruff voice as he studied Stone.

He knew how it had hurt Stone when Leigh Simms had broken his confidence by going public with the story about Castle Sin. All because Stone hadn't returned her feelings at the time. He might not have loved her but he'd come to care deeply for her. He had taken personal care of her the entire time she'd been on the island. When she'd made demands of marriage, Stone had realized he'd made a mistake and she had misinterpreted his actions. Leigh had been livid when instead of offering marriage, he'd banned her from the island and the club.

They had all learned a lesson from that episode. Since then, they assured that they kept their association with the trainees purely professional.

Leigh had retaliated in true woman scorned fashion. The fact that she'd withdrawn the allegations the moment Hawk had offered her the five million dollars Stone had put on the table, had cut his cousin deep. She had proven once again to Stone that no woman could be trusted with his emotions—something he'd learned as a young boy at the emotionally abusive hand of his mother.

"That wasn't loyalty, Hawk. It was greed and we all know how exposed we are to that."

"Maybe." Hawk grabbed another sandwich and bit into it before he continued, "But since then, we've tightened up our screening of new applicants and do intensive background checks."

"That poses the question: why did you approve her application, Stone?" Shane asked. He watched him closely. Stone never did anything without reason.

"I followed her investigation at the time of Leigh threatening to expose us. There was something about her that I found intriguing. Besides that, she's not a virgin to BDSM. She'd been a regular visitor at various exclusive clubs all over Seattle, Club Sensation being one of them. Hence her application." He paged through her documentation. "The fact that she indicated she's a vanilla was the first thing that sparked suspicion."

"*That* sparked suspicion. Not the fact that she used her real name and you *knew* she's an investigative journalist?" Shane prodded.

A Cheshire grin split Stone's lips apart. His usually warm eyes turned chilled as he looked at his oldest cousin. "No, that just made me more adamant to teach little miss know-it-all she should keep her busy nose out of business that doesn't concern her and that the Sinclairs aren't a family to be trifled with." His eyes darkened as his expression turned serious. "To be frank, I'm concerned that there's more behind this than meets the eye."

"Meaning?" Kane leaned forward and pulled the file closer to scrutinize the content.

"I want to know if there's someone else involved and why. Parker found too many discrepancies in the background checks he did. Information black holes, so to speak and too many variables that don't add up." Stone stood up and started to pace.

"You're talking in circles, Stone. Just spit it out," Hawk rasped.

"Peyton Jackson had been deep undercover in Sudan, chasing a story for a year about the U.S. government's involvement in their political upheaval, or so the reports indicated. Then, three months ago, she's suddenly replaced with Luke Bene. It doesn't make sense. She'd already won the confidence of many politicians in the country by then, even hobnobbing with some of them. Why pull her out at a time when she was that close to the core of the problem? Only to arrive on our doorstep now?"

The seven men silently mulled over the information, each studying Peyton's file thoroughly. Shane glanced around the table. "I have to agree with Stone. Something doesn't add up." He tapped a finger on the folder he'd just closed. "For all we know her and sub ST are working together. I just don't understand why."

"I'll be damned if I do," Ace grumbled. A deep frown marred his forehead.

"It's an assumption at this stage, but yes, Parker and I came to the same conclusion."

"I still don't understand why you approved her application if you knew there was a chance she might expose us." Zeke ran his hand through his spiky hair. "Don't get me wrong. I don't give a shit about the world finding out about Castle Sin or that we live a BDSM lifestyle, but I'd prefer to make the decision how and when to release the information myself and not have it splattered all over the news in a biased and unsavory manner."

"Which is exactly why I want her here. I'm going to get to the bottom of this. Parker is looking deeper to see if he can uncover who tampered with their data. Something warns me there's more to this than meets the eye. I'm concerned it might have to do with Be Secure Enterprises' association with the federal government. Keep your enemies close as they say. In the process, Miss Peyton Jackson is going to find out what a real Master/sub relationship is like. Once I'm done with her, she won't want to leave, let alone tell the world about us."

"That spark in your eyes worries me, Stone," Parker said as he looked at his brother. Stone had a dark side, one that he kept hidden from the outside world, but here at Castle Sin, he sometimes let go of the reigns that held back the black Beast inside him. Parker suspected that this time, he wasn't going to hold back; he intended to release the full force of the darkness on the unsuspecting woman.

"You're not the one who should be worried, bro," Stone said with a cold smile.

"Yeah," Parker and the rest of the men chuckled. "If she knows what's best for her, Peyton Jackson would be better off to turn tail and run the moment the boat docks."

Chapter Three

Stone didn't relax once his cousins left to welcome the newcomers. He was in no hurry to follow them downstairs. They would wait until he arrived before proceedings began. He stood at the window with binoculars, watching Danton ease the boat into the docking bay. His eyes narrowed on shining auburn hair as the sun caught the luxurious tresses the moment the tall woman jumped with agility over the rails. She landed like a graceful feline on the wooden dock before the sleek boat came to a standstill.

With an expressionless face, he watched as she turned to stare at the imposing castle. He refused to acknowledge the punch in his gut the moment she tilted back her head and he saw her face. She had a classic Audrey Hepburn kind of beauty, her heart-shaped face enhanced by the deep red of her hair that tumbled in loose curls over her shoulders. The view through the lenses did nothing to blur his reaction to her. Tall, at least five feet seven or eight, she carried her curves with a gentle sway of her hips. She wasn't catwalk model thin but he felt the effect of her rounded hips and full breasts in the twitch of his cock. Not to mention the excited purr of the Beast inside his soul.

Stone had master control over his emotions and body. It shook him that lust exploded in his loins and stirred forgotten emotions in his mind by just looking at her. He'd instantly recognized her from memory and the latest photograph included in her application.

Peyton Jackson.

"Not very clever to use your real name, sub PJ, especially since you're here under false pretenses." His voice sounded deep, guttural and vibrated with a hidden promise in its depth. His eyes turned dark, swirling with silver flashes, like a tumultuous sea during a storm. A grin twitched his lips. "Two can play at this game, little one. You undoubtedly know who we are but probably think we're clueless about you. Let's see how long you can keep up the pretense."

Stone picked up a molded iron half-mask that covered the top part of his face and fitted it in place before he strapped it around his head. They always wore these masks at the initiation meeting. Each cousin's mask was shaped in the form of the animal totem they chose as their Master name in Castle Sin.

Wearing them served a double purpose. Not only did it keep their true identities intact until the new trainees committed their loyalty to them and the program, but it also aided in the mystery, the danger, and the fear among the trainees. In the end, they all came to care for them, not wanting to leave the dungeons but wishing only to be submissive to the Masters who spent seven grueling months to turn them into perfect submissives or slaves.

Tears generally flowed at the graduation ceremony where they were allocated to their private living quarters in the massive five-story medieval designed castle with seven training dungeons and three luxurious Castle Sin Dungeons for members.

One entire floor was dedicated to house fifty full-time submissives and slaves that chose to become Castle Sin employees to serve the exclusive members of the club.

Members were handpicked and invited personally. Only those who could afford the exorbitant fees and wished to be ensured of total privacy and discretion because of their status in the community were considered. It was rare that a Dom who accepted their invitation wished to bring along his own sub or slave. They generally stayed over for a couple of days to play and enjoy their kink with the variety Castle Sin offered.

By the time Stone arrived at the Gathering Hall the seven new trainees were waiting meekly in the Castle Sin present position, standing upright with their hands clasped behind their backs, shoulders straight and eyes lowered to the floor. His approach was so quiet, none of the women were aware of his presence. He stood watching their posture, silently assessing, as did the six men standing around them. Two of the women appeared uncomfortable and squirmed under the intense regard, the other four were relaxed and in true submissive form, awaiting the attention of their Doms.

Stone wasn't surprised to find that Peyton Jackson was one of them. He already knew she was into BDSM.

She's failing her mission so soon, he grimaced inside his mind. He was disappointed in a way, having expected her to play the part of a vanilla sub to perfection and yet, here she was, portraying complete subjugation.

And so the plot thickens, my little dove.

It had been a long time since Stone had felt the excitement of the hunt, circling his prey and finding the weaknesses that would allow him to get inside a sub's head. He experienced it now and it thrilled him with a profound intensity that stunned him.

Fuck, I want this woman.

He listened to the voice echoing in his mind. It had been a forgotten sensation. The lust searing through his entire frame, the thrill of dominating a submissive and the utter satisfaction of watching a woman helpless and writhing in his grasp. A woman he wasn't training but enjoyed for his pleasure.

What the hell, why not? Now that I'm done with acting, it's time to settle down.

He walked around them to stand next to Shane and Kane who faced them, with the rest of his cousins and fourteen resident training Doms surrounding them. Behind them, the sixty odd trainees who were already in various stages of their training, watched silently with the current fifty permanent residing submissives and slaves regarding the initiation process from comfortable sofas on the opposite side of the hall.

"Eyes." His voice echoed deep, guttural and demanding through the acoustics of the large room. He couldn't deny the satisfaction of watching Peyton start when she lifted hers to be caught in the darkness of his gaze that didn't waver from his regard of her.

At first, he was startled at the extreme deep blue of her eyes; beautiful and striking. He blinked and realized they were, in fact, a mesmerizing shade of violet. A wayward thought flashed through his mind whether she was a descendant of Elizabeth Taylor who had the exact color eyes.

She was unsettled. Exactly like he wanted her to be. A raw grin split across his face as he watched her guard rise to hide her feelings from his piercing gaze.

Now that's the kind of challenge I can't resist, little dove. Yeah, Peyton Jackson. You just sealed your own fate!

He looked down the line of women, ensuring he caught each one's eyes before he moved to the next. Between him and Shane, they had an innate ability to read new trainees with that first glance, that first clash of gazes. The seven women's emotions varied from excitement, trepidation, and insecurity, to fear. No different than any of the hundreds of submissives that had walked through the castle doors over the past seven years. Employment contracts were limited from six months to a year, where after new submissives were appointed or old ones renewed. They also trained as many, if not more, submissives and slaves, with no interest in a position at Castle Sin but who strived for perfection.

Their training was thorough—a seven-month process in groups of no more than ten trainees at a time per Master—it was precise and aimed at creating the perfect submissives and slaves. Each trainee spent a full month under the tutelage of one of the Masters of the castle. Only the ones who mastered all the skills expected from each Master ended in the final stage with Stone who did the final evaluations. The ones who didn't pass his muster, either left the island or re-did the sessions they'd failed.

"State your name, surname, age, and the reason you're here." His voice didn't sound remotely like the deep, soothing tone of his acting persona. It was harsh, grating, and brooked no resistance from the women facing him. He held out his hand to the side, smiling warmly at the familiar feel of the hard leather handle of his custom made red crop his assistant training Dom placed in his palm. It was made from tough leather with the clapper on the end covered in hard leather knobs which added that extra sting when needed. The subs have aptly christened it, the King's Sting.

"I don't like to repeat myself," he rasped with his eyes on the woman to the far left. He watched her tongue flick nervously over her lower lip. His smile widened. It was going to be fun mind fucking this little trainee.

"I ... er, my name is Cora Dunning from Louisiana, I'm thirty-two." She shifted her feet but kept her gaze on him. He silently applauded her courage. From memory, he knew she was new to the lifestyle. "I need a place where I can release the boundaries of suppression I've lived under for far too long. I need to be heard, to be understood, and to become the woman I know is desperate to come out of her shell and feel cared for and safe at the same time. I need ..." She swallowed hard. "I'm not exactly sure what else I need, Sir," she ended softly.

Stone walked closer. His large hand cupped her cheek. She tilted her head and leaned into his touch.

"Ah, little one, you might be new to the lifestyle but you're a natural submissive. It's going to be a pleasure to guide you and find exactly what it is you need."

"Thank you, Sir."

She hissed as a sharp sting landed on her inner thigh. She blinked hurt-filled eyes at him.

"Who is your sir, sub?"

Her tongue did another foray over her lips. Stone couldn't resist the unintended invitation. He swooped lower and caught her surprised mouth in a hard and lustful kiss. He fisted his hand in a tuft of hair and tilted back her chin as he lifted his head.

"Keep doing that, little one and you'll be on your back with your legs spread wide, getting fucked like a bitch in heat more times than you can count."

Her breath came in short puffs; her arousal obvious in the tightening of her nipples and the fragrant aroma that filled Stone's nostrils.

"I'm sorry, Sir ... owww!" she screamed as the crack of the crop found its mark on the outside of her thigh. "Master! I mean Master," she finally remembered the warning Danton had issued upon their arrival.

"There's a good girl," he praised and smiled as she sagged in relief against him. "Get back into position, my pet," he warned as he moved on to the trainee to her left. "You."

"Rose Lovett from Miami. I'm forty-four."

The slightly plump but nicely curved woman dared a small smile at the formidable man studying her intently. Her breath caught in her throat as he traced the hard edge of the crop over the full upper slope of her breasts. A sharp sting against her left nipple reminded her to continue. The painful squeak that puffed from her lips stirred awake Stone's cock. Nothing beat the warm effusion of lust that infiltrated his veins from a painful cry in response to his crop. He could feed his arousal for hours with nothing more than yielding impact tools against soft, supple and luxuriously marble-like skin of an errant submissive.

Stone continued down the line, paying special attention to each trainee. He brushed his palm over a straining nipple here, a snap of the crop when needed there, and another heated kiss to unsettle the redhead at the end of the line even further. She had started to fidget the closer he came.

Then he stood in front of her, watching, waiting, his eyes piercing as he stared at her, unmoving like a statue. The rigid line of his jaw offered a fair warning that he was primed and ready to pull apart every lie she was about to spurt forth.

"I'm Peyton Jackson from ..." she hesitated as he tilted his head sideways, allowing his gaze to take a slow, intimate scroll up and down her body. He took careful note of the delicious shudder that caused her body to tremble as his eyes lingered on her voluptuous breasts.

Crack! Crack!

"Fucking hell! That hurts!" she shrieked as two strikes landed with acute accuracy on the tips of her taut nipples when she didn't continue.

"The next ones are going to sting even more if you don't continue, sub," he grated darkly. He had difficulty suppressing his smile at the mutinous expression on her face. She was feisty. The challenge she represented grew exponentially ...

along with the tumescence that caused the space at the crotch of his jeans to shrink.

"I'm from Se—" She clamped her lips around the word as she remembered the lies on her application form. "I'm from Chicago." Her eyelids fluttered at the flash of anger in his eyes. "I recently moved there," she quickly added to save face. She peeked at him through the sooty fan of her long eyelashes and released a relieved breath when he seemed to accept her explanation. "I'm thirty five and I'm here to become the best person I'm meant to be."

She winced at the sharp crack of the crop against his jeans as he continued to study her silently. Her bottom lip disappeared between her teeth as his insolent gaze traveled over her body a second time. He stepped into her, crowding her as he invaded her private space. He was aware of the mammoth effort it took her not to shuffle backwards. It pleased him that she had the courage to stay put.

"And?"

"And ... er, I'm, well ..."

It was obvious that being unsettled didn't sit well with her, something that she'd in all probability never experienced. She had a strong personality, and the research he'd done since Parker had uncovered who she was, showed she was no pushover. She managed to stand firm in a world still ruled by men.

"Come now, sub. If memory serves, your application stipulated that you're an author. Surely you can articulate your reasons better than a few sputtering words?"

Stone deliberately pushed her. He wanted to see how far she would go with her deceit as well as learn her tells. So far, he had an entire arsenal of them in his pocket already. Biting her lip when she was insecure or scared, her eyes flashed when she was irritated, and she stammered with fluttering eyelids when she lied.

Out of the corner of his eye, he noticed sub ST shifting her weight constantly from one foot to the other with one hand covering her mouth. He turned his head and caught her staring at Peyton with a wide-eyed and horrified look. His gaze moved to Ace.

"Correct sub ST's form, please Master Leo."

The Master names referred to their character and strength in relation to the animal kingdom. Ace's referred to the king of the jungle, the lion. He had the same fierce and protectiveness over those he cared about.

Stone watched Peyton's eyes flare as her cousin screamed in response to the four sharp strikes of Ace's flogger landing in rapid succession on the errant arm. Tears filled sub ST's eyes as she quickly corrected her form.

"I'm sorry, Master Leo. Please forgive me," she said in a teary voice. It was well known that she didn't take well to impact tools and always tried to avoid sessions that included training of such nature.

"I'm not the one you should apologize to, sub ST," Ace growled. "You disrespected Master Eagle."

The eagle was a power totem and Stone personified its spiritual meaning to a T. He had insight into the most minute of details to see life from a broader perspective. With the same grace as the mighty bird of prey, he had the knack to make people look inward and allow their hearts to guide them. He challenged as much as he guided.

Sub ST's eyes clashed with Stone's, wide and fearful. "I'm sorry Master Eagle, I didn't mean to be disrespectful."

Stone didn't respond but soaked in the silent communication between the two women as their gazes slinked together. The warning in Peyton's flashed with a spark of charcoal spots in the deep violet of her irises.

"Interesting," he murmured, smiling within himself as Peyton's gaze swung back to his, watching him cautiously. He leaned closer still. "Do you and sub ST know each other, my pet?"

"I ... er, no, Master, we d-don't."

"Hmm." He straightened to stare at her down the length of his aristocratic iron-covered nose. "Lies always come out, sub, and in here, they aren't tolerated."

He crossed his arms without stepping back. His lips twitched as her breath hissed from her lips. He stood so close that his forearms pressed against her nipples, which had gone as hard as stones. They poked with delicious insistence into his skin.

"Yes, Master," she said in a breathless whisper. Her lips pulled in a downward slope. It was obvious that she had never been exposed to such a powerful Dom, who managed to turn her as meek as a lamb while her brain must be screaming out orders in direct contrast to her reactions at the same time.

It was refreshing to witness the effect he had on a woman he felt attracted to. More than that. There was something pulling them closer, an electric force that threaded around them and created sparks of awareness, lust, and expectations he had never experienced before. It was enlightening.

Stone Sinclair had no intention of fighting against it. Rather, he embraced it.

Peyton Jackson stood no chance. His mind was made up. She was going to be his. In every sense of the word. She'd willingly stepped onto his island. He was going to make sure she didn't leave.

At least not until he's had his fill of her delectably sexy body.

His eyes darkened; his voice lowered warningly. "I'm not done talking with you, little dove. You're hiding something and I'm going to find out what."

He stepped back with a satisfied smirk as she started, her face turning pale. He nodded at Hawk who stepped forward.

"From this point forward, you're in training." Hawk looked at each of them. "Until you have passed every section of your training, you're all treated as trainees, irrespective of your current experience as a submissive."

His no nonsense tone silenced any protest the seven women might have had. They stared at him in meek acceptance.

"It matters not whether you're here to learn to be a trained submissive or slave, the basic principles are the same." His eyes moved over the line of women again. "To ensure proper decorum is maintained throughout the training period, you no longer have the use of your name." His eyes narrowed at the twitter that followed his announcement. "Silence!"

His voice grated like a thunderbolt through the large hall, causing the seven women to jump in fright. Their lips clamped shut. "You will only be known and called by the name sub and your initials." He stared at Peyton. "You are sub PJ, and you sub VK." He pointed at each trainee as he christened them with a razor-sharp look, ignoring their looks of disbelief. "You're stripped of your identity because you're all here to find something you feel is missing in your life or grow as a person. You're on the precipice of something new and what could be an exciting existence, but that will be *your* choice at the end. Where you go from here and how you use the power true submission offers you, is in your hands. Until then … your fate and your future belong to us." He looked them over. "Any questions?"

"Yes, Master. Exactly how long is the training going to be?" Peyton asked. She stood upright, with her shoulders pulled back and her breasts pushed proudly forward in a perfect form of present.

"Didn't you read the material you received after your application was approved, sub PJ?" Stone rasped, watching her steadfastly.

Her weight shifted but she bravely lifted her eyes to his.

"I did and it mentioned seven months but ..." her eyes widened as the realization sank in. "Are you saying we'll be in training for the entire seven months?"

"Indeed. One month per Senior Master."

The Beast purred and clawed at his chest to be released at the expression on her face. It fed the sadist in him, the need to completely fuck with a sub's mind until she became lost in a whirlpool of confused emotions; helpless to fight the sensations he'd teach her to crave—all fed by him—him and him alone.

I can't wait to get my hands on her ... or my cock inside her for that matter.

Chapter Four

Peyton was too shocked to respond other than stare blankly at the expressionless mask that made each of the seven Masters look eerie and scary. Not that it mattered. Every single woman in that massive Gathering Hall looked flushed, caught in the magnetism the powerful men represented, the danger that produced a flush of pheromones they were helpless to control. Peyton included.

"It's time for inspection. Strip, slaves."

The order slashed toward them from the mighty king of the castle himself. From the moment he'd snapped the word 'eyes' and she'd looked into globes the color of dark moss growing on the forest ground, she'd known. He held the ultimate power at Castle Sin. The glow that had darkened them almost black as she'd watched, warned her there was a dark side to him. Her breath snagged in her throat in remembrance.

The Beast! Oh, fucking hell! It's him! He's the Beast Danton spoke about! The one he said would take an interest in—oh holy shit!

And, the man behind the mask was none other than Stone Sinclair. She would recognize his eyes and those gorgeous oh-so-kissable-lips anywhere. Her stomach did a flip-flop and continued into a series of somersaults as he sauntered closer. She had to plant her feet into the floor to keep them from slapping a staccato of retreat on the marble tiles back to the speedboat.

"Do you have a hearing problem, sub PJ?"

A whiff of his warm breath caressed her temple as he stopped in front of her. She felt a shudder of arousal through her body. Her nerve endings sparked to life as he trailed a broad finger over her shoulder.

"No, of course not, Master."

"I'm going to say this once. The next time I have to repeat myself, it'll come in the form of punishment. In here, you react immediately when given an order, is that understood?"

Her breasts lifted as she heaved in a deep breath of annoyance. Stone's eyes narrowed, the warning in them was as clear as the blue sky she could see through the large bay windows.

"Yes, Master." Peyton decided to curb her bratty nature. She needed to stay on the island, especially after she'd witnessed her cousin's reaction to the short whipping. She had to get Savannah out of here.

"Then why are you still dressed?" This time the dark growl came from deep inside his stomach.

Peyton looked to the right. All six women were already naked. "You expect me to strip naked," she glanced around the room filled with people. "in front of all of them?"

"Well, this is a pity, I was looking forward to taking you in hand personally. So be it." He looked up. "Danton, take Miss Jackson back to the mainland. Evidently, she came to the wrong place."

"But—" She gulped and her eyes bulged as he wrapped a large hand around her throat and squeezed, forcing her onto her toes.

"But nothing. Either you came here to be trained and are committed to the entire process or you leave."

"I ... please!" she croaked, swallowing with difficulty as his fingers tightened.

"Decide and be quick about it but know this Peyton Jackson, if it's to stay, it will be because it's what *you* want, knowing the next seven months won't be a walk in the park." His nose pressed against hers. "Female wiles will get you nowhere, nor will a bratty attitude, except to either be whipped black and blue or fucked until you pass out. Either way ... choose. Now."

She groped at the small pearl buttons of her blouse. She undid them hastily and unclipped the front clasp of her bra in response. His fingers stroked the back of her neck, briefly, before they tightened again.

"I expect an answer, Miss Jackson."

"Yes, I'm staying, Master."

"Loud enough for everyone to bear witness."

His growl brooked no further resistance, nor did she offer any. She'd realized the moment they'd arrived in the Gathering Hall to meet the Masters and training Doms that these men wouldn't be manipulated or topped from the bottom. Something she'd become known for at the few clubs she frequented. Here, she'd have to be careful not to step on any of their toes. They all oozed confidence; power exuded from them in waves and it was obvious they were more than experienced in training subs.

They were the BDSM lifestyle.

They lived it.

They breathed it.

They were IT.

"I am committed to the training program and I'm staying."

Crack! Crack!

Peyton jumped back a couple of steps, shrieking with pain from the harsh strikes connecting with her just bared nipples. She cupped her breasts, forcing back tears as she dared to glare at the offending Master.

"Lower your hands, sub PJ. In here you don't cover any part of your body unless instructed to. When you respond to any of us, you *will* do it properly. Care to try again?"

Peyton imagined one eyebrow shooting toward his hairline under the offending iron mask. She had only been here an hour and she already hated those silver-gray molds covering half of their attractive faces. She lowered her hands, aware of the burning throb of the stinging strikes across her nipples. She'd be damned if she gave him another reason to punish her again. Like Savannah, she wasn't fond of impact tools but for an entirely different reason.

"I'm committed to the training program and am staying ... *Master* Eagle," she clipped, relieved when his name popped up in her mind. That would teach her to pay better attention. Each Master had been introduced before he had arrived but they were warned Master Eagle was the ruler, the Master Dom, the king of the castle, and not someone to be toyed with.

"That's better." He flicked a finger up and down. "Continue."

Now Peyton wished she hadn't balked against getting naked. She should've known from the thick manual of instructions and explanations that had been delivered to her apartment that this kind of thing would happen. She'd stupidly thought it would only be those who had applied as slaves who would be forced to go naked in public, which was why she'd applied for a position as a submissive.

How mistaken she'd been!

Her hands trembled as she pushed the blouse and bra over her shoulders and felt it slip down her back to slither to the floor. She dragged in a deep breath and reached for the zipper of the skinny jeans that molded to every curvy line of her long legs. Luckily, she didn't have to struggle with shoes first. It was the first thing they had to remove when they'd entered the castle.

If only Stone Sinclair would look away. Her skin already felt too tight for her body. To further exacerbate the matter, she tingled all over, almost like it was his hands caressing every inch of flesh being exposed, rather than his eyes. The dratted man unsettled her, too damn much.

Worse! The fucking man knew it!

If Peyton had been embarrassed to stand bare ass naked in front of roughly a hundred people, she turned into a glowing lobster when Stone walked around her. Her breathing faltered as he brushed his palm over her ass cheeks, the indent of her waist, the soft under slope of her breasts and finally rolling and pinching her aching nipples between his fingers. It was a shock to feel the effect of those tugging fingers all the way to her clitoris which now throbbed incessantly. She sucked in her stomach as his fingers trailed over her belly, to play squiggles on either side of the little nub, which she was relatively sure was so swollen, it must be twice its normal size. It took all the willpower she possessed not to orbit her hips and tilt it into his hand, to force a touch over her pulsing clit.

"Nice body, sub PJ. Perfectly proportioned." His lips flattened as his fingers encountered the soft fluff of hair covering her mound in a thin landing strip. He ignored her squeal as he pinched his fingers around a couple of hairs and yanked them ... *he fucking ripped them*! ... from her body. "Another instruction you chose to ignore, I see."

The smile that curved his lips upward caused a chill of trepidation to course down her spine. It was a grin of such wickedness, she could feel every hair covering her labia shrink back into their follicles.

"Bend over, legs straight and grab your ankles." His voice held a hint of amusement as he waited. The Beast growled in pleasure as her eyes shot to his, narrowing as her lips pursed into a tight pinch.

"I'm not—"

"Dom Evans, please assist this trainee into position."

The dark order still hung low in the atmosphere when a large body slammed into her from behind, grasped her wrists and bent over, forcing her to follow suit. Before she could blink, her wrists were cuffed to her ankles.

Peyton felt her ears go red. There she was, head between her knees, ass up in the air with her naked pussy spread open to a fucking hundred people! Oh, good lord, the embarrassment!

"Hmm … let me see what else I'll find."

She cringed at the deep rasp above her. If not for fear that she'd topple over, she would've jumped out of the way when his warm hand cupped one of her ass cheeks. His huge paw completely covered it.

Holy shit! Imagine that hand spanking—

Her eyes met his sparkling ones. She shook her head. He chuckled.

Crack! Crack!

"Jesus! Owww *fucking* oww!" Peyton screamed as he did exactly what she was about to envision. Pain seared to her brain from where he was rubbing what she was sure was her bruised ass. Only, it got hijacked by the heat surging through her veins to set her loins throbbing.

Noo! Not now, she wailed in her mind. She squeezed her eyes shut, not wanting to witness the glaring proof of her arousal on her labia that glistened with the juices that oozed from between her lips. In the position she was in, she could smell her own lust.

"Well, well, just look at that." A hard boot kicking her foot, prodded her to open her eyes. Her cheeks burned with shame as she looked up at him, well aware of the view he had; one *she* did her best to avoid looking at. "Not me, little dove. This," he said and tapped her labia with his fingers. Tell me what you see."

"Oh lord, you're not serious," she said in a thin voice.

"You will learn that I never say anything I don't mean. Now, I'm waiting."

Peyton cursed quietly and closed her eyes briefly to gather some strength.

"M-my labia are spread wide open and appear to be puffy and darkened," she quickly rambled off the sentence after a glance at her nether region. It was beyond embarrassing.

"And?"

She shot an angry look up at him, which he countered by crossing his arms and spreading his legs wide. A sharp silver streak lit up his eyes.

"It seems you're the first trainee begging to be punished, little dove. Believe me, I'll be more than happy to comply."

Peyton immediately looked away, focusing her gaze on his big ass feet, not surprised at their size. He needed serious planters to keep his massive body grounded. She swallowed hard. If what they said about a man's cock size in correlation to his feet … *Holy shit! Then he must be fucking huge!*

She groaned within herself as another hot flush heated her loins. She bit into her bottom lip as she felt the telltale trickle of her juices from between her labia.

"I'm waiting, slave."

"Master Eagle, please," she pleaded in a small voice, refusing to lift her eyes from their regard of his feet.

"You're an intelligent woman, sub PJ. I'm sure you're aware of the repercussions of standing upside down for too long." The dryness in his voice attested to the fact that he wasn't bothered by whether she toppled over and died at his feet.

"I'm fucking wet, okay!" she snapped, her eyes clashed with his in defiance. "My juices are dripping from my … from between my lips."

"Indeed they are and a very enticing view it is too. Unfortunately for you, seeing as you decided to disregard the instruction to ensure your pussy is clean-shaven upon arrival, I'm going to require assistance with your first inspection."

Peyton cringed as she watched too many feet to count approach and stop beside Stone's. Still, she refused to look at him. It was debilitating to be bent over and watch from between her legs, knowing all their eyes were on her spread open private parts.

Good lord, what was I thinking? I should've known this was way more than any of the club's I'd been to.

That's the problem, Peyton. You didn't think. You didn't even read all those documents, just jumped in with both feet. To the rescue … to your own detriment!

She couldn't even deny the judgment she heard in the soliloquy in her mind. She hadn't read the thick file. At best, she'd skimmed through it, completely disregarding the rules and prerequisites sections. Too much in a hurry to get to the part that stipulated when and where she had to be to join the Castle Sin training regime.

Now, she was paying the price. She suspected this was nothing but a small taste of what the powerful Master Dom—the king of the castle—had in store for her.

"Masters, if you please."

Peyton whimpered as another big pair of boots stepped closer. Warm hands brushed over her flanks, her ass cheeks and thighs before blunt fingers trailed up and down her labia, gently pulling them apart. Her breath hissed from her lips as he pushed a finger deep inside her channel, swirling and brushing it against the satiny walls deep inside her. She all but jumped when she felt him press a finger against her anus.

No! Lord no! Not that, she wailed in her mind but of course, he did. Her ears hot and her cheeks reddened, she could do nothing but meekly accept the intimate prodding of her back hole and vagina. She sighed in relief when he stepped back.

"Done, Master Eagle. Apart from the offending fluff all over her delectable cunt, I can't find any defects," the deep voice of Master Hawk fell to her ears.

"I need to Be Secure. Master Leo, if you please."

By the time all six of the Senior Masters had prodded, patted and swirled their fingers all over and inside her, she had difficulty standing with her knees that threatened to buckle. She was so aroused, her loins throbbed with painful intensity, not to mention the wet secretions that now dripped freely from her exposed pussy to splatter on the sleek marble floor in front of her. She felt like crying when she noticed Stone walking closer. The one rule Master Hawk had drilled into them when they'd first arrived was that they weren't allowed to climax unless given permission. She was so close that just thinking of this man she'd had a celebrity crush on for years, touching her, almost tipped her over.

'Hmm, nice firm ass and thighs, sub PJ, strong muscles. I can almost imagine how hard you'll grip me between them when I fuck you."

Peyton moaned as he brushed his palm over her pussy, from the front to the back, over and over. With every pass, he dipped a finger inside her slit to rub her essence over her throbbing clitoris.

"Please, Master Eagle," she managed through thin lips. Her eyes were scrunched closed in a desperate attempt to concentrate on keeping back the approaching climax. The sharp needle pricks of heat that stabbed at her loins and turned her clit into a hard, little pearl warned her she was on the edge of tumbling over.

"Please what, little dove?"

His voice droned in a grating rasp to find resonance deep in her soul. The muscles inside her pussy clenched, heat exploded in her chest as he hilted three thick fingers inside her pussy, brushing against the swollen ganglia of nerves on the front wall of her vagina. She wailed as he twisted his hand to swirl his thumb over her clit in slow, seductive circles.

"I feel faint ... I can't ..." she groaned as his fingers immediately exited her clinging pussy. Desperate times called for desperate measures.

Besides, she'd lied so much already, another white lie wouldn't make a difference. Within seconds the cuffs were loose and Stone gently assisted her to straighten. His sharp glance turned dark as he examined her flushing face intently. It prodded her to do the next best thing to avoid his too astute eyes. Her legs crumbled and she promptly sat down on the floor.

On the one hand, she was relieved that he'd immediately acted, but her body berated her with every throb in her loins and pulse of her clitoris. The little nub suddenly seemed to have a will of its own— worse—a voice that kept yelling at her, *"Come! I want to come!"*

She kept her head lowered, hiding her face behind the silky curtain of her hair, praying that he'd assume the red flush on her face was because she'd been standing ass upside down for too long and not because of the blatant lie.

Master Eagle, of course, was a Dom first and foremost. He went on his haunches in front of her. It was senseless to resist the hard pinch of his fingers around her chin tilting back her head while he brushed her hair out of the way. He would have none of her hiding from him.

"Eyes," he snapped darkly.

Her gaze lifted and got caught in a piercing look as sharp as a green laser flashing in a black night. She had no control over the darkening blush that once again bloomed over her cheeks.

His eyes narrowed.

She could almost see one eyebrow crawling higher on his forehead.

And just like that, Peyton was screwed.

Her celebrity crush expounded into an attraction so profound, she could feel volts of electricity searing through her body from where his fingers touched her. Her lips separated, her tongue did a quick foray over her suddenly desert-dry lips. His fingers tightened as his gaze followed its path.

"If you believe me to be a fool, you just made a big mistake, sub PJ."

"I don't—"

"Silence! You'll learn that I abhor deceit, however minute it may seem to you."

He straightened but didn't release her gaze. She tilted her head to stare at the man towering over her like a veritable giant. A shiver of trepidation trailed down her spine when his eyes darkened as he looked upon her down his iron covered nose.

"I will deal with you later. You've wasted enough of everyone's time." He gestured to the women behind her. "Get up and stand in line."

He turned to face the trainees, his gaze inscrutable as Peyton struggled to her feet and took her place next to the other trainees.

"For the next two days you'll have the freedom of the island to explore and find your roots in your new temporary home. In three days you'll be evaluated to establish your level of experience insofar as the BDSM lifestyle and being a submissive is concerned. Based on that you'll be allocated to one of the Senior Masters to commence your training along with the rest already in session. Understand this, trainee slaves: disrespect, insubordination, and willfulness won't be tolerated. If you waste the Master and the other trainees' valuable time, you will be treated accordingly. Let this be your warning. Do not ask for punishment with a bratty attitude. You're here to learn and we take your training seriously." Stone ensured he looked at each of the women as he spoke. "Once you've been allocated to a Master, you'll be moved to your sleeping quarters for the next seven months. For tonight, you'll be served dinner in the Concubine Room, where you'll be sleeping." He gestured at Zeke and Parker who waited under the wide arch leading toward the stairs. "Please follow Masters Dragon and Tiger."

Stone watched the women trot in the direction of the two men.

"Except you, sub PJ," he barked as Peyton came abreast of him.

Her footsteps faltered. She looked at him warily. The dark glimmer in his gaze was full of evil intent. She silently cursed her stupidity. She'd pinned them all as powerful Doms the moment she'd slapped eyes on them. Stone Sinclair definitely led the pack. She should've known better than to try and play him with her trickery and lies. He had seen right through her.

"Dom Evans, please escort sub PJ to the Penance Room in my wing. I'll deal with her later. Make sure she's in position for me when I arrive."

He kept his gaze on her throughout. No matter how hard she tried, she couldn't hide the flash of fear. She'd done the one thing she shouldn't have. Drew the Beast's attention, but no, why the hell would she listen to her inner voice? Now, she was dead center, in the eye of the hurricane. She had a feeling she was about to experience the first of the mighty Master Eagle's wrath. She opened her mouth to talk but the warning look from Dom Evans was enough for her to snap it closed.

"Follow me, sub PJ," Dom Evans growled as he turned to leave.

"But what about my clothes," she dared to ask. The rest of the trainees had been allowed to take theirs when they left.

She stiffened as a hard body pressed against her back. The instantaneous sizzling of her nerve endings was enough for her to know who it belonged to. His breath was warm against her temple as he rasped in a deep voice, "Clothes are a privilege earned, sub. One, you have yet to achieve."

"What are you saying?" Peyton lilted, although she feared she already knew the answer.

"Until you act properly, you won't need any clothes." His hand brushed over her taut nipples. "I for one, hope you never do."

Peyton couldn't get away fast enough. She all but ran after Dom Evans as a flush of pheromones heated her loins from that brief contact. She had to put some distance between her and the demon man before she did the unspeakable and climaxed from no more than a brush of his skin against hers.

She had just arrived at Castle Sin and there was already the promise of punishment hanging over her head. She could only hope Master Eagle preferred a flogging or spanking over forced or withheld climaxes. As coiled up as her insides were, she'd fail both of those miserably. No, she'd be much better off if he used those humongous hands on her ass rather than anywhere else.

Chapter Five

"I'm not going to change my mind, Shane. I'm done. I am not doing another movie. I told you when the last one finished that I'm not signing up for another sequel." Stone's stern tone was in contrast to his large body slumping lazily in the sofa at the boardroom in Castle Sin. "You know I never intended to do more than that first movie. I caved in to do the second and was stupid and young enough to let the excitement of the adrenaline to do such a fast-paced action series pull me in for a couple more. But no more. I lost the passion for acting. This, Castle Sin and Be Secure Enterprises, is what's important now."

"I'm with Stone on this, Shane," Hawk said in a low rumble.

"Me too," Parker interjected. "Hell, the attention of all the chicks is great but with all due respect to those of you who are born actors, I've got to work my ass off to get every scene perfect. Besides, like Stone said, Be Secure Enterprises needs us now."

"Why now? You've always coped fine during filming to manage the company in between. It's a couple of months. Come on, Stone, this one is produced in Hawaii," Shane said.

"Because we've just signed a massive contract with the U.S. federal government. It's going to take a lot of time and work to get the project off the ground." Stone sighed heavily. "Look, we fulfilled the contract for all the sequels we agreed upon way back when. I, for one, am not getting trapped into another ass tight agreement for ten more years."

Shane frowned. "You're right. Neither am I. I think we're all ready to lay down the reins as far as the Space Riders are concerned. I'm too old to compete with all the young actors but I owe it to my career to go out with something big."

"Then get them to end the series. Come on, Shane, we've done nine already and that's more than enough." Zeke sat forward and stared keenly at his older half-brother. He'd looked up to him since he was a baby. Following in his footsteps had been a no brainer but only after he'd promised Shane he'd get a business degree. Their mother and Zeke's father had died in a car accident when he was the young age of ten. Shane, twenty-four at the time, had been forced to step in and take care of him. He had just qualified as a psychologist when the part as a young officer in a war drama had fallen in his lap when the producer had seen him act in a community play. He had shot to instant stardom and had been at the top ever since.

Like Stone and the others, Zeke had also started to feel the itch to leave the limelight and acting. He wanted to utilize his skills as a cybersecurity systems analyst and technology specialist. Ever since he'd started working with Parker, who was an absolute genius insofar as software development was concerned, he'd realized it was where his real passion lay.

"Okay, Zeke, I get it and I agree. Most of us have done other movies over the past couple of years but even I'm tired of the Space Riders. To be honest, I've silently been preparing myself to leave the limelight for a long while."

Shane looked at Kane. "You and I have been acting since we were at school." Shane sat down. "I'll speak to the producers. See if they're willing to write Stone and Hawk out of the movie in the opening scene. Come on, Stone. That'll mean two or three days' worth of filming tops," Shane said as Stone frowned darkly.

"Very well. I'll give you that much but not a day more."

"What about the rest of us? I'm not keen to leave now either, especially as we're just about to start with new trainees," Ace said, tapping his fingers on the desk.

"Production will only commence in five to six months. I just received the script and since they'll have to rewrite it to either end the series or adapt it to move on with a new cast, it won't happen earlier than that, Ace." Stone looked around the table.

"Apart from Stone and Hawk, everyone already signed up for this sequel last year. Even you, Parker. So, Ace and Zeke want out too. How about you Kane?"

Kane and Shane were both fifty-one, but Shane was a couple of months older. They grew up in similar circumstances. Their fathers had been military men and were both killed in Vietnam during the fall of Saigon in 1975. Both boys were only eight years old at the time and they were left devastated. They had been forced to mature emotionally as they'd taken on the roles as the men of their houses. They had always been close but that had created a bond between them that had never been broken.

"It's been one hell of a ride but I agree. I'm tired of the pretend life that comes with acting. It's time to utilize our skills to the fullest we all worked our asses off to get in between the movies. You're one hell of a behavioral psychologist, which makes you an excellent strategist in the business, Shane, and I'm not too shabby at finance and budgeting. We all bought into Be Secure Enterprises. It's not fair that only Stone, Hawk, Ace, and Parker do all the work. Let's make the break now. For once and for all."

"Then it's agreed. This is our last film." A profound sadness colored Shane's voice that he couldn't hide from the rest.

Kane felt it flow through him too as their eyes met. It had been a fantastic career for both of them but their priorities had changed. They didn't crave or need the attention or the awards anymore. He smiled at Shane. "Just make sure we go out with a fucking bang, Shane. Nothing short of explosive will do. Let's make sure the script hits it out of the ballpark."

"Enough of Tinsel Town talk," Ace said. "Fill us in on this federal government deal, Stone."

"It's highly secretive. Only the United States president, the secretary of state, and secretary of defense are involved."

Kane leaned his elbows on the table. "Okay, now I'm intrigued. Not to discount the success or competence of Be Secure Enterprises, but the government has strict measures when appointing contractors. How did BSE make the cut?"

"The secretary of state was involved last year when we designed the safety protocol systems for the CIA, which they were quite impressed with. That, combined with the projects we regularly assist the FBI with gave us the edge. Don't forget that we've become known for the work we do for security and civil protection across the globe." Stone smiled conspiratorially. "Now do you understand why we want to concentrate on BSE? The government could potentially become our biggest client, which will stand as our best credential in securing larger global corporation contracts as well."

"Ideally, we'd like the government to offer us a retainer to safeguard and monitor the systems protocol and safety measures of all their divisions. A 24/7 offsite expert on call as well as a phantom eye in the sky, A Cyber Ghost Guard, so to speak." Hawk looked between the men. "If we pull off this project, that possibility becomes a sure thing and it would mean opening branches nationally."

"Not if, when," Stone said as he got up and refilled his mug with the aromatic coffee brewing on the server table. "We're almost finished with due diligence before we can present a proper proposal to the president." He looked at Shane. "That's why Hawk and I can't afford to leave for Hawaii for months now and," he gestured at Parker, "We're going to need him as soon as we get the go-ahead."

"You still haven't told us what the project is about," Ace prodded. He was miffed that he had been excluded, seeing as he'd worked just as hard on growing the company as the three of them.

"I haven't brought you up to speed on this, Ace, and I apologize. You were in Mexico overseeing the final stages of the security protocol at the Department of Security and Civil Protection at the time this came through. With the arrival of the new trainees, it completely slipped my mind." Stone was relieved when Ace visibly relaxed. "Parker, do you mind?"

"Not at all." Parker sat upright and opened the relevant folder on his iPad. "I'll just detail the basic outline for now and email the link of the folder on the server to everyone once the proposal is finalized." He looked around the room. "You're all aware that we've developed a specialized program that had been one of its kind five years ago. Since its inception, we've used it to secure numerous system drives for the FBI and CIA."

He looked at Zeke. "Cybercrime is on the up rise and with anything revolving around technology, hackers are evolving too. They're not the backstreet, young men looking for a thrill of achievement anymore. It's become a lucrative business because through them it opens so many doors to criminals."

"Don't we know it. Computers make our lives so easy but it's a pain in the ass if someone hacks your accounts."

"Which is why Zeke and I have worked on developing a nanotechnology driven security software program. It's completely undetectable and can identify and deflect any threat before anything is breached. We installed it as a test run in a mirror drive of ours and managed to smooth out a few technicalities six months ago. We launched it live on our system and it's been operational for the past four months at the FBI, CIA as well as at DHS."

"And lucky for them, just in time too," Hawk said.

"The FBI and CIA receive hundreds if not thousands of Cyber threats every day. Their overall systems are advanced but as we've been informed, not impenetrable."

"Fucking hell! The FBI got hacked again?" Ace sat forward in his chair.

"Yes, and Homeland Security as well."

"What did they hack?"

"There have been numerous assassination attempts made on the president and his family over the past year," Stone said solemnly. "The secretary of state appointed a black undercover secret service team to guard the president. It consists of a group of fifty men and women that are rotated all the time. Only Madam Secretary and the president have access to the database where the file is containing their details."

"They hacked that drive?" Shane asked.

"Yes, they're after the names to eliminate them to get rid of the president but with our NanoT integrated into the file, they can't crack the passcode to open the file. The NanoT has a tracking strain in every file that's hacked, so we're able to corrupt it remotely, which in this case was done. Even if they crack the code, the content is gibberish. They're now attempting to access older files to try and extract the information that way. We've been appointed to find out where the breach came from and who is involved. We've also been instructed to secure every government division's databases," Parker said with excitement in his eyes.

"Hawk and I are busy designing a comprehensive national strategy to secure every aspect of the government divisions' data," Stone said.

"This is our biggest challenge to date and we're all excited about it. This is what it's about for us, Shane. This is what makes us tick and why we have no interest in acting anymore," Hawk said passionately.

"Hell, I'm excited and I wasn't even involved. Fucking brilliant. Damn, I feel like a father getting his kids' 4.0 GPA results."

Chapter Six

Two days later …

Stone arrived in the Penance Room as silently as the sweep of his namesake, the eagle. His gaze immediately homed in on the tall woman facing the far wall. Her naked beauty shimmered like glowing silk in the dim lights cast by the wall sconces. Her hands were clasped behind her neck with her hair taken up in a messy ponytail. Dom Evans' handiwork, no doubt.

He was enraptured by the deep curve of her spine that pushed her cute little ass outward in the arched position she was standing. He could almost taste the sweetness of the skin of her smooth legs on his tongue as his gaze traced their toned length.

In his mind, he envisioned them wrapping around his waist as he gorged himself on her hot body.

The interior of the Penance Room was as rough and raw as any of the training dungeons. The surface of the walls had the same appearance as the outside of the Castle—large rough stone-like bricks.

Today was day three of Peyton Jackson's stay at Castle Sin. He'd deliberately stayed away from her and kept her separated from the other trainees, letting her expectation build while she had to wait for him in this room in the same position every day for two hours ... only, he never arrived. It was all part of the mind games he loved to play with submissives.

It was against the rough bricks that Peyton pressed her nipples to keep the two pieces of paper that Dom Evans had warned her not to drop in place. Her feet arched prettily as she stood on her toes to keep her shoulders at the indicated height.

He noticed how the muscles in her thighs trembled from the strain of keeping the position. She'd been standing on her toes for over an hour by now. No doubt with the curt instruction from Dom Evans to keep her form until Master Eagle arrived.

"You may lower your heels."

"Shit!"

Peyton was so startled from the deep guttural voice that suddenly sounded behind her that she started and involuntarily stepped back. She spun around, her hands landing on her hips and her bare toes tapped irritably on the plush carpet.

"Damn it! Why do you have to sneak up on me? Now look what you—"

Her gaze finally lifted to his face. It was inevitable that the sight of his mask-less, gorgeous face left her speechless. It also caused a slither of unease to crawl up her spine. He'd taken his sweet damn time, making her sweat for three days to be punished. As if standing in this uncomfortable position wasn't punishment enough!

"Y-you're not wearing your mask," she stammered, lowering her arms. It was a defensive gesture to wrap one around her breasts as the other dropped to cover her girly bits from his piercing gaze.

One eyebrow drifted lazily toward his hairline, like he was saying, *Yes, and?*

"I ..." Peyton glanced around uneasily, not sure what to do. She had never felt this overpowered by any man or Dom for that matter—physically and emotionally, which left her stumped, especially as he had yet to give any indication of what he thought about her. Probably not much, especially as he hadn't been all that eager to see her again. Her eyes landed on the two pieces of paper on the carpet. She grimaced and dared to peek at him.

Gaawd, he's gorgeous! How the devil am I going to keep my libido in check now that he's not wearing that mask?

As much as she hated it at first sight, now she wished he had kept it on. It would be so much better for her sanity.

Not ours! Her slutty ovaries shouted in protest. Peyton ignored their outcry and decided it might be advantageous to keep him occupied before he fixated on her breaking form. She tilted her head sideways questioningly.

"Why did you remove the mask? Surely you had to realize I would recognize you?"

No matter how hard she tried, her eyes had a will of their own and scored him from head to toe, hungrily and, with what she believed to be, an unacceptable amount of pheromones rushing through her body.

What woman could resist him? He had the perfect model face, square jaw, high cheekbones, and straight aristocratic nose with full and oh-so-kissable lips that her tongue flicked in an uncontrolled sweep over hers. She could almost feel his mouth on hers, soft, slanting back and forth in a lustful—

"Oww!" Peyton cried out at the stinging pain on the outside of her left thigh following a quick flick of his wrist. Her eyes dropped to the offending object in his hand. She took back a tentative step.

"What the devil was that for?" she grumbled, refusing to drop her hands from covering her supercharged girly parts.

Dammit! Why can't I react the same way Savannah does to impact tools?

Heat lined every vein in Peyton's body, spurred on by the searing pain from where the thin cane had connected with her skin. It sparked arousal as far as it traveled.

"Your blabbering is going to get you into all kinds of trouble, sub, and your brattiness ... well, let me put it this way. Unless you learn to curb both of those, you'll spend the next seven months either on all fours or on your back with legs spread wide open."

The offending cane rat-a-tatted against his jeans. She bit back a moan as her clitoris throbbed in tune with its threatening thuds.

"I know Dom Evans well enough to realize he gave you an order. Care to enlighten me what it was?"

"I ... ehm ... no!" She jumped back as he lifted his hand clutching the very thin ... "Holy shit!" she squealed as she noticed the reflection of the light on steel. She looked at him in reproach. "That's a steel rod!"

"Stainless steel, yes and a wonderful tool it is. As strong as they come." He held it on both ends between his hands. His biceps flexed but the cane didn't budge. His grin turned wicked at her wide-eyed and horrified look. "As you can see it doesn't bend." He walked closer forcing Peyton to retreat step for step. "That means this beauty can take ..." his chuckle was as deep as it was threatening, "or should I rather say, *give* a decent beating without bending."

"Oh, fuckity fuck," Peyton wailed as her back connected with the rough stone wall. Her hands lifted automatically to ward Stone off who didn't stop until he pressed into her. Her skin sizzled everywhere they touched. She blinked rapidly, unable to prevent her nipples from turning hard as stones and poking into his chest like steel bullets.

"And it's perfect for temperature play too, little dove. Just imagine how it'll feel iced or warmed up ... yes," he crooned as he watched her pupils dilate and her chest heaved with each labored breath she took.

"Y-yes what?" she breathed. Up close, she became entranced with the warm glow in his eyes. They were the glimmering color of emeralds, sparkling like the light of the morning sun on a fresh sheen of morning dew. That churning, passionate green that the ocean turned during a storm.

"I was right about you." He smiled as she bore back into the unyielding wall that now dug painfully into her skin when he lifted the cane and trailed its cold point over her cheek.

Peyton couldn't breathe. It felt like a hand clamped around her chest and squeezed. All because of his closeness, of what she perceived to be the message he portrayed with the cane following the line of her chin, her throat to track over the upper roundness of her breasts. Which of course raced up and down with every breath she took. Could it be, or was she allowing her imagination to run away with her?

She blinked up at him. Her breath caught in her throat at the heated look in his eyes. This wasn't a Dom looking forward to training a sub. This was a powerful Master who knew exactly what he wanted.

And god help her, that look promised all kinds of pleasure and pain, heaven and hell. Her insides coiled. It staked a claim—on her!

Get a grip, Peyton Jackson! Before he really thinks you're a wuss!

She did her best to reign in the emotions that were rapidly spinning out of control. It wasn't fair. She'd had a celebrity crush from afar on this man for years. Now here he was, pressed against her, and what did she do? She shivered and whimpered like a naughty schoolgirl standing in front of the headmaster.

"I don't know what you mean," she said lamely, praying her voice sounded more confident than the squeak she heard coming from her mouth.

"You will in due time, but for now … what was Dom Evans' instruction?"

Peyton's eyes briefly flicked to the two pieces of paper and back to him. She licked her lips as she dragged in a deep breath and rushed off the sentence in one syllable.

"Ihadtokeepthepaperspressedtothewallwithm ynipples."

Stone struggled not to laugh at the disgruntled expression on her face. It was refreshing to have a sub stand up to him. The trainees were usually scared of him. She was brave, yes, but in this situation, not very clever. However it may be, he enjoyed every second of it, knowing the pleasure he was about to experience at the expense of her tender buttocks. His hand tightened around the leather covered handle of the cane. He could feel pricks of heat stab at his loins, resulting in a rapid expansion of his cock, just thinking of watching every stripe turn red on her delectable ass while she writhed with the arousal from the seductively inflicted pain.

She might deny her experience as a submissive and the BDSM lifestyle as much as she wanted, but her body couldn't hide the truth from his perceptive eyes.

Little Miss Investigative Journalist was a masochist. He'd bet the deed of the island on it.

He turned his head to look at the two square pieces of paper on the deep golden carpet.

"What did he say would happen if you failed?" he asked without looking at her. The cane returned to the rhythmic rat-a-tat against his jeans. He could feel her shrink into the wall at the same time as his nostrils caught the spicy bouquet of her arousal. He suppressed a pleased smile with difficulty.

I'm gonna have so much fun with this little dove.

"Don't let me repeat the question, sub PJ, you won't like the consequences."

"He said that …" the hesitation was brief and then she rushed it off again, "myasswouldmeetthesteelbeast." Her voice spiked at the end as she finally made the connection. The steel beast—his stainless-steel cane. "Fuckity fuck," she muttered under her breath then pinned a woebegone look on him. "It's all your fault. You scared the shit out of me. If you hadn't—"

Peyton all but swallowed her tongue as he turned a dark look on her. His chest pressed into hers. She hissed in pain as the roughness of the stone dug into her back.

"What's the first rule of waiting on your Master, sub?"

"N-not to move, no matter what. To close your mind to …" Her voice drifted off at the satisfied expression on his face. He'd tricked her and she'd fallen for the trap—hook, line, and sinker!

Brilliant Peyton! You as much as admitted you're not a BDSM virgin.

"Yes, sub PJ, the quicker you realize lies will only pull you deeper into the muck, the better. I will deal with that later, for now, let's address your—"

"Please, it's not fair. You arrived as quiet as a mouse and …" She lowered her eyes with shame at the disappointment she noticed in his. This was their first encounter, so to speak, and already she'd failed him. She felt miserable and wanted to crawl into a corner.

Stone pinched her chin to force her gaze to his. He stared at her for long moments.

"I want to hear it, little dove," he said softly.

The deep tones of his voice resonated all the way into her soul. She didn't have to ask what he meant. He was too perceptive and without a doubt had recognized the self-castigation in her eyes. The kind of emotions only a true submissive experienced in the wake of failing her Dom.

"I'm sorry, Master Eagle, for trying to manipulate you. I have no excuse and I'll do my best not to disappoint you again."

Peyton inadvertently leaned into his palm as he cupped her cheek. Stone felt the punch of her unconditional subjugation in the tightening of his cock.

"You will listen very carefully to all the rules in the morning, sub PJ, but here are a couple basic ones of mine you'll never break. If you do, you *will* bear the consequences. First of all, never interrupt me when I'm speaking. Don't ever hide your body and its naked beauty from me. In here, your body and every one of the trainees' belong to me." He ignored her stiffening at that piece of information. "When I give an instruction, you react without hesitation or protest. I don't have the time or the inclination to sweet talk you to obey. If you're unhappy or in distress you *will* immediately talk to me about it. Do you understand?"

"Yes, Master Eagle."

"Now, as I was about to say earlier, it's time to address your insubordination in the Gathering Hall in front of everyone upon your arrival."

Her eyes widened. "You mean …" she exhaled slowly. "You're not going to punish me for dropping those damn pieces of paper?"

He shrugged as he stepped away. "It was Dom Evans' instruction, my pet, not mine. It'll be up to him tomorrow morning to decide whether you should be punished."

He smiled with pleasure, all the while feeling her gaze bore into his back. He had no doubt if she had a knife, she'd cut the grin from his face.

Peyton Jackson was going to be so much more fun to mind fuck than he'd originally thought. And he was already enjoying every minute of it.

Peyton had a hard time keeping her expression neutral and not glaring at the offending man. Then the penny dropped. She'd seen Doms mind fuck with subs before and had always prided herself on never getting trapped in their games. Master Eagle was much subtler in his approach. She felt like a fool for not realizing what he was doing. Building up anticipation and fear—for three fucking days!—and then making her believe he was angry at her breaking form from the wall while he had been enjoying her braying like an ass over it.

She watched him saunter towards the box bed in one corner of the room. It was so high it would reach her waist. A black base cover contrasted starkly against the dark gold carpet. Apart from a couple of puffy pillows, there were no covers or duvets on the covered mattress which was the size of two extra-long double beds. She noticed a small set of wooden steps against its side, obviously to accommodate the subs, seeing as all the Masters weren't just all rippling muscles, they were tall as well.

Stone Sinclair was the epitome of all that rippling and bulging muscles, of course. She licked her suddenly dry lips as she watched his bicep flex when he patted the bed.

"Get on the bed, please. Flat on your stomach with your hips at the edge and your legs hanging over."

Peyton shivered at the mocking smile that broke across his handsome face. His eyes flashed a warning as they bored into hers. The blazing fire in their depths threatened to scorch her to the core. She did her best to suppress the panic that surged inside her as she slowly walked closer. She couldn't help but be reminded of a hungry panther that had just spotted his prey and was about to devour it in one ravenous bite.

Her fearful gaze dropped to the silver cane that shined like a jewel against the blackness of the thick mattress cover. For the first time, real fear unfurled inside her. She'd been participating in BDSM activities for four years and believed herself to be an experienced sub who had the bad habit of misbehaving at times. She enjoyed being flogged and spanked, even had taken to the crop but had always shied away from harsher impact tools such as whips and canes. Her skin shrank in agreement.

"I assume you haven't been caned before?" Stone accurately identified her fear.

"You know I'm new to this and—" Peyton bit back the words as she was raked over with a cold gaze of discontent. She winced in memory. She'd forgotten that moment when he'd seen right through her lies.

"It seems I'm going to have to break you of some bad habits, sub. Lying has just moved to the top of the list."

"I'm sorry."

"Yes, you will be … over and over until I'm satisfied no further untruths will fall from your lips. Get onto the bed," he snapped in a dark voice. His fingers curled around the cane as he lifted it from the bed. He didn't say another word. He waited with his body taut like a coiled mamba ready to strike.

Peyton didn't think it would be wise to open her mouth again and seemingly with little effort, she silently lifted the upper half of her body onto the bed and lay down. She felt vulnerable with her ass all nice and naked sticking over the edge and because the bed was so high, her feet dangled in the air.

"Let's try this again. Have you ever been caned before?"

"No, Master Eagle. Whips and canes scare me."

"Let me guess. You always choose lightweight Doms you can top from the bottom." He ran his palm over the round curves of her cheeks.

CRACK! CRACK!

"Ugh! Good god," she puffed as he landed two harsh slaps on each cheek and then proceeded to rub the sting into her skin. She sagged against the bed as she felt the heat penetrate deeper, shooting like a well-aimed arrow directly to her loins, setting them to throb from the start. She gasped as she felt him grab hold of her ankle and pull it to the side, cuffing it with economic movements to a clanking chain. He ignored her protests and repeated the process with the other leg.

Great! Now I'm spread open like a damn Christmas turkey.

Her ears turned warm as she felt him move to stand behind her.

"Do I need to cuff your arms as well, sub?" The question came sharp and crisp; a clear warning echoed at the edge of it.

"I ... ehm, no," she said in a small voice. It was incomprehensible how small and vulnerable this man made her feel. What completely floored her was how the submissive inside her bloomed at it, craved to be dominated in such a formidable way.

"Are you sure? Because let me warn you, once I start your punishment, I won't stop, whether your hands are in the way or not."

She managed to handle the fear at what was to come but the thought of being tied down completely caused her to tremble violently. She'd rather have her fingers broken if she did the unthinkable to cover her ass while he caned her than have that small freedom taken from her.

"I'm sure, Master."

"Very well. I've tied you in this position as it causes your skin and the muscles in your buttocks and thighs to tighten. That way it'll increase the potency of each stroke I give you."

She glanced at him over her shoulder. "S-strokes?"

"Let's call it stinging strokes, my pet. The cane is my first choice of punishment tool, followed by my red crop. The sooner you learn how to accept its bite, the better for your tender skin."

He traced the outline of the still glowing mark of his hand on her cheeks. "Seeing as it's your first transgression, I'll be lenient with you. Be warned, sub PJ, I take every trainee's training here very seriously. I don't punish unless it's necessary but undisciplined actions and insubordination in front of others, will always end in corporal punishment. Your action will determine the severity of such discipline. Do you understand?"

"Yes, Master Eagle," she said. She felt miserable. She was probably the first new trainee to elicit punishment!

She was stumped at the feeling of failure that assailed her. She didn't even know the dratted man, apart from the image he portrayed to the public as an actor, and yet, here she was, splayed bare by the thought that as a Dom, she had managed to disappoint him from the beginning.

It had taken Peyton years to accept the fact that she was a sexual submissive by nature. Proof of that was in her continued returns to BDSM clubs after that first visit to follow through on a lead of a well-known politician indulging in what the public deemed to be unacceptable behavior. She had no legitimate reason to go back, except that the flogging she'd volunteered for, had opened her mind to entirely new sensations and emotions. The story— she never wrote it.

When she'd finally admitted it to herself, her inner submissive strived to be the best that it could be. Just like everything she did in life, she took to it with the same passion. She had always prided herself on the rush of power to give herself over to the Doms she chose, fully embracing the commitment never to disappoint them during their alliance. Although she had a reputation for being bratty, she was also known as a submissive who prided herself on pleasing her Dom.

Until now. She had failed the moment she'd stepped inside Castle Sin.

She had never felt as miserable as she did at that moment.

Chapter Seven

Stone was aware of the turmoil swirling inside Peyton. He was astute in reading submissives and knew now that his initial assessment about her had been spot on. She was a natural sub who took pride in pleasing her Master. The fact that she had failed upon landing on the island, slayed her. It was there in her eyes, in the stilted movements of her body and the way her shoulders slumped dejectedly.

His lips twitched in a cynical grimace. Unfortunately, her lies had brought her to this. Something he intended to get out in the open soon. Once it was resolved, he could fully embrace the path ahead he envisioned for the two of them.

Secretly, he was pleased by her misery of what she perceived to be submissive failure. It meant he'd be able to push her harder and quicker than the rest.

"Before we continue, sub PJ, remind me what safe word we use at Castle Sin."

Peyton dared to glance at him over her shoulder, surprise evident in her gaze.

"King," she said after searching through the frayed emotions casting a gloom in her mind. She blinked at him with a hopeful look on her face. "Wait, are you saying I can use my safe word? Even during punishment?"

"You will always have the right to use your safe word. During the training period, we trust no trainee sub would as it's a time to embrace change and the skills we aim to teach. During punishment, I can only hope you won't use it, that you'll trust me and my skill to read your signs accurately and not to push you past your boundaries. I'm warning you right now, if you use your safe word before you've reached the edge of your endurance, I'll know and I'll be very disappointed." His gaze sharpened. "To such an extent that I'll hand over your training to another Dom. If that's your aim … you came to the wrong place for the wrong reasons. It's your choice, sub PJ. Is that want you want?"

Peyton immediately shook her head. "Of course not, Master Eagle, but it's a relief to know I've got a choice."

Stone nodded regally. With the tip of the steel cane against her chin, he gently forced her to turn her face forward. She took the hint and relaxed back on the bed.

He was pleased to notice how her body immediately stiffened when he spoke in a voice that grated rougher than he intended, "I'm going to give you ten strikes on your ass and legs. The aim is for you to realize and acknowledge your misbehavior. If I feel at the end of the ten strikes your apology isn't heartfelt and honest, I will add an additional five."

"Master, I'm sorry. It was just—"

CRACK! CRACK!

Her scream echoed through the room as he repeated the slaps on her buttocks with a hell of a lot more bite than the first two.

"Like I said earlier, many bad habits. As a seasoned sub you should know when to stop talking, my pet, and you've passed that mark long ago."

He rubbed her cheeks, hard, drawing a tortured moan from her lips. His chuckle attested to the fact that he knew it wasn't due to the burning pain but rather the flush of juices filling her pussy.

"From this point, you ask permission before you speak." He kneaded her soft rear between his large hands. "Although I'm going to keep the impact light, as a rookie to caning, each stroke will leave behind a white-hot line that'll leave a sinking or searing sensation into your body. You'll even experience vibrations throughout your anus and ..." he ran his fingers over her labia, delighted to find them coated with her glistening essence, "this very wet little cunt."

He laughed as she jerked against his hand.

"You'll feel a radiating warmth spread from every welt into your loins. And in the end, my little recalcitrant dove, a feeling of surrender will travel up your spine. Then, you might admit and feel the castigation of your misbehavior wash over you, drowning you in the well of my disappointment in your actions."

Peyton had listened with a beating heart to every word he said. By the time he finished, she was ready to shout her regret to the roof but realized it would do her no good. Not until she'd suffered the consequences of her actions.

She hissed as she felt the cold steel of the cane trace the insides of her thighs followed by soft taps from one leg to the other. It didn't hurt at all but it did cause her to tense her muscles in expectation of the intensity increasing.

Tap-tap-tap-tap.

The sound found resonance inside her mind which was desperately trying to tune out the rapid rise of arousal that heated the blood in her veins. The strokes continued up and down the insides of her legs, the back and outside of her thighs. They sped up as Stone tap-danced the steel rod all over her butt cheeks.

"This was to make you accustomed to the feel of the cane. Now, the punishment starts."

Her cheeks immediately bunched tightly as she turned tense. His palm whispered over her buttocks, now kissed alive and wired, every nerve ending sparked and heated.

If I feel like this now, how the devil am I going to last ten strikes?

Peyton cursed her spread legs, desperate to squeeze her thighs together to contain the flush of desire that heated her loins.

"No, sub PJ, I'm sure you know better than this. Don't tense up or this caning is going to be a lot worse than it has to be," he warned.

SNAP! SNAP!

Before Peyton could brace herself, the first two strokes fell in rapid succession, first across the one cheek and then the other.

"Oww!" she moaned and pressed her face into the bed, her buttocks squeezed tighter as a bolt of white-hot pain blazed from her ass through her mind.

"It seems to me you need to keep your mind busy during the punishment. Relax these cheeks, sub," he rasped brusquely.

"Easy for you to say!" she snapped once the pain finally settled in a hot streak inside her nether region.

"I do recall telling you not to speak, didn't I?"

"Fuckity fuck," Peyton cursed herself for allowing the brat in her to spark to life so soon after guilt had castrated her for her sassy actions. Her hands fisted. She clamped her lips closed.

"Indeed," Stone rasped. "You just added an additional four strikes to your count. Before I continue, remind me why I'm punishing you."

"Because I was insubordinate and disrespectful to you in front of everyone in the Gathering Hall, Master Eagle," she lilted in a small voice. It was evident failing her Dom as royally as she had, didn't sit well with her.

"And?"

"I spoke without asking for permission," she moaned as he ran his hands over her thighs.

"And that awarded you how many swats?"

"Fourteen, Master," she said quietly.

"Good girl," he grated. "I'm punishing you to ensure you'll remember the importance of paying attention to Castle Sin rules as well as following the proper decorum we expect from every trainee sub and slave on this island. Being insolent and insubordinate towards me, the Master Dom, will never be tolerated by any of the Masters here. Do you understand?"

"Yes, Master."

"You will count out the strikes and thank me after each one," he said in a strict voice.

Was he freaking crazy? He wants me to thank him for whipping me?

This time Peyton curbed the natural tendency to speak up and took a deep breath. She couldn't keep her body from going tense as she waited for him to continue the punishing swats. It didn't matter that he was holding back, to her, the first two had felt like her butt was about to split open.

SNAP!

"Holy shit!" she cried out in shock as the steel edge connected with the narrow, creased area where her upper thighs joined her buttocks.

"Count, sub PJ," he demanded

"One, Master," she bit out.

"And what else, sub? Better think quickly or I'm going to start over," he warned, his voice dark.

"Thank you, Master," she added hastily.

He ran his finger over the welt he'd just created causing a fresh flush of pain to sear through her. She was still cursing him in her mind when the next swat landed.

"Two, Master," she cried out chucking in a deep breath. "Thank you, Master."

"I told you not to tense up, little dove. You're making this worse on yourself," he said and then proceeded to strike two sharp swats over both her cheeks in quick succession.

"Three. Four, thank you, Master," she wheezed softly as she struggled to get the words out around the screams she was trying her best to keep contained. She had survived brutal floggings in the past, this shouldn't be as painful as it was.

How many more? Fuck it hurts! How am I going to make it to fourteen?

They hadn't even made five, well seven actually, if she added the first two she hadn't counted. For the first time since she'd embarked on the BDSM lifestyle, she wanted to scream out her safe word.

Stone smoothed his hand over her backside, bringing forth a painful gasp that morphed into a deep moan as he moved lower. He brushed her thighs briefly before he cupped her pussy, covering it completely with his huge paw before slipping his probing fingers deep inside her channel.

"Hmm, for someone new to caning, you seem to be enjoying this. You're soaking wet and I'm practically drowning in the delectable bouquet you emit," he said.

Peyton winced at the disapproval in his voice, although she'd put her head on a block that she detected a trace of amusement in his tone.

She whimpered and was helpless to prevent her pussy from clenching around his fingers as he slowly pulled them out to find the hidden yet unmistakably hardness of her clitoris. She cried out as he began to rub it.

Stop it, damn you! This is supposed to be punishment, not an erotic caning!

Peyton could feel the pressure coiling rapidly tighter in her loins. An insistent throb warned her she was edging closer and closer to a climax.

She sagged into the bed with relief as he removed his fingers, leaving her feeling bereft. Her ears turned red in realization at the loud sucking sound. Her loins clenched and the vision in her mind of him licking her essence from his fingers flushed her pussy yet again. She panted and felt a heated blush crawl up her chest at this wicked display of carnality.

Peyton was still processing it when the next strike thudded even more painfully on the inside of her left thigh. It broke her from the reverie she was wallowing in. Her shriek echoed shrilly in her ears as she puffed in a teary voice, "Five, thank you, Master."

The change of pace sent her for a loop. One minute he turned her on so badly, she wanted to beg for more and the next moment he sent her reeling with pain until her eyes blurred.

"Come now, sub PJ. Stop fighting the pain and embrace it. Allow it to run through you," he instructed as he rubbed the welts on her bottom once more.

"I'm trying, Master Eagle," she bleated.

Get a grip, Peyton. You can do this. You know how this works. Focus! On him, on your punishment.

Once the words echoed in her mind, she realized why she had difficulty concentrating. The frustration emanating from the Dom behind her warned her that he had caught on to it as well. She didn't want to consider the repercussions if she failed this too.

"Clear your mind, Peyton. Now."

The brusque instruction confirmed her suspicion that he was no fool. Using her name even though they were told they never would, warned her that he wouldn't allow her mind to wander during punishment. She closed her eyes.

SNAP! SNAP! SNAP! SNAP!

She gasped out the count as she focused her mind and began to breathe through the pain. Each strike that followed cracked like thunder in her ears but she forced a breath out, feeling the pain radiate through her until it swept a heated trail to throb in her aching pussy.

With quick successive SNAP! SNAP! SNAP! and eleven was done. They weren't as bad as the first eight were. She almost smiled, realizing she finally learned what he had meant by embracing the pain. She kept her eyes closed and relaxed as much as she could, breathing deeply.

"Three more. You're doing very well, my pet."

She moaned deep in her throat as he tapped his fingers over her swollen labia and pulsing clit. She became embarrassingly wet. To such an extent, she could feel the juices trickle from her slit to soak the mattress cover. She jerked as the following two cracked over her buttocks, grunting out the count, breathing harshly until she felt the pain vibrate through every inch of her body, sparking a lust so profound, she wanted to curl into herself.

SNAP!

"Fourteen, thank you, Master," she cried out. She panted as she struggled to control the streak of pain that curled around the pressure in her loins, threatening to push her over the edge. She struggled to catch her breath.

"Nooo! Oh, fuckity fuck, please stop," Peyton wailed as she felt the teasing tap-tap-tap of the cold steel cane all over her labia and finally her clit. Heat exploded in her veins, rushing through her until she felt like one massive pulsing vein. She was inching over the edge and she knew if he continued, she was doomed to fail and climax.

"Master, I beg you. Please stop," she pleaded, her voice as raw as the lust clawing at her loins for release.

"You won't come, sub PJ. Not without my permission," he rasped in a dark voice.

"I can't hold it back! Please stop," she wailed in desperation as the tapping continued.

"You can and you will."

Peyton wasn't as confident as *he* sounded, especially as the tapping stopped only to be replaced by his fingers plunging into her.

"So hot and wet. It seems I'll have to find a different kind of punishment for you, my pet. You seem to take to the cane too much," he mused as he worked his fingers in and out, setting a quick rhythmic pace that had her squeal in ecstasy.

"I have to … come," she ground out through clenched teeth, unable to prevent her hips from thrusting back against his hand in a desperate attempt to force the climax. His thumb brushed over her clit.

"Gaawd!" She jerked frantically as he caressed the swollen nub with every inward thrust of his fingers. "Please, Please," she chanted. The edge loomed closer, she pressed harder, preparing for the pitch into the abyss. "Yes," she moaned as her muscles clenched around his fingers. The impending climax crawled closer but just wouldn't come, it hovered right at the edge, like it was waiting for something else. She tried to wiggle on his hand, thrashing and jerking like a rodeo bull but nothing helped.

She couldn't force herself over. The dark chuckle washed through her and she knew. How, she had no idea, but he had taken control of her body. In the short time since she'd arrived at Castle

Sin, Master Eagle was the puppet master, the only one who could pull her strings.

She shrieked angrily with the realization. Her body was the biggest betrayer. It was waiting on him. On *his* order for her to come.

An order, the continued chuckle told her, that wasn't forthcoming.

"Please," she tried once more, her voice pleading and teary. "Please, Master Eagle, fuck me."

A knock on the door broke through her desperation. She screamed in frustration as he removed his hand.

"Ah, there she is. Regardless of how delightful I find your uncontrolled lust, unfortunately, I have another errant trainee to attend to."

Peyton didn't move as he released the cuffs from her ankles. She couldn't, her body had gone numb, like it went into shock, still pulsing and charged in readiness to come.

"Come, sub PJ, down you come."

Stone assisted Peyton from the bed and held her against his chest until she found her feet. His hands caressed her back, aware of her shuddering form pressing closer. He led her to the sofa and urged her to sit down before he walked towards the door.

His deep voice rumbled in the quiet room but Peyton couldn't make out the words. She began to shiver as she started to come down from the high charge she'd experienced during the punishment.

Then he was there, dragging her onto his lap and cuddling her against his chest. It was all it took to settle her frayed nerves, to prevent her from sinking deeper into sub-drop—that sharp downward spiral of emotions after the rush of adrenaline ended.

Peyton buried her face into his chest, hiccupping and sniffling while her body relaxed into his as he wrapped his arms tightly around her. She could swear he kissed the top of her head. It completely rattled the little composure she had left.

Don't read too much into it, Peyton. He's just doing what any Dom would do after punishment. Tender aftercare. Do. Not. Fall. For. This. Man. Just don't!

It didn't take long for her emotions to settle. She was surprised to feel the tears trickling down her cheeks the moment she could think a little more clearly. Master Eagle's arms loosened. He brushed the hair from her face and pushed back her chin with his thumb.

She tried to smile through the tears, finding comfort in the warmth of his eyes. She attempted to speak, to tell him that she wasn't crying in pain but because she felt overwhelmed by regret for disappointing him.

He quieted her with a finger on her lips before the words formed; his voice sounded deep with soft, paternal tones. "Don't cry, little dove. It's over and you did exceedingly well. I'm proud of how well you took your punishment." He tenderly wiped away her tears.

"I disappointed you, Master Eagle, and I'm sorry," she hiccupped.

"No, my pet. I'm proud of you. This punishment addressed your misconduct and it's over." His gaze darkened. He opened his mouth and closed it again, changing his mind about what he was about to say. "Come, up you go. It's time for you to go to sleep."

"I'm not tired," she protested.

"Then you'll use the time to consider telling me the truth about why you're here." A sharp glance silenced the protest she was about to utter. "This was more than punishment. It was a test to evaluate your level of submission and knowledge of the lifestyle. That secured the first lie you told me." He leaned closer to pin her in place with a piercing look. "If you wish to stay at Castle Sin, you *will* be honest with me, otherwise you'll be leaving much sooner than you'd like."

She hung her head in defeat. The scoop she'd envisioned in her mind was slowly disintegrating in front of her mind's eye. Be it as it may, if she was honest with herself, that wasn't what bothered her the most. It wasn't that she didn't grasp the opportunity to run to the docks and leave, nor was it concern for her cousin, Savannah, and getting her home. It was the knowledge that she wouldn't be able to face his disappointment when she told him the truth. She turned towards the door.

"No. In here."

His grating voice stopped her in her tracks. She pivoted to face him. Her mouth dropped open in shock. She pointed at what she believed to be a huge cage under the bed.

"You … that's a cage," she sputtered in disbelief." Her eyes rose to his. "You're not serious."

Stone's expression remained stoic as he stared at her. His gaze glimmered over the short distance. She noticed the warning flash in their depths when she didn't move.

"Do not let me repeat myself, sub PJ."

He stood next to the bed; the base cover lifted to accommodate the open door of the cage. She took a hesitant step closer, seriously considering telling him she wanted to leave immediately.

"I'd be disappointed if you did, little dove. I thought you had more guts than that."

Peyton pursed her lips as he accurately read her thoughts. She glared at the offending cage. It was large, the same size as the huge bed above it with bars all around. There was a dim light shining from within. At least she wouldn't be left in pitch darkness.

"Now, sub. I've made the trainee wait outside on her knees long enough. You're being extremely inconsiderate." He gestured inside. "There's bottled water and some snacks. If you need to relieve yourself, I'm afraid it's going to have to wait until morning."

"That's extremely unhealthy," she complained.

"And yet you'll do as you're told." The warning was clear in his narrowed gaze.

Get in or …

Peyton got in but she did it muttering her displeasure, "I thought you said the punishment was done. Why the devil do I have to sleep in a freaking cage?"

"Oh, I believe you'll realize soon enough."

Before she could demand an explanation, he locked the cage door.

"I don't want to hear a peep out of you, sub, because if I do, the sub waiting outside will be punished in your stead. Understood?"

"Understood," she snapped, choosing the safe route not to berate him for threatening her with something that unfair. She moved deeper into the cage, relieved to be able to sit upright and not having to crawl on all fours like they did as children.

The base cover dropped back into place and her confinement turned darker. She looked around. The dim light came from two small sconces on the wall. There were pillows and a thick comforter covering a single mattress against the **wall** with the refreshments he'd promised stacked neatly on a narrow shelf beside it. The dark gold carpet covering the floor extended throughout the cage. All in all, it looked kinda cozy. Definitely not what she expected a slave cage to look like in a medieval castle like this.

"Sub ST, come inside, please, and take off your clothes."

Peyton stiffened and quickly shuffled to the bars. She lifted the edge of the base cover and peeked under it.

Fuckity fuck! It's Savannah.

Her mind turned numb as she saw Stone watching her cousin undress with a closed expression on his face. His head turned towards the bed. She dropped the cover and scooted back against the wall, praying he hadn't noticed her playing peeping Tom.

No freaking way! What the devil is he up to now?

Chapter Eight

Stone watched Savannah undress with a mask of impassiveness. His stance was relaxed with his thumbs hooked into the pockets of his jeans.

She was beautiful and looking at her closely, he was startled to notice a slight familiarity of her features to Peyton's. He banked the information for further investigation later. She was also a very troubled young woman. Something he and Shane had identified at their first meeting. Initially, they hadn't wanted to accept her into the training academy but throughout that first assessment, she'd possessed a quiet strength and determination. They offered her a three-month trial training period during which time Shane did regular therapy sessions with her. The purpose wasn't to delve into her troubled soul, but rather to establish whether she was maturing as a potential Castle Sin slave employee.

It was known that his door stood in open invitation, should she feel the need for more intense therapy. So far, Savannah hadn't taken them up on the offer. Tonight, was supposed to be Stone's evaluation to decide if her trial period would be extended or ended.

That was until he'd seen that warning look from Peyton at the Gathering Room when she'd arrived. A red flag immediately waved a warning, confirming his suspicion that there was more to the two women arriving at Castle Sin than they first imagined. Stone intended to find out what. They would soon realize that the Masters of Castle Sin were no fools.

It hadn't been until Savannah knocked on the door that the decision had been made to teach both women a lesson simultaneously.

He had been a Dom long enough to know Peyton was physically attracted to him and that she had no control over her body's reaction to him. He smirked. He knew he had managed to home into that part of her submission only a few Doms managed unless they'd been in a long-term relationship already. He was her body's trigger, his voice, his hands, and his demands; he was going to use it to his advantage—ruthlessly so.

He recalled the pleasure that filled his mind when he realized that no matter how hard she tried, she couldn't curb the explosive lust he'd wrung from her.

Stone wasn't surprised to notice from his peripheral vision the base cover easing up. He knew the moment Peyton peeked out; the soft gasp of breath floated through his mind. A slow turn of his head in that direction took care of her curiosity and it dropped back in place.

He didn't want her to see, he wanted her to feel and experience every sensation and emotion he was about to drag from Savannah as her own, purely by listening. Peyton had still been strung tight as a piano wire when she'd crawled into the cage.

The next hour was going to be fun … for him at least.

For the two women? Well, maybe not so much.

He walked closer to Savannah as she straightened, circling her and tracing her naked skin with his finger as he went. He was pleased with the perfection of her present form.

"Do you know why you're here, sub ST?"

"Yes, Master Eagle," she lilted, lowering her head. Her shoulders slumped dejectedly.

Crack! Crack!

Her cry slammed against the wall as he gave her two quick swats on her buttocks. The white skin immediately glowed bright red in the shape of his handprint.

"You should know better by now. Correct your form, sub."

Her shoulders straightened obediently and she pushed her tits forward.

"Much better," he praised. "Tell me." Stone stood in front of her, watching and waiting.

"Because I did the same in the Gathering Hall when the new trainees arrived. I failed to keep the present form in front of them."

"And why does that anger me?"

"I'm sorry, Master Eagle. I ... AWW shit!" she wailed as he clamped her nipples between his fingers, pinched and pulled them harshly away from her body.

"Answer the question, sub," he said in a dark voice.

"Because it's an insult to the Masters who already trained me. I dishonored them with my poor performance." Her labored puffs sounded loud in the room. "I didn't mean any disrespect. Oww! Fuck, Master Eagle, please! I'm sorry."

"What made you break your form?"

He eased the pressure around her nipples and gently rolled them between his fingers. Her breath hitched at the contrasting sensations bombarding her mind and she couldn't hold back a moan as she flicked an unsure look at him.

"I ... guess I didn't pay attention, Master. I was too ... awww!" She bit her lip, trying to breathe through the pain as Stone placed Japanese clover clamps around each nipple that he'd taken from his jeans' pocket.

"If there's one thing I abhor more than a disobedient sub or slave, it's lies."

Stone hooked his finger around the thin chain connected to each clamp and walked towards the bed, ignoring her cries as the clamps tightened from the pressure exerted on them.

"Bend over, keep your legs straight and place your hands at the edge of the bed." He waited until she was in position. "Spread your legs, hollow your back and turn your feet inward. Wider!" He stood back and studied her form, satisfied when she pushed her ass out a little higher. He rewarded her with two hard swats on each cheek. "Face forward and don't break this form, sub ST, no matter what."

Stone stepped back, removed his shirt and kicked off his sneakers. He flexed his muscles as he walked closer, unbuckling his thick leather belt, he dragged it slowly out of the loops of his pants. Savannah's back straightened at the ominous sound but she didn't look back at him. To further build her anticipation, he flicked the belt in the air; the swish so close behind her brought a fearful gasp from her lips.

He couldn't help but admire her taut and perfectly formed buttocks as his fingertips gently grazed each ass cheek again. Almost as sexy as sub PJ's. He grasped hold of the full morsels and squeezed hard.

"Owww!" Stone reveled in the kickstart his libido received from the painful cry.

"You've been trained with various impact tools before, sub ST and punished with a flogger once. So, tell me, why are you so tense?"

"With all due respect to the other Masters, they're not you. We all fear you, Master Eagle. We've heard the other subs talk about your punishments."

"I only hand out punishments when necessary and they always match the misconduct, my pet. Something that's pertinent to all the Masters here." Stone relaxed his hold on her ass cheeks to brush his palms over the fullness of each one, down her thighs and ended with a sensual barely there tease of her labia. He smiled at her aroused little gasp. It seemed like it didn't take much to awaken desire in these two women. "You should know by now it's imperative to relax your muscles to make a spanking or whipping easier." Stone took back a step and spread his legs.

"You've earned yourself twelve strikes from my belt, sub ST. Even though this is punishment, tell me what will stop me if it becomes unbearable?"

He wrapped the one edge of the belt around his fist. He never used a double folded belt. It didn't achieve the amount of sting he wanted for a punishment.

"M-my safeword, Master." She was unable to hide the fear in her voice. "King."

"I expect you to use it if and only if I push you past your endurance."

"Yes, Master Eagle."

A quick flick of his wrist and the first swat landed across both of her cheeks. It had a soft sting but didn't hurt. Savannah hissed softly.

"I want to hear you count them, sub."

Swish, thud.

"One, Master Eagle."

The next four followed rapidly, spread out across her ass accompanied by her breathless count. Her shoulders relaxed as he continued with medium impact swats.

"Seven," she squealed as the bite of the leather increased against her reddening skin.

Stone stepped closer. She moaned as he ran his hand over her heated ass.

"Hmm, so nice and glowing red, my pet," he praised as he trailed his fingers down the center of her crack.

"Ahh ... Master!" Savannah jerked. Stone knew she was assailed with lust. The spicy bouquet of her arousal filling his nostrils screamed it out at him. He moved his fingers further down to slowly spread her swollen labia and pushed them deep inside her pussy.

"Ah, my pet. This little cunt is hot and completely soaked." Stone smiled as he detected a smothered curse from beneath the bed. He shoved his fingers deeper, growling as Savannah pushed back her hips, forcing them further inside her channel.

"Do not move, sub," he rasped as the belt swished through the air to land with a searing bite at the underside of her buttocks.

She cried out but it quickly morphed to a panting moan as he twirled his fingers deep inside her, pumping fast, chuckling at the squishing sound of her wetness.

"Master Eagle, please!"

"Behave, sub. Try and move that little cunt for more pleasure again and I'll clamp it too."

He smiled at the two simultaneous gasps from above the bed and below as he withdrew his fingers. He rubbed her essence over her clit, then pressed down hard on it. Her hips twitched higher.

The sharp crack of the belt was followed by a loud scream.

"I told you not to move." He continued to torture her clitoris until she was panting frantically.

"I'm sorry, Master Eagle! I'll never break form again but please—I need to come."

"We have five more swats to go. Count."

CRACK! CRACK!

Her voice was thin as she counted the strikes, the impact had increased exponentially.

"What is Peyton Jackson to you, sub ST?"

"M-Master?"

Another brutal strike had the room echo with her scream. She struggled to find her breath but dutifully counted it off.

"Do I need to repeat my question?"

"I … don't know her, Master Eagle," she said quickly.

"And yet it was the sight of her that caused you to break form."

"No, it … AWWW! God please, it hurts!" she screamed with tears streaming down her cheeks as the punishing strike seared like a lightning bolt across her buttocks.

"What did I tell you about lies, sub ST?"

"That you abhorred them, Master," she sobbed quietly.

"You missed two counts. I will continue until you reach the designated number."

The five swats came in rapid succession, just as hard and painful as the last two but Savannah managed to scream out the counts after each one.

Stone dropped his belt on the sofa as he stepped closer. He rubbed her flaming red ass.

"Yes, that's what happens when you blatantly lie to me, my pet," he growled over her sobs, and yet he was pleased by how well she was holding up. She was much stronger than he'd first believed.

"I'm sorry, Master Eagle," she whimpered. Her fingers clawed at the edge of the bed as he continued to stroke her flaming ass, thereby keeping the heat and the sting contained before it traveled through skin and muscle to set off a throb in her pussy.

"You might not like to be whipped or spanked, sub but this proves just how much your body loves it." He slipped his hand between her legs and twirled the tip of his finger inside her pussy. He chuckled and flicked his finger teasingly in and out. Savannah's moan was raw need.

"Deep breath, my pet. This is because of your recent lies," he warned before he fisted his hand around the chain and yanked off the clamps from her nipples.

Her legs gave in as her pitiful scream broke through his mind. She crumbled to the floor. Stone sighed in pleasure as he felt her pain in the tightening of his balls. He didn't move, just enjoyed the sight of the beautiful submissive on the floor. Her legs were spread wide as she leaned weakly against the bed, clutching her breasts. His gaze moved down in full appreciation of how dark her labia had gone with desire and the milky discharge dripping from her slit as proof.

His cock throbbed insistently. He had deliberately not fucked Peyton as part of her punishment but he had no intention of playing the martyr twice in one night.

"You've done very well, little one. Come."

Stone gently picked her up and lifted her onto the bed without effort. Keeping his hand on her stomach to gentle her distress, he kicked off his jeans before he settled on the bed beside her, drawing her into his arms, caressing her back and cooing sweet little nothings against her ear. He enjoyed giving aftercare but only to those he scened with or punished. It offered him the opportunity to tap into the sub's mind, understand her emotions and the depth of her submission.

Stone smiled as he became aware of the excessive rustling of the comforter beneath the bed. He could even hear a fist punching a pillow. It seems Miss Investigative journalist was frustrated, maybe even a little jealous.

"How do you feel, my pet," he asked a little while later.

Savannah peeked at him. "I feel fine, Master Eagle. You holding me and talking to me really helped." She licked her lips. "I'm sorry I disappointed you, Master."

"Did you learn anything from the whipping, sub?" He studied her intently and noticed her eyes become smoky.

"It taught me that misbehavior will be punished. I knew I shouldn't have broken form and yet I did. I'm truly sorry. It won't happen again."

"Breaking form or misbehaving?"

"Er ... both, Master."

"And yet, you continued to lie to me. Is that not a form of misbehaving, sub ST?"

"Master, please, I—"

"Do you know why I didn't end your punishment with strikes across your pussy?" he brushed her off, unsettling her by the change in subject.

Savannah's eyes widened. A soft curse sounded below them. Too soft for her to hear but Stone was so tuned in, he was aware of every rustling move sub PJ made.

"No, Master Eagle," she lilted with her gaze lowered.

"Because I intend to feast on it."

"Y-you do?"

"Yes, my pet ... it's the one thing I most love to do. Kissing, licking and sucking a juicy cunt at my leisure. And tonight, I have all the time in the world."

Savannah just stared at him. He caught another whiff of her excitement teasing his nostrils. A wicked smile twitched his lips.

"So, I'm about to have fun and while I'm at it, I'm going to ask you some questions." His eyes caught hers. "What do I expect from you, sub ST?"

"That I answer your questions immediately and do what you tell me."

"And?"

"I'm not allowed to come without permission," she said in a moaning voice. Her arousal was evident in her nipples turning hard and her legs twitching on the bed.

"Ah, so you have been paying attention to your training. Excellent." Stone prodded her legs as he moved between them. "Spread open these lovely thighs for me, little one. Wider, my shoulders need lots of space."

He could swear he heard a muffled groan from down below but deliberately pushed thoughts of Peyton Jackson from his mind to concentrate on the writhing woman awaiting his attention.

Savannah's carnal cry sounded as he spread open her labia and blew hot breaths on her exposed pussy. Her hips jerked upward in a desperate plea for his touch. He took his time, taking a long lick with his flattened tongue from the back of her slit to the front and back down again. He repeated the sensual torture three times, smiling at the constant flow of her spicy juices coating his tongue from the first pass.

He flicked the tight point of his tongue inside her slit and wiggled it teasingly back and forth. Savannah's hips shot up from the bed.

"Tell me about the redhead sub, my pet," he gruffed against her wet labia.

"Master, please," she moaned her protest at the question. Stone was impressed that she still had such resolve in the face of her heightened arousal to keep up protecting the relationship bond between her and Peyton.

Crack! Crack!

"Gaawd! Oh lord," Savannah wailed as he slapped her nipples hard which resulted in her hips rotating against his mouth.

"Stop moving, sub."

"Yes, Master."

She reached up and clawed at the pillow, her back arched as lust assailed her when he sucked the swollen little nub of her clitoris deep into his mouth without any warning.

"I asked you a question, sub ST." His voice slashed through the air coated in a dire warning.

"I ... she ... she looked familiar, Master ... ohh," she gasped as he nibbled on her clit while at the same time pushing his fingers inside her pulsing pussy.

Stone continued to torment her as he took pleasure in her uncontrolled reaction to his ministrations. He did what he'd promised, he feasted on her pussy for almost an hour, continuously prodding her about Peyton.

Savannah remained steadfast in her responses, keeping them to vague memories but not once admitting to any intimate association.

"Oh god, please Master Eagle. I can't stand it any longer. Please, I beg you! Please fuck me."

Savannah's throaty plea was met by a strangled, "No," from below which brought a delighted smile to Stone's lips.

Ah, yes. Sub PJ is indeed jealous.

Or maybe just envious that sub ST might find the relief she'd been denied.

"Do you want me to fuck you, my pet? Do you want to feel my hard cock slide deep inside your tight little cunt and pound it mercilessly?"

"Yes, fuck yes!" Savannah's passionate cry was once again countered by a vehement, "No," from under the bed. Savannah was too caught up in her lusty need to hear the voice but it sealed Peyton Jackson's fate and hers for that matter.

After all, he did warn Peyton what would happen if he heard a peep out of her.

"Very well. Who am I to deny such an eloquent plea from such a beautiful little sub." Stone sat back on his heels. "Turn over, sub, and get on your knees. I want that ass high up in the air when I pound it." He didn't wait for her to comply. With a hand around her hip, he flipped her over while he tore open the foil packet that he took out of the secret compartment at the side of the bed.

"Spread those thighs wider, sub. Ah, yes," he said as he pressed his cock just inside her hot little slit.

"Yesss! Please, Master, now! Fuck me," Savannah demanded as she tried to push back and force him deeper.

"Oh, I intend to, little one. I'm going to fuck you hard and rougher than any of the Master so far but here's the thing." He pushed her shoulders down so that her ass tilted higher, giving him better leverage. He caught her hands and pressed them against her lower back, effectively rendering her helpless. "Because of your continued lies, you don't get to come. Is that clear?"

"But Master ... ahhh fuck!" she screamed as he pinched one nipple hard and pulled on it with brute strength. "YES!" she shrieked. "I understand."

"Good girl."

He released the pressure and soothed the abused nub with gentle rubbing. His voice turned deeper, amused and rippled with wicked seduction.

"Now, me on the other hand ..."

Peyton was miserable and drowned in the guilt of knowing she was the one responsible for Savannah's punishment. For fear of the repercussions to her cousin if she shouted out the truth, Peyton was forced to wallow in self-recrimination while listening to her cries of pain and even more annoying, moans of pleasure.

She recalled the horrified look on Savannah's face when she'd recognized her among the new trainees. She'd expected that, but what came as a complete surprise was the pleading look that she kept casting her way. Clearly, there was more to Savannah's application as a Castle Sin slave than met the eye. Peyton had every intention of finding out what. Her aunt would never forgive her if she didn't bring back her daughter from the claws of the demon cult, as she referred to people in the BDSM lifestyle.

"You've done very well, little one. Come."

Peyton had done her best to block out what was happening outside the cage. Stone's deep voice filled with tender care, yanked her back to the present. She could see his bare toes under the base cover as he stepped against the bed. Her breath hitched in her throat when soon after, his jeans landed on the floor and he got onto the bed.

No-no-no! Damn you, Master Eagle! You denied me the pleasure. How can you …

She bit her lip and closed her eyes. It wasn't rocket science. Stone Sinclair was a master in mind fucking. He'd already proven it to her. This was just a step up to break her down further. He knew how aroused she still was. *He fucking knew!* Now he was taunting her with the thought that he was going to fuck another woman while she was left high and dry.

Listening to them!

She crawled onto the mattress and yanked the thick comforter over her body. Her fist connected a few times with the pillow … his grinning face the center point of her ire.

"Spread open these lovely thighs for me, little one. Wider, my shoulders need lots of space."

Peyton did her best to muffle the moan that escaped from deep within her throat at the vision his words elicited. She squeezed her eyelids shut but they shot open immediately as the vision of his broad shoulders anchored between Savannah's thighs flashed behind them.

Damn you, Stone Sinclair!

Here she was. So close and yet so far from what she'd been craving for years. To feel the enigmatic and super-hot celebrity's lips exploring her body. Inch by inch, not leaving any crevice untouched.

"Tell me about the redhead sub, my pet,"

Peyton sat up like Jack-in-the-box and waited with bated breath. She could only imagine the state her poor cousin was in by now. How else, with the wicked Master's lips and tongue plaguing her most intimate parts. Licking, sucking …

Oh, for fuck's sake, Peyton! Stop it.

She squeezed her thighs together in an attempt to stay her arousal, the climax that had lingered since he'd almost brought her to the edge, inched threateningly closer with every sensual sound from above.

She cringed at the loud echo of two quick successive slaps followed by Savannah's painful scream. She laid back down and glared at the roof of the cage, very tempted to kick and pound against it. Not that it would serve any purpose, seeing as it was made from the same rough sandstone as all the walls in the Castle.

"I fucking hate you, Master Eagle," she said sotto voce as she listened to the loud sucking and licking sounds he made while feasting on Savannah's nether parts. Her girlie bits tingled in response. She clamped her hands between her thighs, desperate to stop the sensations that surged through her. It felt like he was licking and sucking *her* soft bits, pushing his hot tongue deep inside *her* pussy and ...

She moaned as she felt the telltale wetness of her lust on her hands. She pressed her head into the pillow, trying her best to block out the pleasure rumblings from the couple on the bed.

"Oh god, please Master Eagle. I can't stand it any longer. Please, I beg you! Please fuck me." Savannah's desperate cry penetrated her mind.

"No!" Peyton clamped her hands over her mouth as the word escaped her lips. She stared with wide eyes upwards, praying Stone hadn't heard the involuntary outburst.

"Do you want me to fuck you, my pet? Do you want to feel my hard cock slide deep inside your tight little cunt and pound it mercilessly?"

"Yes, fuck yes!"

"*No*!" This time the word exploded from her lips with even more vehemence as her pussy clenched in reaction to his descriptive response.

Peyton didn't even care if he heard, more than annoyed at her cousin's inability to control her lust. Begging the demon Master to fuck her. Imagine that! Didn't she have any pride?

At that moment, she completely forgot that she had done the same thing not too long ago—begged Master Eagle to fuck her.

Maybe so but he freaking denied me! she wailed in protest.

"Ah, I love the first entry into a hot, tight, and wet pussy. Easy, sub, don't force it. Give this little cunt time to adjust to my size. I intend to ride you hard and fast but not before you're stretched enough to accommodate me."

Peyton slammed her hands over her ears but she had no control over her pussy clenching and lubricating itself, almost like it was preparing for the penetration of his hard cock.

Savannah's moans and cries escalated. Peyton's face bloomed hot red as the sound of slapping flesh reverberated throughout the room. Master Eagle hadn't made an empty promise. He was fucking her ferociously.

With a furious growl, Peyton yanked one of the pillows over her head, hoping to mute out the sound of the copulation that resonated with raw carnality through the room.

Her body pulsed and twitched but she forced herself to ignore it. She had no idea how long the primal coupling took or heard the growling roar when the demon Master finally climaxed.

She'd thankfully and blissfully fallen asleep. Her thighs were soaked from a sticky substance. A sign of a climax that had rippled through her in a wistful dream of her pussy being ruthlessly pounded by Stone Sinclair's lascivious cock.

She was oblivious to Stone unlocking the cage after Savannah had left or that he sat in the opening and looked at her for a long time.

It was a good thing too, as the wide smile on his lips when he noticed her arm still clamping the pillow over her head, would've triggered her ire once more.

Chapter Nine

"What the devil are you doing here, Peyton?"

Peyton wasn't surprised that her cousin attacked her the moment they came face to face the next morning, especially since Peyton had done her utmost to avoid Savannah for the past five years. She did her best to appear normal but it was damn difficult to get the mental conjuring of Savannah being fucked to kingdom come by Stone Sinclair out of her mind. The sounds of their copulation were ingrained in her brain and that made what she pictured even more vivid.

"I can ask you the same question. Your mother told me you're on vacation in the Bahamas," Peyton instinctively knew it would be a mistake to tell Savannah the real reason she was on the island.

Sticking to half-truths would keep her safe from her very astute cousin's inquiries.

She looked around. It was just after eight in the morning and everyone was gathered in the massive Great Dining Hall for breakfast. When she'd first entered, she'd been cast back to the Harry Potter movies. The massive rectangular room was approximately three times as long as it was wide, with a very high roof. The medieval room was contrasted by long rows of modern tables and comfortable chairs that filled the front half of the room with a conversation area closer to the wide arched entrance. It consisted of plush leather sofas, huge wingback chairs with a number of small tables placed between. Thick loose carpets adorned the floors under each group of chairs with the rest of the hall gleaming from well cared for dark wooden floors. The dancing rays of sunlight cascaded through large mullion bay windows, casting the room in a warm, inviting glow.

"My mother? What does she have to do with this? We both know you haven't been to her house in years and don't turn this around on me, Peyton.

If you think you're going to talk me into leaving, you can forget it."

Well, if Stone Sinclair fucked me like he did you last night I might not want to leave either.

Peyton blithely pushed the envy to the back of her mind and gestured around them. She shook her head. "Castle Sin of all places, Savannah? You, who always screamed blue murder whenever your dad took off his belt to spank you?" She noticed the annoyed glimmer in her younger cousin's eyes at her attempt to pacify her. She wondered where her sudden assertiveness had come from. It would probably be frugal to reign in her quest and take her cue from Savannah. "Okay, relax your tight panties. Geez, one would swear you have sole proprietorship on this place."

Savannah crossed her arms over her ample breasts and glowered at Peyton who was amused as the telltale tap-tap of her foot on the floor reiterated her growing frustration.

"You know I've been involved in the BDSM community for a couple of years. When this opportunity crossed my path, I couldn't resist applying. See it as an adventure added to my portfolio," Peyton said with a wink.

Alarm colored Savannah's expression with streaks of panic.

"Don't tell me you're undercover to do a story?"

"You know me, if there's smoke I'll be—"

"NO! No-no-no, Peyton. You can't do a story on Castle Sin or about any of the Masters of The Seven Keys Island. Promise me!" She looked around as her panicked shriek drew attention to them where they stood to one side from the rest. She lowered her voice. "I can't let you do this."

Peyton tilted her head sideways and regarded her silently. A proverbial red flag waved frantically above Savannah's head.

"What's this about, Savvy? According to the others, your group has been here three months. That's way too soon to be this protective over them. Don't tell me you did something stupid and fell in love with one of the Masters." She held her breath, not sure why, but the thought that Savannah might mention Stone's name tore at her heart. "Or," her insides cringed as another thought came to mind, "are you being threatened?"

"Don't be ridiculous! Of course, we're not. We're all here of our own free will. It's not a jail, and anyone who wishes to leave is free to do so at any time."

Peyton's suspicion sharpened. Savannah's response was too vehement and rushed. Her stomach clenched as she came to the only conclusion that made sense. She *was* in love with one of the Masters.

"That's what I don't understand, Savannah. Do you honestly expect me to believe you've thrown away a career as a system analyst at the FBI to work as a slave in an exclusive BDSM club? A career, need I remind you, that you worked like a Trojan to make a success of. You just got promoted to department senior a couple of months ago and now you're here trying your damnedest to dodge whips and floggers?" Peyton shook her head. "Don't bother to deny it. I saw your reaction during our introduction the other day."

Peyton thought it prudent not to divulge the intimate knowledge she had of the whipping Savannah had suffered at the hand of Stone Sinclair. It was still too raw in her mind, and besides, she didn't want to make Savannah feel uncomfortable knowing her older cousin had been privy to the hot and lustful copulation between her and the king of the castle. Not with their history. Pain slashed through her heart. It caught her by surprise. She'd believed she'd managed to put it behind her. Clearly, she'd only been fooling herself.

"Don't think I don't realize you're trying to make me forget about your intentions, Peyton. I'm asking you very nicely. Do not write a piece on Castle Sin and The Seven Keys Island."

"It's a free country, Savvy, and what's happening here is newsworthy, especially because of *who* these men are and how the public—"

"I don't believe my ears. Are you truly that callous? That uncaring to what an article like that would do to all the people who live and work here? All for a moment of fame?"

"Now you're insulting me, Savannah. You know very well I don't write tabloid articles." Peyton bristled and made no effort to hide her indignation. She had always prided herself on the work she did. It was the reason she chose investigative journalism. To tell stories that mattered. To honor those who served the country and fellow humanitarians selflessly and without expectation of rewards. More so, she had uncovered many scams and corrupt government officials and politicians over the years. She was affronted that Savannah would even mention something like that.

"Oh, really? Pray tell, if not for pure sensationalism, what angle are you pursuing with this article? That these men keep slaves under duress? Or are you aiming to go the illegal route and get them closed down? You better think long and hard about this, Peyton. It will affect every single BDSM club out there. If you go public and try and shame them and the lifestyle, be prepared to be cast out and denied entrance to every club out there. You'll become a household name to them—your

BDSM lifestyle will come to an end. No one will ever trust you inside a club again."

Peyton was gobsmacked at the passion with which Savannah spoke. It was more than loyalty and commitment to the training program, her desire to become a submissive sex slave, or even to the Masters. She studied her intently. She almost missed it, but for a brief moment, it was there, buried in the depths of Savannah's hazel eyes.

Fear.

Instinct, as one of the best investigative journalists in the U.S., told Peyton that something or someone was behind Savannah's arrival on The Seven Keys Island.

A commotion at the arched entrance drew their attention that way. Dom Danton led the group of training Doms that arrived for breakfast. Peyton watched in amazement as the trainees scattered and quickly took their seats at the dining tables.

"We should sit down too." Savannah looked around. She looked relieved as she walked towards the tables. "We can't be seen together. I'm not sure how much longer I'll be able to deny knowledge of who you are."

"What are you saying? Have you been interrogated about me?" Peyton felt her face heat up at the lie but couldn't bring herself to admit that she'd been a silent witness to Savannah's punishment at the hands of the Master Dom. "Are you going to tell them I'm an investigative journalist?"

Savannah laughed and said derisively, "I can't believe you're this naive, Peyton. Even if you lied on your application form, you better believe that Master Eagle might already know who and what you really are. Your face is as well-known as theirs. You're *the* CNN investigative journalist. Some of the trainees even recognized you and are wondering what you're really doing here." She slanted a cold look at Peyton. "Thanks, cuz, for wanting to fuck up the first real good thing I've been able to do for myself since I completely destroyed our ..."

Her voice drifted off as a flash of pain pulled Peyton's face into a grimace. Savannah squared her shoulders. "I'm not going to apologize again. I fucked up and I owned up to it. More than that, I've suffered for it for the past five years—more than you'll ever realize." Her eyes teared up. "I've missed you terribly but I understand why you still can't forgive me."

She ran her hand through her hair, the move tired and resigned but her voice remained controlled and firm. "Understand this, Peyton, I won't let you be the cause of another fucked up mistake in my life. I refuse to let you destroy all these people's lives and ..." She clamped her lips together, giving Peyton the impression that she'd almost blurted out the reason she was there. Savannah shot a sharp look at her. "Even if it means I have to rat you out. Just keep quiet. It would be best for both of us if they didn't know we're related."

"I don't understand. What does it matter if they knew we're cousins?" Peyton wanted to keep their familial bonds secret so she could lure Savannah back home but she was curious to know what drove her.

"Trust me, Peyton, you'd rather they don't find out and I can only pray they don't start digging into our backgrounds. Now, just keep your mouth shut.

Better yet, leave!" She pivoted and walked away briskly.

Peyton looked after her cousin with dull eyes. The last thing she'd needed on this trip was a reminder of why her heart refused to become involved with another man. Why the thought of Savannah being in love with Stone Sinclair hurt more than she cared to admit. Peyton had conceded to herself the previous night that she lusted after him and was infatuated with the man. But love?

Not happening.

Not to her.

Never again.

"Have you been able to find out more about the hacker, Stone?" asked Secretary of State, Sheila Madden. "The president is becoming agitated. He's not comfortable keeping this from the cabinet. We need to know exactly how exposed we are and quickly."

"Parker is getting closer. Whoever it is, is clever but from the signature he leaves behind, Parker ascertained that he has inside help."

"Are you saying someone in the bureau is helping him?"

Stone glanced at Hawk, who had accompanied him to Washington DC for the meeting with Sheila and Gary Sullivan, the secretary of defense.

"Not the FBI, no. It seems the culprit is closer to home, Madam Secretary," Hawk said with a wry smile. "The communication he managed to uncover came from Homeland Security offices."

Sheila stared at them, her expression grim. "Do you know who?"

"We do but for now we're keeping it under wraps. We know this person is used as the carrier, in other words, to relay messages between the hacker and the person in charge. In instances like this, that's a rather common practice."

"So, we just allow this person to continue to put the country and their people at risk?" Gary Sullivan barked in a gruff voice. He shifted his tall frame in the chair. "We need to put a stop to it, Mr. Sinclair."

"We already have."

"I don't understand. You just said we can't move on it yet," Gary said.

"We've installed an undetectable firewall." Stone waved off the question he could see forming on Sheila's lips. "It's nanoTechnology Parker and Zeke used to develop a system that prevents it from being detected. If it can't be found, it can't be hacked. The hackers have been trying to crack it for the past week without any success."

"Are you saying you're watching the hacker at work?" Sheila leaned forward, her eyes moving between the two men.

"Yes, that's why Parker is getting close. Another day or two and we'll be able to extract him." Stone accepted the cup of coffee the secretary passed to him.

"What do you mean you extract him?"

Stone looked at Gary Sullivan. There was something about his attitude that caused his sixth sense to spark to life. He never ignored that feeling.

179

"We remove him from his cave. Take away his only form of communication. A hacker is like a fish out of water without his computers." Hawk had picked up on Stone's discomfort and responded with caution.

"And take him where? Why not supply us with the details of his whereabouts and let us pick him up for interrogation? I can assure you we have the techniques to get information out of rats like that much quicker than you," Gary said sharply.

"No, Gary. This is the agreement we signed with Be Secure Enterprises, specifically because we suspected there's a mole in our midst. I just never believed it's someone this close to home."

"But Madam Secretary, surely as the secretary of defense it's up to—"

She held up her hand to silence him. "The order came directly from the president, Gary. This entire project is done undercover, so to speak. No one, and I mean no one in any federal department, is aware of what they're doing and that includes the Cyber Division. They safeguarded the entire governmental systems without the knowledge of our cyber teams. As far as our computer programmers are concerned, nothing has changed, is that correct, Stone?"

"Yes, Madam Secretary. The NanoT system clones the current one and imports the new system as a mirror deflect, by manner of explanation. We can see every keystroke the programmers make and evaluate the authenticity. The technology is so advanced that the moment it detects the possibility of being penetrated, it adapts and immediately attacks what's perceived as a threat."

"At the same time, we receive a warning of the cyber threat at which time our team immediately starts a trace. Combined with the NanoT already in the system, nine times out of ten, we'll clamp down on the hacker in less than an hour."

"Then why haven't you caught the bastard yet?" Gary demanded. He didn't bother to hide his anger. Stone assumed it stemmed from being excluded the day they had presented the project and proposal to the president and secretary of state. They had been so impressed with their visual presentation that they'd immediately signed the contract.

"Because his signature was already part of the system when the NanoT was installed. We had to filter through every keystroke to find the ones that don't belong," Stone explained patiently.

"Had to?" Sheila sipped her coffee, watching Stone over the rim of the cup. "Does that mean you've managed to segregate them?"

"Parker eliminated all internal factors. He was working on the system last night when the hacker logged on. We now know his signature. Parker's busy eliminating the false ones the hacker planted to find the core stream. Once he's done … we'll have him."

"That's brilliant news and a lot quicker than I had hoped for. The president will be pleased." Sheila looked at Gary who snorted irritably. "You should be too. This is a hell of a lot more than any previous effort from the Cyber Division has offered."

"I'm still not happy to leave the interrogation to a team of computer suits, Madam Secretary."

Stone and Hawk struggled not to laugh at the expression on the secretary of state's face. She flashed a quick apologetic glance their way before she told Gary in an acerbic tone, "I suggest you familiarize yourself with the background information about Be Secure Enterprises, Secretary Sullivan, before you make a bigger ass of yourself than you just did."

He stuttered indignantly but she blithely ignored him as she got up and shook hands with Stone and Hawk. "Thank you for taking the time to come out here and personally give me a progress report. Your hours of hard work and dedication to solve this matter speedily is testament to your commitment to our country's safety and prosperity." She dimpled at Stone. "Now, there is this matter of my daughter's fascination with a certain Space Rider." She held up her hands. "Don't worry, I didn't break the confidentiality clause we signed but I did mention I've met you. She would be devastated if I came home tonight without a signature from you on the dashing promotional photo she made me buy at an exorbitant price."

Stone laughed and held out his hand for the photograph. He signed it with a flourish and winked at her. "How about we give her a special photo of her mom hugging the mighty Iron Eagle?"

"Oh, now that would get her braids totally in a twist."

She insisted on photos with both of them while Gary Sullivan watched the trio with growing resentment.

"I want an in depth and deep web background check on Gary Sullivan, Hawk," Stone said as they got into the elevator five minutes later. "There's something about him that's not kosher."

"I concur. I'll contact Ace on the way to the airport."

"I also want details of all his movements over the past year. Where he went, why he went there and who he met. Financials, everything about his wife and kids, and whoever else plays a role in his life."

At the airport, they were dropped off in front of the hangar where the company jet was already ready for take-off.

Chapter Ten

"The top floor is off limits to everyone except the Senior Masters of Castle Sin. If you're caught snooping there, you'll immediately be banned from The Seven Keys Island. Is that understood?" Dom Evans scrutinized the group of new trainees. His dark look warned them that it wasn't an idle threat.

Unfortunately, it triggered the bloodhound instinct in Peyton. She glanced up the stairs, wondering what the Masters of Castle Sin valued so much that no one was allowed up there. She knew it wasn't living quarters, as they'd already visited each Master's wing and was introduced to the different rooms in each, except for the Masters own private apartments, which they were also warned were only entered upon invitation from the Master himself.

Dom Evans didn't afford her the opportunity to ponder it though and ushered them down two flights of stairs to the ground floor and into the Gathering Room where the rest of the training Doms and the Senior Masters awaited them. All, except for Master Eagle. She released the breath she'd inadvertently been holding since they'd entered the Hall. She wasn't ready to face him, not since she was struggling to get over him having had sex with her cousin. It was almost like history repeating itself.

Oh, for fuck sake, Peyton. Get a grip. It's nowhere near the same and you know it.

She resolutely pushed the unwanted memories to the back of her mind and concentrated on Master Hawk who stepped forward and looked them over.

Peyton had been relieved that she'd been allowed to get dressed that morning, albeit in a loose fitting, white sundress supplied by Danton, similar to what all the trainees wore. She shifted her weight, slightly uncomfortable as she felt the whiff of a breeze around her legs, flowing upward to her naked buttocks. It was the two things they were denied, panties and bras.

"Good morning, trainees." Hawk waited until the murmured return greeting quieted down. "I trust you slept well last night and enjoyed the tour of the castle?' He smiled at the confirming nods from the group. "Good. You've been given freedom to enjoy the castle and the beach for the past three days to become accustomed to your new home over the next seven months. Before we continue with your individual evaluations, is there anyone who wishes to leave at this stage?" He looked from one to the next, satisfied when no one stepped forward. "Very well. Be assured that you are free to leave whenever you wish. It was your decision to apply for employment at Castle Sin but if at any point in time you feel you've made a mistake, you're free to leave. Understood?"

"Yes, Master Hawk," they said in unison.

Hawk was the only one whose Master name was the same as his given one. An animal totem he'd lived up to all his life. He had the ability to use the power of focus that made him a very powerful Dom, he took the lead when needed, and he had the innate power to see through emotional barriers.

Peyton had overheard a discussion at breakfast that Master Hawk had the ability to make a submissive fly and reach for the sky while screaming in pain and begging for more at the same time. She had no intention of finding out how though and kept her eyes lowered. She squirmed as she felt his intense regard, wondering what she'd done to deserve being singled out.

She didn't have long to wait for the answer.

"Sub PJ, Master Eagle assured us that he'd taken care of your evaluation last night already. You're to join him at the Waterfall of Sin on the south side of the island." He paused briefly. "He'll commence with your first lesson in fifteen minutes, so don't dally."

"Permission to speak, Master Hawk," Peyton said quickly as he turned away.

"Speak," he rasped, watching her with calculating interest.

"I don't know where the Waterfall of Sin is."

"Danton will accompany you. I suggest you get going. Master Eagle hates to be kept waiting."

Far be it for me to remind you that you just *told me to go!* Peyton snipped in her mind but quickly followed Danton who immediately walked out the Hall through the large entrance area toward the front door.

"Buckle up," Danton said as he cranked the engine of a red dune buggy. "There are some rough patches ahead."

Peyton didn't need to be reminded twice and snapped the safety belt in place. She clutched at the silver steel bar overhead as he pulled away and sped up immediately.

"Is the waterfall close to the beach?" Peyton asked while she silently prayed to arrive in one piece. Danton handled the sporty buggy with expertise but the speed at which he cut the corners made her breath wheeze from her throat.

"It's a coastal waterfall. In other words, the water drops into the ocean from approximately forty feet up."

Peyton glanced at him in alarm. She hated water. Especially the kind that came in masses. She hardly swam in a swimming pool nowadays, let alone the sea. Add height to it and she turned into quivering jelly. Doom hovered over her like a black cloud in the sky as she hung on for dear life when Danton sped up a winding road, higher and higher up the mountain behind the castle.

"Why does Master Eagle wish to see me at a waterfall?"

She didn't take her eyes off the road ahead but felt the brief glance Danton slanted her way. Little did she realize just how much her pale face disclosed or that her bottom lip was turning white from the pressure of her teeth biting into it. She sighed in relief when he slowed a little.

"Thank you," she exhaled. "Oh, freaking gaaawd!" she shrieked with fear coursing through her when she glanced to the right and encountered nothing but sky and the ocean far below.

"Are you scared of heights?" Danton said and eased his foot a little more off the gas pedal.

"No ..." Danton snorted and she acceded, "I'm not," she insisted. "But driving like a lunatic on the edge of a cliff ... not my idea of fun." The words exploded breathlessly as she stared in horror at the straight drop next to her. She didn't even realize her one hand moved to clutch his thigh, her nails digging into the soft flesh. "We're right on the edge. Oh lord, please, Dom Danton, we're going to run over!" she shrieked as she noticed a hairpin bend in the road ahead. She wanted to close her eyes but fear kept them open as wide as saucers.

"Relax, sub PJ, I can drive this road with my eyes closed."

His voice sounded far off as they approached the edge of death, which was how it seemed to Peyton. She finally squeezed her eyes shut and prayed, loud and nonstop.

"Oh, God, please don't let me die today. Please, God, don't let him steer over the edge. I swear I'll be good from now on, just please don't—"

"You can open your eyes, sub. The end of the world has passed." Danton's amused voice broke through her murmurs.

Peyton chose to keep them closed, at least until the dune buggy rocked to a stop. She peeked through sooty eyelashes until her gaze clashed with Dom Danton who watched her with mirth in his eyes.

"I didn't figure you as a scaredy cat. Quite the opposite, in fact." He studied her intently. "Or is this a front to get Master Eagle to be merciful?"

"Gmphf," Peyton snorted and jumped from the buggy to join him on the other side, albeit with rubbery legs, as far away from the edge as possible where he'd parked. "I haven't done anything wrong, therefore I have no reason to beg for mercy." She blinked at him. "Or do I?"

"I can't say but he wouldn't have asked you here to enjoy the view. He loves using this spot to correct a sub's attitude." He scratched his stubble beard in thought. "Or maybe ..."

"Maybe what?" Peyton glanced around with trepidation. If Danton was correct and she was here to be punished or whatever it was Master Eagle did to correct a sub's attitude, she wanted to bolt in the other direction.

"Maybe I was accurate in my first assumption. That you've awakened the Beast in him." Danton leaned closer to whisper in her ear. "If that's the case, little subby, you better grow some hair on your teeth, otherwise he's going to eat you alive."

"Well, him eating me doesn't sound all that bad ... I mean ... oh lord!" she ducked her head, feeling a hot flush bloom over her cheeks as Danton burst out laughing. She cursed the vision of Stone Sinclair burying his face between her thighs, the reason for the unsolicited response.

Peyton tapped her toes on the ground and waited with her hands on her hips for his mirth to subside.

"Dom Danton, when you eventually manage to swallow your laughter, perhaps you could direct me to where I'm supposed to go. Master Hawk made it clear I have to meet the king himself within fifteen minutes." She glanced at his watch. "And time is a ticking," she bit out.

"Keep it up, subby. That kind of tone is exactly what'll get you fucked—often—and not only by Master Eagle." He pointed to a pathway between two rows of palm trees. "Follow that path and don't dawdle. Once Master Eagle hears my whistle, you've got exactly two minutes to reach him."

"How far—"

The shrill whistle from his pursed lips cut off the question. With a glare over her shoulder at the offending Dom, she stomped toward the path.

"Better hustle, subby. It's ten swats for every second you're late."

"I never liked you, you know!" she shouted back at him as she disappeared between the rows of trees. His dark laughter was a promise of future chastisement for her bratty attitude. She cursed herself and she broke into a run. She had to remember he was also a Dom, indeed, listening to the dark undertones in his voice, one to be reckoned with.

She took the curve ahead at full speed and the next moment landed with a loud, "Oomph!" flat on her behind as she ran smack into a brick wall.

"Ouch, freaking hell, that hurts," she grumbled as she pushed upright and looked up ... and up and up. The wall was none other than

Master Eagle's rock-hard body, which by all counts hadn't even shifted an inch when she catapulted into him.

"Freaking asshole Dom," she said sotto voce. Danton had known full well it wouldn't take more than half a minute to reach Master Eagle. She could've walked baby steps and still had enough time. Now she was flat on the ground with a painful butt to boot.

"I don't appreciate mumbling subs. Speak up, sub PJ."

To her surprise, Master Eagle held out his hand and helped her to her feet. She groaned and rubbed her tender behind.

"I'm just annoyed that I didn't look where I was going. I apologize for running into you, Master Eagle." She pouted as he looked expectantly over her shoulder. She took a quick peek herself, wondering if Danton had followed her. "What are you looking for, Master Eagle?"

"Whoever was chasing you. At the speed you were going I expected nothing short of a grizzly bear to come bursting through the trees."

"It's not funny," she defended herself indignantly. "Dom Danton ..." Her voice faded as she noticed one heavy eyebrow crawling higher on his forehead. "I ... ahem ... just didn't want to keep you waiting. Master Hawk allowed only fifteen minutes to get here and since my watch was confiscated, I have no way of knowing how much time had passed," she backtracked quickly, knowing from experience not to bad mouth or complain about one Dom to another.

"Nice save, my pet but beware in future, I don't appreciate sulking subs." He looked her over critically. "I'm glad to see you survived your first night in the cage. You even have a rosy glow to your cheeks.

From embarrassment, yes! For having to listen to you fuck my cousin!

Peyton did her best to keep the salacious thoughts from her expression but the heated blush kept spreading over her cheeks. She squeezed her thighs together as he brushed his finger over her nose. A gesture as light as the flutter of a butterfly's wings and yet it caused her loins to coil so tightly, she was tempted to bend over double. Instead, she wrapped her arms around her waist.

"Present, sub!" he snapped irritably and she shuffled into position. "This is your first and final warning. You were told upon arrival that you'll always stand in this position in the presence of the Masters and training Doms. Don't let me catch you forgetting again, sub."

"Yes, Master Eagle, I apologize," she said demurely, her eyes on his feet.

Good lord! He's wearing shorts and is barefoot. Even his damn feet are sexy as hell. How the devil am I going to keep my ovaries in check around this man?

No need, subby. We're all too happy to do a jiggle and bounce for him.

Oh, good lord, help me! Behave, why don't you?

If we behave any longer, we'll shrivel and die a slow and lonely death.

Oh, just shut up.

"Follow me."

As tall as Peyton was, she still had to walk twice as fast as Stone to keep up with his long strides as he led her through a narrow path surrounded by thick, bushy shrubs.

She shocked to a halt at the sight that met her eyes when they entered a clearing. Water was a force of nature, both beautiful and brutal. The sound of it cascading over the cliff had sounded tranquil from a distance and became louder as they neared but was deafening up close. Her hands involuntarily fisted as she stared at the wide stream, or rather a wild river until it disappeared over the abyss into the ocean far below. This was not a slow-flowing, languid pace, and lax by nature flux of water, no, this one was mighty. Many torrents traveled its path, rapids flicked up against the surface like paint flakes off a distressed door. Boulders rose out of the water like the bows of a sunken fleet, and the roar of the waterfall beat mercilessly against her flailing composure.

It was as if the rushing water conjured torrents of equally powerful emotions in her brain. It yanked her back fifteen years, where awe had first turned to fear and then terror as she, among thousands of others, became helpless puppets against the destructive power of nature.

She thought she'd learned to cope with it but watching the avalanche of water made her feet as heavy as cement.

"Stop dawdling, sub PJ, except if you wish me to add punishment to the lesson you're about to learn?" Stone barked over his shoulder as he continued on and stopped next to a woman cuffed naked to a stainless-steel St. Andrew's cross.

Peyton forced her attention from the water and glanced toward the couple. She started as her eyes got caught by the concerned hazel ones of her cousin.

Shit-shit-shit. He's like a damn bloodhound, Peyton grated to herself, immediately realizing what this was about. *And an asshole*, she continued as she watched the mighty king's hands caress Savannah's nipples until she squirmed against the cross. She resented her body's response to the seductive scene she bore witness to. Her nipples puckered into tight nubs that triggered a rush of heat through her veins. She bit back the moan as her clitoris reacted with a rhythmic throb watching Stone flicking and rubbing his fingers over Savannah's.

"Remove your dress, sub PJ, and stand against the cross. Dom Danton, please cuff her." Stone's eyes pierced through her, the warning at her tardiness for not jumping at his order, rendered her protest into oblivion. She took a deep breath and stepped onto the foothold of the St. Andrew's cross. She hadn't even noticed Danton arriving.

They probably all took lessons in phantom appearance, she thought with annoyance. Her stomach heaved when Danton immediately slipped the leather cuffs around her ankles and secured it to the iron loops of the cross. He straightened and guided her hand upward to repeat the process. Her breathing became erratic as he added a wide waist cuff that secured her tightly against the cross.

"Oh," she gasped as he brushed his palms over her budding nipples. Her eyes shot to his, panting as he smiled while he teased the taut nubs with tugs and pinches between his fingers.

"Relax, sub PJ. This is going to be as easy or as difficult as you make it. I warned you that Master Eagle abhors lies and whether you believe it or not, he's caught onto yours." He leaned closer; his warm breath was hot against her cheek as he nuzzled her ear. Gooseflesh tingled to life all over her body, adding more spark to her already dancing ovaries. "He's not going to let up until either one or both of you confess to what he wants to know, my pet. Be warned, this lesson is the easiest of them all."

A whimper from Savannah drew her attention. Master Eagle was busy pushing a string of thin anal beads inside her rectum, all the while talking to her and pinching her nipples. Peyton grimaced as she watched him squirt lube on a large egg before pushing it deep inside her vagina.

"Both of these are vibrating toys, my pet, as is this one."

This being a butterfly clit vibrator that he placed over her clitoris and secured it in place with straps around her thighs. Peyton cringed at the implication. This wasn't just a lesson in what she had no doubt was climax control but a warning that lies resulted in nothing pleasurable.

"Of course, we can't neglect these delightful little nubs, now can we, Dom Danton?" Stone's deep voice sounded faint and far off due to the thundering cascade of water over the edge of the cliff.

"I agree, Master Eagle. Do you wish me to prepare sub PJ as well?" Danton said once Savannah's cry faded into the atmosphere after Stone had clipped Japanese clover clamps onto her nipples.

"Freaking hell," Peyton hissed as he added insult to injury by clipping three ball weights to each clamp. They were so heavy it pulled Savannah's nipples downward and elicited another cry to marry with nature's symphony in the background. Peyton shivered, knowing the same fate awaited her own poor nubs.

"All except the clamps, please, Dom Danton."

Soon, Peyton's orifices were also stuffed with anal beads and a torture egg that she never believed would fit when she saw it in Dom Danton's hands.

"Oh, hell and damnation," she complained as he strapped the butterfly clit vibrator into place.

"I doubt that, my pet. I imagine hell is a lot hotter."

"I'm so glad you find this amusing, Sir," she snapped. "Oowww!" she cried out as he pinched her nipples hard and then twisted them cruelly. "Okay! I'm sorry. I didn't mean to sound disrespectful," she begged breathlessly. The pressure eased but he continued to pinch them.

"You're a trainee, sub. A willing one who wishes to become a permanent employee as a submissive to serve our members. Your continued sassiness is going to cost you many hours of pain and frustration." He pressed his face against hers. "He might have taken a fancy to you and his Beast might be clawing at his insides to take possession of you but make no mistake, you will follow the same training program as the rest."

"Is she giving you lip, Danton?"

"Nothing I can't handle, Master Eagle," Danton said with a smile as he took back a step.

"Good. While I finish here, please get sub ST in place. Just off center. I want them close to each other."

Danton saluted Stone and walked toward Savannah. Peyton glanced warily at the Master Dom. He regarded her silently for a moment before his eyes took a gander up and down her body. She was helpless to prevent the rosy blush that started at the top of her head and followed the track of his gaze. Even though there was no one around, it felt totally wicked to be naked outside in nature and with a man too gorgeous for words, dressed in nothing but a pair of cargo pants. Her overeager ovaries were doing gymnastics at the sight alone.

She'd seen his naked chest on movie screens before but to stare at the real thing this close catapulted her smack bang into an unexpurgated lustful realm. Hot damn, his broad, perfectly sculpted shoulders, massive biceps and washboard stomach with way too many hard ridges to count, made her break out in a sweat, not to mention the flush of honeyed juices she could feel tingling between her labia.

"I'll ask you the same question I asked sub ST. Is there anything you'd like to tell me about her?"

"Apart from that she's a very beautiful woman, I don't think there's anything, no Master."

"Hmm," he flicked his fingers over her nipples, watching with detached interest as they immediately budded into tight stones. "So, you maintain that you don't know each other?"

Peyton resisted the urge to look over at Savannah. She could feel her eyes boring into her over the short distance.

"Yes, Master."

"For two strangers you had a very heated and urgent discussion before breakfast this morning."

Her heart skipped a beat at the cold, calculating look in his eyes. Somehow, Peyton got the impression that he knew more than he was leading on. Perhaps Savannah had been right and they'd dug into their respective pasts. If that was the case, why didn't he just come out and say so?

Because he's a Dom and trust and communication are key to the BDSM lifestyle. He wants you to tell him the truth.

Peyton knew the little voice inside her was right but if she admitted to Savannah being her cousin, it would immediately lead to more questions. Like why both of them were on the island and why pretend they didn't know each other.

And because we've both lied up to now, they probably won't believe a word we say either way.

She was caught in a catch twenty-two situation. She could come out with the truth about herself but she couldn't shake the feeling that Savannah was hiding something. That the reason for her being here might end badly if she was forced to leave the island now. Maybe it was time to build the bridge of mistrust and resentment between her and her cousin. Time didn't stand still. Besides, they were family after all.

"How do you know about that?" she hedged, daring a quick glance at Savannah, who appeared extremely agitated as the St. Andrew's cross lifted from the ground and gently swayed back and forth from the thick cable it was attached to overhead.

"The entire castle is under CCTV surveillance. Nothing happens anywhere without my knowledge."

Stone's deep voice yanked her attention back to him. She licked her lips. "We were just getting to know each other, that's all."

His sigh dragged from his chest like thick molasses from a spoon.

"No! Please, not that!"

Savannah's shriek once again drew Peyton's attention. Her breath got stuck in her throat, her heart began to race and her entire body turned to ice.

Danton slowly cranked the pulley that pushed Savannah out over the edge of the waterfall, the cross was guided by the thick cable connected from the one edge of the rocky mountain where they stood to the one on the other side of the waterfall.

"Fuck!" Peyton screamed as Stone clipped Japanese clamps onto her nipples without any warning. Her breath wheezed from her lips.

"Breathe through the pain, little dove. Come on, take a deep breath. Good. One more," he guided her with a soothing voice. Just when her breathing settled, he hooked the ball weights onto the clamps.

"Geesus!" she bit out through tight lips as the weights ruthlessly pulled her nipples downward. She closed her eyes, willing the throbbing to stop that sparked to life in her clit as soon as the pain subsided.

Then she remembered what she'd seen and her eyes popped open. She stared in horror at Savannah who was now suspended over the edge of the waterfall. The cross swayed back and forth, probably from the heavy spray of water. Over the distance, she could see her body shimmering in the sun, already wet from the shower and her long hair was plastered to her back.

Stone noticed her tension as he wound a thin chain around her wrist and looped it through two fingers.

"Your application form stipulated you have no triggers, phobias, or fears. Is there anything you omitted to inform us about, sub PJ?"

Peyton heard the words, she even understood them. Her mind screamed at her to tell him, to admit why she, fifteen years after the fact, still woke up in a sweat from nightmares that kept recurring now and then.

She shook her head. "No, Master Eagle."

"You could tell me the truth, sub PJ, and save yourself and sub ST a lot of trouble and frustration."

She swallowed hard. "I've got nothing to tell."

Stone's expression turned stormy, his jaw was rigid as he walked toward the pulley. "Very well, then you give me no choice." He frowned as he noticed her pallor. "I ask again. Do you have any triggers I should know about?"

"I said no!" she snapped, unable to push aside the agitation that threatened to overwhelm her.

"Very well. You will not come, sub PJ, no matter what. The chain I looped around your fingers is your safe word. Yank on it when you have something to tell me or if you wish the lesson to end. If you climax, it will result in punishment later today."

He cranked the pulley and slowly inched the cross with its cargo over the edge of the cliff. Peyton was numb. The thunder of water became frighteningly loud, her breath sounded like a train blowing out steam while she could feel the thump-thump of the pulse of the blood flowing through her veins in her ears. The cross rocked to a stop and eased into a gently swaying motion next to Savannah.

Peyton tried to relax her body, to force her mind to tamper the terror that closed around her chest like a fist tightening and threatening to choke the breath from her body.

"Peyton! Look at me," Savannah's shout was faint over the deafening roar of the water below them. She listlessly turned her head; her eyes were dull as she looked at her. "Pull that chain in your hand! Come on, Peyton. You have to let them pull you back out!"

It was to no avail. It was too late. It had been too late the moment the cross had edged over and the thundering sound of rushing water overwhelmed her. She whimpered as she felt the lash of the water spray against her body; she went into an uncontrolled spasm.

Peyton didn't feel the vibrations of the anal beads, the egg or the butterfly as Stone remotely switched them on. Nor did she feel the pinch of the clamps that tightened with every thrash of her body as she fought against the terror that threatened to swamp over her.

"Peyton, please! Ring the bell! Let them pull you out! Peyton! Do you hear me!?"

Peyton heard the pleading voice but the words were no more than a blur. She was flung back fifteen years, running with her legs that burned from being pushed to their limits as she desperately tried to outrun the mass of water behind her. Her life flashed before her eyes as she felt the liquid lick at her heels. Her body arched in a bow away from the cross as in her mind, her feet got yanked from under her, water submerged her and cut off the terrified scream as she swallowed gallons of the salty substance. Her hands and feet flailed helplessly, desperate for air.

Her raw scream at the memory was muted by the thunderous cascade of water and then she gave over to the dark void that folded her within its cloak of blissful unconsciousness.

Chapter Eleven

"I'm disappointed. I thought she'd be able to last longer before she climaxed," Danton said five minutes later where they sat on a boulder watching Peyton twitching and thrashing on the cross.

"She seemed overly distressed before I pulleyed her out," Stone said. His gaze was glued on the redhead. "Sub ST also looks to be more concerned with Sub PJ than her own predicament."

Stone jumped up from the boulder as Savannah's safe word bell began to ring incessantly. He clicked the remotes to switch off the vibrators as he ran toward the edge, shouting at Danton. "Get her back here, Danton."

It didn't take long to get the cross with Savannah back across the edge, seeing as Danton had already started yanking on the pulley before Stone gave the order.

Stone dragged the St. Andrew's cross clear of the raging river. Between him and Danton they had her loose in a matter of seconds.

"Are you ready to tell me about sub PJ, my pet?"

Savannah shook her head frantically clawing at his shoulders with her eyes glued on Peyton's thrashing body.

"She's my cousin," she cried. "Get her out of there. Please Master Eagle, she's completely hysterical. I beg you!"

Stone looked out toward Peyton who now seemed relaxed against the cross with her head lowered. "She looks quite calm to me, sub."

"NO! You're wrong! She's petrified of heights and masses of water terrify her. Please!" She shook Stone—or rather tried to—in an attempt to convey her urgency. "She was in Phuket when the tsunami hit in 2004! She almost died. You have to get her—"

Stone was already reeling Peyton in. His chest heaved with concern that was at war with the fury and fear inside him.

"Switch off the vibrators, Danton," he shouted as he rushed toward the cross and yanked it the last couple of inches toward him with brute strength. He cursed when he realized she'd passed out. What they had perceived as a climax had been a desperate attempt to ward off the horror that had been blinding her.

Savannah clucked around them to such an extent that she was more of a hindrance than a help.

"Take sub ST back to the castle, Danton," Stone rasped as soon as they uncuffed Peyton. He picked her up in his arms. His way was blocked by a spitting trainee submissive who refused to budge.

"Where are you taking her?" She shrugged off Danton's hand as he reached out to restrain her. "No! I'm not going anywhere. She needs me. NO! Let me go. I have to be here. Come back! We need to take her to the castle," she screamed after Stone, then kicked and bit at the arm that caught her in its grasp.

"Fuck! You little hellion. Calm down, sub ST! Master Eagle has to warm sub PJ's skin. She's in shock and he can't leave it for the time it would take to reach the castle."

Stone was oblivious to the battle Danton had on his hands as he carefully laid Peyton's prone body down on a thick duvet under a thicket of trees that had been placed there in preparedness should it be needed. His expression was stoic as he quickly patted her dry with a large white towel and folded a small turban-style one around her hair.

He pinched her nipple and gently removed the clamps one after the other by slowly releasing the pressure around the nipple to allow the blood to flow systematically back into the abused vessels with little or no discomfort. The vibrators were next and he tossed it all aside before tenderly covering her with a light blanket.

Stone sat down next to her and with firm hands began to massage her feet, rubbing her toes until they got their color back and her skin pulsed warmly under his palm. He moved upward, massaging her legs, taking care not to miss an inch of her quivering, cold skin until he had massaged her entire body with soothing, gentle and rhythmic circular movements aimed at getting her blood flow back to normal.

He knew the moment she came to but didn't stop his tender ministrations and continued rubbing his hands all over her until she moaned and shifted on the duvet.

Their eyes clashed when hers fluttered open. She stared vacuously at him for a few seconds and then she gasped. Her gaze searched frantically behind him as the roar of the cascading water penetrated her hazy mind.

"W-what happened?" she croaked and cleared her throat to give herself a moment to recover from the cold look he cast upon her.

"You tell me, sub PJ." His voice sounded dark, his face grim and his lips drawn in a straight line as he pinned her down with a glacial look.

"I ... ehm ..." She pushed into a sitting position, surprised at how warm and relaxed she felt. Stone moved back a couple of inches from where his legs had been pressing against hers. She realized with a blush that it hadn't been a dream. It was his hands that had been soothing her, rubbing and heating her cold skin.

And she'd been passed out, oblivious to what she just knew would've been an explosive experience.

"I'm waiting, sub."

She cringed at the acerbic sting that laced his words. It warned her that his patience was hanging on a thin thread. She rubbed her forehead and glanced around furtively.

"Where's sub ST and Dom Danton?" she asked in a small voice to give her time to think. The cogs in her brain were desperately searching for a solution to the predicament she was in. She didn't want to exacerbate the situation by lying ... again.

"They returned to the Castle." His retort was short, clipped, and painted with the warning hue of impatience.

"I passed out, didn't I?"

"Yes. The question is: why?" His eyes narrowed as she lowered her gaze to stare at her fingers that alternately fisted and relaxed under his unwavering regard. "I asked you, more than once, if you had any triggers. What was your response, sub PJ?"

"I said I didn't have any." Tears trickled over her cheeks. She looked up as Stone cursed. "I'm sorry. I'm so sorry. I didn't expect … it was … I didn't think—"

"You're right. You didn't think. Do you have any idea what could've happened if you had been alone out there? If sub ST hadn't been there to warn me what was going on? Well? Do you?"

"I said I'm sorry," she cried in growing agitation. "What more do you want from me?"

He leaned forward so fast that she had no time but to gasp and stare at the chips of emerald ice shooting shards of fury at her as he all but bellowed, "Honesty! The truth. That's what I want from you." He got up and towered over her. "But it seems you're not capable of something as simple as that."

Peyton watched him stomp away with long strides. She felt miserable. She'd failed her Dom—big time—and nothing she could say or do now would change the disappointment he didn't bother to hide from her.

"Get dressed, we're going back to the Castle." The white dress fluttered to drape over her legs. "Hurry up, sub," he snapped when she didn't move.

"Master Eagle, I ..." She swallowed her words at the dark frown on his face. She was still too fragile to deal with an angry Dom ready to explode. It was on the tip of her tongue to tell him to turn around so she could dress. The apathetic twitch of his mouth warned her off that notion. It was stupid of course, seeing as he'd seen her naked more than she cared to admit but somehow at this moment, she felt too raw, too vulnerable and exposed. This unplanned emotional breakdown had laid herself utterly bare. His grim expression warned her there was no turning back from this. He had a peek into the window of her soul and learned things she desperately didn't want anyone to know about—him least of all.

She managed to struggle into the dress without dropping the light blanket until she could stand up and let it slip to the ground.

"Let's go."

"What about the duvet and—"

"Leave it." He was curt and morose as he took her arm. She had to run to keep up as he stomped off in a different direction from where Danton and she had arrived. Her legs were still rubbery and about to give in when they reached a clearing. He unceremoniously picked her up and placed her in the passenger seat of the dune buggy that was parked under a palm tree.

She automatically grabbed hold of the steel bar overhead and braced herself for the harrowing trip back to the castle on the edge of the mountain.

Stone noticed her tense body as he cranked the engine.

"Relax, Peyton, I'll take the inland route. No more heights today."

Peyton doubted the words of thanks ever left her mouth. She was too overwhelmed by the heat that consumed her from the sound of his voice. The way her name rolled off his tongue combined with his deep, soothing voice found resonance deep inside her, leaving her to drown in emotions she never expected to feel when she came to The Seven Keys Island, let alone understand.

Stone might have appeared to be aloof to Peyton as he concentrated on the winding road back to the Castle but he was aware of every move she made and every breath she took. He noticed the moment she became tense and the tremors returned to her body.

"The weather here is unsurpassed anywhere else in the world. It's the reason I bought the island and made it my home." He kept his voice deep and even. He chose a neutral topic to ease her back down.

Peyton glanced at him in surprise. "This is home?"

"Yes. It's the only place where I can be myself, away from the hordes of clinging women and fans."

"It doesn't sound like you enjoy the fame your acting has brought."

"I don't. I never wanted to become a household name. It was supposed to be one movie." He shrugged. "But I got caught in the adrenaline rush, the thrill of the stunts and one became nine in a blink of an eye on a night of liquid indulgence. I was pissed off when I slept off my hangover and realized I'd signed a contract for a ten-movie series in my drunken stupor."

"Aren't you concerned that a trainee might spill the beans about The Seven Keys Island and who owns it? Worse, Castle Sin?"

"The NDA everyone signs is airtight. Anyone who even hints at our identities, connection with or the existence of Castle Sin and what we offer here, stands the chance to be tied up in litigation for years and issued such a heavy fine, they'll lose everything they and their families own." He slanted a brief look at her. "No one is here under duress, sub PJ. Every trainee that steps onto this island, does so because they applied to either be trained as a submissive or for employment at Castle Sin should their training be successful."

"Is that why you don't wear the masks once you have each new trainee's commitment to the Masters and the program?"

"Yes. We offer you our trust and in return we expect yours."

There was no threat intended in his words but it awakened her guilt again and she fell quiet. She felt calmer, set at ease by his deep voice that he wasn't angry at her any longer. It didn't help to stop the trembling, though, that seemed to start deep inside her core and rippled outward in constant shudders that shook her body.

Like the first time she'd laid eyes on Castle Sin, she stared at it, in awe as they rounded a curve and it rose majestically in front of them.

Castle Sin was beautiful, built with a panoramic view of the surrounding land. Palm trees surrounded it like great armies defending their citadel. Their armored trunks reached out in the air protectively. This great expanse of green enhanced the soft gray walls of the castle. It was bold on the canvas of the blue sea beyond, just like its owner. It stood there as if conjured from the storybook of a child or the wild imagination of a willing submissive eager to please her king. It was perfect. Every stone was even and square, built with precision, aimed to caress the eyes of those who looked upon its rising towers. And within its walls echoed daily wails of pain, moans of passion, and laughter of companionship.

It shook Peyton how her heart contracted at the thought that this might be the last time she looked on its breathtaking beauty. She blinked away the tears burning her eyes as they entered the backyard. Stone parked in front of the door and jumped out seemingly in one fluid movement.

"Oh! I can walk by myself. You can put me down, Master Eagle," she protested as he plucked her out of the seat and into his arms like she wasn't a five-foot-eight woman weighing a healthy hundred and thirty pounds.

"Are you presuming to tell me what to do, sub?"

"I—"

"Because that would be a very unwise thing to do."

"Let me guess. Punishment?"

"No, discipline in correcting an attitude would be more appropriate."

"Dare I remind you that I just arrived and have received no training whatsoever. You can hardly discipline me for something I haven't been trained ..." Her voice drifted off as his one eyebrow drifted upward, like he was saying, *"Really? You want to go there?"*

"Yes, sub PJ, I'd swallow that lie once and for all if I were you. We both know you're not new to this lifestyle. In fact, I'm willing to bet that you've been a part of the BDSM community for, at a guess, four years?"

The blush that blossomed over her cheeks was answer enough and she was forced to bury her face in his throat to hide her embarrassment. She hated that he was so astute. She stiffened in his arms as he continued up a private flight of stairs.

"But this is the stairway to your private apartments. We're not allowed up here," she protested lamely.

"Except by invitation of a Master." He glanced briefly at her. "You're still in shock, sub. It's my duty to ensure you're taken care of."

"Master, I appreciate your concern but I'll be fine. I just need a hot bath and … oh, my," she sighed as he carried her into a bathroom that could only be called palatial and so big, her entire apartment could fit inside.

"A hot bath is exactly what you're going to get." Stone sat her on a plush ottoman that stood in front of the window that encompassed one entire wall and looked out over the island and the blue expanse of the ocean beyond.

"What a beautiful view," she breathed in, tasting the salt on her lips. She forced the shudder that threatened to regenerate as she stared out to sea. "Such cruel beauty," she whispered, soothed by the sound of water running into the tub behind her. She curled her feet under her and rested her chin on her fists, feeling the tension slowly ebbing from her body.

"Oh!" she started and grasped Stone around the neck as he unexpectedly picked her up again. "You don't have to carry me around. I can walk."

"There you go again, telling me what to do. It seems inevitable that I'll have to discipline this bad habit out of you."

"Oh, my lord," Peyton sighed as Stone lowered her into the bath filled with hot water and fragrant bubble bath that immediately soothed her tortured soul. "This is heaven."

She sank further down until she was fully submerged by luxurious bubbles. She closed her eyes with a delighted sigh as she rested the back of her head against the rounded edge of the tub, blissfully unaware of the silent man watching her with growing hunger darkening his green eyes.

Peyton looked like a mermaid immersed in an ocean filled with bubbles. Her dark red hair had dried on the way to the castle and the windblown and tousled tresses framed her beautiful face like a lover's hand cupping her cheeks. The natural light shining through the window tinted her skin with a glowing marble-like sensuality that to him reflected her inner beauty.

He had never felt this drawn to a woman before. It wasn't just her beauty, it was the natural sensuality that oozed from her that threatened to destroy all the walls he'd built around his heart ever since he was a young boy. A dour memory scorched his mind.

Cynthia Sinclair should never have had children. She didn't know how to be a mother, or a good person as far as Stone was concerned. He could never conjure up one memory of her not belittling him or telling him how useless he was. Memories of how she used to leave him at the young age of seven to look after his one year old brother, hounded him for years. The fear that he wouldn't know what to do if he started to cry and he couldn't get him to stop or that he could suffocate while he fed him his bottle. How he would sit next to Parker's baby bed and watch him the entire night while his mother was out partying with her friends at times when his father was out of town for work. But he couldn't stop loving her through it all. He longed for the day she would hug him like she did Parker or tuck him into bed. It never happened, and he gradually began to believe that he was worthless, a young boy who didn't deserve to be loved. That was how the first bricks around his heart were formed.

John Sinclair, his father, had been devastated when his wife ran away with his best friend, leaving him with a teenage boy of thirteen and his younger brother of seven. He'd seen and lived his father's pain, over and over for twenty years while he endeavored to care for his younger brother, Parker. To keep the ugliness of the world from him while their father wallowed in his wife's rejection at the bottom of liquor bottles. He never recovered. Stone didn't believe he'd ever tried. Booze became his best friend, his lover and the only family he cared about. It had been a relief to Stone when he died, having drunk himself to death.

Stone had no intention of ever losing his soul to such an extent over a woman. It made a man vulnerable and having lived with the destruction it had wrought to his family, he would never open himself to any human being like that. Except for his little brother. He'd give his life for Parker.

He inhaled deeply, focusing his mind to the present and forced back the dour memories. It was in the past. His father had been dead for eleven years. He'd learned to move on. It shook him that the memories which had been locked away in a compartment so deep, chose this moment to surface. Here, now, in the presence of a woman who was a deceiver and a liar.

The soft, flowery aroma of the bubble bath and the vision of Peyton's beauty caused a flush of testosterone to heat his veins. He kicked off his cargo pants and flipped the switch to activate the Jacuzzi jets.

"What? Oh my, Master Eagle, that's just delicious," she said as her eyes popped open and widened. "I ... that is, I mean ... oh freaking hell," she blubbered as her vision was filled with the most beautiful Adonis imaginable—in his full naked glory. Her cheeks turned blood red as he laughed.

"I think it's a little premature, little dove, but I'll be happy to let you be the judge if indeed it is ...

delicious," he said with amusement laced in his voice.

"That's not what I … I was referring to … what are you doing?" she shrieked as he stepped into the tub and pushed her forward gently.

"I'd have thought it's rather obvious. I'm making space for me."

"But you … I … we …"

Peyton felt like a stuttering fool and gasped as he lowered himself into the tub and pulled her into his arms. Her skin sizzled as she leaned against his warm chest, giving in to the desire to feel herself engulfed by his heat.

"Relax, subby. I'm sticky from the salt air and I can't think of a better way to rinse it from my body."

Peyton's resistance edged away with the endearing warmth in his voice and the whiff of breath against her cheek. When his lips trailed tiny butterfly kisses over her shoulder, a delicious shiver trailed down her spine, taking with it the last protest she might have had. His soapy hands gently washed away the salty film from her skin.

"Besides, you're still tense. As I said, it's my responsibility to take care of you. What better way to do it than up close and personal?"

His tongue tickled a sensual play of persuasion against her neck, ending with hot, intimate kisses all over her nape. Her moans escalated as he nibbled, bit and sucked at the tender and sensitive skin, the sweetest spot on her body. She was inundated with shivers of delight. She had no further resistance. If she had, she would personally have banned it all the way to oblivion.

This was what she'd been longing for the night before. To feel his hands and lips on her. Just like this, soft, teasing, gentle and persuasive.

"Master Eagle," she whimpered as his large hands cupped her breasts, teasing the budding nipples with soft pinches and tugs.

"You suffered an ordeal today, sub PJ. Just relax, let me take care of you."

"Yes, Master."

Stone felt the punch of the soft lilt of submission to his expert molding of her desires like never before. It awakened the Beast inside him that he'd managed to keep contained up until now.

He wrapped her silky hair around his fist to turn her head and direct her mouth to his. His lips took passionate possession of hers.

Peyton was lost.

She fell. Hard and fast.

Completely. Just like that.

"Hmm." The desperate whimper followed the butterfly brush of his lips over her sensuous mouth as he ended the sensual kiss. She was ablaze with the exhilaration of his ravishment as she gave into him. All her inhibitions, every single one, crumbled under the weight of fervor that saturated her lips and engulfed her senses.

He nibbled his way across her cheek to suck on her earlobe. His voice was gruff against her temple, "You have the most luxurious skin, little dove. A man could easily become addicted to the aphrodisiac taste of your skin."

Her eyes flickered open to meet his with a languid plea. Her carnal moan floated to the ceiling as she arched her back when his fingers found her nipples once more. The gentle caresses ended in a sharp pinch.

He felt her painful cry in the tightening of his loins, in the growl of the Beast for release. He tugged on the tips, pulling on them until her back arched to alleviate the pain.

"Did I give you permission to move?" His dark voice snapped her out of the fog of euphoria she'd been floating on. The submissive in her reacted immediately and she relaxed back against him, moaning as he kept her nipples extended as far as he could stretch them.

"I'm sorry, Master," she puffed.

Her hips jerked as his hand began to wander over her belly. Her carnal moan rose half an octave as he stroked and probed her fleshy succulence. Her hips canted upward.

Crack! Crack!

"Ooww!" she cried and glowered at him in reproach at the stinging slaps on her nipples. Peyton was slowly drowning in the ocean of lust that swamped her entire being. The hard arousal that poked high up against her back took away her ability to breathe.

"Master, please," she pleaded on a broken sob of lust unbound.

"Please what, little subby? Is this what you want?" Stone was entranced by her guttural moans rising and swerving through her throat as she endeavored not to buck against his fingers. He teased the opening of her pussy with a fingertip, once, twice and then with no forewarning, plunged three fingers hilt deep inside her. He curled his fingers inward, rubbing and patting the swollen ganglia at the front wall of her vagina.

"Ohh fuck!" Peyton screamed, her body solidified as the world tilted around her and she erupted in uncontrollable spasms—her hoarse cry echoing against the marbled walls of the bathroom.

Stone looked on in amazed as she writhed and jerked. She arched hard against his chest while he alternately probed her pussy then strummed her clit until she was so thoroughly bent beyond the boundaries of her own sanity that she climaxed again and again.

Her body was still spasmodic when Stone lifted her out of the tub, dried them off and carried her to his bed.

Chapter Twelve

Stone had no intention of playing the martyr with Peyton, not again. He wanted her too much. The way she'd shattered so quickly had sparked a desire so profound, he knew their copulation would be earth shattering.

The Beast inside him purred with hungry expectation. For the first time, he was tempted to completely unleash the full power of his dark desire on a woman. He suppressed it firmly. Once he did that, there would be no turning back. The Beast would never allow him to let her go.

"Ohh lord, Master Eagle, you feel so good," Peyton moaned as he spread her legs wide and settled between them. Her eyes caught his frown as he stared at her. Realization struck. She lowered her eyes demurely. "I'm sorry for climaxing without permission. It wasn't intentional but I wasn't prepared for it or expected it to happen so fast."

"Are you trying to justify breaking one of the key rules of Castle Sin, sub PJ?"

She dared a quick peek at him through her eyelashes. Her breath caught in her throat. The man who stared at her all of a sudden seemed bigger and as fierce as a wild beast.

"Oh, holy crap," she whispered. Danton had been right! She'd awakened the Beast. Her stomach heaved. She had no idea if it was in fear or excitement at the prospect of meeting the dark side of the man, who up until now, had only been tender with her, even the night before when he'd punished her.

This man, the dark Beast, scared the bejesus out of her as much as he triggered a desire so profound, she had no idea how to compartmentalize it.

"Indeed. You should've stayed away, Peyton. You have no idea what you've just unleashed."

"Master ... oh freaking hell," she protested as he dragged her leg upward and before she realized what he intended, cuffed her ankle to the side of the headboard above her head. "I'm not sure—"

"You know what the safe word is, sub PJ. It's the only thing that'll stop me now,' he rasped. His voice sounded deeper, darker and excitingly evil as he repeated the process with the other leg. Peyton did her best to hide her hands but to no avail. He barked out a condescending laugh and effortlessly caught her hands in one of his huge paws. He pulled her hands over her head and cuffed it to the center of the headboard. She shouldn't be surprised to notice the steel loops specifically welded onto the impressive wrought iron monstrosity of a bed. Stone sat back on his heels and stared at her with glimmering eyes.

Her ears burned as she saw him watching her. She had never felt so exposed. She was completely spread open with her legs hugging her hips. The way he had bound her aided in the slight tilting up of her hips.

"Beautiful." He brushed his hand over her pussy, back and forth. She tried to push down onto the bed to avoid his fingers, still too fragile and tense to accept such an intimate touch. He would have none of it and grinned derisively. "Oh no, little slut, I'm going to have my fill of this weeping cunt."

He brushed his palm over her mound and flicked his thumb over her protruding clitoris. Peyton's hips canted involuntarily toward his hand.

Crack! Crack!

"Ahhoooww!" she cried as he brutally slapped her open pussy.

"You don't move, sub. Not unless I tell you to." His expression remained stoic as he stroked around the hard nub, teasing but barely touching. He taunted her by drawing a figure eight around it until she couldn't keep quiet.

"Please," fell in a pleading whimper from her lips.

Stone ignored her, enjoying her untethered response too much. He could feel the Beast slowly clawing its way out, his lust spiked by her spicy scent. His cock became gorged, swollen and taut as the hot flush of arousal diverged into his loins.

His feathery touch caused all of Peyton's energy to suddenly gush between her legs. Her cry was raw as she fisted her hands when he pressed down on the throbbing fleshy button in an effort to force her hips not to jerk into his touch.

"Hmm, such a succulent little nub," he murmured as he caressed it with slow, smooth strokes.

"You're a demon," she moaned. It felt like he was summoning all her hunger into one spot, feeding it until he was ready to catapult her over the edge.

His dark chuckle was the only response he offered, watching her neck arch as he squeezed her ample breasts with one hand. He rubbed her nipple and then pinched the hardened peak. A satisfied purr sounded inside him as he watched a ripple of pleasure flash over her face;

"Are you still as hot as in the bath, little dove?" Stone rasped and thrust two fingers knuckle-deep into her hot channel. Her cry coalesced with his growl as her heat engulfed and coated his fingers.

"Ah, yes, I see you are and so very eager too."

Her cheeks turned a becoming rosy color as she watched him smooth her warm, wet essence all over her throbbing clit.

"Master, please I need to … uhmmm," she moaned as his fingers closed around her nipple, tugging at it, pulling on it, and pinching it hard.

"Don't come, sub," Stone warned, his eyes glowing as he vibrated her clit with short rapid bursts of his thumb.

She was helpless as he unleashed something wild that ran rampant inside her. It probed the perimeter of her lust, ambushing it into overdrive as it stole away her control.

Never before had anyone been able to tap into her deeper reserve of sexuality and turned her into a mindless vessel. She surrendered to the sting that aroused the untethered lust that surged through her veins.

Peyton shattered.

Crack! Crack!

She screamed as he slapped her pussy in punishment but all it did was fuel her climax. She was still trying to come down to earth when he dipped his head and buried his tongue inside her pussy to suck at her fleshy folds.

"No! I can't ... it's too soon," she begged as she tried to buck and dislodge him but his hands clamped around her hips to hold her in place as he sucked and licked at her juices with gusto.

She cursed her traitorous body's reaction to his callous treatment with a surge of heat that flushed her skin.

"Ah, yes ... such a succulent little cunt." The saturated color of his aroused groan spilled out against her quivering thighs and pushed her closer to the edge.

His crude laughter turned evil as he continued to dine on her like the feral animal that had now been unleashed and drove every action he made.

"Oh god, please," she begged him in a quivering voice; she teetered then fell as he pushed his tongue inside her.

Crack! Crack!

Her cries continued as he didn't allow her to come back to earth. He kept her on edge, slapping her pussy and clit viciously every time she disobeyed his rule and climaxed until all she could do was cry and beg him to stop. Through it all, she never once considered shouting out *king*, the only thing that he'd warned her would stop him. Her labia were swollen and red, painful, stinging, and still she couldn't prevent one climax after the other from rocking through her.

Eventually, he rose over her, his body taut with lust as he sheathed his cock in a condom. He looked at her, enjoying the tortuous expression of overindulgence on her face; his own was pulled into a carnal grimace.

"I'm going to fuck you now, Peyton. Your brains are going to be scrambled I'm going to pound you so hard. This is one time you'll never forget. You'll wake up in the morning climaxing as you'll still experience the feel of me pounding your tight little cunt." His eyes darkened and his voice deepened. "Who am I?"

"Master Eagle," she whimpered, unable to look away from the heat in his eyes.

"No, Peyton. My name. Who. Am. I?"

"Stone … Stone Sinclair."

He smiled with devilish satisfaction, like he had needed her confirmation that she knew his name. He pushed the tip of his cock inside her slit.

She whimpered, surprised to feel fear creeping closer to submerge her now quivering form. This wasn't the man she'd crushed over for years. This truly was a Beast.

"Remember that, Peyton, because every time you hear my name, your cunt will flush with lust," he promised caustically.

"Ahhh, gaawwd!"

Peyton screamed as he slammed home, hilt deep—and lost the tenacious hold he had over the Beast the moment her tight heat wrapped around his length. He drew back, not giving her time to adjust to his massive girth, he began to pound into her.

Hard, sharp jabs that hilted with every thrust.

Peyton was breathless, lost in the euphoric sensations that overpowered her body while her mind floundered for one coherent thought.

"You're so tight, sub, and so fucking hot ... scorching." His feverish gaze met hers as he reached down and brushed his fingers over the fleshy nub, turning her breathing ragged.

"Now, Peyton ... you may come."

His mouth lashed her nipples with long, deep kisses, dosing her with ragged breaths as she gasped for air. The passionate discourse of their moans drifted through the room.

Stone thrust more deeply, pounding harder, exulting in her hoarse cries that washed over him.

Peyton drowned in tumultuous waves of the ecstasy as she gave in to the final demand of a climax on his raw command.

"Stone! Ohohoh!"

Her scream split the room as she gasped for breath.

Peyton had no control over her body but fear of the Beast had dissolved with every touch and demand to burst into unexpurgated lust. She was

247

enraptured by the look on his face, the way the veins in his throat gorged and pulsed with every wild thrust. She twisted and jagged under him.

"More! Fuck me harder, Master. I want all of you," she spurred him on, desperate to experience the full power of the Beast unleashed upon her.

It was all Stone needed. He became mindless—something he never allowed to happen when the Beast came out to play. All that mattered was the moment, the pleasure, the desperation and the screams of Peyton's uncontrolled lust that kept fueling it to want more, become wilder, rougher. The bed slammed against the wall from the force of his thrusts. He powered into her as he lost the ability to control the Beast that now urged him on to pound her with uncontrolled strength and fervent thrusts, chasing his raging orgasm.

Heat tickled at the back of his scrotum to illuminate the rush of arousal blinding him in that moment. It surged through his veins. His primal roar echoed through the room. A sharp pain shot through his head as he came deep inside her.

He slumped over her convulsing body, continuing to jerk the final drops of his release through his turgid length. A carnal groan rumbled from his throat as Peyton's pussy clenched around him with the final spasms of her climax.

The tension and sexual exertion took its toll on Peyton. She couldn't move when Stone uncuffed her and massaged her legs. He went to the bathroom to fetch a cloth only to find her fast asleep when he returned.

His expression was shuttered as he stared at her. He was still stumped by the shattering climax he'd had. All brought on by her demand for more, her desire to meet the full power of the darkness inside him. His instincts about her had been right. She was the woman he had been searching for. The female counterpart to his Beast. His lips flattened.

But fate had a strange way to change one's destiny. She might be the one to satisfy and tame the darkness inside him but it wasn't meant to be.

To Stone, honesty, trust, and integrity had been the deciding factor in all important decisions of his life. He could never trust his heart to a woman who had failed in all three of those traits.

It proved once again that happy ever after wasn't meant for him.

"She has to go."

Shane and Hawk looked at each other. Stone had called them for a meeting before seven in the morning, which in itself indicated a serious matter was at hand.

"I assume you're referring to sub PJ?" Hawk said. Danton had already brought them up to date about the incident at the waterfall. He studied Stone with concerned curiosity. He had never seen him this reserved, closed off, and stoic. He had always been able to read his expression. Today, all he saw was a blank canvas.

"I assume Danton told you what happened, so I don't need to repeat any of it. Our rules on this are clear cut. If any sub, whether she's experienced or a trainee, can't be trusted to be honest with us, especially in regard to something as crucial as triggers, she's removed from the program and leaves the island."

"Is that really what you want, Stone?" Shane asked quietly. He had seen Stone carry a naked Peyton from his private apartment in the early morning hours. Stone had never, in all the years since they'd opened the Castle, taken a woman to his home. He was a very private person and all alliances he'd formed with subs in the past, had been limited to the wing he used for training.

Stone's expression turned grim. "You know how I feel about honesty and trust, Shane."

"Are you taking into consideration the trauma the experience of the tsunami had caused to her at such a young age?" Shane leaned forward, aware of the turmoil scathing at the younger man's soul.

"Because of that, she, of all people, should know how crucial it is to be honest about her triggers. She's not a rookie and she's highly intelligent. I asked her, Shane, repeatedly, before I put her out over that waterfall if she had any. She kept denying it. God alone knows how many more she's hiding from us." He shook his head. "I'm sorry but I can't allow such an irresponsible submissive on the island. One way or the other, it'll filter to the others and cause more havoc. No. She has to leave."

"What about sub ST? She also lied to us." Hawk steepled his fingers together over his stomach. The prospect of the delectable blonde leaving didn't sit well with him.

"That's different and will be handled accordingly," Stone asserted.

It was evident to Shane and Hawk that he'd made up his mind and nothing either of them said would change it. It wasn't that they didn't agree with him. They'd been very stringent about their rules, especially those that could affect a sub's health or cause irreparable damage and harm on a physical or emotional level. They just hated to ban the first woman to bring such fire and passion to Stone's eyes from The Seven Keys Island and Castle Sin. A very slight and unguarded emotion that was hidden to most, but to them, glaring in its desire to find happiness.

"Very well, you're right. We can't look past this but I do feel she should be offered the opportunity to talk about it and offer the proper apologies," Shane said just as Stone's PA, Alexa Silver, arrived with a tray stacked with pancakes and coffee. "Ah, you're a lifesaver, Alexa. I'm starving."

"If I had prior warning about the meeting, breakfast would've been served upon your arrival, Master Fox," Alexa snipped with a pointed look at Stone.

"Don't believe for one moment you're safe from my whip just because you're my PA, little snip," Stone grated with his heavy brows drawing together. He generally didn't dominate her during her official working hours but he was irritated and felt the need to expunge the angry energy that continued to boil inside him ... preferably with his whip in hand.

Alexa immediately lowered her eyes and poured the coffee. "I was just saying," she mumbled under her breath as she passed plates and mugs around.

Stone's sigh was as heavy as an early morning fog around the island during winter. He ran a tired hand over his eyes. He hadn't slept, courtesy of the woman in his bed. He'd preferred to sit and watch her sleep, while he savored the memory of their sexual encounter. Over and over until in the early morning hours, he resolutely locked it away so deep it would become forgotten, never to regurgitate over it again before he'd carried her to her sleeping quarters.

"My apologies, Alexa. I'm in a foul mood. Please ask Dom Evans to bring sub PJ to us."

"Right away, Master Eagle."

"Not Master Eagle … Stone, Alexa. This is the office and I'm your boss here, not your Dom."

She giggled. A rich, bright sound that drew their eyes toward her. Suddenly she didn't appear as dreary and dull as she always did in her pristine corporate suits and tightly pulled back hair. Her eyes glimmered with life and passion. Shane's interest was prickled, not just as a Dom but also from a professional aspect. He'd love to delve deep into her mind and find what made her tick. She was in her late forties, that much he could remember from interviewing her. At the moment, she bubbled with the energy of a thirty-year-old.

"With all due respect, Master Dom. You'll never *just* be my boss."

Stone smiled indulgently as she trotted out to do his bidding. Alexa had been with him for the past three years. She had been one of the first successful trainees to apply for employment as a submissive at Castle Sin. She had filled the position for two years and applied for the position as his PA the moment it became available. She had the perfect credentials, Stone liked her, and they had clicked on a professional level immediately. He still scened with her on the odd occasion or used her for demonstrations during training sessions, but once they stepped foot inside the office wing, they were colleagues.

"Now why is it I wonder, that I've never seen that side of her?" Shane pondered aloud.

"Maybe because you always prefer to scene and fuck the younger subs," Hawk teased good-naturedly.

"Yeah, well, perhaps it's time to start broadening my preferences, especially now that I'm retiring from acting and wish to commit to one woman and settle down."

"What!? No twenty-something tight ass girl to warm your bed as you ease into your old age?" Hawk laughed as Shane scowled at him.

"God forbid. They're fun to play with and fuck but I have no desire to play Daddy to a younger woman. No, when I settle down, I want a mature woman who knows what she wants and isn't shy or scared to tell me to fuck off when I make her mad."

"And you think Alexa is that woman?" Stone asked with a teasing gleam in his eyes. Alexa had more spunk and sass than either of his cousins realized. And she wasn't shy when it came to making demands to be pleasured in bed. He had always thought she would be a perfect match for the oldest Master of the Sinclair clan. He, for one, would be very pleased if they were to find each other.

"She definitely has potential. Maybe a lot more than I gave her credit for." Shane finished the decadent pancakes and pushed back the plate. He stretched out his legs. "Close your mouth, Hawk. I'll be fifty-two in seven months. It's about fucking time I find a woman to love ... before I become senile and then no one will want me."

"You senile? You live too healthy and are too active and energetic to ever get there, old timer." Hawk sighed and slouched lower. "We're all getting older. In all honesty, I'd like a little fluff of my own too ... soon, I think."

Stone didn't say anything. His attention was drawn to the doorway and the arrival of Dom Evans and Peyton.

"Morning, Masters. You asked to see sub PJ," he said as he pushed her into the office ahead of him and waited for her to take the present form.

"No, stay, Evans. You need to hear this," Stone stopped him when he retreated to the door. "Close the door, please."

His eyes moved over Peyton's tense body with slow deliberation. She was once again dressed in the customary white sundress all trainees wore during their sessions. Her deep auburn tresses tumbled in luxurious waves over her shoulders. "Sit down, sub PJ."

Her startled gaze shot up to meet his. Her tongue flicked over her lips in a quick foray to moisten her suddenly dry lips. The darkening blush over her cheeks was evidence of the memory of what they had been doing before she'd passed out the night before.

Evans dragged one of the heavy visitor chairs to the side of the desk, where she would be the center of the three men's attention. She sank down into it with graceful flair, crossed her ankles demurely with her hands on her lap.

"Omitting and denying you have triggers could've ended fatally yesterday. You do realize that, don't you?" Stone began. He appeared relaxed as he leaned back in his chair.

"Yes, Master Eagle." The misery she felt ciphered through every syllable.

Stone's expression didn't change, he just watched her with indifference. He'd already locked the chambers of his heart, this time with an impenetrable shield of armor.

"What triggered it so badly that you fainted?"

Peyton froze as the question floated toward her. She didn't want to talk about it. Not to him because then she'd have to tell him why she'd hid her triggers from them. Admitting that she hated failure went against her nature. In her mind, *she* had failed. Failed to overcome her fears over something that had happened fifteen years ago because she had allowed it to turn her into a weakling instead of facing her fears.

"I don't like waiting, even less to repeat myself, sub PJ."

She stared at him with pleading eyes, hoping to persuade him to let it drop. She filtered through the swirls of color in his eyes, none showed any emotion, zero empathy until one silver flash broke through to shatter her defenses.

Disappointment.

"The cascade of water, the … the height of the cliff," she stammered in a broken voice. She clenched her hands together, closed her eyes briefly and breathed in deeply. "I always used to love the ocean. It was exhilarating to jog on the beach, to feel the water around my ankles. On vacations when I was young, my dad and I would swim out to the deep sea. I loved the challenge ... but that all changed." She stared ahead with unseeing eyes as the memory of that fateful day flashed before them.

"My dad treated me and two of my friends with a surprise trip for my twenty-first birthday to Phuket in Thailand. The sun, sea ... it was idyllic. It was our final day and I went jogging on the beach, like I'd done every morning since we arrived. The weather was sunny with a little breeze, the perfect way to end our week-long trip."

A tiny smile quirked her lips. "California Girls ... it was the song playing on my iPod when I got back to the hotel. I love the oldies, you know. I was singing along when I noticed people screaming and running frantically in all directions. I saw my friends, Pippa and Violet, at the hotel entrance. They were jumping up and down, screaming and waving at me." Peyton started to rock back and forth, the words tumbled rapidly from her lips. "I remember yanking off the earphones as I ran toward them. It was then that I h-heard i-it. The deafening roar of the ocean obliterating everything in its path. I'll never forget that moment when I looked over my shoulder. It was as though fear added a punch to my heartbeat, speeding it up at what I saw. My screams still echo in my ears sometimes and when thoughts of it rush through my mind it takes me right back to that moment, sprinting as hard as I could after my friends who were running up the stairs of the hotel. I remember thinking at the time how senseless it was, us hoping to outrun the wave of destruction. I'll never forget how difficult it had been to breathe with my lungs feeling as it was about to burst from fear, how my legs burned and the desperation that kept me pushing, harder, faster as I took the stairs. The terror that froze my mind when the first spray of the water hit me as I reached the fifth floor will most probably stay with me all my life."

Peyton was unaware of the tears running over her cheeks as she continued, "It's strange how in a situation like that everything seems to happen in slow motion and felt like it was taking a lifetime, while in fact, it was over in a matter of minutes. I'll always remember the desperate screams from my friends higher up for me to go faster and how hard I tried. God knows I did but the water was faster. One moment I was running, the next I got swallowed in a giant hand of liquid death." Her hand trembled as she brushed her fingers over her forehead. "I don't know how but my friends told me afterwards that one of the hotel guests out of sheer desperation leaned over the railing and miraculously managed to get a hold of me. Another man had helped him to pull me out of the swirling mass of water while I had been flailing around in an effort to surface. Violet said I wasn't breathing, that it took them ten minutes to revive me."

A shudder shook her body. She smoothed the skirt of the dress over her legs, using the movement to find focus and calm her mind, a tactic she'd learned during therapy.

"I believed I had learned to deal with it. Accept the fear I now have over the ocean."

"How do you cope with it?" Shane asked, his voice warm and understanding.

She smiled briefly. "I never go to the beach anymore. I haven't set foot in the ocean since that day. I've come to hate island life. Sand, sea, the sticky salty air ... it doesn't excite me anymore. The trip on the boat here ... it wasn't as bad as I thought it would be but luckily relatively quick." Her shoulders hunched. "I guess the roar of the waterfall was the trigger. I remember just before I passed out the feeling of despair and realization that I was about to die overwhelmed me. In that moment, I was back in Phuket, running up the stairs and then the spray of the water hit me and ..."

She lifted tortured eyes to Stone, shocked at the impassive expression on his face, like he felt nothing. Then she realized—he didn't. Her heart plummeted to her feet. She'd fucked up. Royally and Stone Sinclair wasn't about to forgive her now ... if ever.

"I'm truly sorry, Master Eagle."

"You blatantly denied having any triggers even though I asked you, more than once. You endangered your life and worse, you put me at risk by lying to me. If sub ST hadn't been there you could've died and I would've had to live with that guilt the rest of my life." He held up his hand when she opened her mouth to speak. "Severe shock can cause death." He gestured at his cousins. "You're not the first submissive who believed she knew better and kept her triggers from us. We've seen it happen. It's something we'll never allow again."

Stone got up. He towered over her as he looked at her regally. "You proved to us you cannot be trusted; therefore, you're removed from the training program. You'll leave immediately."

"But ... no! Please, Master Eagle. I made a mistake and I'll be forever sorry about that. Please don't send me away."

His lips tightened. "What is sub ST to you, Peyton?"

And there it was. The final blow. The one test she knew she was going to fail. She'd sworn silence to Savannah and she couldn't break it. She hung her head.

"Please don't ask me that," she croaked in a whisper. She hadn't seen her cousin yet and had no idea if she'd said anything to Stone. Although she highly doubted after the way she'd pushed Peyton to silence, she would have.

"More lies. I guess I shouldn't be surprised." A wry smile twisted his lips. "It seems between you and Sub ST, she's the honest one." He ignored her shocked surprise and turned to Evans. "Collect all her belongings and then escort her to the docks. Make sure Danton takes her right away."

"Of course, Master Eagle," Dom Evans said somberly. He took Peyton's arm and pulled her from the chair.

She looked back at Stone but he'd sat back down and was calmly discussing the training program for the day with Shane and Hawk. Peyton was devastated that after the explosive encounter they had the previous night, he didn't even bother to say goodbye.

Stone refused to give in to the turbulent emotions inside him when Evans led Peyton to the door. It was over. He wasn't the kind of man to dwell on what could've been. He ignored the concerned looks from Hawk and Shane and stoically discussed the evaluations of the different levels of trainees.

"You wanted to see me?" Parker said as he strolled into the office. Each Master had an office in his wing that they used for Castle Sin matters.

"I want you to prioritize finding what I now know to be tampered background information of Savannah Thorne and Peyton Jackson. Their connection is a familial one." His voice darkened. "They're cousins."

"How do you know that?" Shane asked with raised eyebrows.

"Sub ST. She was so agitated, I don't even think she realized she told me. Someone went to great lengths to hide it. I want to know why. Those two are up to something and my gut instinct tells me we need to be prepared."

"Will do." Parker turned to leave. "Oh, before I forget. You and Hawk were right to be wary of Gary Sullivan. I found some very interesting connections he made during his visit to Sudan eight months ago."

"What kind of connections?" Stone straightened with interest.

"He had the usual meetings with the ministers and politicians during the planned two-week visit. All the reports I could find indicated he stayed for fifteen days but I stumbled across a flight plan from Sudan to Mexico four days prior to his return. Guess who got off the plane in Mexico?"

"Defense Secretary Gary Sullivan," Hawk said.

"His entire entourage had been left behind in Sudan to wield off any questions about his whereabouts. The biggest trigger here is the man he met in secret at the Hacienda Mexicana Hotel around midnight the day after he arrived."

"Spit it out, Parker," Stone grumbled, eager to hear exactly what they were dealing with.

"Miguel Muerta."

"The crime lord of the La-Muerta Syndicate?" Stone asked with a frown.

"The one and only."

"What else?" Stone shifted in his chair. Suddenly the entire project they were involved in took on an entirely different dimension.

"Apart from a few secret phone calls between the two, nothing else. I'm working on trying to hack into those calls. There might be a way to get the voice recordings but it'll take a couple of days. Oh, one more thing. Sullivan seems to be in constant contact with Deputy Director of the FBI, Decker Cooper."

"Why should that be a flag?" Hawk asked. "It could just be related to a case."

"When I say constant, I mean two to three times a day for the past four weeks. No, there's definitely something more to it."

"Thanks, Parker. Please set up a secure live interface with the secretary of state. She should be made aware of the potential danger he presents."

"On it."

Chapter Thirteen

The ocean breeze whispered like a lover, placing salty kisses on her cheek and tousling her long auburn tresses. Peyton tilted back her head and closed her eyes, for once allowing herself to feel what she used to love so much when she was younger. The teasing caress of nature, the vastness of the sea surrounding her.

Her sigh was softly deflating; like the tension had lifted yet left her overwhelmed with melancholy instead of relief. Her eyes opened to watch with a feeling of detachment the calm surface of the sea passing by, here and there brightened with little flags of white where small waves rippled playfully.

"It's not the end of the world, little one."

Danton's deep voice floated toward her as if from far away. He stood at the helm and steered the speedboat with confidence … just much slower than when she'd arrived. A wry smile twisted her lips.

I guess I should be grateful he was there and understands how I feel. Juicy news must travel fast in the Castle. Everyone probably already knows of my failure.

She looked back over her shoulder. The Seven Keys Island appeared like a large green speck on the horizon. Danton had no idea just how bad it was. She hadn't even grasped the magnitude of leaving until the boat had pulled away from the dock.

"No, I guess it's not but it feels like it is," she murmured softly.

She knew she had no one to blame but herself. She had failed, miserably because she'd been too hard-headed and proud to own up to her fears. She'd been successful over the years to pretend that she'd had a hold on them. It worked, purely because she avoided placing herself in situations where they would be triggered.

Therein lay the root of her screw-up. She should've known better. She knew the dangers of triggers in a BDSM scene. She was a grown up for heaven's sake, a thirty-five-year-old woman who had always owned up to her behavior. This time she'd allowed her emotions to get the better of her. She felt it racing through her again, just like at the waterfall—cold, fearful, anxious—and instead of admitting to Stone the terror gripping her, she'd backed away.

The act of a coward.

Shame washed over her. She'd failed to be the warrior she had become over the years since the ordeal in Phuket. A strong, assertive woman who knew what she wanted and went after it with all guns blazing.

Not this time.

Instead, she'd shown the frightened young woman within, damaged and afraid, the twenty-one-year-old one, who still had nightmares about the dark tunnel she'd floundered in during those long moments of near death.

"You blatantly denied having any triggers even though I asked you, more than once."

Stone's cold voice echoed inside her mind. There had been no reproach, no accusation in his tone. He had stated a fact. She still didn't know why she hadn't told him of her fear of falling water and heights. Perhaps in her naivety, she'd believed the way he'd secured her to the St. Andrew's cross would be her safety net.

"You endangered your life, and worse, you put me at risk by lying to me. If sub ST hadn't been there you could've died and I would've had to live with that guilt the rest of my life."

Peyton shivered as the guttural voice rasped through her brain. She felt as gutted now as she had the first time he'd said it. It had never crossed her mind that there were more factors than her own triggers involved until that moment. For the first time, she realized just how dangerous it could have turned out by lying about her fears.

No use bleating over it now, Peyton. You fucked up, you have to own up to it and carry the consequences.

If only Stone casting her aside so easily didn't hurt so much. That made the entire situation so much worse. Her soft moan dissipated into the wind at the memory of the previous night that kept replaying in her mind like a movie on a loop. She'd been in the lifestyle long enough to know that what they had shared was more than rough and kinky sex. So much more. It had been special, explosive; something that didn't come along easily nor something that happened to everyone.

It hurt that Stone Sinclair obviously hadn't felt the same. Not that it should surprise her. He was a powerful Dom, a Master of fucking with a sub's mind and the kind of man every woman yearned for. He had the pick of the crop from the submissives on the island and by all counts, they stood in queue for his attention.

The sounds of laughter and loud music yanked Peyton back to the present. She was surprised that they'd arrived at the marina of the Margaritaville Key West Resort on Key West where Danton had picked them up five days earlier. She was startled to realize her stay at Castle Sin had only been for four nights. It felt like much longer, especially since she'd managed to lose her heart in such a short time span.

Whoa! Where the hell did that come from? I'm not in love with Stone Sinclair. I'm in lust with him. I celeb fangirl over him with a very high octave kind of emotional lust but love, it definitely isn't. It can't be. Can it?

"Let's go, subby."

Peyton took Danton's proffered hand, grateful for the assistance as she suddenly felt rattled and weak in the knees. She followed him blindly until she realized they were walking in the opposite direction and not toward the shuttle.

"Wait! Where are we going? I need to get to the airport."

"Master Eagle said to take you to his unit at Sunset Key Cottages." He glanced at her. "You've suffered an ordeal, little one. He offered for you to stay for a week, relax, and have a vacation before you head home."

Peyton was too surprised to protest as he unlocked the door and waved her inside. She stared around in awe. It was as luxurious as it was homey.

"I don't know what to say. I didn't expect him to offer me such kindness after …" She swallowed her misery.

Get a fucking grip, Peyton. You sound like a spineless wimp!

Danton dropped her bags in the main bedroom and turned to her. He brushed back her windblown hair. "As Master Eagle, he's unmovable and strict, especially when it comes to safety and honesty. It's one of the most important traits he values in the people he allows close to him." He smiled gently. "As Stone Rothman, he has a heart of gold."

Peyton was startled to hear his acting name. She'd become so used to thinking of Stone as the real him that she'd forgotten who he was to the rest of the world. Not that she believed Danton didn't know the Sinclairs' true identity but she wasn't about to blurt it out to him.

She went cold as another memory burst to the surface of Stone demanding his name from her.

"No, Peyton. My name. Who. Am. I?"

"Stone ... Stone Sinclair."

She'd blurted out his real name, not Rothman, not realizing at the time that once again he'd caught her out on a lie. Now he knew without a doubt that she'd been on the island under false pretenses.

"I can't stay here," she croaked. It didn't feel right, not since she'd realized that he knew she was a complete and utter liar.

"Don't be silly, Peyton. You need some rest and since you planned to be on the island for a long period, there's no rush to get back home. Take the offer. No one will bother you here. Master Eagle will be busy with the trainees, so you don't have to worry that he'll come here." He smiled gently. "It's a pity. I had believed you're the one who could thaw his heart. He needs warmth, love, and caring in his life. He's been living in the cold and alone for far too long."

Peyton leaned into him as he hugged her. It felt good just to be held.

"Drop the key at the reception desk when you leave. They've stocked the kitchen with supplies but if you're not in the mood, there's a very nice restaurant on the premises." He brushed his lips over her forehead in a brief kiss. He pressed a business card in her hand. "I'm only a phone call away. "Take care, sub PJ."

Peyton felt bereft when he left. It had been too easy to be drawn into the camaraderie and feeling of belonging at Castle Sin. She supposed it was for that reason there were so many eager women who applied for permanent positions as subs. She still wondered how she got selected in the first place. The documents in Savannah's file had indicated there was a very long waiting list.

She spent the afternoon in listless limbo. She was numb from thinking too much and roamed from one room to the other. It didn't help that she felt Stone's presence in every one of them. There were small things that indicated his personal touch. Beautifully framed photographs of special places from all over the world, which she instinctively knew he had taken himself. An out of place rug here, an intricate ornament there—things that stood apart from the stylishly decorated home.

"It serves no purpose to stay. It's only going to be torture knowing he has slept in the same bed, used the shower … no, it'll be better for my sanity to go home in the morning."

Her mind made up, she prepared a light prawn pasta dinner and went to bed early.

Though her eyes were open, she couldn't think of why; it was still pitch-black outside, apart from the silver beam of moonlight shining through the window. Her heart pounded, her mind raced, inundated with wild scenarios. It felt like a hypodermic of adrenaline had been pumped into her carotid.

Something had woken her up. She pushed upright and strained to see into the moonlit darkness, her ears pricked for any sign of an intruder.

"Nothing. Relax, Peyton. You're chasing ghosts in your sleep," she berated herself sotto voce. Her breathing rate began to settle. She dropped back onto the pillow and closed her eyes giving in to the drowsiness dragging her under.

Not for long though. Her senses were now too aware and she couldn't slip back into the realm of sleep. Then she heard it. She froze at the sound of breathing that wasn't her own. It had a heaving vibration, rapid and harsh, like a man who had sprinted into the room.

Before she could act, a hard hand closed over her face, cutting off her ability to breathe. She struggled, her eyes stretched open wide with fear. Her nose filled with the strong scent of cigars on the hand that covered her mouth and nose. In the almost blackness her eyes strained for some sign of what was to come.

"Hmmph!" Her muted cry sounded pitiful as she kicked out, desperate for air.

Help! Somebody help me! I don't want to die! Her desperate cries echoed only inside her mind. She struggled and tried to comprehend what was happening but it was like trying to grip tightly onto sand. The more she squeezed her mind for a way to escape, the more it slipped through her fingers.

She kicked out again and this time her heel connected with something soft, maybe an inner thigh.

"Fucking bitch!" a dark voice growled furiously in the stillness of the night. Peyton was frantic, her lungs felt like bursting, the blood pumping through her veins sounded like a formula 1 race car in her ears. She increased her struggles, thrashing and clawing at the hand holding her down.

"Behave," the voice barked softly. "Stop struggling, woman, and I'll take away my hand." He pressed his face close to hers. "Scream and it'll earn you a fist under the chin."

He chuckled evilly as she continued to struggle, desperation to fill her lungs with oxygen made her deaf to his threats.

"Better yet, I'll indulge in something I can at least enjoy."

His hand moved suggestively over her hip to cup her breast and squeezed. Peyton stopped breathing and turned to a statue.

"Tie the bitch up, let's get this over with. There's no time for your games. I don't wish to be caught here in daylight."

"Pity," he grated. The hand fell away at the sharp order from the doorway. "Yes, Boss."

"Ms. Jackson, I suggest you take his warning to heart and keep quiet. He's going to take his hand from your mouth, scream and I'll let him loose on you."

The hand lifted and Peyton gasped, heaving in deep gulps of air. She moaned as the brute yanked her hands in front of her and tied her wrists with zip ties. He forced her into a sitting position. Her eyes frantically searched the room for the second man,

"Who are you?"

"Who I am is no concern of yours, Ms. Jackson. What's of importance is what you're going to do for me."

"What do you want with me?"

"You should've stayed on the island, Ms. Jackson. It cost me a lot of money to ensure your application was in this group of trainees approved."

Peyton frowned. Castle Sin didn't advertise publicly, or anywhere on the web for that matter. Trainees were recruited through appointed BDSM clubs only. It had been all in the file Savannah's mother had given her. It was how she'd gotten a foot into the door—or so she'd believed.

She'd visited Club Sensations in Seattle, the same one where Savannah had been recruited. The file had contained very detailed information of the kind of submissives that would be successful applicants for employment at Castle Sin. She'd practiced every action, gesture, and reaction that had been detailed in the file. Words and hints of her desire and need to break away from her unfulfilled life. Everything that would ensure she got the attention of Hunter Sutton, the owner. It had taken four visits for him to notice her and another three before he approached her.

"I don't understand."

Peyton had been in dangerous situations before, chasing stories, but this was on a different level. This time she was on the receiving end and it brought a completely new dimension to light than reporting on it happening to someone else. She shuddered as she felt the leering eyes of the bulky man standing by the bed on her, posing the kind of threat she refused to consider. She blithely ignored him and kept her gaze on the tall and dark figure of the man in front of the window. Strategically placed so that his face was completely in the dark with the moonlight shining through the window, casting him in a silhouette of approaching doom.

"Did you honestly think someone as clever as your cousin would leave a file with information about a place like Castle Sin out in the open?" He laughed derisively, "For her *mother,* of all people, to find?"

Peyton went cold. Now she knew without a doubt that her suspicions about Savannah had been correct. Someone had a hold over her. And here she was facing that frightening man herself. To make matters worse, it seemed he had, unbeknownst to her, been playing her like a puppet too.

"So, I was right, Savannah isn't at Castle Sin because she chose to go there."

"See, Rusco. I told you this woman is sharp."

"So, you did, Boss."

"Enough chit-chat. You'll go back to The Seven Keys Island, Ms. Jackson. Your presence there is of cardinal importance."

Peyton barked out a sardonic laugh. "You didn't do your homework properly, did you?"

Crack!

The slap came out of nowhere and so hard, she was flung off the bed on the opposite side. Before she could find her bearings, Rusco yanked her up so roughly that it felt like her arm was being torn out of its socket.

"Ahhh," she screamed as he flung her on the bed, her abused shoulder taking the brunt of her weight.

"Get the fuck up," Rusco snarled and pulled her upright. "You will treat the Boss with respect, *capiche?* One more snide remark from your pretty little mouth and I'll be too happy to shove something in it to keep you quiet."

Peyton covered her throbbing cheek with her hands. She could feel it swell under her tentative touch.

"I expect an answer, bitch."

Peyton cleared her throat and croaked out, "I understand."

Her initial assessment of Rusco had been wrong. She had thought him to be rough and uncouth but behind the bulk and brute strength was housed an intelligent and sharp mind. The way he articulated himself spoke of an educated man.

She looked at the dark figure in front of the window. "I've been banned from the island. In case you didn't know, those men rule Castle Sin with an iron fist and strict rules. I broke a primary one. There's no way they'll allow me back."

"Oh, I do believe Stone Sinclair will take you back. He's never been this enamored with a trainee before."

"I ... how do you know that?" Peyton waited with bated breath. It didn't take a genius to figure out he had eyes and ears on The Seven Keys Island. It meant that whatever she and Savannah had been drawn into, had something to do with the Sinclair cousins, but she'd be damned if she could hazard a guess at what it was.

"Let's just say I'm a very resourceful person."

"I don't understand what you want from me, from us? Whatever you believe my cousin and I can do, or that we have any influence over those men, you're wrong."

"I'm never wrong, Ms. Jackson. The two of you were chosen for a reason. We need both of you on that island, inside Castle Sin for it to work."

Peyton leaned forward, concern for Savannah raced like wildfire through her. "Look, I don't know what you think we can do but I'm not a spy or an influencer of any kind in that place. I only lasted four days for heaven's sake."

"Ah, but that's where you're making a mistake. You might not be a spy but you're like a bloodhound. You've unraveled mysteries, political and government corruption no one even thought of over the years. That my dear, has set you apart from most journalists out there—you're the best influencer I could have hoped for."

"In a newspaper, a magazine and on television, yes! But not … I don't even know what it is you want from me!"

"All in good time. You have the sharp mind to search the castle, or the entire island if needed, to find what we're looking for. Your very clever and compassionate cousin is there to ensure you do my bidding. You two, my dear, are going to play a key role in changing the way the government of the U.S. operates for once and for all."

"Savannah knows why she's there?"

"Yes. Unfortunately, your arrival took a little longer than anticipated but that couldn't be helped."

"At a guess, I'd say she didn't know I'm supposed to be her sidekick," Peyton said dryly.

A slow anger began to burn inside her. She didn't want to believe that her own flesh and blood would be a traitor to their country. Pieces of brief conversations they'd had in the past surfaced in her mind. Savannah had been very frustrated with certain aspects and limitations of her job. God forbid that she'd become involved with the wrong people because of that.

No! You're being ridiculous. She would never do something like that. The harsh berating from her inner voice worked to ease her troubled mind. They might have drifted apart over the past five years, but Savannah would never stoop so low and betray her country.

"Look, this is ridiculous. You can't force me or Savannah to do this. I'm not going to—"

"Before you make any rash decisions, my dear, I suggest you try and get a hold of your aunt. She might be able to shed some light on why your cousin agreed to do my bidding." He nodded at Rusco who threw a cellphone on the bed. "That's a secure satellite phone with only one number where you'll be able to reach me. You have one week. Don't dally longer than that, Ms. Jackson. My patience has been running very thin over the past couple of months."

He walked closer with long measured strides. "One more thing, my dear. Don't get it into your head to go to the authorities. I have more than one trump card to play should you be that stupid. You started your job in Sudan, why do you think I brought you back to the U.S?" His laugh was evil as he reached the door. "Untie her and be quick about it. I want to be on the plane in ten minutes. It's almost daybreak."

He cast a dark look over his shoulder, nothing more than a glint in the darkness.

"Don't make me wait too long, Peyton. Your cousin might just have to suffer for it."

Chapter Fourteen

"Answer your goddamn phone, Aunt Vera!"

Peyton's voice echoed through the open space of the great room in the cottage. She listened to the raw quality of the cry floating back to her.

"Fucking hell!" she growled as she slammed the cell phone onto the counter. She leaned against it, her shoulders hunched and her head hung with the despair that had been creeping over her. She'd made close to two dozen phone calls to her aunt since eight that morning. To no avail. She didn't answer, nor had she responded to the myriad of messages she'd left.

It didn't make sense. In the two months leading up to her leaving for The Seven Keys Island, Aunt Vera had phoned her four to five times a day to ensure she was going. Now, when she could have news on Savannah, she didn't answer. The feeling of doom that had settled heavily in the atmosphere since the two men had left, thickened, threatening to choke her.

She heaved in a deep breath.

Crack!

"Ugh! Shit," she cursed at the pain that surged from her fists to her brain as she slammed them forcefully on the marble kitchen counter.

Peyton had never felt this helpless. The air seemed to become stifling and with her breathing harsh in her ear, she stumbled through the wide-open sliding doors onto the wrap-around patio. She hung over the railing, heaving in deep breaths. For once the salty air of the ocean soothed her mind.

"Think, Peyton! There has to be something you can do."

Her eyes drifted out to the shoreline, watching the waves break around the rocks in the shallows, their foam crests becoming chaotic lace over the blue. Her eyes flickered, mesmerized by the lazy, yet beautiful patterns. In that moment, every swirl, every unpatterned movement of the water, choreographed her thoughts.

She racked her mind for some clues, anything, that could help her find a piece of sanity to hold onto in a scenario she was completely floundering about. Some small token of hope that she might save Savannah from becoming a game piece in a dangerous plot.

"Don't be stupid, Peyton. She's already a game piece and from what the bastard said last night, so are you! COME ON! Think-think-think!"

She paced the front of the cottage until her legs burned, her mind chasing one possibility after another, only to discard every single one. It was useless. She had no idea where to begin, what or who was involved.

"I need to do some digging, get into my folders, Maybe there's something ..." Her voice drifted off as something the man had said burst to the surface.

"You started your job in Sudan, why do you think I brought you back to the U.S?

A cry of disbelief escaped her lips and she covered her mouth with a trembling hand. Her voice broke through in a muffled, horrified gasp, "Oh my god! Sudan! How did I miss that?"

But she knew how. At the time she was too busy fighting off the lecherous hands of Rusco that had found their way between her thighs. The fear of rape had taken precedence in that moment over listening to his boss' grating announcement.

"I need a laptop. I refuse to allow those bastards to take over Savannah's and my life, to ruin Stone's happiness or worse, hurt him and his cousins."

Within minutes, she'd hailed a cab and was on her way to the city center to buy a laptop. She had contemplated bringing hers but had decided against it. She hadn't wanted to risk it being confiscated and locked away. There was too much information she couldn't afford to lose, or for that matter, have anyone snoop about and find her valuable sources. It could potentially put many people in danger. She started making notes on her mini iPad in the cab, her mind racing a mile a minute.

At least she found a straw to grasp onto. Now, she had to find the bale of hay it came from.

Peyton ran a tired hand over her eyes. She felt defeated, totally drained from the energy that usually sparked life into her. The moment she remembered the comment from the Phantom—as she started thinking of the man of the night before— she made the connection. Well, kinda made the association. The same conclusions she'd reached in Sudan. The one that made her contact her editor at CNN with excitement prolific in her voice. She still recalled their discussion.

"I found the connection, Cyril," Peyton said. She lowered her voice and looked around to ensure there was no one close by that could listen in on the conversation. She'd learned to be over-cautious the past eleven months of her stay in Sudan, a North-African country that was locked in a year-long state

of emergency in response to months of protests nationwide and calls for the president's resignation.

"Are you safe, Peyton? I just heard the news that the Sudanese President Olar al-Hasham has been arrested and forced from power in a military coup."

"Don't worry about me. I managed to find refuge in a safehouse; a local family that provides shelter to protesters and reporters."

"For God's sake, just stay under the radar, please. If they find out who you are, it could mean your death."

"Listen to me, Cyril! I don't have a lot of time. I don't want to raise suspicion by disappearing or being caught on a satellite phone. There's more going on here than we initially thought. The U.S. government's involvement in their political upheaval has been blown out of proportion by the Sudanese Defense Minister and his cohorts."

"Are you saying they're blaming the U.S. for the violence reigning in the country?"

"It's the only way they can justify not complying to the key U.S. requirements of human

rights protections and practice. The reports filtered to the U.S. have been rigged. The U.S has nothing to do with the protests. It began over a rise in the cost of living and I have personally witnessed, photographed, and video recorded the indiscriminate violence from the Sudan security forces against their own people."

"You need to get those reports and recordings to me asap, Peyton, and then get the hell out of there," Cyril said urgently.

He had become like a father to Peyton, always worrying and being overly protective when she went undercover. This time, she needed his support and concern. She was scared shitless. In all the years of chasing stories, this had been the worst. She had seen things, inhumane acts that she'd never thought one human being could force onto another. Death and destruction was a daily threat. She'd been living in rising fear over the past two months and now that she'd dug deeper and found the coup d'état, she knew her head would be the next one on the block if she was caught with that information.

"I found something else, Cyril, and I need more time to verify the information."

"Peyton, you uncovered what you were sent for. We now have the proof the government has been looking for. Get your ass back here!"

"No, you don't understand. This is bigger and potentially crippling to the U.S.," she cried passionately. She hunched down against the wall, looking around cautiously all the time.

"What are you talking about?"

She could imagine Cyril's hulky body sitting forward with his elbows leaning on the table, a tell-tale frown bonding his thick eyebrows into a straight line.

"Cyber threat, Cyril. Do you recall the 2014 breach at the U.S. Office of Personnel Management, in which personnel records and security-clearance files for at least twenty-two-million people were compromised?"

"Vaguely."

"The information was extremely sensitive. Security applications are over a hundred pages long and it contains information stretching from mental *health history to criminal records, financial data, drug and alcohol use, assignment and work history, family member names, personal references, and fingerprints—you name it, it's in there."*

"Now that you mention it, I recall the buzz about it at the time."

"Yes, it caused a major upheaval because, with that kind of detailed information, any foreign government or organized crime syndicate getting their hands on it could potentially use the data to identify U.S. operatives, particularly those in intelligence roles."

"Are you saying someone hacked the federal government records again?"

"From all the information I've uncovered so far, it looks like it and here's the best part ... the Department of Homeland Security is aware of it."

"And you believe the Sudan military is involved?"

"Yes, I uncovered proof of them being associated with the La-Muerta Syndicate."

"The Mexican crime lords trying to overrun the mafia in the U.S? Fuck, Peyton, that's huge! If they

get their hands on intelligence operatives' information—"

"That's not what they hacked, Cyril. This is bigger, closer to the White House and involves a corporation in the U.S. whose ownership information is locked tighter than a nun's vagina. Look," she glanced around again, smiling at a passing group of children, "I can't talk about this over the phone. It's too dangerous. I'll compile a detailed report but I need at least another couple of months to dig up as much information as I can. Just inform your contact at the FBI about the potential danger, and in my opinion, a spy in their midst. They might want to lodge an internal investigation in the meantime."

"Very well. You have one month and—"

"That's not enough time to—"

"Thirty days from today, Peyton, not a day longer."

Peyton exhaled slowly, her eyes were locked on the flight of a seagull, drifting lazily over the ocean.

"But I never got thirty days. Two days after that phone call, Luke Bene arrived and I was exiled on the next plane back to the U.S."

No amount of pleading or anger could sway Cyril Douglas to send her back. He cited it had become too dangerous for her and that Luke would take over the investigation into the cyber threat and she should finalize the piece on the rest. He'd put her on eight months paid leave, claiming that she needed to recoup from the ordeal and harrowing conditions she'd lived under for a year.

The very next day, she'd received the hysterical call from Aunt Vera that Savannah had been abducted.

"It was all just too well timed to be a coincidence. Freaking hell! Is Cyril involved?"

She listened to her own cry floating off into the warm air. She was sitting in the comfortable sofa on the patio, the laptop open in front of her.

No, she discounted that thought immediately. Cyril had just become a grandfather and he would never jeopardize his family's safety. He was the least corrupt person she knew.

"But what if he's in danger because of the information I uncovered?"

Peyton's hands trembled as she dialed his cell number. He answered on the third ring.

"No, Ms. Jackson, you can't come back to work. You need to rest and recoup," he said by way of a greeting.

She couldn't help but smile at the sincerity in his voice, laced with real concern for her wellbeing. She relaxed somewhat.

"I know, I know but that's not why I called."

"Peyton Jackson, I know you as well as your own father. You won't just phone to chat."

"You're right, I'm not. I need to know what happened with the information I uncovered in Sudan. Has Luke found anything else?"

"No, Luke returned within two weeks after you. The violence had run out of control and his life was in danger. We weren't prepared to take the risk."

"I understand and I'm glad he's safe. And your contact in the FBI? What did he say?"

"They're investigating but we were warned to back off. That it's a matter of National security and tampering with such information could be detrimental in them identifying the culprits."

"I see. He ... er ... he didn't give you a hard time about it? Threatened you or something?"

"No, my dear. As I said, we decided to let it go. Now, tell me what you've been up to?"

Peyton spend another five minutes lying to him about being in the Caribbean but thought it better that he didn't know here she was.

After she ended the call she contemplated the situation further.

"It has to be someone in the FBI, maybe his contact. How else would the Phantom have the power he flaunted about last night? Yes! He has to be a spy or a double agent, freaking hell, most probably working for that Mexican syndicate."

Peyton opened the web search engine and typed in the address to her secure cloud account. She systematically worked through the files containing the information about the cyber threat she'd continued to delve into over the past two-and-a-half-months since her return.

She went cold as she scrutinized the document with the notes on the corporation involved with the federal government. Someone had tampered with her files. All the information she'd dug up about them since her return was gone, wiped from the document! She frantically searched the rest of the folders, furious but not too surprised that everything else she'd added since she'd been put on forced vacation was gone.

"I've been hacked! Someone got into my account. Shit!" She looked around. "Where did I put my cell ... ah," she dug it out between the cushions of the sofa and searched for the number she was looking for. "Please, please answer, Dancer," she murmured softly as she pressed dial.

"Long time no hear, Chica," the melodious lilt filled Peyton's ear. Peyton had stopped trying to tell her to stop calling her the ridiculous name.

"Oh, thank heavens you answered."

"Easy does it, little birdie. You sound stressed. Tell Dancer who stole your bright light."

"Someone hacked the secure cloud account you set up for me."

"It wasn't me, Chica. I just set it up and then forgot about it."

"I know but I need you to find who did."

"I can try but if someone was clever enough to hack into that account, chances are they left no trace behind."

Peyton listened to the sound of Dancer's fingers flying over her keyboard. She was a pro hacker, one of the best there was and as much of a shadow as could be. Peyton had no idea where she called home. She wondered if anyone did. They only met face to face once, at a remote location of Dancer's choice. She had offered her services to Peyton as a CI, an offer she'd gladly accepted. Dancer had supplied invaluable intel over time, with the understanding that she would never be abused as a hacker. They had formed a bond of mutual respect for boundaries, one that continued to get stronger over time.

"They deleted information from documents and some files. Would you be able to recover it?"

"If, and that's a big if, I can find the hacker I might. Give me an hour. I'll get back to you."

The connection ended in Dancer's usual abrupt way, her focus already completely on the job at hand.

Peyton closed the cloud account and paged through the notes she'd made. Something didn't add up. Homeland Security was aware of the alleged hack. Why would they involve an outside company for assistance when they have a Cyber Division specifically equipped to deal with cyber-attacks?

She glanced at her watch, surprised to realize it was already past four in the afternoon and she was no closer to finding a solution than twelve hours earlier when she'd staggered out of her bedroom after the two men had left.

She grabbed her cell phone when it rang. "About damn time," she muttered as she recognized her aunts smiling face on the screen. "Aunt Vera, I've been out of my mind with concern. Are you okay?"

"Peyton, where are you? Please tell me you managed to get Savvy off that island."

Peyton could hear the panic in her voice, the soft wheeze as she whispered loudly into the phone. She frowned.

"Aunt Vera, what's going on. Why are you whispering?"

"Peyton! Did you get Savannah back?"

"That's it. I want to know now what the devil is going on. Talk to me, Aunt Vera. I can't help if I don't know what's really happening with you and her."

"Darling, please, I can't tell you. It's too dangerous and I'm ... God! I should never have involved you. Get off that island, Peyton before you—"

"It's too late. I'm already involved and I know you don't just want Savannah off The Seven Keys Island because of the BDSM club and what she applied for. Talk to me! Let me help!"

"I can't." A soft sob escaped her aunt's lips "It's too dangerous."

"Aunt Vera, I was banned from the island for breaking a cardinal rule. I'm in Key West at the moment."

"Oh, thank god. Did you see Savvy? Is she okay?"

"She's fine but I had visitors in the dead of the night last night. They informed me you can tell me why Savannah is on that island."

Silence followed her accusing tone. Peyton waited, praying that her aunt had some information that could shed some light on the identity of the Phantom.

"They threatened her," she admitted finally, so softly that Peyton had to strain to hear the words. "If she refused to do their bidding, they told her they'd kill me and ... have you sold into the sex trade in the East."

Peyton was racked by cold shivers. Visions of the horrors she'd seen sex slaves forced into in the past blinded her for a moment. She forcibly shook it off.

"Who are they?"

"Peyton, please—"

"And how do you know about it? Surely Savannah wouldn't have told you?"

"She didn't."

"Talk to me, Aunt Vera! Who are they?"

"Someone at the Bureau."

"The FBI? But she works there! Why would they blackmail her into something like this? She's not a field agent."

"No, but she'd also joined a BDSM club last year. I never knew about it until I got an email with pictures, videos …" She inhaled deeply. "This was after she'd disappeared. After that I received a phone call. The man warned me to listen carefully and do exactly what he expected from me … or I would never see Savannah alive again."

"So, because of being in the BDSM lifestyle, she was the perfect candidate to get on the island." Peyton suspected Savannah had to join the lifestyle, otherwise she'd never have been selected as a possible recruit.

"I didn't want to do it. I swear to you, Peyton. I never wanted to put you in danger but then they …" Another sob reached Peyton's ears. "The accident your father was in that put him in ICU … they did it. He boasted about it afterward, warned me how easy it is for them to snuff out a life. They already too Savannah's ..." Peyton frowned as her aunt swallowed her words and then rushed on hastily, "She was next if I didn't convince you to go to the island and bring her home. I'm so sorry."

"Oh, no. Are you saying my dad's life is in danger? As well as yours and Savannah's?"

"I'm hoping they'll leave all of us alone now that Savannah is on the island."

Peyton struggled to breathe as the seriousness of the situation expounded exponentially.

"And you have no idea who the man is?"

The hesitation was brief but enough to scream out the answer. A door slamming in the background caused a gasp of fear to echo toward Peyton.

"I've got to go. Be careful, Peyton. I can't expect you to go back. I'm an old woman and if this is the end for me, so be it but you and Savvy ... *oh no.* He's here. Be safe."

"Aunt Vera!" Peyton shouted into the phone but the silence was a deafening sign that the connection had been cut.

"They've got her. Someone is holding her captive." She jumped up and started pacing. She was devastated. The accident almost killed her father. It was two months later and he was still recuperating in a rehabilitation center.

"They ... whoever the fuck they are ... are ruthless. I can't leave Savannah to deal with this. God knows what they'll do to Aunt Vera if I refuse and Dad ..."

She all but pounded on her cell phone when it rang again.

"I managed to find an IP address, Chica, but somehow I don't think this'll come as a surprise to you."

"It's from the FBI," Peyton said dully.

"Bingo! But brilliant me managed to get past all their tight firewalls."

Peyton stilled. She clutched the phone harder. "You know who it belongs to."

"I do indeed. You better sit down, Chica. This is gonna rip the floor from under you."

"Spit it out, Dancer."

"Your cousin's boss, Chica. Deputy Director of the FBI, Decker Cooper."

Peyton sank into the sofa, completely defeated. There was no way DC, as he was called by everyone, could have known about Peyton's involvement or knowledge about her discovery in Sudan, except if he was Cyril's contact or Savannah had told him.

If it *was* her, it meant she was in on the scheme and not an innocent used as a game piece in a bigger plot. That thought disturbed her more than she cared to admit.

She still couldn't figure out what they were looking for on The Seven Keys Island. Nothing she'd uncovered at the time had led there or to the Sinclair cousins.

She was now more confused than ever.

Chapter Fifteen

"Baby girl! This is a pleasant surprise," Tom Jackson exclaimed when Peyton found him in the recreation hall playing a game of cards at the Swedish Center for Health and Fitness in Seattle the following afternoon. The accident had caused severe damage to his legs and it had been a long and painful process up till now. Peyton was relieved to see that he had advanced to crutches already.

"Look at you! All dapper and energetic. I'm so happy you've improved so quickly," she cooed with a wide smile. She hugged him so hard that he groaned in pretend agony.

"Easy there, love. These old bones are still a little fragile," he teased as he hobbled on the crutches toward the lounge area and sat down. "It becomes too painful if I stand for too long," he explained at her inquiring look.

Peyton couldn't stay away. She couldn't think straight after the news from Dancer and had booked a plane ticket to Seattle immediately. She had to ascertain for herself that they were safe.

"Don't rush it, Dad. There's nothing chasing you to go home."

"I'm improving by the day. As pleasant and friendly as everyone is here, it's not home, my girl. An old man like me prefers his own bed at night."

She laughed and squeezed his hand. "You're far from old. Come on, be honest, it's that new neighbor of yours that you miss, not your bed." Her eyes glinted playfully. "Except, of course, if she's in it with—"

"Shut your mouth, young lady!" He shook a stiff finger at her. "Young people of today ... tsk."

Peyton peeled with laughter. "Young? I'm thirty-five, in case you forgot. A spinster by all counts, and besides, what's wrong with a little hanky panky between more ... er ... mature people?"

Tom just shook his head but laughed along with her. He studied her as their laughter dried up.

"Aren't you supposed to be on vacation in Key West? Don't tell me Cyril is sending you into another violence riddled country."

He seemed genuinely upset. Peyton realized for the first time under how much strain her chosen career had placed him. The concern and worry he must suffer every time she went undercover for a story.

"No, no, I'm still on a break. I just needed to come and check on you before I flew off to my next destination," she quickly reassured him.

He spread his arms wide. "As you can see, I'm as fit as a fiddle. A couple more weeks and I'll be ready to dance the samba."

"How much longer will you be staying here for treatment?" Peyton needed to know he'd be safe from further harm before she decided what to do. At least here, he was protected and safer than home alone.

"Two months," he grimaced. "They want to make sure the bones heal properly and the steel rods they implanted aren't rejected by my body."

"Still? After all this time?"

"They're cautious, because of my age, which puts my mind at ease. Don't worry, love. I'm not going to run out of here before I can walk normally again." He shrugged and smiled. "It's like a vacation close to home. I get to swim, sit around in a jacuzzi and get spoiled with good food I don't have to prepare myself."

"I'm glad." She cleared her throat. "I went past Aunt Vera's place on the way from the airport. Her place is locked up tight. There's not even a sign of her yapping dogs."

"Oh, she took off to visit her friend, Lisa in Chicago. It's her big seven zero birthday this month, so she invited her over for a couple of weeks to celebrate."

"Strange that she didn't tell me about it when I went to say goodbye," Peyton mused.

"She was probably a little distracted by Savannah taking a long leave of absence from work to go on that hike across the mountains in India. You know how she worries."

Peyton's heart sank into her shoes. Now she had confirmation that her aunt was in more danger than she'd wanted to believe. She had been abducted and kept somewhere against her will.

Deep inside she had known she had no choice but to do what Phantom demanded.

To find a way to get back to The Seven Keys Island and Castle Sin.

"You took your sweet time to contact me, Ms. Jackson."

Peyton cringed at the evil candor of the voice echoing through her mind. Not evil, no—cruel and vibrating with a promise of violence.

"Did you enjoy your visit with your father?"

She froze and cursed within herself. Of course, she should've known they kept an eye on her. She'd become an asset to them. She, more than most people, had learned over the years that criminals always protected their own interests. She hadn't rushed back to Key West. She'd stayed and visited her father every day while she continued to dig for information. With Dancer's help, she was hoping to narrow down the identity of who could potentially be the Phantom or the leak in the FBI.

"What do you want me to do?"

"Ah, I'm glad you decided to join our little adventure."

"Listen here, you fucking asshole, I'm not joining anything. You're forcing me into it, but mark my words, your day will come. I sure as hell hope I'm there to witness you fall."

His laughter sounded as cruel as she imagined him to be. She morphed from cold to freezing in a nanosecond. She shivered as she listened to him enjoy her despair.

"I like my women feisty and you have just issued a challenge, my dear. You and I … we're going to have some fun before this is over."

"I'd rather slit my throat."

"Ah, well, fucking a hot cunt while the blood is spurting out at the same speed as my cock driving into it … that sounds like fun, sweetheart."

"You're a sick fuck," Peyton managed to sneer. The vision he painted made her want to gag.

"Enough small talk. Time is running out and I need to see some results. You and your cousin had better find what I'm looking for and fast, otherwise …"

"Otherwise what, you coward! All you can do is issue threats, hurt people in your quest for who knows what. That doesn't make you a man or powerful. What it does is prove you're a disgrace to mankind."

"You seem to think I issue idle threats, Ms. Jackson. You will learn very quickly that I don't play around."

"Just tell me what the fuck I must do next," she shouted at him. The thin thread of control she'd been hanging onto for the past six days was ready to snap.

"Get your ass back on that island and no, don't ask me how. I got you there the first time, now you better find a way. Be warned, my dear, without you, your pretty cousin serves no further purpose to us." The silence was measured. "I don't suppose I need to spell out what that means, do I?"

"No," she whispered as she sank onto her knees, clutching her heaving stomach. "No, you don't."

"You have two days to find a way to get on the island. After that ..."

The connection died with the threat echoing over and over in her mind.

It took over an hour before Peyton was calm enough to get up from the floor. She took a long hot shower, standing under the spray of scalding water. In a way, the scorching cascade against her skin was to punish herself for putting her father and aunt in more danger.

She slipped into a soft chiffon dress that floated around her ankles and caressed her still sensitive skin with sheer luxuriousness. She was unaware of how the dark yellow color of the material inflamed the hue of her hair, completing her ensemble in a picture of sensual seduction.

She walked through the cottage, listless and unsure how to proceed. She had no idea how to convince Stone to allow her back in the training program. Her heart punched hard against her chest as he appeared in her mind's eye.

"God, I want him so much. I know it's insane but I feel him, deep inside me, with every breath I take, with every beat of my heart."

She moaned as she sat down in the plush chaise lounge. She tucked in her feet under her and relaxed with her eyes closed. The desire to go back to the island had nothing to do with the threats hanging over her head. It was all about him and how he had made her feel, how she *still* felt.

Come on, Peyton. It's just sex. Hot and explosive, never before experienced sex, but carnal pleasure none the less. Nothing more.

"God, how I wish that was true," she responded to her inner voice.

It was incomprehensible that she, Peyton Jackson, a thirty-five-year-old woman could be head over heels with a man she barely knew. There was no doubt in her mind that the experience she'd had with Stone was more than just sex—so much more. During that explosive encounter, there had been a connection, an emotional and maybe even a spiritual bond that was formed.

"I can't do this," she wailed. "I can't go back there and be involved with him, not if it means I'm putting him in potential danger too."

Peyton sighed heavily and sat up. The only way she could live with herself, was if she went back as a trainee and avoided contact with Stone Sinclair at all costs.

"But how? How do I get my ass, as the bastard so eloquently said, back on the island?"

"I'm only a phone call away."

The gruff voice echoed back at her. "Danton! Of course." She jumped up and went to rummage through her large shopper bag for the business card he'd given her. "Got it!" she exclaimed and held it up in the air.

"Danton Hill, CEO of Diamond Hill Enterprises." She frowned at the card. "Diamond Hill? Why does that sound so familiar? And why the devil does a CEO of a company babysit a bunch of grown men on a remote island?"

She pushed the questions aside and dialed the number.

"Sub PJ, it's about time you called."

"I ..." she stared at the phone in her hand for a stumped second. He sounded irritated but happy to hear her voice. "I'm not bothering you, am I?"

"It's a little inconvenient but you're not bothering me ... hold on a sec, I need to move out of the room." She heard his murmured voice in the background followed by footsteps and a door closing. "Are you ready to come back?"

"Is that even possible? Master Eagle made it very clear what I had done was inexcusable. They all agreed for that matter. He banned me, Danton. How can I just merrily waltz back into Castle Sin?"

"Are you still at the cottage?"

"Yes."

"Don't go anywhere. We'll be there in an hour."

"We? Danton, what do you mean by—"

"See you then, sub PJ."

"Wait! Who the devil is we? Danton Hill, don't you dare hang up on me!"

"Be sure to remind me to address your disrespecting tone once you're back on the island."

With those words and a wicked chuckle, he did just that. He hung up on her.

"Typical Dom!"

Peyton couldn't sit still after that. She paced, she sat at the pool's edge kicking at the water, she drank two glasses of wine—for some Dutch courage of course—and paced some more.

"And I thought the saying goes that time is fleeting! It's dragging slower than a tortoise through tar!"

Peyton couldn't help but be concerned. What if Danton's *we* included Stone? She wasn't ready to face him, not here in this gorgeous little cottage that was a personification of him as a man.

Not the actor, nor the powerful Master Eagle.

Just him.

Chapter Sixteen

"M-Master Fox! I didn't expect to see you." As always in the presence of this older and formidable Sinclair cousin, Peyton felt small and vulnerable. The combination of warmth and intelligent awareness in his eyes constantly made her feel that he could read every thought in her mind.

She flicked a reproachful glance at Danton who responded with a sardonically raised eyebrow. She bit back the snort at the deliberate reprimand it represented. She had no idea how these Doms did it but that slight act all but barked out the warning, *Watch your step, sub.*

"Why would you have?" Shane sat down in a plush bucket chair with his back toward the ocean.

"Take a seat, Peyton. We have a couple of things to discuss."

She was thankful for the order and plonked down on the sofa ungracefully, seeing as her legs had started to wobble the moment she'd noticed him following Danton inside.

"Danton mentioned that you wish to return to Castle Sin. What makes you believe we'd allow you back? Do you perhaps feel we were unfair in our assessment that led to our decision?"

Peyton's shoulders hunched forward; her chin lowered. She hated the feeling of failure at his words. She had screwed up big time. As a submissive who always prided herself on being honest with the Doms she scened with, the fact that she'd lied to the one Master who floored her mind, dragged her into a deep well of despair. She wondered if she'd ever be able to forgive herself. Worse, she knew Master Fox was right. What she had done, didn't deserve a second chance.

"No, Master Fox. I honor your decision and I admit I'm completely to blame for it. I have no way to justify my action, except that over the years I had honestly come to believe that I had conquered my fear of the ocean. I suppose I became complacent over the years and because the trip on the speedboat to the island wasn't as harrowing as I had thought it would be, I thought I could handle it. I actually enjoyed the ride on the boat, if I'm honest with myself." She noticed his eyes flash. "I guess I was naive in thinking that."

"Yes, Peyton, you were."

He studied her with a shuttered look on his face. She hated that she couldn't read the expressions of any of the Masters on the island.

"Did you go for therapy after you returned to the U.S. at the time?" Shane asked in a quiet voice; a smooth, rich tone that found resonance deep inside her, calming her, assuring her of his support.

"Yes, for five years." She frowned. "The therapist believed I was strong enough to discontinue the sessions. That I had perfected the techniques she'd taught me to repel the fear at the first sign of panic."

"Was reacquainting you with the ocean part of her therapy?"

"No." Peyton shook her head. "Water, yes, using a pool. Not that I swim all that much since either."

"You didn't conquer your fears, Peyton. You suppressed them. You told us you don't go near the sea or the beach anymore. For someone who loved swimming in the ocean and spending time at the beach ... that should've told you something."

"I know you're right. I just never ... I guess I used focusing on my career as an excuse not to have to deal with it."

"You were told Castle Sin is on an island. You knew you would be surrounded by the ocean and still you came. Why, Peyton? What drove you so hard that you would put yourself through something that absolutely terrifies you?"

She squirmed in the seat unable to tear her eyes from his searing gaze. *Good lord, he's got the bluest blue eyes*, she realized with a start. She shook herself out of the fascination and concentrated on the matter at hand—the conundrum that could go either way. This was it. The big test from the one Master, who apart from Master Eagle, was the most perceptive. He would know if she lied and then she could kiss goodbye any chance of getting back to Castle Sin.

"My aunt asked me to …" She swallowed hard. It would be better to stick to the truth as close as possible. At least that way, it'll ease her mind that she wasn't lying … too much.

"To what?"

"My cousin is on the island and she was concerned that she was throwing her future away by … by becoming a submissive employee at Castle Sin."

"Ah … and let me guess. Your cousin is sub ST?"

Peyton nodded, feeling miserable that she'd done the one thing Savannah had pleaded with her not to. Now that she knew why, she at least understood Savannah's reason to keep their connection a secret.

"Mind if I join the party?"

Peyton got such a fright from the dark and angry voice booming through the room that she jumped to her feet and stood in the present position.

Shane and Danton looked at each other with broad smiles. It was the only confirmation they needed that Peyton Jackson had fully committed to Master Eagle as a submissive—unbeknownst to herself, of course.

"Sit down, Peyton," Stone said, with what she perceived in her fragile mind, to be suppressed violence.

Her legs gave way at the order and she collapsed back on the sofa. She clenched her hands together, keeping her eyes lowered to the floor. She was too scared that one look at the gorgeous man would make her swoon.

I missed him. How could I have missed him so much?

It was the one thought that kept milling through her mind. She had only been on the island for four days, kicked off on the fifth and scened, or rather, was disciplined, by him twice. That doesn't account for the sparks that sizzled between them at the introduction ceremony in the Gathering Hall on her first day. Or the explosive sex that had left her flayed and vulnerable. That was the minimal contact she'd had with him, and still, she had felt the void of not seeing him, not feeling his presence and hearing his deep, grating voice.

"So, now you're prepared to admit sub ST is your cousin? Why now and not when I asked you before we banned you from the island?"

Peyton didn't miss the cynical intonation in his voice. She cringed in lieu of it. She didn't want to but she knew she'd have to carefully weigh every word she said and story she told. She couldn't afford to be caught. She had to get back on The Seven Keys Island.

"I—"

"Eyes," Stone snapped and waited until her tortured gaze lifted to his. He felt the effect of those violet eyes, that glimmered like a dark amethyst, in the tightening of his loins, the heavy throb of his heart beating the blood flowing through his veins. "Lie to me, Peyton, and I'll know."

It wasn't an idle warning. She knew he would be able to. She just prayed she'd pull this off without compromising her cousin. She had no idea what they truly knew about Savannah's background.

Instinct told her they wouldn't know about her position at the FBI. She had to do this!

"I went to Castle Sin to get Savannah and convince her to come back home with me. Aunt Vera is very concerned over her health."

Peyton unknowingly chose the one word that was her saving grace, seeing as they believed Savannah had applied for a position at Castle Sin to overcome the pain after her divorce.

"Your cousin is thirty years old, Peyton. Surely, she can make her own choices in life?" Shane interjected.

"I agree, but I couldn't say no to Aunt Vera. She has been like a mother to me since my mom passed away when I was fifteen. I could see how worried she was and ..." She waved a hand in the air. "I had to at least try."

"The discussion you had with her in the dining hall I asked you about was heated. I assume she's not ready to leave?" Stone watched her closely.

"No, she's not."

"Then why go back?" His eyes darkened. "Since that's the only reason you applied for a position at Castle Sin in the first place. Whatever reason do you have to return now?" Stone was surprised at the eagerness with which he awaited her response. Something deep inside him, not to discount the growling Beast, needed to know if he in some way had something to do with it.

"Before you answer, there's something else I need to know."

Trepidation ran down her spine in a shiver that shook her body. Her fingers turned white from clasping them so tightly they started to hurt.

"Yes, Master Eagle."

"You claim to be an author, yet you arrived without a laptop. I find it hard to believe that a writer would be on sabbatical for a year-and-a-half. Care to enlighten us about that?"

Peyton cleared her throat, her back straightened and she tilted her chin in a show of pride. At least she could own up to who she really was and the reason why she had free time at the moment.

"No ... that was a lie." She saw the flare in his eyes and realization sunk in. "But I guess you already knew that."

"Indeed, but I want to hear from you why an acclaimed and Pulitzer Prize winning investigative journalist from CNN would willingly give that up to spend over a year working for the pittance of your salary at Castle Sin."

The hurt accusation in his eyes stumped her. It wrapped around her chest like a vice that slowly clamped tighter and tighter her until she couldn't breathe. She heaved in a deep breath.

"Or is this another undercover story you're working on? Exposing the Rothman celebrity cousins for monsters who harbor unwilling sex slaves? Is that it?" His voice lowered in a deep growl. "Tell me I'm wrong, Peyton. You, who admitted knowing what my real name is," he accused with suppressed violence in his eyes.

"No! I only know your real name because I did research about the island once my aunt told me about it. It's who I am. It's what I do!" she cried passionately. She exhaled slowly. "I was in Sudan

working undercover for a year. I experienced and …
and saw things over there … inhumane and ugly
things. We lived in fear every single day we were
there. We never knew if the people who gave us safe
harbor would rat us out. I found out about the lies
they fed to the U.S. government but it took all that
time to find confirmation." She hesitated and then
continued softly. "I was also on the verge of
uncovering something big, a conspiracy that
threatened the safety of all U.S Citizens but … I was
pulled out and replaced. My editor and the station
felt I needed a break since I'd gone from one
assignment to the next over the past five years. They
put me on forced paid vacation."

She looked at him beseechingly. "I won't deny
that I immediately made the connection that
Rothman was an assumed name you used as actors.
It couldn't be coincidence that the Closed
Corporation that owned The Seven Keys Island
listed seven Sinclairs as shareholders with the exact
same first names as the seven Rothman cousins. I
… had every intention of doing a story but only after

proper investigation into what is really going on there. Now ...”

“Yes? Now what?” he rasped.

“I have no desire to anymore,” she admitted softly. It would be wrong, like Savannah had said. She couldn't destroy all the lives of the people who had made The Seven Keys Island home. Who depended on the emotional support and care they received from the Masters and training Doms. If there was anything she'd learned in the short time she'd been there, it had been that.

“I believe her,” Shane said, stretching out his long legs lazily. He winked at her as she looked at him in surprise. She'd completely forgotten about their presence.

“For what it's worth, so do I,” Danton added gruffly.

Stone slanted an amused look his way. “Yeah, and we both know why.”

“Hey, she's got a hot ass, Stone, what can I say?”

Peyton had no idea what the joke was that made the three men chuckle ... except that she had a sneaky suspicion it was somehow at her expense. Stone's mirth died as his gaze caught hers again.

"Now, I want your answer, Peyton. Why do you wish to return to Castle Sin, if not for a story or to convince your cousin to leave?"

She blinked—once—and then and there decided the hell with it. This was her one chance to fight for something good in her life. Her one chance at becoming the submissive she knew she was meant to be—his and only his. And maybe, just maybe the only chance she had at happiness and … God willing … love.

"Because of you, Master Eagle."

Stone's body turned to stone. His jaw appeared to be carved out of marble, and his eyes …

Lordy help me, I could climax just from the heat swirling in his eyes!

Peyton began to despair when he continued to stare silently at her and then he pointed to the floor in front of him.

"On your knees."

"Well, Danton, my boy, I guess that's our cue to leave," Shane chuckled as he got up.

"Yeah … pity though. It's just getting interesting."

She was deaf to their taunts and scrambled to her feet to kneel in front of Stone. Her hands were clasped behind her back and her chin tilted upward to keep eye contact with him.

"Good girl," he praised and stroked her hair.

"Damn, Shane. You sure we need to leave?"

"Yes, Danton, he's sure," Stone said. He didn't bother to check if they had left before he continued. "So, you wish to return because of me. Care to elaborate on that?"

Peyton knew her cheeks were glowing with the realization of what Danton and Shane perceived was about to happen. The hard ridge of his tumescence pressing against his jeans attested to his arousal. It gave her the courage to continue.

"I've been intrigued by you for years. Not the characters you played or the fact that you're an actor. You, the man. Now, having met you and … experienced you as a powerful Dominant, I can't walk away. I don't want to! What we had that last night, for me, was a revelation. It was so much more than just sex and kink. I felt closer to you than I've ever felt with another man. There's something between us. I don't know how to articulate it, maybe, some kind of emotional bond. I owe it to myself to explore it." She hesitated and then rushed on. "And I'd do my best to make you realize it too."

"How long have you been in the BDSM lifestyle, a submissive?"

"Four years," she admitted shamefaced.

"The question is, do you wish to return as a trainee or as my submissive?"

"I ... wha—what do you mean as your submissive?" Suddenly she was short of breath. The possibility that there just might be a future for her with this wonderful man winked at her on the horizon.

Stop dreaming, Peyton. In the end, you're going to be part of his downfall. You're still lying to him— by omission!

Her spirits dropped to the floor and she prayed he didn't notice. She had to get back on the island because someone was holding a spear over her head—but more than anything—she wanted to be his.

His submissive.

Just ... *his.*

Peyton had a hard time curbing the excitement that was hard at war with the denial inside her mind. She wasn't going to lose hope. Given time, she'd have to find a solution to the problem at hand. To ensure he, his family, the entire Castle Sin was safe from harm, and maybe, just maybe, he might not end up hating her in the end.

"Just what I said, Peyton. The only way you'll set foot on my island and inside Castle Sin is as my permanent, live-in submissive with a signed contract stipulating all my rules."

His large hand wrapped almost completely around her throat. She scrambled to her feet as his grip tightened and he pulled and dragged her against his chest.

"For a non-negotiable period of two years after which we'll decide the road ahead." His lips brushed over hers. "But that doesn't mean I won't insist you attend certain training sessions with the other Masters."

"Two years?" her eyes had widened with every word he uttered.

"Not negotiable." Stone was pleased that it was the only thing that concerned her and not the fact that he demanded her submission to him.

"But what about my career?"

"You can do that from anywhere but I expect you to discuss every assignment with me before you accept it. That's what a relationship is about, Peyton. Communication, trust and respect."

"I ... this is rather sudden and unexpected. I mean, don't get me wrong, I'd be delighted to say yes but I got the impression from the other submissives that you're a confirmed Dom bachelor. That you have no interest to form a Dom/sub relationship with anyone."

She searched his eyes, desperate for some spark, some indication of returned attraction. Not surprising, there was none. As always, he kept his emotions locked away deep inside his soul.

"Why now and why me?"

"Don't search for something other than what it is, Peyton. A Dom/sub relationship. I'm not offering you love and I never will. It's one emotion that makes a man vulnerable. I'm officially retiring from acting with the next movie. I'll die in the opening scene, so will Hawk. We've wanted out for a long time. It's time to concentrate on running our company and maybe settle down. Who knows, that emotional connection you spoke about, might just ensnare me too."

His fingers caressed the side of her throat, the upper curve of her breast as he noticed with pure male satisfaction the rapid rise and fall of her chest, the small gasps of breath puffing from her lips as he tilted her chin to stare into her eyes.

"You're a very beautiful woman, Peyton, and I'd be lying if I didn't admit to the attraction and lust I feel for you. Understand one thing very well. I don't tolerate lies. One more from these pouty lips and you're out ... for good."

Before she could respond his mouth caught hers in a kiss that shattered any will to resist, any thought that she may very well lose any chance at a happy ever after with him. She reveled in his arms around her, confident and hard as he pressed her closer. She was overcome with a rush of helplessness, a sinking yielding, a surging tide of warmth that left her limp. She moaned as he caught her hair in his fist and pulled, the kiss intensified, his lips demanding and so hotly passionate all she could do was cling to him. He became the only solid thing in a suddenly dizzy swaying world. He forced her lips wider, surging deeper until wild tremors danced along her nerves, evoking sensations she'd never experienced before.

She stumbled as suddenly he was gone, leaving her with a cold shiver of denial washing over her. Her entire body crackled like a live wire, ready to explode at the slightest provocation.

"One more thing that's not negotiable. You will attend sessions with Shane to overcome your fear of the ocean and deal with the trauma of the tsunami." His eyes trailed a slow path up and down her body, leaving heat in its wake. "The boat leaves in fifteen minutes. If you're not there, I'll accept that you're not interested in my offer."

It took a full two minutes for Peyton to realize she was still gaping at the door after he left.

"I'm ... going to be his submissive." Her raw voice echoed back at her. A wide smile threatened to split her face in two. "Fifteen minutes! Oh shit!"

Peyton jumped up and with trembling limbs haphazardly threw her clothes in the suitcases. She was slipping a pair of silver sandals on her feet when the dreaded call sounded from her handbag.

"What?" she snapped into the satellite phone as soon as she'd dug it out.

"Such heat in your voice, my dear. Talk to me, what happened?"

Peyton felt deflated. All the joy that had just filled her entire being disintegrated with the realization that this man was her puppet master. The fact that he knew Stone had been there terrified her. He had power and connections, that much she knew. How was she going to keep everyone safe? How was she going to prevent Stone from coming to hate her?

"I'm waiting, Ms. Jackson," the voice sneered in her ear.

"I'm going to the island. What do I do?"

"When you're sure no one can overhear, tell your cousin, Storm Chaser."

"Storm Chaser. That's it?"

"Yes, she'll understand and explain everything you need to know. Well, then, my dear. I suggest you hustle. Stone Sinclair isn't known for his patience."

Chapter Seventeen

Peyton stopped mid-step as she walked into Stone's room from the bathroom. She was still in awe of his apartment. The space was enormous and the rooms very big, decorated in different shades of autumn. Splashes of color were added with scattered pillows, plush carpets, and majestic oil paintings.

But that wasn't what left her gasping and staring like a love-sick teenager. She's seen him dressed in tuxedos on television, in jeans, and naked but none of that prepared her for how Master Eagle looked dressed up for Castle Sin's dungeon. The black leathers hugged his buttocks tightly, round, firm gluteus maximus that rippled as he slipped on a leather vest over his broad shoulders. She licked her lips as his biceps bulged and rippled.

She didn't even notice her fingers losing their grip on the towel she'd wrapped around her when she'd stepped from the bath. It slithered down her body to pool at her feet.

"My memory didn't deceive me," Stone said in a gruff voice, having turned around at the slight noise she made. His eyes dropped to her perfectly rounded breasts, the coral tipped nipples standing taut under his gaze.

"I can say the same, only I've never seen you in leathers before. You look … dangerous, Master Eagle."

Stone smiled as he stared at her. His gaze traveled upward from her small feet, committing every scrumptious inch of her lithe form to memory. Her legs were lean with perfectly rounded calves. He licked his lips at the succulent perfection of her clean-shaven pussy between her legs, before his eyes traced her toned stomach, small waist, and gorgeous full breasts, to her delicate jaw. He could still remember the sweet taste of her skin, the velvet softness under his tongue.

She's perfection and completely impervious to the effect she has on me.

Lust excoriated his body uncomfortably, like a sunburn against linen. Almost like a persistent and painful throb, instead of a pleasurable one. For once, he reveled in it.

"I see you shaved your pussy, little dove." He chuckled as her cheeks bloomed. "Pity. I was looking forward to removing every hair with tweezers."

"You're not serious?" She visibly cringed at the thought and with eyes wide, grabbed the towel and quickly wrapped it around her, watching him warily. He couldn't contain his mirth and laughed. She used the towel as a protection mechanism in case he found something else on her body to taunt her with.

Her eyes remained fixed on him; her lips curved up in a shy, yet sensual smile of pleasure at his obvious appreciation of her body.

Fucking hell, this woman is going to have me in flames before we even walk into the dungeon.

He listened to the sound of himself dragging in a breath, how it married in the atmosphere between them with hers that puffed from her open lips. He felt his flesh squirm as shards of heat set alight his lust.

Peyton shifted her weight, pursing her lips, exulted at the look in his eyes. "You're staring. I never pictured you as a Dom who would be struck mute by a naked woman," she lilted.

He noticed her nipples had turned to stones, poking against the towel as a low laugh rippled from deep inside his chest, a sensual purr that reached to her soul. His cock twitched in eager anticipation; the Beast inside clawed like a tiger in captivity, eager for another chance to come out and play.

Peyton couldn't withhold a carnal moan; an acknowledgment of his mastery over every sensation she felt running ubiquitous through her body. His lips were just too tempting and reminded her of the lustful kiss they'd shared in the cottage earlier. Her eyelids closed in an attempt to bring her raging libido under control.

She soon realized it was a mistake as suddenly she was yanked against his rippling chest. His mouth covered hers but so briefly that his lips were gone before she could fully savor his taste, his essence. She shuddered in the aftermath of that brief, yet promising touch.

"Don't assume too much about me, little dove. You'll realize soon enough that I treasure every woman for her beauty, and yours ... is beyond words," he drawled. He slid his tongue sensually along the inviting curve of her lower lip.

Peyton was overwhelmed if not tantalized by the scent of primal machismo and confidence that oozed from him. It was a heady combination of power and sexual prowess, of credence and virility. It made him even more irresistible. It was the verification she needed that he was everything she'd always imagined the man of her dreams to be.

"Get dressed, my pet. Hawk has our contract ready to sign. I want it done before we indulge in the dungeon of Castle Sin."

"You make it sound like it's a legally binding contract," she hedged, suddenly scared of the repercussions of such a commitment, especially in light of the untruths she still harbored.

"Of course, it is. I wouldn't have it any other way."

"Hawk is an attorney?"

"A very good one. Enough hedging, Peyton." He gestured to the bed. "You have ten minutes."

"Ten minutes? That's hardly enough time to brush my hair, let alone put on my makeup."

His laughter sounded like a musical symphony to her ears. He tapped her on the nose. "You don't need makeup, baby."

"But I can't appear in front of strangers with a naked face," she wailed, as vain as any woman who prided herself on her appearance, especially in front of the cameras.

Stone cupped her cheeks and kissed the tip of her nose. "You're beautiful *au naturale*, little dove, besides, would you rather have a fresh and clean face or walk around the majority of the evening with runny makeup and mascara?"

"I'll have you know, Mr. Sinclair," she declared haughtily, "I use only the best, organic brands. They don't run, not even in the heat."

"Ah, but what about tears and spittle running into your eyes and ruining all that work?"

"I ... you mean we're going to scene? Tonight?"

"Yes, and do a demonstration for the members. Your choice, my pet. Don't make me wait too long. You don't want to add punishment to the lineup." He strolled toward the door. "I'll be waiting for you in Hawk's office."

"Wait! Where's his office."

"I'm sure you'll be able to find your way there, seeing as you just wasted all of the ten minutes you had to get dressed. But I'll be lenient and allow you an additional five. Two strikes with my red crop on your pussy for every minute you're late, sub."

Peyton stamped her foot as she watched the door close behind him. Her gaze fell on the—

"What the bejesus is that? I'm not wearing this... this piece of ... of *string*! Is the man totally crazy!?"

She twisted the ensemble this way and that in her hands, her mouth gaping open. Now, generally, Peyton was no prude and liked to dress in skimpy, tight leather outfits when she visited the clubs in

Seattle but this! There was no way she was wiggling the pieces of string between her little tush. A sly smile curved her lips. Her eyes caught the watch on the bedside table.

"Shit! Two minutes wasted. Well, Master Eagle, you didn't say where or *how* I had to wear this pretty piece of purple string, so ... I'll just slip on this black and purple set of satin lace panties and bra UNDER it."

Peyton blithely ignored the little voice cautioning her that seeing as that was the only *garment* he'd left on the bed; the intention was to *only* wear it.

"At least he has better taste in shoes," she mumbled once she'd managed to get the stringy leather harness on over the lingerie without strangling herself. She stepped into the black high heel pumps, relieved that he hadn't opted for stilettos. With her height, she rarely wore too high a heel.

On the strike of ten minutes after the allotted five allowed, Peyton knocked on Hawk's office door.

"Enter," his gruff voice called out. Her fingers trembled as she pushed it open, suddenly not as confident about her act of defiance. She winced when Hawk burst out laughing which of course, made Stone glance over his shoulder. If she hadn't been so nervous, she would've noticed the twitch of amusement on Stone's lips before it flattened into a disapproving line.

"I'm looking forward to the spice your relationship is going to bring to Castle Sin, Master Eagle." His gray eyes traveled leisurely over Peyton's body. "Very much indeed."

She squirmed under Stone's frosty reception and cringed as his inscrutable stare swept over her to further erode what little confidence she had left.

Stone, on the other hand, was stunned by her beauty. The purple of the lingerie added a sensual glow to her luxurious skin and darkened the sheen of auburn in her hair just that little extra. Angelic, was the word that came to mind. For the second time in a short period, he had trouble breathing.

He felt his loins start to throb as he followed her tongue in a nervous sweep over her pouty lips.

The little minx knew she was pushing his boundaries. He couldn't help but admire the courage she had to defy him. It was an act of stupidity on her side but courageous nonetheless.

He pushed back the chair so that he could look at her without craning his neck. He stretched his legs and steepled his hands over his …

Holy hotness, that eight pack looks so yummy.

Peyton cleared her throat and reluctantly dragged her gaze from his corrugated abs to clash with his baleful eyes.

Behave! Good lord, the man looks like a demon ready to devour me and all you can do is jiggle around in my loins like cheap whores! Peyton had to try but she didn't think the beratement did her any good; her ovaries acted like energizer bunnies on steroids.

"My memory must be failing. Remind me, sub PJ, what did I leave on the bed for you to wear?"

Peyton looked at her feet, the toe of her shoe digging into the thick carpet. She clamped her fingers tighter behind her back.

"I ... er ... what I'm wearing, Master Eagle." She dared a quick look at his face and swiftly backtracked, "Or at least, thepieceofstringthatcutsintomyass," she ended in a rushed mumble.

Stone fought his mirth not to join Hawk in his delighted laughter, keeping his face drawn into a disapproving frown. In his mind, he chuckled. He found her habit to string an entire sentence into one-word endearing. It pleased him that although she showed obvious respect and wariness toward him as a Dom, she still retained her cheeky sassiness, even blatantly flaunting it in small acts of defiance. Unfortunately for her, it was something he wouldn't tolerate.

"I just assumed you forgot to add the rest, Master, and took it upon myself to complete the ensemble."

"I see." Stone got up and walked around her. "What do you think, Master Hawk? Do you believe I forgot to add the lingerie to the leather harness I personally went to Key West for to purchase this afternoon?"

"Knowing how precise you are in choosing your sub's outfits, I doubt it, Master Eagle."

"Do you hear that, sub PJ?"

"Aha," she puffed as he hooked a finger in the back of the purple thong and pulled it so hard, it slipped between her labia. She went onto her toes to alleviate the pressure, he pulled harder. Peyton moaned pleadingly.

"Please! You can't expect me to walk around wearing nothing more than a couple of strings," she protested breathlessly, completely caught off guard by the pulse of awakening lust inside her loins.

"I can't?" This time there was no mistaking the amusement in his voice. "These so-called *strings*, sub, are handmade leather. Specifically crafted to my instructions into a harness to fit your delectable body and enhance your beautiful tits and draw attention to your bare little cunt." His fingers tormented each body part he listed. "Not to mention the enticing contrast of the dark purple against your satiny skin." He faced her with a haughty look. "Now, tell me again that I didn't think your ensemble through properly."

"I apologize, Master Eagle," she said in a breathless whimper. "I didn't mean to insult you."

"On the other hand, seeing as you don't know me that well as of yet, I'll let this one miscalculation slip and not punish you. However, you will remove the sexy lingerie." His eyes held hers captive as he prompted Hawk, "Scissors, please Master Hawk."

"No! I'll remove them. They're my favorite pair and very ..."

Her voice dissipated as she watched in disbelief as the two pieces of purple satin and lace become little slithers of color floating toward the carpet with a couple of quick snip-snip-snips from the scissors in Stone's hand.

"I can't believe you just did that," she huffed.

"Maybe next time you'll think twice before you defy me, little dove. Now, let's just fix the harness ... ah, yes ... and over here as well. Perfect," he said as he stepped back and regarded her naked body, prettily enhanced with a very thin leather harness crisscrossing her skin.

He gestured toward a chair. "Sit down, Peyton. Hawk will explain the details of the contract and answer any questions you might have. Then we'll discuss our limit list."

Peyton took the time to read through the contract while she listened to Hawk briefly explain the key aspects. It was a very detailed agreement that covered everything from Stone's expectations insofar as decorum and submissive protocol was concerned, what was accepted, what wasn't, and what would be considered as a breach of contract from both parties. It set her mind at ease that it wasn't a one-sided contract and protected her interests as much as it did his. She knew *she* would be the one to cause the dissolution of the contract because honesty and truth were two of the main components listed as *the* important characteristics expected from both parties.

Stone and Peyton signed the three copies of the contract with Hawk as witness. He handed each of them a copy, filed away the third and left, leaving them to finalize the discussion around the limit list.

Peyton took the list Stone handed her and paged through it. "There are three pages," she said in awe, her eyes widening at some of the items listed.

She noticed that every item on the third page was ticked as a hard limit, half of the ones of the second page as well but no ticks on page one.

"That's a complete list of most BDSM practices. We don't limit our members to what's allowed, with the understanding that all hardcore activities will only be performed in the presence of a Club Monitor."

"And they're happy with that?"

"Yes, but the majority of our members don't embark on the heavy hardcore practices." Stone gestured to the papers in her hand. "Our relationship's foundation is built on trust, mutual trust, which is why I discounted all the activities I have no interest in and will never do. The others are what our scenes, discipline, and punishments will consist of."

"And if there's anything on there I won't do?" she asked as she ran her finger down the list, relieved to notice that asphyxiation, golden showers, waterplay, and cutting were off limits to Stone as well.

"Then you need to tell me now so we can discuss it."

"And the scenes? Are we going to talk about them in advance?"

"Part of our relationship, in the beginning, will be you learning to trust me, to offer yourself to me unconditionally and give me ultimate control. You don't have to think when we're in a scene. You only obey and allow yourself the freedom to feel, without thought or hesitation. That, my pet, will be your offer of complete submission. Trust in me to know what it is you and your body need at any given time." He cupped her chin to look into her eyes. "I'll never hurt you, Peyton … well, not more than you can bear," He smiled wickedly. "But I'll push your boundaries, make no mistake about that. Therefore, I need you to indicate on that list which of the items you're not comfortable with so I'll know to ease you into them."

Stone didn't rush Peyton and patiently discussed all her concerns in regard to the items she wasn't comfortable with. Once they both agreed on everything, they signed the limit list.

"On your knees, Peyton. Nadu, please."

She didn't hesitate and sank to the floor, her back straight, and legs spread apart with her hands resting facing upward on her thighs. Her gaze was dutifully lowered to the floor.

"Eyes, little dove." He smiled as she looked up. "I have a desire to hear your commitment to me from your sweet lips."

"Yes, Master Eagle." Notwithstanding the circumstances she was forced in or the fact that their relationship would be cut short too soon, Peyton couldn't deny the joy that played havoc with her emotions as she stared into his eyes. This was where she was meant to be. With him as his submissive. She was going to embrace every precious moment she had with him.

"Do you accept me as your Dominant, your Master, Peyton? Do you pledge to be my submissive and offer me your trust, to know what's best for you, to care and protect you and be in control of your body and all the pleasure it needs? Are you freely offering to please and fully submit to me?"

Peyton shivered as his deep voice found resonance deep inside her, his oath wrapped around her soul in warm assurance. He cupped her cheeks, gently rubbing her temples. Every nerve in her body burned hot and smoldered, inflamed in molten plasma. It heated the shell of her core from what wasn't a seductive caress, but to her, his briefest touch was the conduit that sparked her desires.

"Yes, Master Eagle, I accept you as my Dominant, my Master. I solemnly pledge to be your submissive and offer you my trust that you'll know what's best for me." Her voice was hoarse and she had to clear it before she could continue. "To care for and protect me. I gladly give you control over my body and all the pleasure it needs. With this pledge, I offer myself freely to you and commit my full submission to you as my Master."

Stone pulled her to her feet and sealed their commitment with a deep kiss that once again caused her toes to curl and her body to tremble from deep within.

"Have you thought of a sub name for the club, my pet?" Stone asked as he lifted his head. "Seeing as you're no longer a trainee, you'll need one."

"Oh, not really, but I've been using Pandora up to now."

He smiled. "Hmm … like Pandora's box? I always think of the mythical story when I hear that name. No, I don't like it. I don't see you as an evil woman that releases sickness, death, and many other unspecified evils into the world. I think of you as something sweeter, softer … and juicier." His lips twitched. "Petals." He brushed his fingers between her thighs, his fingers gently probing apart her labia. "Like these succulent pieces of flesh."

Stone pulled a choker out of his pocket. Peyton's eyes widened as she watched the glittering reflection of the lights on it.

"In Castle Sin, it's customary to collar a sub in a committed relationship with a Dom or Master. That way, every member will know you belong to another and won't bother you."

Peyton couldn't help but lean closer and gently touch the small stones placed in a diamond shape along the dark purple leather collar with a pearl-shaped drop stone in the center. She gasped as she realized that what she'd perceived as an amethyst stone was, in fact, a purple diamond. Similar to the one her father had given her on her thirtieth birthday, just much, much bigger.

"I ... I can't accept this." Her eyes lifted to his. Filled with wonder and swirling with regret. This wasn't just a collar he'd picked out randomly. It was special, custom made and the kind a Master would offer to his sub as a sign of commitment, love, and honor.

"Why not?" Stone frowned as he looked at the collar in his hand. "I had it made especially for you. The leather is the exact color of your eyes. Don't you like it?"

"W-when did you have it made?" she hedged for time to sort through her frayed mind.

"Today. It was a rush job but it's exactly what I asked for."

"It's beautiful, it absolutely is but it's too expensive. I just can't ... it's just—"

"Nonsense. Money isn't a factor to me. Making sure you're collared as my sub is. So," he placed it around her neck and snapped the clip closed behind her neck, "you'll never leave our room without wearing this, is that understood?"

"Yes, Master."

Peyton looked into his eyes, and in that moment, she felt a tremor of emotion so adverse, she couldn't breathe. A connection of so much more than a touch, it threaded together her soul with his. His confidence, his passion, and his entire temperament lured her into him. She coveted his deep soothing voice and craved the warmth emanating from deep within him. In that instant everything paused and she knew she belonged right there, with him. His moss green eyes locked themselves in her mind. She couldn't deny it any longer. It wasn't admiration or a celeb crush, nor the physical attraction she felt for him. She was falling for him.

Hard, like a shooting star.

Chapter Eighteen

"How did you worm your way back onto the island, Peyton? Damn it! Can't you take the hint? The Masters don't want you here, I sure as hell don't! Why don't you just go!?"

Peyton was shocked at how close to unraveling her usually steadfast cousin was. She looked around to ensure no one was listening and spat out the code, almost like she was extracting a parasite from her body.

"Storm Chaser."

Savannah took back a step; shock pinched her face into a grimace. She shook her head. "How is this possible? Please, Peyton, tell me they haven't gotten to you too."

"The question is, how could you have become involved with something like this? You work for the FBI for heaven's sake!" She gestured around. "For that matter, what the hell *is* this! I don't even know what I'm blackmailed to do."

Savannah touched the glimmering large diamond resting snugly in the hollow of Peyton's throat.

"You're wearing a collar." Her eyes lifted to stare at her. "Who did you commit ... oh lord no. Peyton! Not Master Eagle?" She was so agitated she twirled around in a circle. Her breathing was labored as she faced Peyton again. "I don't believe this. How did it happen?"

Peyton briefly explained what had happened since she'd been banned from the island and how she'd managed to get back there. She told her about Phantom and his threats but she omitted how Aunt Vera was held somewhere in captivity and the fact that her emotions as far as Stone was concerned were totally fucked up.

"Do you have any idea what he would do if he found out you lied to him ... again! Not just embellished the truth or omitted it but outright lied to him when you committed to becoming his submissive? You've been in the lifestyle for years, Peyton, you know a Dom doesn't commit to a relationship unless there's complete trust. And Master Eagle? How can you do this to him?"

Peyton's eyes narrowed on Savannah. Jealousy sharpened her voice. "Don't tell me you're in love with him?"

"Don't be silly, but I've come to care for him, for all the Masters, and I don't want to see any of them hurt."

"Really? So, whatever the fuck it is we're supposed to be doing here isn't going to hurt them? Emotionally, physically, or their reputation for that matter?"

"Peyton, you have to understand. I don't have a choice. If I didn't agree, my mom, you, Uncle Tom … and … and …" Tears filled her eyes.

"And?"

Savannah shook her head. The struggle to find her composure was painful to witness.

"You said no at first, until they almost killed my Dad," Peyton said dully but was glad that Savannah wasn't a willing participant in this entire mess.

"I wish there had been another way but when I realized how ruthless they are … I couldn't take the chance that they would hurt my mom and what they threatened to do to you? I wouldn't have been able to live with myself."

Peyton carefully studied her. She couldn't shake the feeling there was something more than just threatening the three of them.

"And they knew you well enough to know that. Who are *they*, Savannah?"

"The less you know the better. No, don't give me that look. I'm not giving you a name." She gave a stiff shrug. "I don't even know who are all involved. I've only had contact with one man, and believe me, it's someone you don't want to mess with."

"Don't worry, I believe you. If Phantom and he are one and the same, I have no doubt how cruel he can be." She noticed Savannah's eyes move over Stone and three of his cousins at the bar. "I did omit things, Savvy, but I didn't lie to Stone when I made the commitment to be his submissive. It's something I desire with everything in me."

Savannah's head turned back and she stared at her for a long while. She had a pensive look on her face. "You've celeb crushed over him since you were twenty years old. Don't confuse that with something more, Peyton. Don't fall in love with him. Rumor is, like his name, his heart is made of stone. You'll only get hurt … again."

I'm afraid it might already be too late for that.

"I need to know what I've been dragged into, Savvy."

"Master Eagle is on his way over here. We'll talk in the morning. I jog to the top of the hill behind the castle every day before breakfast. Meet me at the front door at seven."

"Jogging? Really? You know how I feel about running."

"Yeah," Savannah chuckled. "Nowadays, you only run when someone or something is chasing you."

"Exactly."

"Time for our scene, Petals," Stone said as he reached them. "Sub ST, Master Hawk requested that you join him in the bondage room for a demonstration."

"Of course, Master Eagle." Savannah smiled at him and quickly trotted off to find Hawk.

"How many demonstrations do you do in one night?" Peyton asked as she followed Stone through the large reception hall of Castle Sin toward the massive wooden door on the other side. It stretched the entire height of the wall and was as wide as two garage doors.

"Only one." He nodded at the two bulky men, dressed like Roman soldiers, who stood guard at the doors. They opened them immediately and Stone edged her inside with a guiding hand against her lower back.

"Does that mean we're not doing one anymore?"

"No, I'd rather concentrate on our scene."

"And my punishment?" she asked tongue in cheek.

He chuckled and tapped her on the nose. "I'm feeling generous tonight. I'd rather concentrate on our scene, so, no punishment but don't for one moment think this will happen again."

"I wouldn't dare and … oh, my lord!" she exclaimed and looked around. Her head snapped from side to side to take it all in. The trainee tour hadn't included member dungeons at Castle Sin because the newbies weren't allowed to set foot inside until their first month of training had been successfully completed.

The dungeon was as medieval as the rest of the castle. Huge arches led from one massive room into the other with wide hallways forking in various directions. The furniture was a mixture of large sofas and chairs in shades of black and dark green with a variety of dark gold and copper fabric covered plush chairs placed in between. Thick Persian carpets offered added warmth to the seating areas. Small lantern lights on numerous little tables along with big sconces on the walls offered the dim lighting in the entrance hall. Soft murmurs came from a few couples that were seated and in the process of aftercare.

Then other sounds and smells penetrated Peyton's mind. The wicked sounds that made it Castle Sin. Gruff voices snapped out orders, cries and screams echoed from one of the hallways, laughter came from the large adjacent room. She felt excitement rife through her as she detected numerous benches, stockades, St. Andrew crosses, and different kinds of torture chairs.

It embodied what the wicked Masters of Castle Sin represented—the smell of sweat mingled with leather, the sound of pain, excitement and pleasure—this was their territory, their playground.

"It's rather overwhelming," she lilted as she followed him into the adjacent room. "I've never seen a club of this size before, or one that felt like raw power, pleasure, and pain all melted into one."

"That's a rather accurate assertion and exactly what my aim was when I designed the dungeon."

"You designed it?"

"The castle too. This is what I envisioned and wanted. I was lucky enough to find an architect who could turn my vision become a reality."

"Oh," Peyton eyed the table Stone stopped at warily. "Exactly what's our scene going to be, Master Eagle?"

"Edging. I want to gauge how far I can push you, how much you trust me to know when you've had enough. Ultimately, to see if you'll give me what I need tonight."

Peyton shifted her weight. She wasn't a lover of climax control, of any kind, whether it was forced or denied, she hated them. She firmly believed all subs agreed with her.

"Sometimes, not often, I love to watch and tonight is one of those nights."

"Someone else is going to edge me?"

"No. I'll be the one awakening your lusts, Petals. Satisfying them on the other hand ..."

Peyton felt a punch in her stomach as he allowed his sentence to hang. Refusal was her immediate reaction, but as she looked into his eyes, she was shocked at the myriad of emotions that ran through her. At the top of the list was the desire to please her Master. She heaved in a breath. She would never have believed she'd be excited to be fucked by another man while her Dom watched.

Oh, freaking hell! That's exactly what he wants! She only verbalized it when the thought flashed through her mind. She blinked at him.

"Y-you mean you're not going to be the one ... that you expect me to ... that—"

"Yes, Petals, Master Bear will do the honors."

Peyton searched her memory. During introductions, they were only given the Masters' club names. Master Bear was none other than Kane, the second oldest of the Sinclair clan. She relaxed somewhat. She'd always liked all the cousins and he was one of her favorites as an actor. The strong, silent, brooding type that had the ability to see deep inside your soul, as some tabloids referred to him. The tension eased from her shoulders. She'd always been very pedantic about her sexual partners, which was why her initial reaction had been negative but now she didn't think she'd mind all that much.

Stone pinched her chin and watched her with blazing eyes. "Is that going to be a problem, Petals?"

"No, Master Eagle. If it's your desire to watch me fuck Master Bear, then it's not a problem." A small frown marred her brow. "Although I'm a little confused."

"About what?"

"One of your rules is that no man is allowed to touch me, yet you wish another man to fuck me. I don't understand."

"My control, my decision, little dove, always. Unless I give permission, no Dom or Master, my cousins included, are allowed to touch you. I'll decide when, where, and how." He patted the padded tabletop. "On your back, Petals. I want full access to every girly part of you. We don't even have to waste time removing clothes. Now do you see why I chose this pretty harness for you?"

"Yes, Master," she muttered as she climbed onto the table.

"No, leave on your shoes. There's something about a woman with heels being fucked that's very sexy." He grabbed her hips and pulled her towards him until her buttocks were at the edge of the table. "These pretty knees go up and over the stirrups," he said as he guided them in place and strapped her legs to the supports. "So pretty," he chuckled when she whimpered as he pushed the stirrups backward which spread her legs wide apart, exposing her pussy and tilting her pelvis upwards. He walked to the other end of the table and bound her wrists with the leather cuffs attached to the table. He moved to stand next to her, his fingers drawing gentle circles on her stomach.

"From this point forward, your mind is clear. Your head is with me, in this scene all the time, is that clear, Petals? You follow my instructions and keep your attention on me, nothing else. Understood?"

"Yes, Master."

"For now, I need your lower body completely immobile," he explained as he tightened a strap around her waist which effectively made it impossible to move her hips. "Normally I would blindfold you, but tonight I want to see the desire and lust built in your eyes," he said as he ran his hands over her body. He feathered his palms over her nipples, once, twice before he splayed his fingers over the tips.

"Hmm," she moaned and arched her back, the only part of her body she could move, to press her breasts harder against his hands.

"So eager, my pet and we've barely begun," he teased as he pinched her nipples gently with one hand while he ran the warm palm of the other up and down her spread open pussy.

Peyton shut her eyes and desperately squeezed her inner muscles in an effort to contain her rapidly rising lust but it was a wasted effort. Her arousal glistened on her labia, coating his skin with her juices as he took another pass.

The spicy, yet honeyed smell tantalized Stone's nostrils.

"I love the bouquet of your arousal, Petals. It's rather intoxicating." His voice sounded strained as he dipped the tip of his finger inside her slit to swirl it around teasingly. "It seems it's going to be a lot quicker to push you to the edge of desperation before you beg me to allow Master Bear to fuck you."

"Master Eagle, I don't like this," she protested. "In fact, I hate climax control."

"Edging is a little past climax control, my pet. I suppose that means you've never experienced it?" She shook her head and moaned as he cupped her breasts to flick his fingers over her distended nipples. "I'm going to push you to the point of an orgasm and yank you back just before you tumble over until the only thing that fills your mind is the need to come, to have a cock fuck you so hard that you lose all control and come again and again."

She groaned as he tweaked her nipples, nibbling a seductive path with his lips over her torso to flick the tip of his tongue into her belly button. Her breathing increased as he slicked a path down the center of her stomach to lick her fragrant pussy. Using the flat of his tongue, he stroked it from the bottom of her slit to her clit. He repeated it, watching with satisfaction how her labia darkened, puffed up and pulled apart.

He looked up, feeling himself falling deeper into the tentacles of her seductive web. She looked hot, sexy with her lips reddened and her cheeks flushed from the lust that coursed through her veins. Her breathing hitched and puffed fervently from her lips.

"Please," she whimpered, straining against the bonds to try and embed his teasing fingers inside her. She was desperate for a harder touch, a deep penetration as her mind became flushed with the memory of their night together. When he'd let loose the Beast and fucked her until she didn't know where he ended and she began. But it was all for naught; he ruthlessly played with her body as promised, pushing her to the edge, ignoring her pleas, he just started again and again. His lips teased, his fingers aroused and his tongue …

"Ahh, Master!" she shouted as his lips latched onto her clit for the umpteenth time. He sucked it, using hard and deep pulls that caused ripples of heat to surge through her veins.

"I love how succulent and tasty this little nubbin is, my pet," he murmured as he lapped at her clit, swollen from his intense treatment.

Peyton watched in wonder as his eyes darkened, homing in on her distilled essence. His nostrils flared wide as he inhaled her intoxicating bouquet.

"Fuck, you smell so good!"

"I can't anymore, please Master Eagle. I need … ohh fuck!" she cried. Radiant heat seared the inside of her loins and surged upward into her chest in pulsing emanation that caught her breath as he pressed his tongue deep inside her pussy, licking and teasing the silky folds, boldly supping the elixir he found there.

"Master Eagle please, please, please," she begged as he forced her labia further apart, sucking her clit as he plunged two fingers inside her and fucked her with a wild, rough rhythm.

"Please what, Petals," Stone rasped against her heated center as he mercilessly gorged on her pussy, causing her to spiral out of control.

"I need to come, I need … please, I need you to fuck me!"

"Ah, little pet, almost there … but not quite, I see," his voice deepened as he latched onto a nipple, sucking, biting and shaking his head while he pumped his fingers inside her.

She screamed, she cursed, all the time amazed that no matter how close she thought she was, nothing she did could push her over. He was always aware, just that split second too fast and pulled back, keeping her there, just there, teetering on the edge.

Her mind blank, she recalled what would offer her the relief she was desperate for, what he desired and wanted from her.

"Master Bear! Please, Master Eagle, I need Master Bear to fuck me. God damn you! Let him fuck me!"

Her words still echoed around them, when Stone uncuffed her arms and legs and gently massaged her stiff muscles. She moaned, all the while twitching under his ministrations. Her eyes feverish, she begged once more, "Please Master Eagle, I need Master Bear to fuck me. Now, I need him now!"

"I'm here, little one."

Peyton's eyes searched for the man with the gruff voice and sighed with relief as Stone stepped out of the way and Master Bear took the spot between her legs. She clamped her thighs around his hips to force him closer.

"Ahhh," she screamed as he repaid her with two hard slaps on her tits.

"You don't get to dictate how I fuck you, sub. Turn over. I want you on all fours."

Peyton didn't even protest, she flipped over and stood on her hands and knees, her breathing labored. She had never in her entire life been this desperate to climax, to be fucked, hard, deep and nonstop.

She whimpered, listening to the crinkle of paper and then she felt Master Bear press his large cockhead against her very wet slit. She pushed back against him, forcing him in deeper.

Gawd, he's just as big as Stone!

"Down you go, my pet. I want this little cunt open wide and accessible for my cock," he said as he forced her down with a firm hand on her shoulders until her cheek rested on the padded leather top of the table.

"No. I want to see your face. Turn your head this way, Petals."

Peyton blindly followed Stone's order, realizing that he had sat down in a sofa against the wall, his legs spread out to watch.

"Please, Master Bear, I can't stand it any longer. Fuck me!"

"You may come at will, Petals," Stone laughed with a wicked glint in his eyes. "Over and over, my pet."

"Freaking hell!" her scream echoed to the high rafters and punched Stone's libido sky high as Kane slammed into her, setting an immediate rhythm that lifted her clear off her knees. Her body shook and she clawed at the table.

"Ah, fuck, that's beautiful," Stone rumbled as he watched her splinter apart under Kane's onslaught. Her face pulled into a grimace of pleasure as she tried to ride through the climax. He smiled. She would soon learn it wouldn't be as easy as that. He sat back to enjoy the show. He reveled in the smooth lines of her back as she arched and jerked with every powerful thrust of Kane's cock deep inside her. The sound of slapping flesh was like a melody of lust that kept feeding his own. His dick was hard, twitching with every scream from her rosy lips as Kane forced climax after climax from her before his roar merged with hers and he spilled his load deep inside her.

Stone didn't move. He watched as Kane gently pulled out and wiped Peyton's pussy clean with a warm cloth a club coordinator handed to him. His soothing voice calming her, traveled to Stone but his eyes didn't waver from hers, which were still feverish as she stared at him, pleading silently. His chest filled with warmth, his cock surged as fresh blood punched into it and swelled it even bigger. He'd hoped she'd react like this. That one wouldn't be enough ... maybe not even two.

"Master, please," she whimpered as Kane walked away.

"More?"

"Yes," she exclaimed. "Please, I need more. I'm desperate, please, Master."

He didn't move, her body twitched on the table as she pushed her clit against the padded top.

"Who do you want this time, Petals?"

"Anybody. I don't care who! Just get someone to fuck my pussy. I beg you!" Peyton was in a vortex of lust that ate away at her loins, that clawed for release so violently, she wanted to curl up in a ball and cry.

"No, little dove. I chose the first time, now it's your turn."

"Master Hawk! I want Master Hawk to fuck me."

Stone nodded at the coordinator who stood to the side and she rushed off to find Master Hawk. By now a crowd of members and submissives had gathered to watch but Peyton was oblivious, her attention fixated on her Master.

When Hawk arrived, she was dripping wet with lust, her hips danced up and down as she slammed her clit against the table in an attempt to climax. She didn't dare use her hands to try and bring herself off. It was another of Stone's rules. She wasn't allowed to masturbate without his permission. That she could even remember it in the state she was in stumped her.

"Turn around, little one," Hawk rasped as he gently assisted her onto her back. He brushed his hand over her wet labia. "Fuck, Petals, you're scorching hot."

"Please hurry, Master Hawk, I beg you." Her voice was hoarse from all the screaming and cries Stone and Bear had drawn from her. When he ignored her and continued to enjoy the wet heat against his palm, Peyton took matters in her own hands and unzipped his cock.

Hawk took back a step. "No. I didn't give you permission to touch me. Do you want me to leave?"

Peyton felt like bursting into tears. "No, I'm sorry. Please don't leave."

"Lay back and put your feet in the stirrups." Hawk sheathed his cock while Peyton hurriedly got into position. She was deaf and blind to the excited twitter of the crowd watching. All that mattered was his cock and the relief he would bring. He stepped between her legs, pushed back the stirrups that tilted her hips higher. He thrust his cock slowly inside her hot little slit.

"Eyes on me, Petals." Again, she obeyed Stone's command. Her head turned and she looked at him. Hawk plunged inside, hard and to the hilt at the same time as Peyton realized Stone was pumping his huge cock in his hand. It spiked her own arousal to such a height that her scream was as unexpected as the climax that rippled through her.

"Well, Master Stone, I have to applaud you. You've got one hell of a sub here."

That was the last words Hawk uttered as he began pounding into her, watching with amazement how her body jagged and twisted, helplessly caught in a flurry of climaxes she seemed to have no control over. It caught him for a loop and he increased his speed, powering toward his own climax that shuddered through him quicker than he would've liked.

Stone's body was flaming hot by the time Hawk strolled away. He was completely entranced by his sub. His instinct about her had been spot on. He had known she'd be strong enough to survive his dark Beast, the pleasures he would derive from scenes just like this and more, so much more.

"Please, Master," Peyton sobbed. Tears fell from her cheeks as she stared at him, her stomach heaved from exertion and her legs were still splayed open after Hawk had wiped her clean. Her hips jerked and she whimpered.

The Beast growled, ready to pounce and possess. Stone suppressed the desire to do his bidding.

"More, my pet?"

"I … can't believe it … it's … ooohh gaawd," she wailed as a flush of lust flooded her pussy, dripping in a steady stream from between her swollen labia. She was on fire. Every cell in her body thrummed with heat and all sound and physical sense of where she was and what she was doing was subsumed her in a wave of unbridled lust. "Yes, YES!"

"Who this time, Petals?"

"You, my Master. I only want you. Please … I need … the Beast."

The Beast howled his pleasure as Stone got up and walked closer, his steps measured, his hand still pumping his cock with lazy movements.

He brushed a hand over her labia, noticing how swollen they were. He spread them apart, as his Beast roared with joy at the sight of her red, well used pussy. His cock surged to full capacity as he noticed her eyes glimmering, begging for him to end her misery. He pulled out a condom and within seconds sheathed his rowdy cock.

"Easy, little dove," he soothed her as her breathing spiked the moment he pressed his large mushroom shaped cock between her labia. Her breath hissed from her lips as he pushed forward, slowly, watching her wince as he settled balls deep inside her. His cock tingled excitedly, spurred on by the voice inside him to pound her into kingdom come.

He looked into her eyes, their amethyst color darkened to a deep violet with the turbulent emotions wreaking havoc inside her. Her pussy clenched around him, released and clenched like it was begging him to fuck it. His finger traced her lips, around her jaw and tenderly wiped away the tears from her cheeks. Still, he didn't move inside her.

Nor did she. All she could do was wait, no matter how her loins begged for release, how intense the shocks of exhilaration flooding her lower body were. Now that he was there, inside her, none of that mattered. She breathed in slowly and the tenseness flowed from her body. She was at peace.

He was there and she was his.

Body and soul.

A calmness washed over Stone as he felt her relax, the wildness dissolved from her eyes and then—there was just them.

Man and woman. Master and submissive, staring at each other. In that moment, they acknowledged to each other that there was a bond between them, a thread stronger than the Beast inside Stone, a connection that soothed it to stillness but could awaken it just as easily.

He leaned over her, dragging her hands over her head and steepled their fingers together in a gentle caress that was in total contrast to everything she'd experienced this evening. Her heart skipped a beat as he planted soft kisses all over her face, her eyes and finally her lips.

"You are so beautiful, baby."

He began to rock into her, with slow, even strokes that awoke her desires, no matter that she was swollen and raw. All she felt was him, his heat and how completely he filled her. Not just her pussy but her heart, her mind, and her soul. She clung to his shoulders as he sucked her nipples until she writhed under him, racing toward the edge once again.

"Do you have any idea how arousing it was to watch you climax, knowing it was me you want, my body, the only one that would be able to offer you what it really needs."

He reached between them and toggled her clit as he thrust into her with hard, fast jabs. Her back arched, she wrapped her long legs around his waist and guided him in the race to an explosive orgasm. One where the world fell away under them as they clung to each other in the throes of shared passion.

His finger traced the purple diamond in the hollow of her throat.

"I have you now, Peyton Jackson. You are mine."

Chapter Nineteen

"Good lord, Savvy! Since when have you turned into a marathon athlete? Don't forget that some of us are normal human beings, not fitness ..." she panted to drag in a deep breath, "maniacs like you."

"I'm not a maniac but jogging helps me think and relax," Savannah said as she sped up the incline.

"You know when you said to join you *jogging*, I assumed it would ... be at a normal ... *slooow* pace," Peyton complained through gasping breaths as she tried to keep up with her cousin. She was shocked just how unfit she was. Her, Peyton Jackson, who used to run for miles every morning when she was younger.

Savannah slanted a glance at her and smiled briefly.

"If you stopped complaining so much, you would be able to keep up. We're not even running that fast."

"See! There it is. We're supposed to be jogging, not running!"

Savannah conceded and reluctantly slowed down. It always helped to keep her mind clear the harder she pushed her legs. It was easier to concentrate on the lactic acid burn in her thighs than the fucked-up situation she found herself in. In the desperation and concern over her mother and ...

She forced her mind to go blank and concentrated on the fact that her cousin had now been drawn into as well.

"Maybe it's time you started getting fit again. This little hill hardly ..."

Savannah looked around as she realized Peyton wasn't jogging beside her anymore. She stopped and shook her head as she walked back to where she was lying spread-eagle on the grass next to the gravel road they'd been following. Her chest was heaving and her labored breathing was in harsh contrast to the chirping of the birds in the trees.

Peyton's hands fluttered in the air in an *'I give up'* sign as Savannah sank down next to her. "I'm done! My legs … just gave in."

"Must be from all the exertion of that scene last night. Fucking three Masters one after the other? Geez, Peyton!" She looked at her askance. "It's a wonder you can even walk this morning," she teased.

"Believe me, I know!" Peyton sat up, glad she could hide her embarrassment behind the red tint of exertion on her face. "The clubs I frequented hadn't prepared me for Castle Sin."

"Castle Sin or Stone Rothman?"

Peyton shrugged. "Probably both. I think I understand now why all applicants, even experienced submissives, must pass through the training program. This place … it's so much more intense than other clubs. The Castle Sin dungeon … lordy me, I've never seen some of the equipment they have in there."

"All custom made from designs of the seven Masters themselves." She glanced briefly at Peyton who was still studying her.

"Who would've guessed the Rothman cousins have such a wicked side to them?"

Peyton started as Savannah repeated their surname. Evidently, she wasn't aware of the cousin's real identities. Either that or she was gauging Peyton's reaction. Her expression gave nothing away, though, as she sat looking out to sea far down below.

"Some days I'd stand on the edge over there," Savannah pointed to the highest point of the hill to their left, "and stare down into the crashing waves below, fighting the urge to jump, to end this nightmare. Maybe if I had, everybody would be safe and you wouldn't be here."

"Don't talk shit like that, Savannah. You of all people would never give up, for no reason."

Savannah took a deep breath and with a brief glance at Peyton tackled the huge white elephant that had kept them apart for the past five years.

"You never gave me the opportunity to explain. Not five years ago or every time I tried over the—"

"I don't want to hear it, Savannah. It—"

"No! We're family and I love you like a sister, not a cousin. I fucked up, badly, I know, but we can't do what they expect us to do with this gap between us, the mistrust … the hatred."

"I don't hate you, not anymore. Come, let's continue to the top." Peyton started to get up but sat back down as Savannah continued in a raw voice.

"I swear I didn't know you and Roger were engaged, Peyton. I knew you'd been dating casually when I'd left on that assignment to Russia but you never, not once in any of our emails, or Skypes told me how things had developed between you." Tears filled her eyes. "When I returned, I was such a mess, I couldn't think straight. Things happened over there …" She swallowed hard and clasped her hands together. "Anyway, when I came back you were doing an undercover story in Los Angeles. I got so drunk that night and yes, it's no excuse for what I did, but he never, throughout the night at the club or when he took me home ... not once did he tell me he was your fiancé." She closed her eyes briefly. "The next morning when I woke up and saw you standing over the bed; the shock on your face, just briefly, before it turned to anger and then hatred, I was confused, so confused ... until I noticed the ring on your finger and realized I was in his house—"

"Our house. It was our house," Peyton said tonelessly.

"I wish I could turn back the clock and do it all over, Peyton, but I can't. I can only keep telling you how sorry I am for the heartache I've caused you. I would never have slept with Roger if I had known about you." She dragged in a deep breath. "Why? Why didn't you tell me you and he fell in love and got engaged? We used to share everything and yet you kept the biggest and happiest development in your life from me."

"I knew you were in a difficult situation in Russia. How unhappy you were that the FBI had forced you to move there for ten months and work with the undercover field team. Your mom and I didn't want to make it worse by burdening you with my happiness." She sighed heavily. "I had never felt as betrayed as I did looking at you … sprawled naked all over the man I loved—and I did at the time—with all my heart. He was my first real love; did you know that?" She waved her hands in the air. "I was devastated, broken by the deceit of the two people I loved the most in the world. That's why I started taking on all the out of country undercover assignments. I ran away from the hurt and from facing the fact that I had failed."

"No, Peyton! You did nothing wrong."

She smiled wryly. "Oh yes, I was the one who had failed to see the signs. It took you that morning to finally open my eyes. I saw the devastation and shock in your eyes when you realized what I was doing there, what I meant to Roger. I had suspicions about him sleeping around by then already, but it was easier not to admit it. To allow the pain and hate to blacken my heart, to toughen it up so it would never happen again." She looked at Savannah. "I ran away from the biggest failure I couldn't face. The one I should never have allowed to happen, Savannah. You. I failed you."

"No, you did what anyone would've done in your situation and I don't blame you. Can you ever forgive me, Peyton?"

"There was never anything to forgive, not once I realized Roger was the liar, but I didn't have the guts to face you, to admit I had been wrong. How could I, after all the ugly and dreadful things I said to you?"

"No more. It's over, in the past. Can we move on and maybe one day find that camaraderie and love we lost along the way?"

"I'd like nothing more and, Savvy, we never lost the love, we just had to find each other again."

They hugged for a long time, both relieved that finally, they'd been able to clear the air.

"Did you know Roger got married a year later, divorced two thereafter, remarried last year and is again in the process of getting divorced?" Savannah said against Peyton's hair.

Peyton pulled back, laughing gaily. "Well, that does it. How can I be angry or resentful to you if all you did was save me from a loser?"

"You should … look what I've got you into now again," Savannah said with a concerned frown.

"We both know this isn't your fault. What I'd like to know is how the bastard got us on the island. The man who came to me, claimed he paid millions to get us here."

"I've wondered about it too. He must have a contact on the island but I'm not sure who. All applicants are accepted and approved by Stone."

"Via email?"

"Yes. Wait, are you thinking it could be their hacker that managed to get our applications in and it didn't go though the normal channels?"

"It's all that makes sense. I just don't know. They're aware I'm a journalist, I admitted it to Stone but what about you? Do they know you work at the FBI?"

"No. The bastards created an entire new profile and background for me." Savannah quickly filled her in on the details of her cover. "They apparently did it in such a way that there's no trace of any family on my side, which means they tampered with your information on the web as well."

"In other words, even if Stone did a background check they wouldn't have picked it up?"

"Exactly."

I think it's time you tell me what's going on, Savvy."

"Cybercrime and this is big. It involves the FBI among others."

Peyton sat upright and stared at her, in a way relieved that her suspicions had been confirmed. It all evolved around the cyberthreat she'd uncovered in Sudan that concerned the federal government and involved the La-Muerta Syndicate.

"I'm sorry, Peyton. I have no fucking clue why they even chose me in the first place."

"To get me here," she said, lowering her head dejectedly. "It's because of me you're in this situation, why our families are in danger. I'm the fucking reason!"

"I don't understand," Savannah said in obvious confusion.

Peyton briefly explained what she'd uncovered while in Sudan, that she'd been pulled out just as she was to dig deeper and promptly put on long vacation when she continued to push to stay on the story.

"It's not just someone in the FBI, Savvy, it involves the La-Muerta Syndicate."

"The Mexican crime syndicate that's been trying to take over the U.S. Mafia?"

"The same." Peyton stared at the mirror like surface of the ocean. "I still don't understand what we're doing on The Seven Keys Island."

"Okay, let me tell you what I know. Homeland Security was hacked at the same time as the FBI—the cyber threat you uncovered. Because it's DHS, it was kept under tight secrecy, to prevent mass hysteria. The federal government, specifically the FBI and CIA have been using the services of a private company for the past ten years to install certain security systems and to protect top secret files. They've designed specialized programs the FBI and CIA used to eliminate threats. The moment DHS was hacked, they were called in to safeguard all federal cyber systems across the board, but by then, they'd already managed to hack certain files."

"What did they get?"

"The files that contain the details of the phantom special forces team guarding the President of the United States."

"Phantom SFT? Since when?"

"Since there have been numerous threats made on his life. They're so deep undercover they're undetectable and the president himself doesn't even know where they are. They've already prevented three attacks on the president and his family's lives over the past six months."

"Why don't I know about this?"

"Because it's been kept out of the media."

"Are you saying they now have the information of every member of that special forces team?"

"No, that's the thing. Apparently, the security company used advanced NanoTechnology that was integrated into those types of system files automatically. The CIA Cyber Division and the government system divisions, don't even know it's been installed or picked up on it, it's that advanced."

"So, they added NanoT protection to certain system files of the FBI and Homeland Security, including the one the hackers got and I guess, whoever is after the information needs the key to the technology to unlock the files?"

"Yes, and since those were hacked, they've installed the same technology across every federal division's database. The hackers have been trying to crack the new firewall to get in and recover older data that could assist in identifying that team. So far, the best of the best can't even find a needlepoint access."

"And we're on the island because?"

"The company, Be Secure Enterprises, operates from somewhere on this island."

"Like hell they do." Peyton gestured in the air. "Look at this place! It's a private island with one massive castle on it and nothing else but mountains and fresh air ... not to forget surrounded by an ocean." She got up and stomped off a couple of steps. "And where the devil would any of these Masters find the time to run a company of such magnitude? They've been filming blockbuster movies year after year."

Savannah threw her hands in the air. "I don't know! I've been trying to tell them that. I've been all over this island and I can't find anything. But you know there's one area no trainee, sub or slave is allowed to step foot in."

"The top floor." Peyton looked back toward the castle in the distance. "I suppose it could be. I guess that would explain all the satellite dishes on top of the roof and towers all over the place." She looked at Savannah. "What exactly is the instruction, Savvy? What are we supposed to do?"

"Plant a virus in their system."

Peyton laughed. "How fucking stupid are these people who're behind this? If they can't crack the NanoTechnology firewalls at the FBI or DHS, how the hell do they think we'll be able to plant a virus here, where I'm sure they have even more advanced firewalls and antivirus programs that'll immediately detect a threat? And what are they trying to achieve with a virus? Surely a company like Be Secure would have their data backed up on cloud servers?"

"I have no idea but that's what he ants and it's what we have to give him."

Peyton's eyes narrowed. Who is he?"

Savannah shook her head. "The less you know, the better. I'm not putting you in more danger than you already are."

"We're in this together, Savvy."

"I'm not telling you, Peyton, and that's final."

Peyton couldn't stare her down or intimidate her to divulge the name, so she didn't even bother.

"How are we supposed to load the virus?"

"With an advanced wireless attachment, a box the size of a thick A5 book, that has to be secured to their main server. From there, they would be able to remotely access it and download the virus."

"That makes no sense. Why don't they just attempt to remotely download the virus, especially seeing as they've locked onto the location of the company?"

"I asked them the same question and was told to shut the fuck up and do as I'm told, or else …"

Peyton's eyes widened. She caught Savannah's hand and pulled her to her feet. "Come, let's get back to the castle. "I need to see that box, Savannah. I don't trust this. Something doesn't make sense."

"I agree but I've already tried to see if I can open it. It's completely sealed. It looks like a normal external drive."

"I still want to see it." Peyton picked up the pace, the bloodhound in her smelled a rat. She just hoped and prayed that this time, her instincts were wrong.

"Have they found the servers yet?"

"Give them time. Peyton Jackson just arrived on the island yesterday. She needs to get the details of what they're there for from her cousin first. You'll have to be patient. They can't just disappear and go searching for it. They have to attend their training sessions otherwise they'll draw attention and that's the last thing we want."

"What makes you so sure Peyton will find what Savannah couldn't in three months?"

"Savannah was the bait to get her cousin there. Peyton is the bloodhound and with her there to search for it, I have no doubt we'll manage to disable their servers soon. Once we do, I intend to bring her here and then she's going to play a key role in our future plans. Don't forget that. You have to think about what the main goal is."

"Yes, and that's what concerns me. Miguel Muerta is becoming impatient. He's lost too many men over the past six months from failed assassination attempts. You have to push them for results. I don't want to end up shark bait because he believes we're stalling."

"He should learn patience and start thinking. Rushing this isn't going to give him the power he's after."

"When are you going to realize this isn't just about usurping the U.S. Mafia by framing them for assassinating the U.S. president?

"I fucking know there's more to it, I'm not an idiot."

"Then you better prove that by getting results. If we don't have something to give him soon ..."

"Tell him to ease off the attempts until we've eliminated Be Secure." He smiled. "Our two girls will get the job done, mark my words. None of those horny Sinclair cousins will be able to resist two hot pussies like theirs."

"God, you're such a fucking prick. They're surrounded by willing women. They train hundreds of them. They've got all the cunts they want. Two more isn't going to make a difference."

"Fuck you."

"No, it's time you get your head out of your dick and start thinking with your brain. If we fail Miguel Muerta, there'll be no accolades for us, no chance at his support to get the Presidency and you know why?"

"I'm sure you're about to tell me."

"Because we'll both be fucking dead."

Chapter Twenty

"I warned you that there'll be training sessions I'll expect you to attend, Peyton."

"I know but I honestly don't understand why. You know I've been a submissive for four years and besides, as your permanent sub, I'm automatically disqualified for employment at Castle Sin, aren't I?"

"That goes without saying." Stone took a bite of the scrumptious eggs and sausages on his plate.

She tsk'ed and stabbed at the fruit and yogurt she'd selected for breakfast while watching him with brooding eyes. Of course, the dratted man had to look sexy just sitting there chewing his food! Her mouth watered as her eyes followed the rhythmic movement of his square jaw that enticed her gaze to inch higher and fixate on his full lips. Lips that earlier that morning had lapped and tickled her clit until she was on the verge of combusting.

Not that she was complaining. It was the first time in her life she'd been woken up by a hungry mouth feeding off her throbbing pussy that he'd subtly been preparing while she'd still been asleep. Except, he hadn't given her what she'd craved. No, he'd denied her his cock and used his lips and mouth to force one climax after the other from her.

It had taken two days for her to recover from the shattering edging scene, especially as Stone hadn't stopped there. He'd carried her to his room and continued to gorge his cock inside her for hours thereafter. For the first time since she'd joined the BDSM lifestyle, she'd learned that when a Dom said he was going to fuck a sub raw, it wasn't an empty promise.

Still, she was healed and would have preferred a good hard fuck that morning, which she had no doubt he knew, but in true wicked Castle Sin Master style, preferred to prolong her suffering.

She sighed and forced her thoughts back to the topic at hand.

Normally, Peyton wouldn't mind attending a training session. It was quite fun to be part of such a close knit and wonderful group of trainees but she had something much more pressing to do. She had to find the operation's hub of Be Secure Enterprises. The subtle searches that she and Savannah had done under the auspices of jogging hadn't brought any results, nor had peeking around corners and under stairs. If BSE operated from The Seven Keys Island, it had to be from the top floor of the castle.

Her mind drifted to the satellite call she'd received the previous morning.

"Time is running out, Ms. Peyton and I'm not receiving any progress reports from either of you. Maybe I should pay your father a visit in the morning."

"Look, what the hell do you expect? That there's a door that says: Be Secure Enterprises. Please knock to enter? We're looking but we have to be careful, unless you want us to raise suspicion," Peyton snapped into the satellite phone.

She looked around, but there was no one in sight. From her vantage point on top of the hill behind the castle, she would see someone coming a mile off. It was just after breakfast and the Masters were all involved in training sessions, which had offered her the opportunity to slip away from under Stone's guard. He'd instructed her to rest until she was fully healed but she didn't want to take the chance at being overheard in the castle and told him she was going for a walk.

"Listen to me very carefully. I need access to that fucking server before the end of this week. If you're not up to the task, I'll send someone else and … well, let's just say, repay you and your cousin for disappointing me in a very appropriate manner. Do you understand?"

"I understand." She didn't need him to spell it out. If they failed, both their parents would pay the price and once they set foot on the Mainland, most probably them too.

"Daydreaming, baby?"

Stone's deep voice yanked her back to the present. She smiled at him, basking in the pet name that fell so naturally from his lips. It warmed her from the inside out and obliterated all the years of loneliness after the Roger fiasco. It offered her hope that maybe her heart wasn't as cold and cut off as she'd made herself believe over the years.

"Hmm ... maybe." She had been surprised when he'd told her that morning he didn't expect her to call him Master all day, especially when they weren't in the dungeon.

"Still confused about our discussion this morning?"

"Not confused, just caught me off guard, to be honest."

He pushed back his empty plate and took a sip of coffee.

"This is more than Castle Sin, the BDSM club, it's our home, Peyton. I'll always be your sexual Dominant but I have no interest in a 24/7 Dom/sub relationship."

He took her hand and traced sensual circles on the inside of her palm. The tender caress impacted a sucker punch directly to her heart. His eyes were warm as he watched her.

"I'm not getting any younger and I want at least three children before I'm fifty. For me, this isn't a fleeting experiment, Peyton. I'm in it for the long haul. If you don't feel the same way, you better tell me now."

Peyton was too stumped to reply. When she'd signed the agreement with him and verbally confirmed it, she'd meant every word, even knowing that it could lead nowhere ... because once he knew why she was really there, he'd come to hate her. It wouldn't even matter that she'd been blackmailed. He'd warned her the high value he placed on honesty and trust.

To him, it would be confirmation that she didn't trust him to be honest enough and warn him about what was happening. But, how could she? She had no idea where Aunt Vera was kept or had any guarantee that he would be able to save her.

"We hardly know each other, Stone. How can you be so sure I'm the right woman for you? I'm not exactly as young as those supermodels you're usually seen with around town," she hedged as she scrambled to bury the pain that burst to life inside her, knowing such happiness with him wasn't meant to be.

"They're part and parcel of the promotional package, Peyton, and you should know that. Do you honestly believe I'm the kind of man who would be bothered with a young girl who wants nothing more than to be pampered and put on a pedestal?"

She tilted her head to the side and pulled her hand free from his. She traced her sharp nails over his forearm. A tingle of feminine power sparked to life inside her loins as his eyes flared.

"So, you'd rather opt for a spinster with two cats." She dimpled at the darkening of his eyes. "I should warn you, Master Eagle, I bite and have been known to scratch," she lilted in a sensual purr.

"I've always been rather fond of little kittens." His long arms reached easily across the table to pinch her nipples, smiling as she gasped and bit her lip. "And it's going to be such a pleasure to make you crawl and beg," he promised in a deep growl. "As meek as a little kitten."

"Oh ..." she licked her lips as he rolled the taut nubs seductively between his fingers. "I'll have you know, Master Eagle, two can ... ooww, *gaawd*," she all but wailed as he pinched her nipples hard and pulled them away from her body, aided by the crop top she wore with no bra.

"And if you're a good little kitten ... I might just allow you to purr."

Peyton was oblivious to the rumble of voices surrounding them in the Great Dining Hall. All she was aware of was him, his forest green eyes scorching into hers, and how the pain he elicited rocked her with the giddy rush of sexual adrenaline. She wiggled in the chair, moaning as the pressure increased.

"Like now," he said with a Cheshire grin splitting over his face. "Come for me, Petals ... Purr, baby."

Her eyes widened and a raw wail exploded from within her chest as shards of heat began deep in her loins, spreading like wildfire to expand into her chest. Stone shook her tits, hard. Peyton clutched at his forearms unable to tear her eyes from his as the world tilted. She was shocked as she felt the ripples of a climax roll through her, like a slow wave ambling lazily to shore. He pulled and shook. A second wave crashed to shore, completely splintering her apart.

"Yes, my little kitten, purr ... just like that."

Stone got up and pulled her to her feet. "Let's go, baby. We don't want to be late."

Peyton had just managed to catch her breath, still completely shattered that she'd climaxed with no clitoral aid and blindly stumbled after him, her earlier protest forgotten. She'd heard of nipple climaxes and even though the pain had been blinding, it had spiked her lust instantaneously. It blew the belief that nipple climaxes only happened with slow intimate caresses, sucks and nibbles, to smithereens.

Stone chuckled at the flabbergasted look on her face. He tapped a finger on her nose. "Have you still not realized it yet, baby?"

"Realized what?"

"You're a masochist, Petals. Maybe still a closet one, but you, my little kitten, come off explosively with the added incentive of pain."

Peyton opened her mouth to protest but closed it again. It was pointless to deny it. She'd suspected it for a long time but no Dom until Master Eagle, had ever forced her to acknowledge it.

"Why do I have to attend this specific training session?" she opted to mumble instead. He'd very effectively distracted her from their earlier discussion. She glared at him as realization struck.

Damn it! He did it again. Completely fucked with my mind!

And your ovaries. Don't forget about that.

"Imagine my surprise to realize when I studied your application again last night, that after four years as a submissive, you're still an anal virgin. Therefore, seeing as I'm craving to fuck this sweet little ass of yours, you're attending this session on how to prepare for anal penetration."

"Fuckity fuck."

Stone's deep laughter carried them inside Master Bear's dungeon where the training session was about to start.

"Ah, Master Stone, I'm glad you and Petals decided to join us. Please, I'd like the two of you on the platform over here. You'll be our demonstrators today."

"I'll have you know there was no decision made about this," Peyton mumbled as she dug in her heels.

It didn't faze her Master. He merely picked her up, hitched her effortlessly over his hip and carried her like a log … *a fucking piece of wood* … to the platform. She huffed and glowered at him as he plonked her down on top of the padded table.

"A glare is as disrespectful as open insubordination, sub. I suggest you check your attitude, and quickly before I decide to skip the preparation training and show these trainees how a Castle Sin Master fucks a sub's ass … especially a brat like you."

"Let's begin. All trainees, please remove your clothes." Master Bear eyed Peyton who refused to budge. His eyebrows drew into a disapproving line. "You too, Petals."

The warning was crystal clear. She wasn't a trainee anymore but as the sub of Master Eagle, she was expected to set an example. She refused to look at Stone, she was still peeved at him for once again having tricked her. He knew this would happen, that he'd not have to convince her to participate. Hence, she was left with no alternative but to obey.

"By a show of hands, how many of you have had training on anal sex?" Master Bear asked, not surprised that of the ten trainees, only the two older women put up their hands.

"And how many have had anal sex?"

Again, the same two hands were raised. Master Bear regarded Peyton with a smile when he noticed her disgruntled expression.

"Well, this is going to be fun," he said.

"More than you know, Master Bear," Stone agreed wholeheartedly, leaving Peyton completely caught off guard by the naughty boy look on his face.

One would swear he was about to open his first Christmas present!

Peyton had always shied away from anal sex because to date, she hadn't felt comfortable with any of the Doms she'd scened with to pop her cherry, as they say. Now, it filled her with mixed emotions. It wasn't the act that worried her as much, it was because she'd had no time to emotionally prepare herself for it. If she was totally honest with herself, she'd always wondered how it felt, especially the times she watched other subs totally fall apart during anal sex when they climaxed. It brought another vision to mind that caused her ovaries to perk up like a row of little Jack in the boxes.

Behave, damn it, before I make a fool of myself in front of everyone.

Hell no! We've been waiting for double penetration for ages! Two holes ... two cocks! C'mon, Peyton, do the math.

Whores! That's what you are. Slutty little concubines!

Unfortunately for Peyton, the intimate soliloquy she was having with her libidinous ovaries had an adverse effect on her body. Something the sharp eyes of her Master didn't miss.

"Do I assume you're a little excited about the demonstration, my pet?" he rasped in her ear.

"What makes you think that, Master Eagle?"

"These delightfully perky tits of yours, little dove."

"Er ... why do men always assume a woman is aroused just because her nipples are taut." She looked at him in a haughty fashion, her nose tilted just so. "It's naught but a chilled draft in thine castle that's causing the tightening of mine bosom, Master," she articulated in her best Victorian lady voice.

Stone's laughter rumbled from deep within, like the rolling of thunder in the distance—low and warm, flowing over her like the sweetest of honey. It was a sound that infiltrated every cell of her body, that firmly entrenched and threaded into her soul, a sound that she immediately craved to hear again as it slowed to a chuckle.

Peyton could only stare at the handsome man who, in that instant, morphed into the most gorgeous mythical god sent down to earth to bless her with the sound of his mirth. In that moment, she fell … harder and deeper than she'd ever thought possible.

He leaned closer, their breaths mingled as he said in a raw voice, "That does it, sweetheart. You just sealed your fate." He kissed her—hard and passionately—just once and then tapped her on the nose, a tender smile curving his lips. "Don't say I didn't warn you." He kissed her again. Short and sweet.

"Oh!" she gasped as the next moment, amid the delighted laughter of all the trainees, he toppled her onto her stomach and pulled her onto her knees. "Ouch!" she shrieked as he added two painful slaps on her behind just for good measure.

"That's because you've just wasted Master Bear's time."

"Me? I'm not the one who boomed with laughter like a veritable … *owww!*" she screamed as two more vicious slaps landed on her still flaming buttocks.

"Keep going, sub and I'll ask Dom Danton to put something in your mouth to keep you quiet."

Peyton thought it wise to clamp her lips tightly together.

"Thank you, Master Eagle, for demonstrating the perfect way to heat up a sub's ass in preparation, especially a recalcitrant one." Master Bear teased as he walked closer. He looked at the trainees. "Have you all prepared for this session after breakfast with a flash enema?"

"What? Wait, not me! I—"

"Shall I call Dom Danton, Petals?"

Peyton swallowed her protest and lowered her shoulders back onto the table. The brief possibility at a respite to be excused was doused to cinders. She jerked as Stone ran a finger up and down her crack.

"I know you spent some time in the bathroom this morning, so for the purpose of this session, you'll be fine, sub."

Oh lord, I'm never taking a crap again when he's anywhere in the apartment!

Peyton couldn't believe he'd said it out loud and buried her face in her arms, listening to the giggles erupting around them.

"The key to anal penetration and sex is communication and lube, lots of lube, especially if you're new to it. It's important to talk to your Dom during the process, listen to his words, respond to his prompts and most of all, let him know what you feel. It matters not if it's pain, pleasure, or fear. He needs to know so he can address all those issues as part of the scene." Kane looked around the room. "Trainees, get on the tables in the same position as Petals." He tapped Peyton's inner thigh. "Open those legs, sub. Much wider, please. That's better."

He waited until the ten Training Doms assisting him had assured the women were in the correct position.

"Today, we're going to start you off with a training anal plug, so that you can get used to the feeling of something foreign in your ass."

Peyton listened to the deep sound of Dom Bear as he continued to talk, it lulled her into feeling relaxed and at peace. For that brief moment, she forgot about the threat hanging over her and Savannah.

She hissed as Stone ran his finger along her tight hole.

"Easy, little dove. Stay relaxed and this will be as easy as pie."

Peyton was too shocked at how that lightest touch of his finger made her asshole quiver with excitement to respond and relax.

"Hmm ... now isn't that a rewarding sight," Stone acknowledged her reaction with a deep rumble.

"We're going to start by stretching your sphincters. It's a ring of three muscles around your anus. It's important to take it slow, easing you into the feeling, one finger at a time. Too fast and it'll hurt and burn like the devil itself, so subbies, relax those tushies of yours and let the Doms take care of you."

Peyton gasped as she felt the coldness of the lube on Stone's finger as he rubbed it on and around her tight rosette. She started to tremble as he squirted a generous amount on his finger.

Oh shit, oh shit, oh shit!

She moaned as she felt his lips brush the back of her neck.

"Relax, baby and it won't hurt ... too much."

She shrieked as he slowly pushed his finger inside her ass ... without stopping.

"It burns," she complained and jerked as he slapped her ass hard.

"Relax, Petals."

No matter how hard she tried, she tensed when he began to pump his finger in and out of her asshole. It didn't take long for the burn to turn into heat. She breathed in deeply, savoring the sensations that surged through her. It felt much the same as the thin string of anal beads they'd stuffed inside her at the waterfall, only warmer, much warmer. She squealed in surprise as he immediately added a second finger inside her ass and began to thrust, slowly stretching the tight ring of muscles. He timed the third finger perfectly as she began to push back against his hand. This time she cried out and stiffened. Every muscle clamped around his fingers and he growled.

"No, don't fight the sensations, my pet. Easy there, little one," he crooned as he gently plundered her anus with rhythmic plunges, alternating with scissoring his fingers to stretch her wider.

"Stone, I'm sorry to interrupt but I need to urgently speak with you."

Peyton didn't pay attention to the voice; her focus was on the myriad of sensations overwhelming her mind. She whimpered as Stone pulled out his fingers.

"Regretfully, I'll have to ask Dom Danton to take over. Don't worry, Petals, he loves anal and will prepare you gently." He stepped away and removed the surgical gloves he'd worn for the demonstration. "Danton, be sure to leave in the glass trainer plug for me to remove tonight."

"Of course, Master Eagle. It'll be my pleasure."

Peyton moaned as once more her back hole was stretched to accommodate Danton's thick fingers. He began to thrust and soon she relaxed, soothed into an arousal that she'd never believed could be as profound from having something stuck up her ass.

"A satellite phone? Not one of ours?" Stone asked as he stared at the recording of the signal Parker pointed out on the large screen in his office. He was surrounded by at least ten monitors and the entire one wall consisted of television screens that showed CCTV footage of every area of the Castle and island.

"Definitely not. Ours are synchronized with distinctive signatures. This is not one of them."

"And this signal is from when?"

"Yesterday morning. I usually don't check for satellite signals but something caught my eye when the system pinged from a cell phone call one of the trainees just made."

"Another anomaly. All the trainees are supposed to be in sessions at the moment. Is the call still in progress?"

"Cell is active, yes," Parker confirmed.

Stone took out his cell phone and dialed Hawk's number. He answered on the second ring.

"What's up?"

"Are there any trainees that are sick or not in their allocated sessions at the moment?"

"No, they're all accounted for. Why? You sound concerned."

"We've picked up a cell phone call that's still active."

"Hold on, Stone. Sub ST just walked into the dungeon." Stone listened to Hawk asking Savannah where she'd been. He couldn't hear her response but Hawk snapped at her to go back to her station. "Claims she was in the ladies' room. I'll be right there. Parker, in the meantime, check if her claim is true."

"Already on it," Parker said as he typed in various commands and the footage on the screens moved back fifteen minutes. They were watching Savannah rush toward her sleeping quarters when Hawk joined them. Parker kept typing in commands to follow every step she took.

"She looks upset," Hawk said as he observed her pinched face as she stared at the phone in her hand.

"She's more than upset. She looks horrified," Parker said and zoomed in on her face. "She's crying."

"There! The phone just rang." Hawk pointed to the screen.

"I don't like to invade the trainees' privacy to this extent but we've had our concerns about her and Peyton for two weeks now. Can you obtain a voice recording of that call?"

"I can try but it might take me a day or two. Because we decided not to monitor their calls just screen them, I didn't set up the system to hack and record their calls." He noticed the disappointed expression on Stone's face. "It's doable, it's just going to take time."

"Do it and see if you can trace where that call came from." Stone's attention moved back to the green signal on the screen.

"Is there a way you can trace the location of the actual satellite phones," Stone asked.

"Is that possible if they're switched off?" Hawk asked as he leaned over Parker's shoulder.

"It depends on the phone. The modern ones look exactly like a smartphone, which I suspect was used. Especially if they didn't want to draw attention to it."

"Yes, and?" Stone prompted him impatiently.

"It might work if I ping it using the signal and the signature that makes it up, so … let's see. There! It worked." Parker stiffened and looked at his brother. "The phone is in your apartment, Stone."

Stone was already stomping toward the stairs. The short path back to the castle took half the time it normally did. His anger drove him as he stormed into his apartment, directly to the walk-in closet. He knew every nook and cranny of this castle and based on the location of it on the screen, there was only one place it could be. He stopped in front of the vanity in the corner.

His hands trembled as he stared at his reflection in the mirror. He looked like a man on the verge of committing murder. He had no idea how Peyton had known about the hidden compartment underneath the vanity but it was where he found the satellite phone.

Stone stared at it with anger unfurling inside him. His hand tightened around it with such force the phone broke into two pieces, the glass of the screen cutting a deep slash into his palm. He watched in detachment at the blood oozing from the cut. He didn't feel it.

Not the pain in his hand.

Nor the debilitating slash through his chest.

He should've known better. He should've kept his heart safe and secure behind the wall he'd built around it years ago.

His eyes lifted to stare at himself in the mirror. His lips flattened as he recognized the haunted look. Only this time, it was his eyes looking back at him, not his father. For the first time, he had an inkling of what his father must've felt.

Once again, he learned the same lesson, but this time, the hard way.

Love made a man vulnerable.

He was the idiot, the stupid one to believe he'd accurately read the signs and commitment of her body, her uncontrolled passion and her willing submission. To his detriment what he had believed to be ... love in her eyes.

Lies. All lies.

The broken satellite phone hit the mirror as he flung it from him with all his might. It shattered his reflection into pieces as shards of glass splintered to the floor.

"Stone! Good god, you're bleeding." Parker rushed over as he and Hawk finally caught up with him.

"She lied to me ... again."

Chapter Twenty-One

Peyton had no idea where Stone had disappeared to but her sixth sense warned her something was amiss. This was reiterated when instead of leaving in the glass anal plug as instructed by Stone, Danton removed it. His expression was stoic as he brusquely told her the training was over while the rest of the group was still practicing.

It had bothered her at first but she'd brushed it off the moment she stepped outside Master Bear's dungeon. This was the perfect opportunity to intensify her search. She walked around the castle, popped in at all the Master's dungeons to appear like she was interested in the training sessions.

"Hold on, where are they?" she wondered out loud as she looked around Master Ace's dungeon. In the five dungeons she'd visited, the training Doms were attending the sessions but there was no sign of any of the Castle Sin Masters.

"Dom Evans," she called out and rushed over to him as he was about to step outside. "Do you know where Master Eagle is? Or any of the Masters?"

"They're at a meeting with their agent on the Mainland about the shooting schedule and script of their new film. They should be back late afternoon."

Excitement brightened Peyton's face. She smiled at him as he nodded and left.

"Peyton!"

She searched for the voice and found Savannah skulking behind the stairs. "Savvy? What's wrong? You're as pale as a ghost," she said as she reached her. "And you're trembling."

"We need to find that server and quickly, Peyton, or my mother is dead."

"Don't be silly. They won't take away the only leverage they have over us, and besides, I told … Savannah, stop crying. Come on, we'll find it. You just have to be patient."

"I'm not the one who needs to be patient! Don't you get it? Our lives mean shit to them. Our parents' lives mean shit to them," she cried passionately.

"Something happened that you're not telling me."

Savannah pushed her cell phone into Peyton's hands.

"They've beaten her up." Her bottom lip quivered. "She's not as strong as she used to be. She won't survive another one like that."

"Oh, my God."

Peyton felt the despair take over every thought, every feeling until she was completely numb as she stared at the video recording. The beating was brutal with no regard to the fact that Aunt Vera was a seventy-two-year-old woman. A vicious fist against her nose flattened her on the dirty floor, blood splattering everywhere. She covered her face with her hands, sobbing uncontrollably. The hard boot kicking her in the stomach pushed her over and she thankfully passed out. Peyton raised tortured eyes to Savannah.

"I'm so sorry, Savvy. This is all my fault. If I hadn't found that information in Sudan—

"No, it's not your fault or mine. We're not the reason any of this is happening. We're just game pieces." She dragged in a deep breath, trying to calm herself. "You know as well as I do … we're not going to walk away from this alive. They won't let us, even if we find what they're after."

"Savvy, let's not panic." She sighed as Savannah slumped against the wall in defeat. "I know you're upset because of this," she pointed to the cell phone in her hand, "but I for one am not going to give up that easily. I'm not ready to die and neither are you. We're going to fight this and we *will* see our parents again. Alive!"

"Are we? Don't you get it? We're collateral damage. Plain and simple. The only thing I'm hoping and praying for is that they'll at least let my mother and Uncle Tom go." The haunting look in her eyes attested to something more profound dragging her under.

Peyton didn't respond. From what she'd seen on the video, although the man beating Aunt Vera up had his back to the camera, he wasn't wearing a mask. From his body shape and profile, it was the man she'd christened the Phantom. Savannah might be denying the reality of it but Aunt Vera knew who he was. There was no way she'd be left alive.

"The Masters are on the Mainland and will only be back late afternoon. We won't have a better opportunity, Savvy. We have to get on the third floor. It's the only place we haven't searched."

Savannah looked around. "I can't. I'm scheduled for two training sessions and I've already been caught once this morning. He called me on my cell, Peyton. Two more days. That's all they're giving us and then ...

"Then what?"

"He said if he can't get access to the server, he's going to blow the entire island into the sky."

"Oh, please! He'd have to be very powerfully connected to ... Savvy? Who the fuck is he? I want to know now!"

"Just believe me when I tell you that he has the power to do what he threatens and no one will blink an eye."

Peyton felt like tearing out her hair with frustration. She had as much right to know who threatened their lives as Savannah. Trying to keep the name from her wasn't going to keep her alive.

"It makes me wonder why he hasn't already done that, Savannah. They have the coordinates of the island. What could be easier than that?"

"I've asked myself the same question over and over. All I can think of is that they're under pressure to get access to Be Secure's server. Maybe it's about more than unlocking files, they might be after the development schematics of BSE NanoTechnology."

"Yes, and a way to unlock secret information that could help them ... God help us ... the La-Muerta Syndicate. The connection I found! If they obtain access to secret government information ... do you have any idea what that means, Savannah?"

"They'll have the power to control the President of the United States." Her voice sounded dull, filled with acceptance.

"We can't allow that to happen."

"How are we supposed to stop it? If we don't do what they say ..." She yanked her phone from Peyton's hand. "She's dead."

"And if we do, millions of people will die and suffer under the secret regime of a Mexican crime syndicate."

Peyton looked around. Her cell phone vibrated in her pocket. She frowned as she recognized the number as the rehabilitation clinic where her father was. Doom clawed at her as she answered.

"Ms. Jackson, I'm afraid I have some bad news."

"What happened? Is my father okay?"

"He's had a very bad fall. He slipped and he fell down a flight of stairs."

"His legs? Did he damage them again?"

"I'm afraid your father is in a coma, Ms. Jackson. At this stage, the doctors are doing tests and scans. I'll let you know as soon as I have news."

Peyton ended the call. She looked at Savannah who immediately noticed the defeat in her eyes.

"Uncle Tom?"

"We need to find that server, Savvy. There's nothing either of us can do to prevent those bastards from getting what they want. I can only hope that the technology is designed in such a way that it has a destructive mechanism of some kind."

"What about the crime syndicate?"

Peyton shook her head. "I can't let my father die, or Aunt Vera." She headed for the stairs towards Savannah's sleeping quarters. "Where's that box? I'm going to find that fucking server today, even if it kills me."

Savannah carefully extracted a shoebox from the closet and handed it to her. "It'll attach magnetically to the back of the server. Before you place it, flip the small switch at the bottom of the box."

"That's it? How do I know it's activated?"

"There should be a blue light flickering next to the switch. Be careful, Peyton. Even if they're not here, there are cameras everywhere."

"It doesn't matter anymore. Stone will find out sooner or later. Nothing I do or say is going to change how he'll react. You better get back to the training dungeon before someone comes looking for you." She smiled wanly. "Don't worry, Savvy. I'll be careful."

Peyton knew the window of discovery was very narrow, so she didn't bother wasting time and ran up the stairs to the landing level on the third floor. She looked around indecisively as she stood facing a large, stylishly, handcrafted wooden door.

"Hopefully I won't come face to face with a large staff complement when I open the door. Ah, well … I'll just have to wing it if asked what I'm doing here," she mumbled and opened the door. She sighed with relief when it slid inward silently.

"What the …"

Peyton stared at the entrance hall in what appeared to be another private home. Her eyes widened as she took in the massive chandelier hanging from the roof, intricately designed with the most beautiful crystals. A grand piano stood in front of the wall of windows overlooking the ocean in the distance.

"This is definitely not the reception area of a security company," she whispered as she walked down the hallway to find the entire floor converted into a stylish and modern home with five bedrooms, four full bathrooms, a fully-equipped kitchen which formed part of what she assumed was a great open room, encompassing a dining room and lounge. The walls were painted in soft shades of white with the most beautiful ceilings and floorboards in contrasting darker colors. There wasn't a piece of furniture anywhere except in the final set of rooms she found.

"Oh my god, it's a baby's suite," she cried out in awe as she walked around the rooms, her eyes wide. Hand carved toys were displayed on shelves, rocking chairs, baby cribs and bassinets—all crafted by a loving and precise hand—absolutely took her breath away.

Stone's voice echoed in her mind.

"This is more than Castle Sin, the BDSM club, it's our home, Peyton. I'm not getting any younger and I want at least three children before I'm fifty.

"This is the home he spoke of. This is where he wants to live with h-his f-family."

Peyton felt the walls close in on her as tears trickled over her cheeks with the realization that she would never share it with him. This perfect, beautiful and well thought out designed home that had stolen her heart the moment she'd stepped through the door.

Her heart slowly tore in two. She'd found love, the kind that only came across a person's path once in a lifetime and it wasn't meant to be—not for her. She clutched the shoebox against her chest and ran out the door, her chest heaving as sobs finally broke through her resolve.

She ran aimlessly and when she finally stopped, she battled to breathe and her legs burned like fire. She looked around, realizing that she must've run in circles as she found herself a couple of feet on a back road behind the castle.

"Why!?" she screamed to the heavens, her voice painted black with the loss she felt. "Why can't it be me?" she ended in a soft whisper and sat down on a large boulder next to the road. She stared with longing in her eyes at the large windows of the third floor of the castle.

A forlorn sigh escaped her lips and she forced herself to rise. She looked at the box she still clutched in her hands.

"I'm going to find you, you bastard, and even if I end up in jail for the rest of my life, I'll fucking kill you for what you did to Aunt Vera and my dad."

She listened to the hoarse oath floating to the sky. She'd failed—everyone. Savannah, her aunt, her father and most of all, Stone, because after all this, she still hadn't found the server room of Be Secure Enterprises.

A movement caught her eyes. Peyton started and ran to hide behind a shrub, staring with wide eyes at the side of the hill suddenly opening. She felt like she was watching a movie. It was so unreal that she furiously blinked her eyes, but it was still there. A secret hatch door under the cover of the greenery of the hill. She stiffened as Danton exited and quickly secured it again before he jogged back to the castle.

"I found it," her voice floated with dull tones back at her.

She hadn't failed. She could still save her aunt and father, maybe even walk away from it all herself … then why did she feel so totally and utterly miserable?

Looking around cautiously, she made her way through the thicket to the side of the hill. She waited breathlessly for several minutes before she approached the section where the door should be. Nothing. She couldn't even see a line in the green foliage that covered the area to find the door. Her heart sank and with a raw cry thumped her fist in frustration against the greenery. A soft click penetrated her numb mind. She took back a step and with her heart in her throat, heaved in a breath as the hatch door slid open. She silently ran down the short stairway only to encounter another obstacle. Large aluminum elevator doors that opened with a retina scan. Her shoulders slumped.

"So close and yet so far."

She sat down on the bottom step and rocked back and forth. There was nothing more she could do. She had tried and her best effort hadn't been enough. If only there was someone she could reach out to for help.

There is, Peyton. Just trust him. He's your only hope.

"He'll hate me," she moaned at the soft voice in her mind.

You won't know unless you try.

"No, I can't. I have to think of Savannah too."

With a heavy sigh, she stumbled back up the stairs. Maybe they'd be satisfied with the exact coordinates of the bunker. It was worth a try.

"It's the only hope I have. If they won't accept it … then it's over … for all of us."

"She's going to the top floor. I'll stop her," Ace said and stomped toward the door. The seven cousins were in the underground Be Secure bunker, the third story down in the operation's room.

"No," Stone's toneless voice barked across the room. "Leave her. I want to see what she does. Today Peyton Jackson and Savannah Thorne are going to talk, even if I have to put them over the fucking waterfall again."

No one responded to Stone's threat. Usually, it wasn't something they would take seriously. He wasn't the kind of man who would use a person's fears against them, but this time, they weren't so sure. They had never seen him this quiet, unmoving, and completely devoid of any emotion. It scared the shit out of them.

They watched in silence as Peyton made her way from one room to the other. A vein pulsed in Stone's temple at her reaction to the baby suite but he remained completely impassive otherwise. His eyes followed her tearful flight outside as she ran up the circular path toward the hill.

Stone crossed his arms over his chest as Parker used the real time Geosatellite system to follow her until she stopped running. He stared at her pensively.

"She's clutching that box as if her life depends on it. What the fuck is in it?" Zeke wondered out loud.

"We have no idea but Savannah gave it to her. It sure as hell isn't a pair of shoes. That, I'm willing to bet money on," Ace sneered.

"Danton, I want you to go outside and walk back to the castle," Stone said quietly.

"But she'll notice him and know about the bunker," Parker protested.

"And if she tries to get inside, we'll know the reason why the two of them are on the island," Hawk caught on immediately.

"Are you saying they've been planted to spy on us?" Shane stared hard at the screen. He felt betrayed. He had believed her desire to be with Stone had been real. It seemed Peyton Jackson was a better actress than any of them.

"We've designed the most advanced software technology, Shane. The kind that would be dangerous in the wrong hands," Stone looked at Danton. "Go."

Danton raised his fingers in a salute to his forehead and left.

Seven pairs of eyes watched with disappointment as Peyton entered the bunker a short while later as soon as Stone had flicked the switch to open the latch door. His expression was inscrutable as he stared at her rocking back and forth on the bottom of the stairs when she realized she had gone as far as she would be able to. The dejection was evident in her hunched over shoulders as she disappeared back outside.

"Now what?" Kane's voice cut through the thick silence that followed her path back toward the castle.

All eyes turned to Stone who still hadn't moved. He stood like a statue for a long while before he turned to face his cousins.

"Have you managed to find out anything more about the two women, Parker?" His voice clipped out gruffly.

"Yes. Peyton had been honest about Savannah's mother caring for her as a mother when hers passed away. Her father was an oil rigger and away from work often. I'll skip the menial stuff to what I'd just uncovered about sub ST. Peyton might have lied, but she's the bigger liar." He briefed them about her position at the FBI, the special undercover assignment she'd been to in Russia years ago and that her mother had suddenly disappeared around the same time Peyton came to Castle Sin.

"Russia? Why would a system analyst go undercover in the field? Do you think that's why she's here? That she's a double agent?" Kane asked speculatively.

"Unlikely," Stone said. "And Peyton? Is her father still alive? Our initial checks indicated he was dead."

"He's alive but was involved in a hit and run two months ago. There was also an incident at the rehab center where he's recovering. He's now in a coma." Parker punched in a code. "Listen to this. Peyton received this call from the rehab minutes before she tore up the stairs to your house."

"They're being blackmailed," Stone said as soon as the call finished.

"What are we going to do?" Hawk asked.

"I don't know. I need time to think this through. Madam Secretary has confirmed that there's a covert team watching Gary Sullivan. We got approval directly from the president and have cloned Sullivan's phone and sim card, so, we have access to every call he makes and every keystroke on his laptop. If he's involved with Aunt Vera's disappearance, he might lead us to her. Parker, please update the secretary on that so the covert team knows to inform us if they find her. Ace, get a security team on Peyton's father, 24/7. If anyone tries to get to him, the order is **lethal force**. Everyone else, keep your eyes and ears open. Anything that looks even remotely suspicious, let me know." He strode toward the elevator and said over his shoulder. "Hawk, I want you to personally guard Savannah Thorne. Don't let her out of your sight."

"No problem. It's time her reins were cut short," he grumbled as he followed Stone into the elevator.

Chapter Twenty-Two

Stone stopped in his tracks as he reached the landing on his way to the private stairs that led to his apartment. He had given instructions to Danton that Peyton must be moved to the trainee sleeping quarters. He didn't want to see her tonight. He had too much to work through in his mind. She might be blackmailed but she still didn't trust him to come to him for help.

But there she sat. On the bottom of the stairs, still hugging the shoe box against her chest. She stared vacuously in front of her.

"Peyton?" His voice slashed through the silence like the crack of a whip. Her head lifted and for long moments she just stared at him. Her cheeks were stained with dried up tears.

"I need to tell you something. I need your help and I … I can't lie to you … not anymore."

Stone felt like the weight of the world just lifted off his shoulders. His heart felt lighter, like the doom that had wrapped around it since that morning was slowly disintegrating.

"Come, let's go upstairs," he said as he walked closer.

Peyton didn't budge but her eyes remained glued on him.

"I didn't lie about why I came here at first. My aunt truly asked me to bring Savannah home, but when I arrived here and saw the fear of discovery in her eyes, I instinctively knew something was wrong. She asked me to keep quiet about us being cousins. I didn't understand why until I had to leave the island."

Stone sat down next to her, not touching, but close enough to offer her his warmth and understanding. He listened to the halting story fall from her lips. Fury burst to life inside him at the fear he detected in her voice of the night the cottage was invaded.

"They're going to kill Aunt Vera and my dad and there's nothing I can do to stop them. Nothing!" She bit her lip. "Savannah received a video clip this morning. They beat her up, Stone. A helpless seventy-two-year-old woman. Oh god, she looked so frail, so hurt!" Her eyes teared up. "She won't survive another beating. I don't even know if we're going to ... if she's still ..."

Stone drew her against his chest.

"Shh, baby, I'm here. We'll find her, I promise."

"If only Savannah would tell me who the man is that forced her into this, but I think she's more scared of him than anything."

"Savannah knows who he is?"

"Yes, Aunt Vera too. The man who beat her up wasn't wearing a mask, Stone. They'll never let her live. I recognized his profile on the video clip, it was the same man that came to the cottage." A sob racked through her body. "We're nothing but collateral damage and my dad ... I thought he'd be safe at the clinic but he's not. He's not!"

Stone could see the rising hysteria in the wildness of her eyes and the trembling of her body.

"All of this ... it's my fault. I'm the one who brought this on everyone and now the entire island is in danger. Everyone here ..." She slammed her fist against her thigh. "I'm to blame, if I hadn't dug into ... in Sudan, I shouldn't have ... but no! I'm always out there, looking for a story. It's because of me ... Savannah, Aunt Vera, my dad ... me! I brought it home with me. I don't know how to fix this. I'm so scared and we only have two days otherwise ..."

"Calm down, Peyton. Take a deep breath." Stone cupped her cheeks and tilted her face to look into her eyes. "Tell me what they're looking for."

"It's dangerous! We're not only talking corrupt officials, Stone. This is high up, I know it! And it involves ... "She took a deep breath, "It involves the La-Muerta Crime Syndicate."

"What do they want, Peyton?" His voice darkened but his eyes remained warm.

She shook the box. "Be Secure Enterprises. I didn't even know you owned a company let alone that it's here on the island. That's what they're after.

It's … it's what I was looking into in Sudan before I was pulled out. Those files they hacked, it's connected in some way to someone high up in the FBI who is involved with La-Muerta. We're supposed to attach the unit … I suppose some kind of satellite signal, to your server, which they'll use to remotely download a virus into your database, but I …"

"Yes?"

Peyton looked at the box. "When I realized I couldn't get into the bunker I was going to send them the coordinates, hoping it'd be enough …" She blinked sadly. "But I can't do it. I can't betray you any further. Not after I saw …" Her eyes wandered up the staircase to stare at the upper level. Her smile was tremulous. "It's so beautiful up there." She felt tears burn behind her eyelids and fiercely blinked them away. "I'm sorry I lied to you and more than anything that I won't be sharing that wonderful home with you," She looked away, unable to decipher the emotions in his eyes.

She tapped her fingers on the box "I have a funny feeling about this, Stone. Something tells me it's not a satellite signal unit."

"Let me see."

She opened the box reluctantly and watched in trepidation as Stone removed the book size black unit. It was about nine by six inches big with no distinctive marks.

Stone brushed his finger over the small switch at the bottom as he turned it in his hands. He heard the soft buzzing click and froze. The fucking thing was touch activated! He'd heard that sound many times during the four years directly after school when he was in the Marine Corps while on tour in Afghanistan—a remote missile beacon.

"Don't! That's how it activates the ... oh no," she cried as the blue light immediately flickered a couple of times in rapid succession and then at longer intervals. "I've seen something similar ... in Sudan ... NO!"

She grabbed it out of Stone's hand before he could stop her. His entire body went cold as he jumped up and sprinted after Peyton already running down the stairs.

"Peyton! Get back here. Goddammit, give me that thing!" he shouted with fear threatening to cripple him.

"No! We have to get it out of the castle. Off the island."

"Peyton, listen to me! Stop!" He followed her through the entrance hall where numerous trainees, training Doms, and three of his cousins stood chatting. Ace moved to cut off Peyton but Stone's voice stopped him.

'No! Leave her. Tell Parker to be ready to activate the shield. Block all communication off and to the island. Get everyone inside the bunker. MOVE Ace," he shouted as they gaped at him chasing after Peyton.

He sped up, calling her name. Fear clawed at him that he wouldn't catch her in time, that he wouldn't be able to save her.

"Peyton, let me get rid of it. Stop, for fuck's sake!"

"No! It's my fault it's h-here. I have to d-do it," she shouted back breathlessly as she pumped her legs furiously, fed by a heavy shot of adrenaline and fear.

He caught her as she stumbled onto the marina. He wrestled the unit out of her hands, cursing as the blue light turned red. The missile was homing in. He didn't stop running. He ignored the white streak high in the sky that inched closer, faster than he was comfortable with. He drew back his arm and hurled the unit out to the sea, the hours of lifting heavy weights and strength training in the gym paid off. It might just be their saving grace. If the missile wasn't meant to destroy the entire island, they had a chance. He watched it fly through the air in a perfect arch, then turned and picked Peyton up who had followed him to the edge of the wooden marina. He started running toward the castle but changed direction and headed towards the large boulders to the left when Peyton's voice penetrated.

"Oh god! It's coming!" Peyton screamed as the white streak took form as it catapulted closer. Its aim—the black unit that splashed into the water a good two-hundred-and-fifty-feet away.

He hit the ground and covered her body. He suspected that the missile had a proximity fuse to detonate automatically within a certain proximity of its target. The next moment his theory turned out to be true as a deafening explosion ripped through the air, just above the surface of the water. The earth shuddered, accompanied by Peyton's fearful scream as the blast wave sucked out the air from around them. Within seconds a deafening silence followed and then the sound of rushing water. Stone was up and yanked her along as he started running, knowing what was coming.

"Run Peyton and don't look back."

Peyton's heart stopped in that brief moment of realization. The explosion was smaller than she'd expected it would be but it would still cause a shock wave in its wake.

"Not again. God, no," she whimpered as she ran after Stone, her hand clasped firmly in his. This time she didn't look back, she just ran as fast as she could until they stumbled inside the castle. Stone didn't stop, he kept running through the hallway, the kitchen and out the backdoor. Water flooded the backyard but he didn't stop until Hawk and Parker slammed the heavy latch door of the bunker closed behind them where he'd stood waiting. They urgently ushered them inside the elevator.

Stone wrapped his arms around Peyton's shivering body, hugging her close as she clung to him.

"It's over, baby. You're safe. Everyone on the island is safe."

"For how long?" she sniffed. "They'll realize soon enough the missile missed the island and then?"

"That missile wasn't meant to sink the island, Stone. It had a specific purpose," Hawk speculated.

"Yeah, BSE's operation's hub … more specifically, our server and all our technology." He rubbed some heat into Peyton's cold arms. "Stop worrying, Peyton, the cloud will stay over the island for a couple of days. Even if they had eyes on it via satellite, they won't be able to see anything."

"How is that possible?" Peyton asked with a frown.

"Zeke and Parker developed a NanoT shield. It'll reflect only a vivid cloud image back via satellite. It'll give us time to get those bastards," Stone said with vehemence.

Peyton shivered. "Do you trust everyone else on the island, Stone?"

"Why do you ask?" He leaned back to stare at her.

"I got the impression from what the Phantom had said a couple of times that he had inside information to what's happening here. He knew things about what's going on between you and me. Things Savannah never told anyone ... there's someone here who's a traitor to you, Stone."

"Fuck, just when we thought we had everything under control. Parker, block all communication to and from the island. Hawk, please take Peyton to her cousin and make sure they're given something for shock. Then get the entire BSE team to meet us in the ops room."

"I'm staying with you," Peyton said with an obstinate look on her face.

"No, baby. I've got work to do and you'll be a distraction. We have to make sure those bastards are put behind bars. Our window of advantage is small. We need to utilize every second of it."

"My father ..."

He cupped her face and kissed her lips tenderly. "He's safe, love. We've put a security team on him inside his room this morning already."

"How did you know where he is?"

"We'll talk about this later. Go."

He watched her walk away with a shuttered expression. Maybe, just maybe, there was a chance at happiness for him after all.

"Decker Cooper," Hawk said as he walked into the ops room.

"DC? The deputy director of the FBI?" Stone stopped the clip he'd been listening to of the call Savannah had received earlier that day.

"Yes." Hawk gestured to the visual of Savannah. "He's the one who has been threatening her. Her own fucking boss." The frown on his face promised violence. "She's not saying anything but I have a feeling he has some hold over her other than the threat of her mother."

"When are we moving on them?" Ace said.

"Not until we find out where Savannah's mother is. It's too risky to apprehend them before that. Under the circumstances, neither is going to admit to being involved and it could take days, if not weeks to crack through their armor." Frustration weighed heavily on Stone's shoulders.

"What about the meeting Sullivan had with Muerta? That's more than enough proof that he's involved with a criminal." Kane said as he walked into the ops room.

"All we have is a visual satellite shot and it's so grainy that a good advocate would be able to put doubt in a jury's mind," Parker said as he brought up the photo on the large screen.

"And Sullivan would most probably claim that he was meeting with him to discuss amnesty if he kept his business out of the U.S.," Zeke interjected.

"Bullshit. We all know that was nothing but a smokescreen the government used a year ago to entice criminals to come out of their holes," Parker exploded, the most passionate of them all when it came to cartels.

"We know that, but Sullivan will try anything to absolve himself." Stone stared at the photographs of Sullivan, Douglas, and Vera Thorne on the screen. "Parker, that facial recognition program you just developed, how fast can you use it to link to the GEOsatellite system and do a search throughout Washington DC and Seattle areas?"

"Searching for those three? Live feed can cover the areas in one search within thirty minutes, going back a week or so might take a couple of hours." He tapped on a monitor on his desk. "But I know where Sullivan is. I've got a 24/7 link to his phone's GPS. According to that, he's currently at Finca La Magdalena Country Club in Homestead Miami."

Parker started the search as he talked. "I'll include Florida in the parameters, just in case."

"In Miami? At the same time a missile is launched to blow us out of the water? That's no fucking coincidence, I tell you," Ace said.

"Bring up the video clip of Vera's beating. See if you can confirm the silhouette of the man as belonging to either Sullivan or Douglas. Both have similar builds and it could be either of them. If it's possible, it'll tell us who the mastermind behind this fuck up is. He's the same one who threatened Peyton at the cottage with his henchman in tow." Stone looked at Shane.

"I need you to chat with Peyton and Savannah, Shane. They're both highly emotional at the moment."

"Got Douglas, Stone. The fucker is also in Miami. He just passed through a traffic cam on 136th Street, two blocks from where Sullivan is. That's *no* fucking coincidence," Parker sneered as he flipped the live feed onto the overhead screen. "Let me see if I can get a lock on the registration of the car he's driving." His fingers flew over the keyboard.

"Got it. Now we'll have him in our sights wherever he goes."

"Danton, fire up the chopper. Everyone but Shane and Parker, gear up. I want to be in the air in five minutes. Hawk, speak to Madam Secretary and arrange for an extraction team to be on standby in that immediate area and a SWAT team to assist us. Parker, you'll be our eyes on the ground. Based on the timestamp, that beating took place this morning. My gut tells me Vera must be somewhere close by. Shane, we need twenty minutes to get over that area, then I want Peyton to make a call to tell them the entire bunker has been destroyed and that Hawk, Parker, and I were down there when the missile hit. Once they have confirmation from her that the damage is done, they'll start eliminating their collateral damage."

"And Vera would be first on their list," Hawk said with a furious glint in his eyes.

"Not to be a stickler for details," Kane interjected, "but won't they insist on proof? A photo perhaps?"

"They have access to satellite view which will produce the cloud image, but you're right. Parker, use Photoshop and create a photo with a crater on the far side of the island. Don't let her send it unless they insist." Stone stalked toward the elevator. "Let's move. Douglas just stopped at the Rancho restaurant in Homestead and Sullivan is on the move too. Let's assume they're meeting there for lunch. I want to be in the area by the time they're finished. Hustle!"

They were in the air when Parker's voice crackled in Stone's ears. "I've got a lock on Sullivan's vehicle too. He's definitely on his way to meet Douglas. I also locked onto a Jeep that left the Country Club the same time Sullivan did. It's heading out toward the Everglades Trail."

"Good work, Parker. Keep on him and let me know the minute he stops. We have to be on him before Sullivan gives the order to finish Vera."

Stone stared in silence out over the passing landscape below, his mind clear and calm. Time was your worst enemy in situations like these and he couldn't allow himself to lose focus.

"We fucking got them, Stone. All the motherfuckers!" Parker's excited voice bleated in their headphones

"Easy on the ears, little cousin," Kane said with a start at the sudden interruption to the silence.

"Here's one more, not so much a coincidence, for you. Miguel Muerta just got off a private plane at the Miami Homestead General Aviation Airport and from the direction his vehicle is traveling, I'd guess he's meeting up with those other two bastards as well. And yeah, I included him in the facial search as well."

"I always knew brains ran in the family," Zeke teased. "Fucking brilliant work, cuz."

"Pump this fucking chopper, Danton. I have a feeling that things are going to happen fast," Stone rasped. "Proud of you, little brother."

And he was. Parker grew up without a mother and a father, seeing as theirs were always drunk. It hadn't been easy for either of them but Parker had turned into a strong, confident and brilliant young man.

"You did well, Stone. It was your guidance and strength that shines in that young man," Kane said quietly. They all knew how hard it had been for Stone to take charge at the time.

"He turned out well and all through his own hard work and determination," Stone said.

"Don't discount the role you played. You were still a boy yourself when you had to start taking care of him. If not for you, who knows where he'd have ended up."

"Yep, I agree. Thanks, big brother, you know I love you, but for now, can we please get back to our three bastard crooks?"

"Shoot," Stone said with a thick voice.

"How far out are you? Muerta isn't going to the restaurant. His vehicle just turned into 207th Avenue towards the Coptic Trail Head Lodgings. Wait, he's just turned onto a side road. I'm sending you the coordinates. There's a house there on the edge of the Everglades Trail. That's where he's heading. Sullivan and Douglas just left Rancho as well. It'll take them five minutes tops to get there. Better hustle, guys."

"We'll be there in six minutes. Has Peyton made that call yet?" Stone asked with concern.

"She's just about to. They've had to go and fetch Savannah's satellite phone in the castle seeing as someone broke hers."

"Hold back on that call for another ten minutes. We'll be in place and ready to roll. Any news on SWAT, Hawk?"

"I just sent them the coordinates as well. They're two minutes out."

"Perfect. Tell them to set up a perimeter around the house, ready to go as soon as we arrive."

"On it."

"Good work everyone. Arms up, we're going in hot but be on the lookout for Vera Thorne. I don't want her getting caught in the crossfire."

"You've had enough time to get this done. I'm not waiting any longer. It's time to make our move. With all the political upheaval in the country at the moment, the time to strike is now. You're already the best candidate to win the election but I need to make sure President Grayson isn't reelected by a stroke of luck."

"It's done. The missile released less than an hour ago. You can relax," Gary Sullivan snapped. He stood on the verge of becoming the most powerful man in the United States and the quicker Miguel Muerta realized that, the better. In the position as the President of the United States, he'd demand to be respected, and feared crime lord or not, he better give it to him.

"You seem a little uptight, Sullivan. Didn't everything go according to plan?" Miguel asked with narrowed eyes. He had learned in his position to read people and Sullivan was an open book. He snorted within himself. He was already developing a sense of importance but he'd soon realize that he wasn't the one who would be in charge. Oh no, La-Muerta had it all planned out. Gary Sullivan might be the next President of the United States, but he, Miguel Muerta, was going to be the one waving the scepter of power.

"Everything went exactly according to plan— my plan in case you forgot. I'm the one who planted the information for that nosy little journalist to find and set her up to be the key player in executing it. I've been trying to eliminate BSE from the first time they were used to install a security protocol for the FBI. It was me who set the ball rolling a year ago already. Don't you ever forget that, Miguel. I'm the one who approached you, not the other way around."

"So, have you received verification that the missile hit the target? Or are you just assuming because it exploded that your plan has worked?" Miguel asked with obvious cynicism.

Satellite visual confirms the cloud blast cover over the island," Decker Cooper interjected.

Sullivan's cell phone rang. He glanced at it irritably. He smiled. "I'm sure my girls on the island are about to give us all the confirmation we need." He flicked his finger over the screen and put it on speaker. "It's about time, Ms. Jackson."

"You fucking bastard! I was almost killed. Or was that the plan, you useless piece of shit!?"

"Yes, I can see you have the little woman right where you want her," Miguel snorted with a grin.

"But you didn't. What's the extent of the damage, Ms. Jackson? And don't even think of lying to me," Sullivan warned in a dark voice.

"The company is ... was run from a three-story underground bunker. The entire fucking thing was blown to smithereens ... along with Stone Sinclair, his brother, Parker and Hawk Sinclair."

"Well, I couldn't have asked for more. You and your cousin did brilliant work, Ms. Jackson. You're free to leave the island and go home. I hope we'll meet someday."

"You bastard! Just like that? You fuck up our lives and you think offering a few pleasantries are enough? That we're expected to just go on like nothing happened?"

"Yes, that's exactly what I expect. I suggest you forget about me and the past couple of weeks, otherwise you might end up like the three Sinclair cousins."

"Where's Savannah's mother? I know you abducted her," she said with suppressed anger rife in her voice.

"Aren't you the clever little birdie," Sullivan taunted. "I believe I'll hold onto the old lady a little while longer. Just to make sure you and your cousin don't flap your lips."

"Look here, you motherfucker, I—"

"Enough! I want proof, Ms. Jackson. Send me a photograph of the crater and make sure there's something that'll show me you're there. Don't think to fool me with some Photoshop bullshit. You have five minutes … or your poor aunt might suffer under my fists again."

He ended the call and sat back with satisfied glee glowing on his face.

"You're going to leave them alive? Are you fucking crazy?" Miguel exploded.

"I'm not an idiot. They'll be taken care of as soon as they set foot on the Mainland. Now, I think it's time to take care of the old woman. We don't need her anymore and I'm sure Lewis is tired of playing nurse."

Sullivan got up and stretched his tall body. The future winked bright and filled with power unbound in the distance. The very close distance. Wrapping his hands around the old woman's throat to watch as her life drifted out of her eyes as he strangled her would be a celebratory present for a job well done.

One moment he was heading toward the hallway, the next all hell broke loose. He reached for his gun.

"Touch that thing and you're dead."

His disbelieving eyes clashed with green balls of fire that shot promised death in his direction … and not an easy one either.

"You! The fucking bitch lied to me! You're not dead!"

Two rapid shots sounded from the back of the house.

"Perimeter secure. Package secured and alive," Ace's voice sounded in Stone's ear. He sighed with relief. Vera Thorne was alive. His eyes turned murderous as Sullivan tried inching closer to the door.

"Go ahead, Sullivan. It would give me the greatest pleasure to shoot both your knees out." He barked out a laugh at his expression. "No, you bastard, I have no desire to kill you. That'd be too easy for you. You and your cohorts are going to rot in jail."

"I'm not going to a fucking American jail," Muerta shrieked. A round echoed through the room as both Hawk and Kane returned fire when he spun around with a gun and started shooting. He went down like a log … dead before he hit the floor.

"If you think you're going to put me in jail, you have a surprise waiting for you. We're here purely to eliminate a threat against the United States of America. I'll be sure to mention that you're the one who rid us of this scumbag once and for all," Sullivan said as he kicked the lifeless body of the crime lord on the floor.

Stone's smile was one of pure pleasure. "Keep dreaming, Sullivan. We're not amateurs. We've got solid proof of your involvement." He nodded at the SAT commander. "Take these pieces of shit out of here."

"She's alive but in critical condition. MedEvac is already on the way with her to the nearest hospital," Ace reported as he walked into the room.

"Good job, everyone. Now, let's get home. We've got a marina to rebuild."

Chapter Twenty-Three

The atmosphere in the King's Dungeon of Castle Sin buzzed with excitement and gaiety. The large events room thrilled the submissives with the feeling of dancing on Northern Lights; beneath the dry-ice smoke swirled an array of blues, acid greens, hot pinks, and gold. The music played over the dance floor as if it had fused with the bodies swinging to the eclectic tunes.

There were as many couples dancing as there were lounging on the outer edges of the room at the comfortable seating areas. Trainees were running around, serving food and drinks to the members and full-time submissives.

Now that the threat against Be Secure Enterprises and the United States had been eliminated it was time to relax. Vera was still in hospital but out of danger and Tom, Peyton's father, came out of his coma and was also on the mend. The only issue they'd been unable to resolve was the possibility of a traitor on the island. Stone and Danton had installed additional security monitors and cameras as a safety measure. If there was someone who wished them harm, one way or the other, he or she would slip up and they'd know.

Everyone was having fun ... except the two cousins in the stockades on a raised platform in the middle of the room. They were naked, with their necks and hands locked into the wooden blocks and their naked pussies on display with their ankles cuffed to leg spreaders, shoulder width apart.

"Master Eagle, I'm sorry to intrude but Petals respectfully requests her Master's presence at the ... er ... platform of voyeuristic torture. Her words, not mine," Jenna, one of the trainees in Savannah's group quickly said at his amused look, but she couldn't keep the smile from her lips.

Stone hid his smile. Peyton had been very verbal about having her tush on display since she'd been locked in the stockade an hour ago.

"Thank you, Sub JC. Please inform Petals that I'll be along shortly to water and take care of her flowery petals." Stone chose his words with deliberation. He didn't have too long to wait as he watched the lithe black-haired trainee report back to Peyton.

"Flower my ass! He can go and ... and water his dried up old ... old *sausage*!"

Members close enough to hear burst out laughing. Over the past three weeks, they'd gotten used to the bratty submissive of the Master Dom. Some said she deliberately pushed his buttons to awake his Beast. She so loved to play with that part of the mighty king of the castle.

Tonight, though, she was going to luck out. The Beast was at rest and the Master himself looked forward to teasing his recalcitrant sub with a promise of something he knew she was yearning for. His cock twitched in eager anticipation.

But first, the sassy cousins must learn that Masters Eagle and Hawk didn't tolerate insubordination. It seemed since they reunited and put the past behind them, they had teamed up to torment every single one of the Sinclair cousins.

"Are you guys ready?" Stone asked the six men lounging around him, sipping their drinks.

"Hell, yes. I always loved a game of dip and sip." Kane said with an expectant look on his face.

"And this time there'll be twice as much fun to be had," Shane agreed and got up. "Well, what are we waiting for? Kane and I take first dips."

"Yeah, let the golden oldies heat up the feast and us young bucks will enjoy the fruits of their labor," Zeke teased his brother.

"Fuck off, little brother." He walked past him and ruffled his perfectly spiked hair.

"Hey! Not the hair, dammit!"

"Golden oldies, my ass. We can teach you a thing or two, you little shit." Kane followed Shane's example and flattened Zeke's hair.

Zeke laughed but didn't bother to check his hair. In his younger years and as part of the character he played in Space Riders, he had a thing about his hair. It was always perfectly styled and woe be the one who dared to mess with it. Nowadays, he didn't care anymore, hence the short spiky style but the *older generation* kept teasing him about it.

The seven Masters jumped onto the large platform and began to circle the two women who were eyeing them warily. A crowd almost immediately began to gather around the platform.

"Would you care to explain why you're about to be punished, Petals?"

Peyton awarded Stone with a chilled glare. "If you need me to remind you, Master Eagle, I should start feeding you more leafy greens to help prevent further cognitive decline. Heaven forbid that I end up with a senile Master before my next birthday."

Crack! Crack!

"Ooww! Freaking hell, who slapped me? This is so not fair," she bemoaned her fate at being unable to see what was going on behind her.

Stone stood in front of them at the edge of the platform while the other Masters continued to circle them, watching, smiling devilishly ... in Peyton's opinion ... *freaking scary!*

"I'm waiting, Petals."

Peyton watched the dreaded red crop tap-tap against his leathers. She'd heard much about said crop and had examined it in detail, but to date, she'd managed to avoid feeling its sting. Something told her she wasn't going to be as lucky tonight.

"We, that is sub ST and I, were unfortunate enough to encounter you and Master Hawk upon our arrival at the King's Dungeon earlier tonight. We took affront at being told to crawl down the stairs."

Giggles from submissives watching, tingled through the atmosphere. They found Master Eagle's sub delightful.

"And exactly how did you express your so-called affront?" Stone asked with suppressed amusement.

"We preferred to hop down the stairs like bunnies."

The crowd burst out laughing. Even Savannah and Peyton couldn't withhold their own snickers at the memory, especially when they recalled the disbelieving look on the two Masters' faces.

"Personally, Master Eagle, I don't see why you're so upset. I mean we offered you quite the enticing view of our bobbing ... eh ... chest attributes instead."

"What my verbal diuretic cousin means, Master Eagle, is that we were insubordinate toward you and Master Hawk," Savannah chipped in before she caused more punishment to befall them. The Masters circling them were an ominous promise in itself. She for one didn't want to push the formidable Master any more than necessary.

"Indeed, sub ST. Therefore, the two of you are the game pieces in a little punishment game we like to call; dip and sip." He watched them, waiting for his words to sink in before he continued with an mocking glint in his eyes. "It's easy enough to understand. One Master will dip his cock in your hot little cunt while the other sips on your honeyed lips, then another Master will dip his rod inside your tight throat while yet another will sip on the spicy juices from your pussy, and so on and so forth."

Master Hawk stood next to Stone. "During the entire punishment, you're not allowed to come. Do not even bother to ask for permission because it's denied upfront."

"Should you be so unwise as to disobey that order ..."

Crack! Crack!

The two women jerked at the sharp snap of the red crop against Stone's leathers.

"The King's Sting will take a nip or two out of the disobeying pussy." Stone regarded them regally. "Any questions, subs?"

"How many times are each Master going to ... er, dip and sip?" Peyton asked in a morose tone.

"As many times as they wish over the next hour."

"What? No, Master Eagle, please. That's just ...tommmphff," Peyton's protest was cut short by Master Kane who pushed his cock into her mouth.

He tapped her under the chin.

"Open wide, Petals, I'm going in all the way."

Peyton concentrated to keep her jaw slack as he pushed his huge cock slowly down her throat, then she gagged as a hot tongue lapped and tickled the opening of her pussy.

"Easy," Kane cautioned but he didn't pull out. As soon as she managed to control her gag reflex, he thrust in all the way.

Peyton was thrown for a loop almost immediately. No matter how hard she endeavored to concentrate on the cock fucking her throat as a mechanism to keep her arousal at bay, her body demanded otherwise. A surge of heat stabbed at her loins as the Master pushed his tongue inside her slit, all the way in and back out, imitating sex. He latched onto her pussy and sucked, alternating with nibbling on her clitoris. Peyton went on her toes as pleasure tiptoed all over her body. Just when she was about to combust, Master Bear pulled out of her throat and the hot mouth left her pussy feeling cold and bereft.

It was a feeling that shook her, knowing there was no way she'd be able to hold back her climax for an hour of such torture.

"Drink, sub," Master Kane tilted a bottle of water against her lips and she dutifully swallowed.

She was still catching her breath when a hard cock entered her pussy, stealing her breath with its smooth entry.

"Ah, I've been wondering what these pouty lips taste like," Master Fox said as he hunched in front of her. "Open those pretty lips wide, little one and make it worth my while." Then his lips covered hers and he kissed her, slanting his mouth back and forth, stealing her breath with a dominating demand she had no choice but to obey. She moaned as she was pounded from behind, hard, quick snaps, followed by a slow, easy rhythm. She decided there and then that the seven cousins were demons ... every last one of them.

It didn't take long for the two women to start thrashing in the stockades. The seven Masters and Dom Danton were experts in arousing games and they enjoyed playing with the cousins.

They both lasted for a grueling forty minutes and both were blindsided by the same two Masters. Eagle and Hawk. First Savannah with Master Eagle taking a dip down her throat and Master Hawk sipping her pussy, and with Peyton they were in reverse positions. The moment she felt the familiar hard heat of her Master slide inside her, she had no control and wailed into Master Hawk's mouth as a climax rippled over her.

She was still assailed by shudders in the aftermath when the strikes fell onto her swollen labia.

Crack! Crack! Crack! Crack!

"Fuck! Fuck! Holy shit!" she screamed as her pussy exploded with pain. She could swear she felt the little hard knobs of leather on the clapper where they landed.

She wasn't given chance to catch her breath before a mouth latched onto her blazing pussy to lick and suck with gusto and a cock fucking her throat.

I won't come again, I won't. Holy shit, that feels sooo good, she moaned inside her mind and then immediately fell back into repeating the mantra, *I won't come. I won't come.*

"Time, Masters."

Both women sagged with relief when Stone announced the end of their punishment.

"What do you have to say, subs?" he asked in a stern voice.

"We're sorry for being insubordinate, Masters Eagle and Hawk," they quickly said in unison.

"Thank you for making us see the error of our ways," Savannah ended in a rush as Master Hawk frowned at them.

Peyton clamped her lips firmly together. She'd be damned if she thanked them for punishing her.

"Very well," Stone said and picked up Peyton as soon as Master Danton had released her from the stockade. He carried her to the corner where Kane and Shane were already having a drink.

"We ordered a couple of snack baskets. The dip and sip has made us ravenous," Shane said teasingly as Hawk joined them with Savannah in his arms. Neither of the women found it funny and their expressions said as much.

Shane just laughed and relaxed in the chair.

Peyton snuggled against Stone's chest and breathed in his smell. She closed her eyes and drifted off to sleep, relaxed and happy for the first time in many years.

She started awake when Stone placed her on a bed. She looked around sleepily, blinking as she noticed Danton close the door of the room and walk closer. They were in the King's Den private room in the dungeon. A big room with large pieces of furniture, sofas and chairs and a bed, double the size of a king sized one.

"This is a c-cozy room," she stammered as Danton sat down on the other side of her. She looked from one to the other, her emotions at war with each other, excitement, trepidation and fear all mixed into one.

"Dom Danton is joining us for the remainder of the evening, my pet.

She glanced at Stone with a mixture of wariness and surprise. His look darkened when he detected a slight tremble in her body. He tipped her chin to ensure he was the only one in her vision.

"Do you trust me, Petals?"

There it was. The question he'd never asked her in all the time she'd been on The Seven Keys Island—it was such a loaded question, but in this case, a relatively easy one. She did trust him, explicitly, but freaking hell, he could've warned her what he had in store for them tonight.

"Explicitly, my Master," she lilted.

"This will be an explosive experience for you, baby and an indulgence I particularly enjoy. I've been preparing you for a while now. You've come to love anal sex and I promise you, double penetration by two cocks is going to blow your mind."

Stone kissed her briefly. "I'm a possessive man, Petals and I'll never agree to you fucking another Dom unless I'm part of it. My cousins will always be part of your punishments, demonstrations, and at times, some of our scenes. Apart from them, Danton is the only Dom I'll ever allow to fuck you. Do you understand what I'm saying?"

His eyes were trained on Peyton. He could see she was a little agitated but still offered him a tremulous smile.

"Yes, and I assume that means you're saying we'll never be exclusive."

"Not in the usual meaning of an exclusive Dom/sub relationship as you understand it. From the moment I collared you, I stopped fucking other subs in Castle Sin, Peyton but as with you and my cousins, so will I be involved with whoever their partners are. In that sense, we won't be exclusive. Outside of that, I'll never fuck anyone else for as long as we're together."

"Thank you, Master Eagle." A trickle of excitement started at the back of her spine. When he'd told her to do the enema earlier, she'd thought it was because he intended to fuck her ass. Just the thought of being sandwiched between these two huge men made her ovaries stumble and stutter.

"Are you up for a threesome with us, Dom Danton?"

"It'll indeed be an honor, Master Eagle, but only if your sub is comfortable with me," Danton said with a sideways glance at Peyton.

"Well, my pet. How do you feel with Dom Danton as our partner tonight?"

Peyton smiled at Stone. For the first time, she felt secure in the knowledge that he cared for her. It was there in his eyes and he floored her every time he switched gears and made tender and gentle love to her. Nothing could match the emotions that overwhelmed her though when he unleashed the Beast and became rough and wild and turned her body inside out; all without hurting her.

He had become like a sexual need to her, her drug, and a certain must have in her life. If she was honest with herself, she couldn't wait to experience what she knew would be rapturous sensation of double penetration. Her first experience in the ultimate pleasure of being fucked from both sides.

"I like Dom Danton, my Master, and I'm comfortable with him joining us."

The men undressed, but Peyton's eyes were glued on Stone as he removed his shirt and kicked off his shoes in easy masculine moves. He was a delicious specimen of manhood with his bulging muscles and broad chest that tapered into narrow hips. She licked her lips as she noticed the rippled movement of his abs as he sat down next to her.

She jerked as Danton pressed his hard body against her back. His arms circled her waist to cup her breasts. His breath was warm against her temple.

"You're trembling, Petals. Do I scare you?"

"No, Dom Danton. I guess it's just a foreign experience ... looking into my Master's eyes with another man caressing me."

"You're a beautiful woman—very enticing, my pet," Stone said as he tweaked her nipples that Danton offered up to him. "You have the kind of beauty that sets a man's blood afire without any effort, and yet, sometimes I get lost in the innocent glow about you."

Danton squeezed her breasts as Stone trailed his palms with feathered lightness over her nipples. His deep voice relaxed her and she leaned back against Danton's brawny body, feeling the heat of his hands penetrate her skin. She bit her lip as effervescent heat rushed in waves through her body. It was the first time she was caressed by two men simultaneously. It threatened to spin her arousal out of control

Danton nibbled on her earlobe while Stone leaned in to suck and nibble on her nipples.

"Fuckity fuck," she moaned as every action of theirs spiked her lust at such an alarming rate that she sat trembling, completely at the mercy of two gentle giants.

"I love the rosy hue of arousal all over your body, little dove," Stone murmured against her breast.

"Dom Danton knows how to create magic with his hands and you, my Master, have the master touch," she hissed when he brushed his fingers over her labia.

"Swollen from indulging too much in the Events Room, I see," he teased as he toggled her clitoris.

Peyton was too aroused to respond to his taunt. She looked at him with feverish eyes and then she was in the middle of the bed with their hard bodies pressing against her. Their huge tumescence stole her breath.

She moaned when the two men licked a slow path over her chest to kiss the underside of her breasts.

"Oh lord," her voice was raw, overwhelmed by the sensations awakened by the tender caresses from two men at the same time. Her breasts had always been sensitive to touch. Now, with both of them nibbling and kissing her slopes, she craved more. Their lips tugged on the needy tips and then sucked them into their mouths with evident lust.

"God, yes," she cried out and arched her back, only to suck in her breath as her legs were dragged apart and two hands slipped between her thighs. One rubbed and stroked her clit, while the other slipped two fingers inside her, pumping gently.

"Master Eagle, please. I can't, this is too much and I need … I don't need more foreplay. I've had more than enough. Please," she begged with a raw quality in her voice that told of the unbridled lust raging through her.

Peyton trembled in desire and need. She caught their eyes and was overwhelmed by the coalescence of joy and triumph flooding her mind. She was caught off guard as she realized then, they were as excited and aroused as she was, entranced by her reaction to them.

Stone settled on his back and prodded her to straddle him, which she did with feminine grace and sat staring into his eyes with Danton on his knees behind her. She hissed as his hands closed around her hips to lift her over her Master. Her eyes followed Stone's movements as he guided his cock to the sweet entrance of her pussy.

"I love that you're always so hot for me. She's ready, Danton and I know how she loves a hard entry."

His words were still wrapping around her mind when Danton lowered her with one hard heave, embedding her fully onto Stone's cock.

"Fuckity fuck," she whimpered.

"Easy, little one," Danton gentled and kissed her behind her ear. Her head rolled back on his shoulder as she grinded her hips against Stone's, reveling in his large cock speared inside her.

Stone pulled her forward, to wrap his lips around a taut nipple and suckled like a baby. Peyton gasped at the unexpected squirt of lube on her puckered hole. Her body tingled with anticipation as Danton gently prepared her.

"Remember to talk to me if we hurt you, Petals," Stone reminded her gently.

Peyton was oblivious to his words, too caught up with Danton lifting her off Stone's cock until only the tip remained inside. Stone continued to suck her nipples, lazily tweaking and pinching the other between his fingers.

She whimpered as Danton pushed the spongy, bulbous tip of his cock forward.

"Come on, baby. You know what to do. Push back against him."

Peyton blindly followed his instruction and sighed in relief when he settled hilt deep inside her.

"Holy shit," she wailed as Danton pushed forward, embedding her on Stone's cock once more. "Full," she gasped. "Too full."

"Just relax, baby and feel," Stone guided her as Danton slowly dragged his cock back, ensuring that every nerve ending inside her ass and pussy flared to life. Stone pushed in and they set a slow rhythm—plunging in and out, in opposite directions.

She tossed and turned in pure undiluted ecstasy. Catching her open mouth with his, Stone plundered her mouth.

"You're breathtaking, baby," he murmured through short bursts of breath.

Peyton was on fire. She gulped as their velvety steel rods plunged deep inside her with long rhythmic strokes. The thrust of their turgid lengths built the pressure inside her loins to a height previously unknown to her; filling every inch of her and flooding her mind with ecstasy.

"I need more. Please, my Master," she pleaded.

Stone was elated at her surrender. They increased the tempo but continued the gently rocking rhythm. Peyton floundered as raw need pierced her loins. Her lower body throbbed in profound pleasure. She knew the end was near when Danton reached around her hip to rub her clit.

"Please, Master. I need to come," she cried, her nails digging into Stone's chest.

"Come, Petals," Stone rasped as he sped up.

It was all her body needed. Peyton was assailed by a myriad of sensations. She panted breathlessly as she felt her muscles gather, fed by the insurmountable pressure from the two cocks plunging into her. In desperation she tried to suck in a deep breath, but as unstoppable as waves upon sand, the orgasm rolled over her. Spasm after spasm shook her body. Her cry carried through the room as she slumped weakly forward, bucking like a wild filly between the two strong bodies. Her blazing eyes locked onto Stone's face. She choked out a scream as a surge of warm liquid erupted from inside her.

"Fuck me, I've never felt such a hard climax," Danton said with his face drawn into a tortured expression, as he pinched back his orgasm. He pulled back and watched as Stone powered into her with strong, upward thrusts. The hot spurt of his ejaculate triggered another climax for Peyton. Her cries and his growl echoed through the room.

Danton thrust home amid their cries and plunged inside her with fierce strength, to drive her to an uncontrollable climax that rippled through her and tossed her high into the cloud of blissful ecstasy. He kept plowing her body until the familiar flashes of heat flared in his chest; wave upon wave drowning him in a state of rapturous elation. His eyelids fluttered and twitched as the dam inside him burst. He roared when the world around him came to a grinding halt and all his energy was concentrated on that rush of heat, from deep inside his loins, which erupted deep inside her bowels. Pulsating streams of hot viscous semen spewed out, his body shuddering with the intensity of his release.

Peyton slumped onto Stone's chest, purring happily as his arms wrapped around her to hold her tight. A feathered kiss on her shoulder accompanied Danton pulling carefully out of her ass.

"Thank you for the honor to be your first threesome, little one."

"No, thank you, Dom Danton, for making it such an unforgettable experience."

Danton smiled and with a salute, picked up his clothes and left the room.

She closed her eyes and reveled in Stone's body and his arms holding her tight. Her life had come to fulfillment. She had come full circle. She had learned to forgive and to forget. Most importantly, she'd come to love again.

She kissed the center of his chest.

"I love how you Dominate me, Master Eagle." She hesitated and heaved in a deep breath. "And I love you, Stone Sinclair."

His body froze and Peyton went cold. They had never mentioned the L word and maybe she should've waited. Maybe it was too soon—

"Please sit up, Petals," his gruff voice rumbled from deep within his chest.

She reluctantly straightened. He brushed her hair from her face, his expression solemn.

"Now, look me in the eyes and repeat what you just said."

"I love how you Dominate me, Master Eagle, and I love you, Stone Sinclair."

His smile was heaven and earth; his eyes offered her the universe. He cupped her face. "And here I was going to give you at least six months to get used to me and pray that you fell in love with me." His face turned serious. "I made an oath to myself that I'd never allow my heart to open itself to a woman. I'd experienced first-hand the devastation my father suffered when my mother left him and swore I'd never leave myself that vulnerable. I didn't believe I knew how to love ... at least not a woman." He smiled gently and kissed the tip of her nose. "Until you came into my life. I love how you submit to me, Petals and I love you, Peyton Jackson."

Peyton's heart erupted in a staccato of drums inside her chest. Joy flooded her mind as she gave him a blinding smile.

"I don't need time, Stone. I've wasted too much of it in my life. With you, I want to treasure every moment, every second we have together." She traced the straight line of his nose. "Besides, you're not that far away from fifty and if we have to produce three children before then ... we better start ... hey!" she broke out in giggles as he flipped her over onto her back and entered her still pulsing pussy with one hard thrust.

She stroked his bulging biceps as he held himself above her. Her breath got stuck in her throat as she noticed the dark look in his eyes, the evil twist on his lips.

A wicked smile twisted her own upward. "I thought you said the Beast isn't going to come out to play tonight."

"Ah, but then I didn't know you were going to issue such a blatant challenge, baby. And you better believe the Beast is hungry and completely up for the challenge."

He dragged his cock back slowly and with his eyes holding hers captive, he smiled. That naughty boy grin that completely twisted her ovaries in a knot.

"Ready, Petals?"

"Oh, fuckity fuck."

"Indeed."

The End

Read on for and excerpt of HAWK, book 2 in the Castle Sin series.

Excerpt: Hawk: Castle Sin #2

CHAPTER ONE

(Please note, this excerpt is unedited.)

"Let me go, you big bully! This ishn't Castle Sin and you have no right to ... hic ... order me around on the Mainlan'."

Savannah Thorne struggled against the hard hand locked around her elbow. She looked up as the Goliath of a man suddenly stopped and she stumbled into his chest. Her attempt at an immediate retreat was stemmed as he yanked her closer. His nostrils flared and for the first time since she'd arrived at Castle Sin on the private island, Seven Keys, in Key West, she feared this man.

Hawk Sinclair, aka Rothman as he was known as an actor, was one of the owners of the exclusive BDSM club and training facility for submissives. He never showed his emotions, much like the rest of his six cousins who were part owners in the club. To see him this furious shocked her ... to almost sobriety ... but not quite.

"I said to lemme go," she tried again but a lot less vehement and wary.

"For as long as you're a trainee at Castle Sin you remain my responsibility. You *will* follow our rules, sub ST, especially insofar as your own safety is concerned. Or is that what this is? An attempt to be kicked out of the program and off the island?"

"I have a name and sinche we're not on the island, ushe it!" she snapped—albeit ineffectively as her slurred speech doused the irritation she tried to portray. The hard glint in his eyes warned her it might not have been clever to throw caution to the wind.

"You're so fucking drunk, I doubt you even remember your own name. What the hell is the matter with you?

Hawk had never been this close to losing his temper. It tampered with his equilibrium because he always had the utmost control over his emotions but then he'd walked into the bar and saw the beautiful blonde woman completely sloshed. It brought back memories he'd locked away to the deepest compartment of his brain—ones that had been forbidden to ever surface. That she had the ability to reach that deep inside his mind, infuriated him.

"Shay it. I wanna hear you shay it ... jush once."

He pressed his face close to hers and sneered, "I don't accommodate drunks. We're leaving and—"

"Shavannah, my name ish ... hic ... Shavannah! Shay it, damn you," she bleated and slammed her fists against his chest.

"Is there a problem, missy?"

Hawk's arms wrapped around her and he held her against his chest in a strong protective cocoon. The natural instinct of the Dom in him was to protect and care for his sub, or trainee as the case may be. The power in his body and the rhythmic beat of his heart was the conduit that made

Savannah lose the tenuous hold she had over her frayed emotions. The sobs started from deep within her soul as she burst into tears.

"She had too much to drink, which if you were a responsible bartender, would've noticed long ago and refused to serve her more fucking booze."

"Looky here, Mister, who do you think … hey! Let go!" The man cried, his eyes wide as Hawk fisted his shirt at the front of his chest and yanked him closer without letting go of the crying woman.

"I'm the man who's about to beat the shit out of you if you don't fetch this lady's purse." Hawk shoved him away with a disgusted snort. "Now, before I lose my temper," he snapped when the man stood like a statue, staring at him in fear.

"Relax, Mister, I'm going," he said and quickly went to grab Savannah's large shopper bag from the booth where she'd been sitting most of the day drinking.

"Has she eaten anything at all?" Hawk glared at the offending barman who kept loitering and barring his way.

"Not that I can remember. Hey, you can't just leave, what about the bill?"

Hawk had earned the name Hawk at College from one of his professors, because like his totem animal, the Hawk, he always observed before taking action. He studied each situation thoroughly before making any rash decisions and he approached life with skilled precision. He was no fool and didn't hesitate to take the lead in situations when required. This time, he struggled to free himself from the mental block that rose as a protective barrier when he found Savannah as drunk as a skunk.

He turned on the barman like his bird totem, swift, decisively, as he swept down onto his prey.

The barkeep retreated hastily.

"You run a cash per order only bar, shithead. I've been here numerous times myself, so don't insult my intelligence. I'm not going to tell you to get out of my way again."

He began to walk, grunting irritably when Savannah stumbled as he dragged her along, still crying pitifully. He picked her up and shouldered his way past the man like he was nothing more than an irritating barfly.

"I'm s-sorry. I didn't mean to—"

"I suggest you just shut the fuck up. My patience is hanging on a thin thread as it is." His cold gaze cut into her with razor sharp warning. "Don't test me, sub. At this moment, all I want is silence. Say one more word and I'll dump you in the goddamned ocean." He snorted as his eyes trailed over her disheveled hair. "And I won't even blink if you drown in your drunken stupor."

Hawk made no effort to hide the disgust from his voice. It had been at his insistence that the employed submissives or trainees were limited to one drink at the members' dungeons per night and one glass of wine at dinner. His cousins had all agreed. They ran a tight ship; the training was grueling and they didn't have the time or the patience to babysit drunk or tipsy women. In the five years since they'd opened Castle Sin, this was the first time one of the women became completely intoxicated.

He jumped effortlessly into the speedboat waiting at the dock of the Margaritaville Key West Resort on Key West. Danton Hill, the senior of the training Doms at Castle Sin and the Security Director of the island, shook his head as he watched Hawk sit Savannah down in the back seat and strapped her in.

"Let's go, Danton. I need to get back to my training session." He pushed a plastic bucket into Savannah's hands. "If you wanna barf, make sure you do it in there," he growled before he took a seat in the front next to Danton and blithely ignored her.

His jaw turned rigid as he listened to the sounds of vomiting before they were even halfway to Seven Keys Island, owned by his cousin as well as his best friend, Stone Sinclair. Him and his six cousins combined, owned forty-five percent to his fifty-five of Castle Sin but Stone was the sole owner of the island.

He refused to turn around and assist her. Her pitiful sob penetrated and took him back ten years.

"*Goddammit, Vee, again? What's your excuse this time?*"

Hawk stared at his wife with growing anger. She had just come out of rehab two months ago. This time he'd believed her when she'd promised it was the last time. She claimed she'd realized she was destroying their lives, their happiness. He'd been over the moon. They'd been married for five years, and it had been anything but moon shine and roses. She'd hidden her drinking habits from him while they were dating. During the year Vee and Hawk had lived together prior to the wedding, he'd missed it due to his rigorous work schedule, juggling to fulfill the contract with Marvel Studios. Eight years earlier, he and his cousins were drawn into acting in the blockbuster series, Space Riders on a whim. Also, he and Stone had started the company, at that time.

When he'd returned from shooting a movie a year into their marriage, he'd come to a shocking realization. His wife was an alcoholic. He'd done his best to help her, to guide her and be there for her through her first rehab stint. It had been a waste of time. She began to drink two weeks after returning home. So it continued every year she gave in to his urgings and tried to stop.

"You doan unnershand, baby," she wailed in a drunken voice, rocking back and forth in their modern home in Beverley Hills. A home he'd paid millions for because it was the one she wanted ... and he hated. He would've preferred to live in the hills of Santa Monica but it was too far away from the hustle and bustle of stardom for her. Vee thrived on it and lived the life of a spoiled rich man's wife.

"No, Vee, I don't, so why don't you explain it to me?" Hawk stood watching her, rooted to the spot in the arch leading into the grand open room. He hated the stench of imbibing, especially on a woman. The fact that this was his wife, made it twice as hard to swallow.

"I'm shorry I dis-shappointed you. I tried, I did, babe! Pleashe believe me."

She looked at him with her big Bambi eyes but this time he was unmoved. He'd reached the end of his tether. He couldn't continue like this, constantly worrying, wondering when she was going to do something stupid in a drunken state, babysitting her *when she was too drunk to help herself. Intimacy in their marriage had become a chore because if she wasn't drunk, she was lethargic. The past two months had been different. He'd begun to hope … until now.*

This was it. He'd had enough.

"Itsh like a drug, Hawk!" She pleaded as she realized he hadn't moved, that he stared at her with an impassive expression. "I can't stop."

"No, Vee, you don't want to stop, that's the difference. Becoming a drug addict is a choice a person makes the first time they give in to it. You can stop but you refuse to admit how big your problem is. It's always one more with you. One more drink, Hawk, just one more chance, Hawk. How many one mores are there going to be before you drink yourself to death?"

Her eyes widened as she shook her head. "I'll never go that far. I know when to sht … hic … shtop."

"No, you don't. Look at yourself. Jesus, Vee! Is this what a woman looks like who knows when to stop?"

"But thishh ... hic ... ish the lass time," she said, struggling to her feet. She stumbled toward him.

Hawk was hard pressed not to step back when the drunken fumes filled his nostrils. He reached out and placed his hand on her shoulder, keeping her at a distance.

"Why should I believe you? What makes this time so different? You've been in rehab six times over the past four years. It hasn't helped. What's going to make you stop now?"

She attempted a smile but it was more a lopsided grimace as she was overcome with hiccups. Hawk cursed; he shouldered her out of the way and strode to the bar. He returned with bottled water and shoved it into her hands.

"Drink this."

Her lips pulled into a disgusting sneer but one look at the anger swirling in his eyes, she conceded and took a few small sips.

"Well? I'm waiting," Hawk snapped impatiently. All he wanted to do was leave. To pack his bags and go. He'd had enough.

"I went to the doctor thish morning," she said, wringing her hands. She blinked at him with growing fear. Another attempt at a smile as she reached out to touch his chest. He remained aloof. "I'm pregnant, babe. We're gonna have a … hic … baby."

Hawk felt the punch of fury explode inside him. What should've filled him with unbound joy, delivered in a drunken stupor, made him see red.

"You're pregnant? And this is how you react? By getting sloshed? Do you even fucking know what it could do to a baby? Do you even fucking care?"

"I know and I'm sh-orry! It wash jush so … overwhelming … I needed … I had to—"

"Had to celebrate by getting drunk. Congratulations! You just potentially caused permanent harm to our child!"

"You're mean," she began to sob. "You doan even try to unnershtand."

Hawk didn't try to stop her when she stumbled to the front door and ran outside into the dark night. He was too disappointed, too tired to care. He should be shouting with joy at the prospect of becoming a father but all he could think of was that she'd never be a good mother. He finally realized she'd never quit drinking. The fact that something this joyous moved her to grab the bottle instead of staying steadfast, realizing the responsibility that came with a child, was the only proof he needed.

His body turned to stone for a brief moment when the sound of screeching tires and a scream echoed through the front door. He tore outside and ran out to the street. Vee laid in a crumpled, bloodied broken bundle in the middle of the street. Her sightless eyes stared toward the stars.

His world crashed around him as he stared at her mangled body, tears running down his cheeks. In one blind moment of rage, he'd pushed her over the edge.

He caused her death.

Hers and the life of his unborn child.

"Hold on, sub ST, we're almost there."

Danton's gruff voice yanked Hawk back to the present and Savannah's pitiful crying. He cursed, kicked off his shoes and ripped off his shirt.

"Hawk! Hey, what the fuck, man!"

Danton's voice drifted across the ocean as Hawk's body hit the water with a perfectly executed dive. Since the accident the ocean was the one place where he could find solace, a little release when he felt the darkness cloud his mind with memories that tried to escape his mind. With the guilt that had been hounding him for the past ten years.

He pushed his arms faster, cutting through the water like a motorized fan, his body was tight as a coiled spring. His chest burned but he didn't let up, he forced himself to move forward at a speed that drowned all thoughts, all sorrow and pain from his mind.

Everything he'd managed to keep suppressed for the past five years and all it took was to see the first woman since Vee who had managed to set fire to his veins, as drunk as a skunk.

Struggling to breathe, Hawk clawed his way onward until he reached Seven Keys Island and stumbled from the surf. He fell onto his back, trying to catch his breath.

He had finally believed he was ready to move on. He smirked.

"Not with Savannah Thorne, I'm not."

Hawk had no intention of ever becoming involved with another alcoholic. No matter how he lusted after her.

All Savannah wanted to do at that moment was to crawl into a dark cave and hide for the rest of her life. She had never felt this miserable and drunk.

Good lord! What was I thinking?

She moaned as the boat hit another wave and her stomach heaved for the umpteenth time. Bile rose in her throat and she leaned forward, hurling into the bucket that already bore witness to the many times she'd already vomited in the short time they'd been on the sea.

The sob tore through her chest without forethought and then the dam burst ... again. She couldn't stop the tears and she didn't bother to try. Through watery eyes she watched a tense Hawk jump up, kick off his shoes, and yank his shirt over his head. All in a what appeared to be one smooth move, he dived into the ocean.

"Oh god!" she cried in apprehension. Danton's hoarse cry echoed in her ears as she leaned over the side, frantically searching for his body. She sighed in relief when he surfaced a short distance from the boat and started to swim in the direction of the island, which in her estimation was still miles in the distance. His movements were confident as his hands cut into the water with what she had no doubt was fury.

She cringed at the memory of the look on his face when he'd seen her slumped in the booth at the bar with a glass of whiskey in her hands.

It wasn't the kind of expression she'd wanted to entice from him, not from Master Hawk and most assuredly not from the man, Hawk Sinclair.

"He's very angry at me, isn't he?" she said in a small voice. Danton didn't respond and she leaned back with a sigh. Maybe it was a good thing he didn't hear the question. She'd already made a big enough fool of herself once today.

"Anger is putting it mildly, little one. I've known Hawk for eight years and I've never seen him like this."

Oh, that's just great. I've managed to wake up the demon in him.

"I'm sorry. It was a stupid thing to do," she said as he docked the boat at the recently rebuilt marina at Seven Keys Island. She looked back over the ocean. Her bottom lip suffered the worry as she searched for Hawk. The black dot coming closer in the distance set her mind at ease.

"I'm not the one you should apologize to and yes, it was." Danton secured the boat and held out his hand. "Come, let's get you inside. You need a hot bath and loads of coffee." His gaze lifted to the man rapidly approaching. "You need to get sober and quickly."

"Shouldn't you go back and fetch him? He's still miles out and must be dead tired by now." The trip from the Mainland and the fresh sea air had done wonders to sober her up. She took his hand and carefully got off the boat. She might feel better but her body was still suffering from the shock of all the liquor she'd forced down her throat.

Danton barked a short laugh. "I value my life too much, little one. No, he needs to vent and that's how he does it." He took her arm and assisted her up the winding pathway toward Castle Sin.

"What do you mean I need to get sober quickly?" she asked as his earlier words penetrated.

Danton slanted a sideways look at her. "You didn't honestly believe there won't be repercussions of you leaving the island with one of our members without telling anyone, did you? Besides that, you know the rule about liquor for as long as you're a trainee or an employee at Castle Sin." He shook his head. "I'm afraid you're in for more than a lecture from Master Hawk, little one. You'll appear before all of them and you better be prepared at the possibility of being kicked off the island."

Savannah stumbled alongside Danton, her heart missing a beat as she listened to him. She initially came to the island because she'd been blackmailed into it by her ruthless and corrupt boss at the FBI, Decker Cooper. He had been in cahoots with Secretary of Defense Gary Sullivan at the time. They had formed a coalition with a Mexican Crime Lord, Miguel Muerta to assassinate the President so that Sullivan would take over. How they believed it would be possible, she had no idea, except if they intended to kill the Secretary of State as well.

She was just relieved that the Sinclair cousins had helped them when her cousin, Peyton Jackson, had spilled the beans to Stone. He acted immediately when he heard how the two of them had been blackmailed to blow up the cousins' business, Be Secure Enterprises, which operated from an underground bunker on the island. Sullivan and Cooper needed to eliminate the nanotechnology the Sinclairs had designed and installed at DHS that blocked their access to government files.

It had been a relief to hear they were both behind bars but with it came a devastating problem that had crippled Savannah's strength. Her uncharacteristic imbibing came after Decker Cooper made it clear over the phone that morning he wasn't done with her and refused to divulge the information she was desperate for.

She didn't want to leave Castle Sin, not since she'd realized how Hawk Sinclair affected her. He was the first man who made her heart beat faster, who was the reason she could dream at night again.

Of love, happiness and a life without threats and ugliness.

Decker Cooper had shattered all those dreams … again, for the second time in her life.

Subscribe to my newsletter here and be the first to know about new releases:

www.linzibassetauthor.com

More Books by Linzi Basset

For Amy – Their Beloved Sub – Book 11
Dark Desire Novels
Enforcer – Book 1

Their Sub Novella Series
No Option – Book 1
Done For – Book 2
For This – Book 3
Their Sub Series Boxset

Their Command Series
Say Yes – Book 1
Say Please – Book 2
Say Now – Book 3
Their Command Series Boxset

Paranormal Books
The Flame Dragon King - Metallic Dragons #1
Slade: The First Touch
Azriel: Angel of Destruction

Romance Suspense

The Bride Series
Claimed Bride – Book 1
Captured Bride – Book 2
Chosen Bride – Book 3
Charmed Bride – Book 4

Caught Series
Caught in Between
Caught in His Web

The Tycoon Series
The Tycoon and His Honey Pot
The Tycoon's Blondie
The Tycoon's Mechanic

Standalone Titles
Her Prada Cowboy
Never Leave Me, Baby
Now is Our Time
The Wildcat that Tamed the Tycoon
The Poet's Lover
Sarah: The Life of Me

Naughty Christmas Story
Her Santa Dom
Master Santa

Box set
A Santa to Love – with Isabel James
Christmas Delights – with Isabel James

Books Co-Written as Isabel James

Zane Gorden Novels
Truth Untold

The Crow's Nest – A journey of discovery on the
White Pearl

Christmas Novella
Santa's Kiss
Santa's Whip

<u>*Box set*</u>
A Santa to Love – with Linzi Basset
Christmas Delight – with Linzi Basset

Poetry Bundle by Linzi Basset & James Calderaro

<u>Love Unbound - Poems of the Heart</u>

About the Author

"Isn't it a universal truth that it's our singular experiences and passion, for whatever thing or things, which molds us all into the individuals we become? Whether it's hidden in the depths of our soul or exposed for all to see?"

Linzi Basset is a South African born animal rights supporter with a poet's heart, and she is also a bestselling fiction writer of suspense-filled romance erotica books; who as the latter, refuses to be bound to any one sub-genre. She prefers instead to stretch herself as a storyteller which has resulted in her researching and writing historical and even paranormal themed works.

Her initial offering: Club Alpha Cove, a BDSM club suspense series released back in 2015, reached Amazon's Bestseller list, and she has been on those lists ever since. Labelling her as prolific is a gross understatement as just a few short years later she has now been published over fifty times; a total which excludes the other published works of her alter ego: Isabel James who co-authors.

"I write from the inside out. My stories are both inside me and a part of me, so it can be either pleasurable to release them or painful to carve them out. I live every moment of every story I write. So, if you're looking for spicy and suspenseful, I'm your girl … woman … writer … you know what I mean!"

Linzi believes that by telling stories in her own voice, she can better share with her readers the essence of her being: her passionate nature; her motivations; and her wildest fantasies. She feels every touch as she writes, every kiss, every harsh word uttered, and this to her is the key to a never-ending love of writing.

Ultimately, all books by Linzi Basset are about passion. To her, passion is the driving force of all emotion; whether it be lust, desire, hate, trust, or love. This is the underlying message contained in her books. Her advice: "Believe in the passions driving your desires; live them; enjoy them; and allow them to bring you happiness."

Stalk Linzi Basset

If you'd like to look me up, please follow any of these links.

While you're enjoying some of my articles, interviews and poems on my website, why not subscribe to my Newsletter and be the first to know about new releases and win free books.

Linzi Basset's Website and Isabel James' Website
Linzi Basset Twitter and Isabel James Twitter:
Friend Linzi on Facebook or Friend Isabel James
on Facebook
Linzi's Facebook Author Page and Isabel James'
Facebook Author Page
Linzi on Amazon and Isabel James on Amazon
Linzi All Author-Page and Isabel James All Author
Page
LinkedIn
Instagram
Goodreads
BookBub
YouTube
Pinterest
MEWE:
Linzi's Lair on MEWE

Like my Facebook pages:
Linzi's Poetry Page
Club Wicked Cove

Club Alpha Cove
Club Devil's Cove
Castle Sin Series

AND, don't forget to join my fan group, Linzi's Luscious Lair, for loads of fun!

Don't be shy, pay me a visit, anytime!